MENGELE'S
LEGACY

MENGELE'S LEGACY

David J. Weinberg

Rutledge Books, Inc. Danbury, CT

With the exception of Doctor Joseph Mengele, and Doctor Von Verscher, all characters within this book are fictional. Any resemblance to a person or persons, living or dead, is coincidental.

Copyright © 2001 by Hashoah, LLC.

ALL RIGHTS RESERVED
Rutledge Books, Inc.
107 Mill Plain Road, Danbury, CT 06811
1-800-278-8533
www.rutledgebooks.com

Manufactured in the United States of America

Cataloging in Publication Data
Weinberg, David J.

Mengele's Legacy

ISBN: 1-58244-185-5

1. Fiction.

Library of Congress Control Number: 2001094465

Dedication

This book is dedicated to the millions who have died and now lie in unnamed, unmarked graves. May this book be a testament to how interconnected we all are. It is also dedicated to the scientists and research professionals who refuse to stop asking questions, even if those questions are controversial or unpopular.

ACKNOWLEDGEMENTS

As part of my research for this novel I have drawn on many different sources. The character of David Dunlevy was inspired by the work of Professor Peter H. Duesberg of the University of California at Berkeley. Doctor Duesberg makes some very compelling arguments against HIV/AIDS hypothesis. His book, 'Inventing The AIDS Virus', asks questions that have not been addressed by the mainstream medical community.

Much of my research on the HIV virus was centered around the work of Doctor Martin Nowak and Doctor Andrew McMichael of Oxford University. Details about Doctor Mengele's life after the Holocaust came from 'Mengele, The Complete Story' by Gerald L. Posner. The charactor of Brian Crighton was drawn from Ian Malcolm, a character in Michael Crighton's Jurassic Park. Ithamar Pollansky was drawn from my undergraduate organic chemistry professor, Ithamar Pollak, and Mrs. Pollansky was drawn my parents' landlady, Eda Schlossberg (may she rest in peace).

However, this book is entirely fiction, as are all characters except Doctor von Verscher and Doctor Mengele. The views expressed here are my own. Theories about the existence and functioning of ' Mengele Cells' are also mine, as are any factual or scientific errors.

I would   like to acknowledge the neighborhoods of my youth, Westville, New Haven, and Woodbridge, Connecticut, and Brooklyn, New York.

From this point on, there are no more Africans, Germans, Russians or Americans. There are no more Black or White, Jew or Gentile. From this point on there are only two types of people, those with this cellular mutation and those without. And it is spreading. Be afraid. Be very afraid.

— Doctor David Dunlevy, *Good Morning, America*

"If I am not for myself, who will be for me?
And if I am only for myself, what am I?
And if not now, when?

— Hillel

PREFACE

Mengele's Legacy was conceived after the release of the movie, *Schindler's List*. Steven Spielberg showed the movie to students in Southern California. Several students laughed and were disruptive. Mr. Spielberg took them aside and the students wanted to know why they should care about the killing of some Jews.

I do not know how Mr. Spielberg responded. He should have told them that if the Nazis' had won the war, other races would have followed the Jews into extinction. And so *Mengele's Legacy* was born.

Is Doctor Joseph Mengele really responsible for AIDS? Let me respond with two answers. First, hate and prejudice are very much like viruses. Once one of us is touched, we are all at risk. The modern Jew asks, "How could the world have let the Holocaust happen?" The answer is quite simple; even here in America the Jews of Europe were somebody else's problem.

As importantly, I believe that many of mankind's current ills can be laid at the feet of Nazi Germany. So much intellectual brilliance was extinguished, it is impossible to comprehend what would be scientifically and socially possible if there were no Holocaust. Perhaps diseases such as cancer and AIDS would have already been solved. We will never know.

Not all holocausts take place on the battle field, or in the crematoria. Just as the world turned away from Jews in Europe, we now turn a deaf ear towards an Africa that is under attack. There are those who are genuinely concerned and involved. There were also those who risked everything for the Jews. Both groups comprise a tiny minority.

Why should we be concerned with AIDS in Africa? The most selfish answer is that Africa could very well be a harbinger for all of humanity.

This book is a work of fiction and, like all fiction, it was written to entertain. Izzy Slesinger comes to discover how interconnected we all are. Connectedness is the underlying theme that I have built into this novel. As I stated earlier, once one of us is touched, we are all at risk.

Be afraid. Be very afraid!

— David J. Weinberg

Chapter 1

Thick, gray clouds enveloped the island of Manhattan. The first few drops splashed softly, giving no indication of the impending downpour. Doctor Isaiah Slesinger clutched his coffee cup tightly, hoping its warmth would chase away the early autumn chill that had washed over him. He stepped to the window of his office just as the rains intensified. A parade of black coffins inched slowly down First Avenue. Isaiah, or Izzy as his friends called him, could clearly see the white letters that spelled out AIDS on top of each coffin. From his vantage point on the third floor of The Viral Research Institute (VRI), he could feel the pain that was etched into the faces of so many marchers in New York's Gay Pride parade.

Izzy was no stranger to the ravages of the disease. As director of protein coding at the Institute, cellular reproduction was his specialty. Over two decades he had broken down the amino acid chains in the proteins of red and white blood cells. On four different occasions Izzy had been nominated for a Nobel Prize in Science. So far he was zero for four. He referred to himself as the 'Susan Lucci' of the sciences. However, the losses came as no surprise. It was always the 'disease' guys who won. Izzy's specialty was the study of healthy cellular protein reproduction. While breakthroughs in disease research were certainly splashier, understanding healthy cell function was vital to building defenses. With only thirty amino acids in human proteins, researching their coding seemed rather simplistic when he first arrived with his doctorate in molecular biology and biophysics from Yale. Twenty-three years of intensive twelve-hour days had passed in a blink of an eye. A new century had dawned and his group was just starting to make sense out of the sequences.

The Viral Research Institute was a one-of-its-kind facility. Technology went beyond cutting edge. A climate controlled basement housed dozens of interlinked IBM and Hitachi super computers. These computers were linked with virtual-reality, holographic image processors. Protein chains could be mapped out three dimensionally, or transferred to high-definition liquid-crystal-displays which offered six thousand different shades and colors for encoding each protein. Powerful electron microscopes tracked every aspect of cellular function. Each day brought hundreds of new discoveries. Old theories were discarded as easily as day-old bagels. However, despite the high-tech wizardry, and the tens of millions that had been spent, thousands of questions about protein synthesis and metabolism within the cells remained unanswered.

Some of the best and brightest minds in the United States worked at The Institute. Izzy's place was at the top of the list. The Institute recruited Izzy right out of graduate school. Such a thing had never happened before, or since. A research Ph.D. from the Ivy Leagues wasn't nearly enough to gain a position. Only the most disciplined and detailed scientists were recruited. Truth be known, Izzy was the best of the best. Researching proteins was much more than a vocation, it was his life's blood. It had been that way for as long as he could remember. Scientific discovery was an adventure. He likened his explorations to "Columbus, with the entire new world ahead of him."

Izzy could still see those first amoeba in his mind. His father bought him his own light microscope for his ninth birthday. It was an expensive present, especially for the son of a Singer sewing machine salesman. However, Izzy's father, Ira, never let his family do without. Opening the box that contained the microscope was exciting. Izzy dashed around their apartment in Brooklyn, grabbing samples of everything that would let light shine through. His older sister, Shana, howled when he snuck up behind her and pulled a single hair from her head. . . at least it was supposed to be a single thread. Izzy could hardly contain himself when he discovered the single-cell amoeba which darted about in a drop of Brooklyn tap water.

His academic abilities earned him a spot in the prestigious Brooklyn Technical High School. At first, his mother didn't want him to go there. It meant traveling by himself on the subway, through some of Brooklyn's toughest neighborhoods. However, Izzy lobbied hard, and finally his mother relented. Those subway rides were Izzy's first experience with the world that existed outside his neighborhood. His early mornings were spent sandwiched between whores who were returning to Manhattan from tricks in Brooklyn. The crackheads were worse, staring numbly around the train cars through shark dead eyes. The key to riding the subway was to keep a blank expression on your face. A smile or a frown could attract unwanted attention and confrontation. Izzy became a master at conjuring a poker face. It was a skill that would serve him well in both the world of science, and in his private relationships.

There are many women who have a need to fathom the unfathomable. Despite being an enigma, Izzy never lacked for female companionship. A spark of the devil stirred in his soul, a wanderlust that showed through the poker face. That little bit of light in Izzy's gray-green eyes acted like catnip on women. However, relationships were often short and physical, confined to brief orgasmic coupling. It didn't take long for Izzy to tire of a woman's company, finding that most women found protein research to be boring. For the women, the spark in Izzy's soul always remained just that, a spark. Since he was never willing to invest the work to turn that spark into a flame, they never seemed terribly upset when he moved on.

It hadn't always been like that. Once, Izzy had been in love. Her name was Emily Driscoll and she was a first year graduate student at Yale during Izzy's fellowship. Even though it was the 1970s, Emily was more a child of the sixties. Her flowing golden tresses were always worn straight, never in a bun or braided. Her outfits varied from a variety of Grateful Dead t-shirts to a selection of flannel from the L.L. Bean catalog. She was one of three students in Yale's very first class of environmental lawyers, and she was determined to clean up the world.

She was the only woman to have ever intimidated Izzy with her intellect. She was as adept with biology as she was with the arcane world of tort law. To make matters worse, she was also the girlfriend of Izzy's off-campus roommate, David Dunlevy. Dave was about as different from Izzy as different could be. He was a tall, curly-haired, surfer from Newport Beach in California. He had literally breezed through attaining a 4.0 grade point average. His hobbies were listening to Jackson Browne's music, smoking grass, and getting laid. Many a night Izzy lay awake, listening to Emily's screams as she and Dave made love.

Izzy didn't understand it, couldn't comprehend it. Certainly Emily must have been aware of his interest. Surely she must have seen the spark that every other woman saw. But it was never destined to be. When Dave left Yale for a Fellowship at Duke, Emily left with them. Eventually they both moved to California, got married, and started on the business of raising a family. Izzy remembered it all as he reflected on the briefness of life as the coffins passed directly below his window. The rains had turned into sheets of water, intensifying the agony of the marchers in the parade.

A ringing telephone snapped Izzy backed to the present. He

struggled to swallow and tapped a button on his speaker-phone. A sultry female voice emanated. "Izzy, it's Lauren."

Izzy rolled his eyes back and forth disdainfully. Lauren was the latest woman that Izzy's friends had fixed him up with. They all took pity on him because he was still single. Perhaps he didn't mind being single, did they ever think of that? "Yeah, Lauren, what's up?"

"I really had a great time at the Guggenheim fund raiser. When I didn't hear from you. . . " Lauren let the sentence trail off, hoping that Izzy would finish it with something promising.

Unfortunately, Izzy had already made a list of the things they had in common, which weren't many. Therefore, he had grasped her image mentally and placed her in the reject pile. "Uh, I know you're not going to want to hear this. I don't think you and I are right for each other."

"You know this after one date?" The hurt in Lauren's voice was palpable.

"You're a beautiful, intelligent woman. A lot of men would kill to have. . . "

"Ugh," Lauren interrupted. "Save me that condescending crap. Mark my words, this is the very last time I go out on a blind date." There was a loud click and the phone line went mute.

Izzy stared at the phone for a moment. He replaced the receiver in its cradle as he turned again to look out the window. The last of the parade finished passing, and Izzy could just make out the long line of coffins several blocks in the distance. At last he turned from the window, deciding that he had better get to work before another Sunday was lost. He took a seat at his desk and grabbed for the latest copy of *The Journal of the American Virological Society*. Under the magazine was a small, clasped yellow envelope. There was no mailing address, no return address, nothing but Doctor Isaiah Slesinger printed in red ink.

Izzy opened the envelope and withdrew its contents. A single, slim paperback book entitled *Cat's Cradle* by Kurt Vonnegut. Izzy peered inside the envelope for other contents and found nothing. When he opened the front cover of the book he discovered a note which read, "Understand Ice-Nine and you will understand AIDS." Under the note was a one-word signature, "Heneke."

"Heneke, Heneke," Izzy thought to himself. He knew the name, but couldn't place it. The Institute phone directory came up blank. He placed the book down on his desk and shrugged it off. Getting caught up on articles that he should have read months ago needed to be the priority. Izzy made it through exactly three pages of the scientific journal when his curiosity got the better of him. He picked up the Vonnegut book, turned off the lights in his office, and headed home.

The rains had subsided, eliminating the need for an umbrella. When Izzy passed the East Side Deli he stopped and went inside. The deli was crowded, but mostly with people who had come in for a meal. On weekends, most people eat in the deli. Izzy was the only person in the take-out line. While he waited for his tuna sandwich, he fished out a creme soda from the back of one of the vending cases. Clutching the can in his left hand, Izzy used his right to open the slim Vonnegut book and began reading.

"You want a pickle with this tuna?" The man behind the deli counter startled Izzy and he jumped a little as he closed the book.

"Yeah, half-sour."

The deli-man quickly wrapped a pickle and placed it in brown bag along with the tuna sandwich. A moment later Izzy was back on the street. He mulled over the Ice-Nine concept in his head as he continued towards home. In Vonnegut's story there were many different kinds of ice. Ice-Nine had a melting point of one-hundred and thirty degrees. More importantly, it was seed which could teach all other water molecules to align themselves in an Ice-Nine matrix. Such a matrix could freeze all liquid water on Earth. While it was quite an effective doomsday scenario, there were no apparent parallels with AIDS.

On East 23rd Street Izzy passed an outdoor news stand. The headline on *The New York Times* caught his eye. It read, "Doctor Pieter Heneke wins war on HIV." Izzy clutched at a copy of the paper and began skimming its contents. Finally he could place the Heneke name. Doctor Pieter Heneke was program director in charge of protein research at Kaiser Pharmaceuticals in Dusseldorf, Germany. There had been a symposia on viral proteins in Vienna. Izzy thought back to the conference which had to be more than three years ago. He recalled Heneke to be an older gentlemen with very sad eyes.

"Hey, you browsing or you buying," the news vendor wailed in a distinctly Brooklyn accent.

Izzy reached into his wallet and pulled out four singles. "Sorry," he replied as he placed the bills on the newsstand's counter.

The man behind the counter looked shocked. "An actual customer. Most guys drop the paper back on the pile. People in this stinkin' city think news is free. Go figure!"

Izzy nodded and shrugged his shoulder. He tucked the paper under one arm and continued on his way. It was a short walk from the newsstand to his one-bedroom apartment in a luxury high-rise on East 23rd Street. Izzy held the brown paper lunch bag with his teeth while he slipped his key into the deadbolt lock on the front door. Once inside, he proceeded to the living room, dropping the lunch bag on his large, wave-shaped, contemporary sofa. The sofa, which had no back, acted as a make-believe Maginot line, dividing the room into two halves. On one long wall sat the entertainment console which housed state-of-the-art audio components and over 3000 compact discs. Tightly packed bookcases lined the other wall. His custom designed computer, with a dedicated T-1 interface to The Institute's mainframe, sat on an antique oak desk. The contradictions in furniture styles were very much in keeping with Izzy's personality. He refused to be tied to convention, or others' perception of what was acceptable.

Izzy sat on the sofa. He lifted the sandwich and soda from the bag as he started to concentrate on the article in *The Times*. Heneke claimed that Kaiser had perfected a new type of protease inhibitor, one that would eliminate the presence of HIV. Izzy couldn't believe it. He knew about Kaiser from their work with artificial blood products, their specialty. How could such a small pharmaceutical company come up with such a breakthrough, especially since that breakthrough eluded thousands of researchers at major pharmaceutical companies, prominent universities, and over forty governments. To the best of his knowledge, Kaiser had never released any anti-viral medication. In the modern world of cost-competitive pharmaceutical medicine, you stick to what you do best, or you disappear.

Even more of a mystery is why Heneke had sent him the book. Izzy remembered exchanging pleasantries with the elderly German scientist, but nothing more. His train-of-thought was interrupted by the ringing of the phone which emanated from speakers hooked to the computer. Leaping from the sofa he tapped a couple of keys on the keyboard which deactivated the computer's built in answering machine.

"Hello Izzy?" The voice belonged to Izzy's older sister, Shana.

"I'm here," Izzy mumbled as he took a gulp of soda to wash the tuna fish down his throat.

"Did you send a check to Dad's temple in Brooklyn?"

Izzy hastily pulled open a drawer on the computer desk and removed his checkbook. "Uh, I was going to write the check tonight and put it in the mail tomorrow."

"Don't forget, Rosh Hashanah is at the end of the week and we shouldn't look like *shnuras*." Shana had just used the Yiddish word for 'cheapskates.'

Izzy sighed. "I said I would write the check tonight."

"And what about tickets for services? You got them?"

Izzy was about to tell Shana that he was thinking of skipping services, but he knew it would only start an argument. "Yeah, I got my tickets."

"Good," Shana replied with relief. "I do not have to remind you that you are the only son of a Holocaust survivor. Papa needs you to be in temple to say a proper kaddish."

"Why do we do this every year?" Izzy questioned as he became aggravated with his sister.

"We're doing nothing," Shana replied flatly. "Is it so terrible if I worry about my little brother? Now, if you were married I wouldn't have to worry."

Izzy could feel the tension in his head building. "Shana, wish Mitchell and the girls a healthy new year and a hearty *l'shana tovah tikatavou.*"

"Maybe you'll meet a nice woman at temple."

"I'm hanging up now." Izzy tapped the computer keyboard and the phone went mute. It took him several moments to calm down. It seemed to him like the whole world was intent on seeing him married. He liked being single. Did they ever think of that? When the throbbing in his head began to subside, Izzy decided to call Dave Dunlevy in California. Dave hated the HIV/AIDS hypothesis and railed against it publicly at every opportunity. Certainly he would have something to say about Heneke's pronouncement.

Dave picked up the phone on the first ring. When he heard his old friend's voice he knew what the first question was going to be. "I know why you're calling, and don't even ask it. The yahoos in my department are already speaking about Heneke like he was the messiah. I, myself, am not buying it. How is it this new protease inhibitor can eliminate viral replication, and yet it is nontoxic to the cells themselves? This is exactly the same claim that FDA made about AZT, and we all know how toxic that turned out to be. I want to see Heneke's data! What about modeling? Any clinical studies? Any double blinds?"

The questions were coming so fast, Izzy couldn't get a word in edgewise. When Dave finally took a breath, Izzy grabbed the opportunity. "When was the last time you saw Heneke?"

Dave fell silent as he thought. "I'm not sure I've ever met him."

"Sure you have," Izzy countered. "At that viral thing in Vienna."

"Oh yeah! God, that's maybe two or three years ago. You say I met Heneke?"

"Maybe it was only me. He seemed like a very thorough scientist."

Dave chuckled. "I don't care if he seemed like Louis Pasteur. Even if everything he says about this new wonder drug is true, which I doubt, it still doesn't mean that eliminating the virus will do anything to help sick patients." Dave's skepticism of the HIV/AIDS hypothesis was always near the surface.

There was a knock on the front door which convinced Izzy to cut the conversation short. "Gotta run, Davie. Someone's knocking."

"Pork fried rice."

"Excuse me?"

"Pork fried rice," Dave chuckled. "Break the Yom Kippur fast with pork fried rice. That way you don't have to worry about the first sin of the new year. Carpe diem, Izzy."

"Oy," was Izzy's reply as there was another knock. "California Jews, now if that's not an oxymoron. Gotta run, I'll call soon."

Izzy opened his front door and found a tall, gaunt looking gentlemen in a dark suit waiting on the other side.

"Can I help you?" Izzy asked politely.

"I'm looking for Doctor Isaiah Slesinger."

"You found him," Izzy replied.

The stranger produced a CIA identification card which had his picture on it. "I'm agent Hafler. I was wondering if I might have a few minutes of your time."

Izzy stepped back and let Hafler enter his apartment. He offered him a cold drink, but the agent declined.

"It has come the attention of the CIA that you recently received a package from Doctor Pieter Heneke."

Izzy looked stunned. "The CIA knows about it? How?"

"We have been watching Doctor Heneke's work for quite some time. Can you tell me what was in the package?"

Izzy led agent Hafler into the living room and retrieved the Vonnegut book. The agent opened the front cover and read the note. He subconsciously nodded to himself and then slipped the little book into his jacket pocket. "I'm afraid that I am going to have to take this as evidence."

"Evidence? Is there a problem?"

Hafler hesitated before he responded to the question. "I'm afraid that Doctor Heneke has been murdered."

The blood immediately drained from Izzy's face. "Murdered?"

Hafler nodded. "His car exploded this morning as he was preparing to leave the Kaiser facility in Dusseldorf. There were many witnesses."

"Do you know who is responsible?"

"I'm not saying we know anything. We're looking for answers, anywhere and everywhere. Fortunately, the viral research community in America is rather small."

Izzy didn't know why, but somehow he could sense that agent Hafler knew a lot about what was going on. "I will cooperate in any way that the CIA sees fit."

Hafler smiled and handed Izzy his card. "You hear anything relating to this, call me."

Hafler extended his hand and Izzy shook it. "Let me ask you one thing. Ice-Nine, do you know what it means?"

The agent's eyes went cold, almost like shark eyes. He stared blankly at Izzy and replied in a monotone. "If I told you, I would have to kill you." It was the cheesy kind of comment expected in a Hollywood movie, and not a good movie at that. However, from the expression on the agent's face, Izzy could see that he was serious. It was more than enough to cause a cold shiver to run down Izzy's spine.

Chapter 2

T A-KI-AH... The short, piercing, staccato blast of the ram's horn stirred Izzy from his trance-like state. Most of the seats in the sanctuary of the East Side Synagogue for Reform Judaism were filled as the shrill sound of the shofar reverberated off the thirty-foot high walls. Rosh Hashanah was heralding in another year. With it came a call for repentance. Izzy's tickets placed him at the back of the temple, in a row of plastic folding chairs. Those chairs were set up for the overflow crowd that only shows itself on the High Holy days.

The Rosh Hashanah service was Izzy's favorite, full of powerful prayers that called Jews back to God. The shofar blasts awakened the soul. Unfortunately, Izzy could not escape the image that had formed in his mind of Heneke's car exploding. Even within the synagogue, the fiery inferno haunted him. He watched his fellow congregants praying from within a dreamlike state. If not for the blast of the shofar, the entire service might have passed without Izzy even noticing what had gone on.

After the first blast of the shofar, Izzy noticed a woman of breath-robbing beauty. She was seated on his right side, three seats away. Her face, which Izzy could only see in profile, held strong features. Her chin was distinct, without so much as a hint of flab. High cheekbones made the eyes, which were accented with long, dark lashes, seem deeply set. Long, raven black hair cascaded down to the shoulder blades. Every once in a while Izzy would let his eyes dart to the right. He strained to see if he could pick up the woman's voice during responsive readings. He could see her lips move, but could not make out the sound of her voice.

After the service concluded, Izzy lost track of the woman as she disappeared in the multitude that was making a hasty exit. He lingered inside the sanctuary, taking his time to fold his tallit.

He carefully tucked the prayer shawl into its protective, velvet bag. The tallit had been a present from his father, presented at the start of his Bar Mitzvah at the age of thirteen. Thirty-four years later and the prayer shawl still looked as if it had never been worn. Izzy resolved that in the coming year he would attend services more often. It was an old promise, taken each year in good faith, but quickly forgotten as he settled back into a hectic work schedule. When Izzy left the temple it was almost deserted. He stepped out of the sanctuary feeling that the new year was going to bring enormous change. It was a feeling, no, more of a sensation that he couldn't shake or explain.

At two in the afternoon Izzy returned to his apartment. He searched for lunch in the refrigerator. His fingers groped the precooked kosher chicken that sat at the back. The bird was still mostly frozen, a consequence of having the refrigerator on its coldest setting. Izzy pulled it from the refrigerator. Hoping that it would be defrosted in time for dinner, he placed it on top of the radiator in the corner of the kitchen. On top of the refrigerator sat a bakery bag. He grabbed it while inserting his hands inside to examine the pieces of rye bread. He removed them, tore each into pieces, and then placed the pieces back in the bag.

Late in the afternoon Izzy reassembled with the synagogue congregation by the East River. About thirty people stood around the rabbi. Each person held a bag of bread. The rabbi said a quick prayer and the congregation dispersed along the bank of the river. Each person began throwing the bread into the water. The ritual symbolized the tossing off of sins so there could be a clean slate for the new year. Izzy made his way to a secluded spot. He noticed the woman he had seen in synagogue. Casually he walked to where she stood. She busily tore pieces of black bread, which to Izzy's eye looked homemade. Black bread is a Russian specialty, and Izzy assumed she was part of the Russian Jewish community that had emigrated to the United States.

"Is that homemade Russian black bread?" Izzy's question seemed innocent, but it brought a sharp and heated response.

"Latvian black bread." There was both pride and defiance in the woman's voice, and she spoke with a deep Soviet accent. She tossed a handful of torn bread into the water and watched the current pull the bread away. Several fish swam close and they devoured her bread.

"That is supposed to mean you will have a good year," Izzy offered after the fish finished the last of the bread.

"In Riga we knew very little of custom," she replied with just a hint of sadness in her voice. "Once Riga had many Jews. Not many remain."

Izzy nodded solemnly. He knew that Riga's Jews had been per-secuted and exterminated in large numbers by both the Germans and the Poles during Hitler's reign of terror. He tried to change the subject by extending his hand and introducing himself. "Doctor Isaiah Slesinger."

Despite delicate hands graced with long fingers, the woman grasped Izzy's hand with surprising power. "I am Doctor Oksana Zibrova."

"M.D. or Ph.D.?"

"I am an oncologist at New York University Hospital." Oksana was pleased to see the look of admiration in Izzy's eyes. She had worked hard to establish herself within the American medical com-munity. However, despite all her hard work, she knew that many of her male colleagues dismissed her as a pretty female Russian token on the NYU staff.

Izzy looked into Oksana's eyes and decided to take a chance. "It is considered a mitzvah to invite a stranger into your home on the high holidays. No one is supposed to be alone on Rosh Hashanah. I'm not making a big dinner, but you are more than welcome to join me."

The invitation took Oksana off guard. She had dated quite a few American men in her three years in America. She found most to be wanting, both intellectually and sexually. However, she found the twinkle in Izzy's eyes to be quite appealing. Besides, only a real swine would try a seduction on Rosh Hashanah. With caution she accepted. "That is a very kind invitation, Doctor Slesinger."

"It's Izzy."

Oksana turned her head from side to side rapidly "Is he? Is who?"

Izzy laughed. "No, that's my name, Izzy. It's short for Isaiah."

Oksana also chuckled. "Okay, Izzy. I would be most glad to join you for dinner."

Neither Oksana or Izzy said much on the walk to his apartment building. Each appraised the other carefully as they walked side by side. Oksana liked the fact that Izzy was trim. So many middle-aged American men were obese. She also had to confess to herself that she enjoyed falling back a step and watching Izzy's buttocks move up and down as he walked. There was nothing she liked better than men with strong, tight asses. She especially enjoyed what she saw when Izzy stepped on the elevator and turned back towards her. As he turned, the pleats in the material of his trousers pulled tight across his groin.

Izzy opened the door to his apartment and immediately noticed the small, yellow, clasped envelope sitting on the floor. The envelope had no address, no postmark and no return address, indicating that it had been hand delivered and slipped under the door. Suddenly Izzy felt a bit nervous, and exposed. As soon as Oksana was in the apartment, Izzy quickly closed his door and locked it. Before closing the door, he looked up and down the outer hallway in both directions. Despite having only met him an hour ago, Oksana picked up on the fact that he seemed unnerved.

"Is something wrong?" Oksana asked as she stared at the letter that Izzy held between now sweaty fingers.

"I'm hoping not," Izzy replied as he ripped the envelope open. There was a small, unlined index card in the envelope. On the card was one sentence: "Jesse Owens is alive and well in Buenos Aires. Heneke." Izzy walked into the living room and slumped down on the couch. Oksana sheepishly followed after him. All the color had drained from his face, and Oksana was thinking that perhaps it would be best if she left.

"Doctor Slesinger, maybe we should do dinner another time."

Izzy looked up from the couch. He shook his head as he let the index card drop onto his coffee table. "Nonsense, I'll go into the kitchen and get started on dinner."

Oksana couldn't help but look at the card once Izzy had left the room. She read it quickly and called out to Izzy in confusion. "This is good news, no?'

Izzy stepped out of the kitchen and looked toward the sofa. "What did you say?"

Oksana held up the card. "This Jesse Owens is a friend of yours?"

Izzy shook his head from side to side. "Only Jesse Owens I know was an Olympic athlete. He's been dead for a good number of years."

"I do not understand," Oksana replied. "The note says that he is alive."

Izzy pondered Oksana's words. He shrugged his shoulders, "I'm at a loss." Realizing that he had not been an attentive host, he took a step towards the wine rack that sat on the wall of the hallway. "Can I get you something to drink? I've got a pretty good selection of cabernet."

Oksana was still not sure that she should be staying. "Maybe it would be better if I left?"

"Absolutely not," Izzy replied vehemently. Then his voiced softened. "I would very much like you to stay for dinner."

Oksana relented. "Would you have anything white, but not too dry?"

Izzy fingers darted from bottle to bottle. He removed a dusty Riesling from a small vineyard in Washington State. "One bottle, a very nice little Riesling. Mostly drink reds myself." Izzy tapped the top of the bottle to his chest. "One glass a day, for the heart. . . "

Oksana stood to her feet and walked the short distance to Izzy's side. "There is no clinical proof that there is any difference between reds or whites."

Izzy looked shocked. "Really? I distinctly remember hearing that reds were better. It was on "60 Minutes" a couple of years ago. I think it was a French doctor. He seemed so certain."

Oksana chuckled briefly. "The French are certain of everything. They know as little about wine as they do about women."

Izzy wasn't about to touch that one and he let it go. He disappeared into the kitchen and returned a moment later carrying two glasses. He handed Oksana her glass and led her back to the couch. Oksana took a seat and glanced again at the index card.

"Who is Heneke?"

"Doctor Pieter Heneke," Izzy offered. "Doctor Heneke was just in the paper the other day."

"The German scientist who invented the new protease inhibitor? Is he a friend of yours?"

"Met the man only once," Izzy replied. "And I was told he was dead. This note obviously proves otherwise."

Oksana looked at Izzy with heightened interest. "I have many sarcoma patients with HIV. Does the medicine really work?"

"I have no idea. It sounds too good to be true."

"It would be very sad if it is just another false promise."

"What is sadder still is that Heneke is obviously sending me some kind of message. I'm just too dense to figure it out." Izzy excused himself and disappeared into the kitchen to make dinner.

The chicken that sat on top of the radiator was now fully defrosted. It took all of fifteen minutes to heat the bird in the oven, and make some potatoes in his microwave. Apple slices were placed on a small plate of honey. When all the food was on the table, Izzy asked Oksana to come into the kitchen.

A challah bread sat in the center of the table. Both said the blessing over the bread in unison. Izzy lifted his glass and offered a hearty, "L'chaim." Oksana replied with, "Nastrovia," and they both dipped slices of apple in the honey. After dinner, Izzy and Oksana returned to the living room. Oksana sat next to Izzy and he thought about draping his arm around her shoulder, but he resisted. "Uh. . . I know you hear this all the time, but you are so incredibly beautiful."

Oksana blushed. The wine had started to loosen her inhibitions. Worse, the twinkle in Izzy's eyes was becoming harder to resist. She twisted her head around to look at him. The next thing she knew, she had her tongue probing the back of Izzy's throat. The kiss was intense, but short. Oksana pulled back abruptly, embarrassed by her bold behavior. "I am sorry. I do not normally do things like that."

Izzy smiled broadly as he made note of the flush on Oksana's cheeks. He moved close and initiated a kiss of his own. This kiss lasted longer, and Izzy could feel the pressure of Oksana's full breasts pushed up against his chest. For a moment he thought of the bedroom, but instantly he dismissed the idea. His entire life had been made up of torrid, short relationships. Realizing that satisfying physical lust on a first date can often kill a relationship, he resisted. Looking at Oksana, he felt something, something deep. He couldn't put it into words, not even to himself. It gave him cause for pause. "Perhaps we could break the fast together after Yom Kippur. I could buy some bagels and kippered salmon."

Again Izzy took Oksana off guard. She was hoping that he would have followed his deeply probing kiss with a different suggestion. Something that might be just a bit more satisfying than smoked fish and bagels. This Doctor Slesinger was turning out to be far more complex than she imagined. And, at that very instant, it was quite frustrating. "I would very much like to share some bagels. Maybe next time you would like to see my apartment?"

Izzy nodded in agreement. "I'd enjoy that. I just need a second to freshen up, and then I'll drive you home."

Oksana objected, "I live all the way out in Brighton Beach. I'm just a block from the subway near the boardwalk. I'll take the train home."

Izzy shook his head. "The subway? At night? I won't hear of it."

Chapter 3

Originally, Izzy planned to spend the second day of Rosh Hashanah by his favorite mountain stream in the Catskill Mountains. Going off into the mountains allowed him a chance to clear his head. In the tradition of most Israelis, and unlike most other American Jews, he only went to synagogue on the first day of Rosh Hashanah. The second day was reserved for quiet introspection. There was no place better for that than under a bright, blue sky. However, Izzy couldn't get Heneke out of his mind. Therefore, he abandoned his plans for a day in the country and settled himself in front of his computer monitor.

The T-1 line hooked to Izzy's computer gave him instant access to the world of cyber space. He typed "www.Medicus//German.com." and a main menu screen instantly appeared. Izzy accessed the author menu and typed in "Heneke, P." Thirty-nine titles filled the screen. Izzy scrolled down using his mouse, noting that the earliest paper was written in the early 1940s. While the titles were in English, the papers themselves were all written in German. Fortunately, Izzy's access to the computer system at work eliminated the foreign language barrier. He highlighted the most recent of Pieter Heneke's publications and downloaded the entire document to his computer. Logging into the language database stored in the mainframe at The Institute took less than thirty seconds. Six minutes after he sent the document out, a passable translation in English was sent back.

The article was entitled "Absence of Genotypic Resistance to mRNA Mutation in African Populations." Izzy had to struggle through the paper. It was typically German; unbelievably detailed, accurately documented, and painfully verbose. There didn't seem to be anything earth shattering in the paper. Heneke had discovered a gene-based anomaly that made African populations more susceptible to mutations of their ribonucleic acids. Medical science had documented many examples of genotypic differences in various populations around the world. If it weren't for a curious research footnote, Izzy would have moved on to the next article.

"Dr. M.J., et al, 1938. mRNA similarities in twin biological units." The entry was more than curious, it was damn peculiar. First off, the date had to be wrong. American experimentation, showing the hereditary nature of DNA, didn't occur until 1944. Avery, Macleod and McCarty were able to transform the character of one pneumococcus, a bacteria, into another distinct type. Experimentation with mRNA didn't start in America until the late 1950s. If the date was correct, Germany would have had a twenty-year head start on the rest of the world in the area of genetics. Such a head start would have propelled Germany to a sole leadership position in gene therapy, and that clearly was not the case.

More troubling was the use of twin biological units. Izzy knew that the Germans had experimented on people during the Second World War. Was it possible that Germany was experimenting with the mRNA of live people? The thought made him shudder. He was about to try and access the paper by Dr. M.J, et al, when the phone rang. A tap of a computer key and the panicked voice of Doctor Richard Levine, chief administrator of The Institute poured forth from the speaker.

"Izzy, you there?"

"Yeah, Rich, I'm here. Is there a problem?"

"You need to come in, now!" The anxiety in Rich's voice caused a shiver to run down Izzy's spine.

"Okay, I'm on my way."

Izzy didn't even bother shutting off the computer. He grabbed his car keys and he was gone.

Fortunately, traffic in the city was light. When he reached The Institute he found a police blockade in front of the building. Izzy zipped his baby-blue BMW Z3 convertible into a spot by a hydrant. He jumped out of the car and was immediately stopped by two police officers. It took several minutes of flashing his identification before the police would let him into the building.

Inside the lobby, Doctor Rich Levine was in a panic. As head administrator of The Institute, his responsibilities were mostly organizational. The majority of his time was spent lobbying for money, either from the government or private individuals. Not a week went by when he wasn't at some major social event or fund raiser. Rich was more hands-on than most administrators, but nothing in his career had prepared him for the hostage situation that was playing itself out inside of Izzy's office.

Rich spotted Izzy, as did a tall, black man in a dark gray suit. They both converged on him at the same time. The black man offered his identification. Izzy noticed he had a small, gold earring in one ear, and a nasty looking scar on the side of his neck. "Doctor Slesinger, I'm detective Adam Rodman with the 123rd precinct. We have a hostage situation."

Izzy glanced at Rich who nodded his head. "A hostage situation?"

The detective opened his note pad and began reading. "At approximately 1:15 p.m., an unknown white male, approximately 5'10" entered the building. He accosted a young woman named Ann King at gun point and forced his way past security. The gunman has barricaded himself and Ms. King in your office. His one demand is to see you."

Izzy looked horrified. He knew Ann as the young research intern in the electron microscopy unit. While they weren't acquainted on a social basis, he knew that she was from a small town in the mid-west. He also knew that she found New York more than a bit frightening. He couldn't imagine the kind of terror she was experiencing at being held captive at gun point. "You don't know who this guy is?"

"Not a clue," detective Rodman replied.

"And what exactly is it that you want me to do?"

"We want to get you in a flak jacket with wires. We'll send you inside. Hopefully, you can convince the gun man to let the girl go." Rodman motioned to a uniformed officer who walked over with a thin, bullet-proof vest.

"That's supposed to protect me?"

Rodman frowned as he took the vest from the other officer. "Actually, the vest is mostly to protect the radio transmission wires."

A real look of concern spread across Izzy's face. "And what's to protect me?"

"The guy knows we have the floor sealed off. He knows he can't escape. This guy specifically said he needs to talk to you. Somehow I don't think he's out to hurt you."

"Unless he's a homicidal maniac," Izzy said half-kidding as he stripped off his shirt. Rodman helped him into the vest, and then Izzy put his shirt back on. "Anything else I need to know?"

Rich Levine sheepishly pushed his way into the conversation. "The guy's sick. I got a glimpse when he ducked into your office. His skin looks funny, maybe anemia."

"Great," Izzy chuckled. "A sick homicidal maniac." Izzy paused by the elevator as Rodman gave him final instructions.

"Remember, try to get him to release the girl."

Izzy nodded and stepped onto the elevator. He could feel his palms begin to sweat. He lightly tapped the button for the third floor. The elevator came to a halt and the doors slid open.

Cautiously, Izzy stepped out. He turned to the right, then left, and stopped twenty feet short of his office. He had expected to find the door closed, but it was open. And laughter was coming from inside. Izzy slowly stepped into the doorway. He was surprised to see Ann King sitting in his chair, convulsed in laughter. Her captor, who stood on the other side of his desk, spun towards the open door and pointed his pistol. Izzy froze in place and Ann's laughter abruptly halted.

"Are you Doctor Slesinger?"

Izzy nodded very slowly as he studied the man closely. He guessed him to be in his early fifties. He had a receding hairline which was mostly gray. He also had several small open sores on his forehead. Those sores were of a type that Izzy had seen many times, Kaposi's Sarcoma.

"I'm Izzy Slesinger. What can I do for you?"

An outstretched pistol motioned for Izzy to come into the office. The gunman released Ann, who scrambled to her feet and quickly scampered out of the room. The pistol was now pointed toward the now vacant chair. Izzy took his seat and waited, carefully observing his captor. Izzy did his best to fight off the beginnings of a tension headache while he watched the gunman silently pace. After what seemed like an eternity, the man spoke.

"I need the sequence."

"The sequence?" Izzy asked with a confused look on his face.

The man took a step closer. "I am Doctor Hans Van Bassen. I know Heneke has been in contact with you. I need the sequence."

"I have no idea what you are talking about."

Doctor Van Bassen cocked the trigger of the gun and pointed at Izzy's temple. "I need to repair my protein sequence. Do not play games with me!"

Izzy gulped hard. "And just how do you repair your protein sequence?"

Doctor Van Bassen looked at Izzy in amazement. He dropped his arm with the pistol. "You really don't know, do you? You were my last hope." Van Bassen fell silent. His eyes took on a far away look and the muscles in his face relaxed. Without another word he lifted the pistol, placed the barrel in his mouth, and pulled the trigger.

"Don't do it," Izzy cried too late. The back of Van Bassen's head exploded open and he crumbled to the floor. Izzy was at Van Bassen's side in less than a second. A moment later, a fully armed SWAT team charged the office. Izzy looked up at the heavily armored officers and shook his head. "He's dead."

Ten minutes later Izzy was seated in Rich Levine's office. He sat numbly, staring straight ahead. Detective Rodman and Rich Levine stood nearby. Rich spoke to the detective in hushed tones.

"I'm worried about traumatic shock. I'll sit with him for a while. If he doesn't improve, I'm going to call an ambulance."

Rodman handed Rich his card. "The body's going to the coroner for an autopsy. If he comes around, I want to speak with him." Rich agreed and shook the detective's hand. Rodman then departed the office, leaving Rich alone with Izzy. Rich pulled up another chair and sat directly at Izzy's side. He cleared his throat and spoke in a very soothing tone.

"Izzy, can you hear me?"

Izzy nodded his head slightly, but remained mute.

"You've been through a horrible trauma. It's going to take time for you to be able to function normally."

Izzy blinked rapidly as his head rotated towards Rich. "Did you hear that?"

Rich listened, but heard nothing. "What?"

"The sound of the shofar. I can hear it. It sounds so mournful." Izzy turned his head and drifted back into mute silence. Rich placed a hand on Izzy's shoulder.

"In a little while I am going to take you to the hospital."

Rich's statement snapped Izzy out of his trance. "Hospital? I'll be fine."

"Probably," Rich replied. "But I'm not taking any chances. No way am I letting you spend the night alone. You need supervision. Is there someone I can call?"

Izzy thought for a moment, but came up blank.

"Fine," Rich concluded. "I'll drive you home in that little toy convertible of yours. I'll call Susan and have her pack some of my stuff and bring it to your place."

"Not necessary," Izzy interjected as he stood and took a shaky step. Rich grabbed his arm and steadied him. "It's either me, or I call your sister in Pennsylvania."

Izzy let out an exasperated sigh. "Take me home, daddy!"

It was a little bit past five when Rich pulled the little blue convertible into Izzy's garage. He was absorbed in Izzy's discussion about Heneke. So absorbed that he didn't notice his wife, Susan, was parked in front of the house in the family Jeep Cherokee. Susan stepped down from the Jeep with a bemused expression on her face. She opened the backdoor of the vehicle, pulled out Rich's suitcase and a bag of groceries, then proceeded up the walk to Izzy's building.

"You drove right by me and didn't even notice," Susan spoke petulantly, stepping right by him when Rich opened Izzy's front door. She placed the suitcase in the living room and then found her way to the kitchen. Izzy came out of his bathroom and was surprised to find her unloading a bag of groceries.

"Susan? What are you doing?"

Susan turned towards Izzy. In her hand was a loaf of pre-sliced rye bread. "I figured that you were going to need some food. I bought some cold cuts, some bread. . . just everyday stuff."

"That's very nice," Izzy commented as he opened his refrigerator. The shelves were all quite full. "However, I think you can see that your husband won't starve."

Rich walked into the kitchen and his wife turned towards him. "You told me that Izzy ate a lot of bachelor food!"

Rich looked embarrassed. "He does!" Rich paused and looked

at Izzy for support. None was forthcoming. "At the office. . . all he eats are donuts."

"That's all anyone in the office eats. Remember when I brought in those Canadian smoked meats. I had to take them home. Nobody touched them." Izzy paused and helped Susan find space in the refrigerator for the American cheese she had brought. He was a bit stunned by the volume and selection of foods. "Rich, how long you planning to be here?"

Rich walked over to the refrigerator and pulled out a peeled baby carrot from an open bag.

"I figure a couple of days," Rich offered as he popped the carrot into his mouth.

"A couple of days? You have to be kidding. I'm perfectly fine!"

Rich wagged a finger in Izzy's direction. "Can't be too careful."

Susan edged closer to the two men and interjected herself. "I gotta run. I left the kids with my mother." Susan gave Rich a quick peck on the cheek and headed for the front door. A moment later she was gone.

As soon as the front door was closed, Izzy parked himself in front of the computer. Rich came into the living room carrying two hard salami sandwiches on fresh Kaiser rolls. Izzy was back at work on his internet search. He ran the initials M.J. through a scientific web crawler. He set the search parameters for Germany, between the years 1935-1945. The search came up a blank. Rich wasn't terribly surprised. Medical research conducted in Germany during World War II remained a mystery to the rest of the world. Rich pointed out that it seemed doubtful that the Germans could have been working on anything substantial, especially considering that their resources were split between the war and destruction of the Jews.

Izzy was about to go back to Heneke's journal article when his email indicator started flashing at the bottom of the screen. Izzy moved his mouse arrow to the appropriate icon and accessed his email. There was only one message and it was short: "Jesse Owens was Ice-Two. Ice-Two started AIDS. Heneke."

Both Izzy and Rich stared at the message for a long time, neither saying a word. Finally, Rich tried to put words to the jumble of ideas that filled his head. "Okay, Heneke wants us to believe that Jesse Owens started AIDS. Jesse Owens? Jesse Owens? Does he mean the Olympic athlete?"

Izzy let out an exasperated sigh. "His last message said that Jesse Owens was alive and living in Buenos Aires. Now I don't know that much about Jesse Owens, but I do know that he's dead. Died of lung cancer in 1980. I checked it out."

"Maybe what Heneke is saying is that Jesse Owens was the first host for the AIDS virus. Maybe his cancer was AIDS related?"

Izzy laughed sarcastically. "I've never heard of even one AIDS related case of lung cancer. It's got to be much simpler than that, and somehow it ties back to something that happened in the thirties. If I could get my hands on that original footnoted research I'm sure that I'd find some answers."

Rich took a big bite of his sandwich and headed for the kitchen to get a beer. When he returned he had the "tuned-in" look in his eyes. "What is the one thing everybody knows about Jesse Owens?"

"No idea," Izzy replied while shrugging his shoulders.

"Owens destroyed the myth of Aryan superiority, and Hitler hated him for it. It took the Nazis months to rebuild morale. If not for Jesse Owens, Hitler could have started his war offensive much sooner. Perhaps those couple of months were the difference between the German's defeat and victory."

"And what does any of that have to do with AIDS?"

Rich Levine shook his head. Neither he nor Izzy could see any connections. Since Izzy was convinced that the answers were to be found in the science of the past, Germany's past, he knew the next place that he had to look.

Chapter 4

The oak trees on Sachem Street in New Haven, Connecticut were shedding leaves quickly as Izzy dropped the BMW into reverse and backed into a spot that was just big enough for his tiny convertible. The briskness of the fall wind caused him to pull his windbreaker closed as he dropped several quarters into a parking meter. It had been years since he last had been in New Haven, and he hoped that he remembered where to go. He stood motionless for several moments, trying to jog his memory. He didn't even realize that he was being watched. As he finally decided to turn to the left, he was approached by a young woman.

"Nice car," she said in a voice that was both seductive and slightly foreign. "I hope you have it alarmed."

Izzy nodded. "Bought it in the city. They don't even let cars out of the showroom without alarms." Izzy was about to walk away, but the young woman blocked his path and looked up into his face. "Is it fast?"

Izzy shrugged and decided he couldn't pass up the opportunity. It was clear that the woman was trying to make conversation, and flirting with a pretty college coed was a tonic for his middle-aged ego. "Needs bigger balls," he said matter-of-factly. "It looks hot, but it's got little tiny cajones."

The young woman didn't so much as blush at the double entendre, and replied with one of her own. "Perhaps she'd scream if you clutched while dropping the stick more quickly? I'd be happy show you."

Izzy was a bit flustered by the young woman's forwardness. If he hadn't had other things on his mind he might have permitted himself to take the girl for a ride. Instead, he just leaned a little closer and said, "Let me give you a piece of advice. Stay away from middle-aged men with beemers. Go after some young stud with a Mustang. You'll get more bang from your buck."

Izzy turned away from the girl and began walking up the sidewalk. The young woman called after him.

"Hey, isn't that supposed to be bang *for* your buck?"

Izzy glanced back over his shoulder with a playful smile on his face. "Think about it!" he shouted back. After walking about half a block he realized that he had turned in the wrong direction and changed course. When he passed by his car, he noticed the young woman he had been speaking with had moved to a grassy spot. She was seated underneath an oak tree. In her hand was a thick, heavy hardcover book which she was intently reading. As Izzy passed the oak tree the woman looked up from her book and smiled.

"I thought you might have turned in the wrong direction."

Izzy paused and turned towards the girl. "Were you talking to me?"

The young woman rose to her feet and came close. "You looked a little lost when you got out of your car. Can I help you find something?"

Izzy nodded. "I'm looking for the molecular biology and biophysics department. I think it's in the Kline Biology Tower. At least that's where it used to be."

The girl pointed a finger up the street. "Half a block up that way. I'll show you since I'm headed to the science library anyway."

"That would be very nice," Izzy replied graciously as he extended his hand. "I'm Doctor Isaiah Slesinger, Class of 71."

"Jean Dulac," the young woman replied as she began to walk up the street. Izzy followed after her, appraising her for the first time. Her light brown hair was cut short, just below the ear. Izzy guessed that she was about 5′ 4″, with the physique of a well-trained athlete. His eyes glanced down to her buttocks which looked highly muscled even through her loose baggy blue jeans. It was her thighs that grabbed his attention because they bulged largely, completely out of proportion with the rest of her legs.

"Perhaps a long distance runner," Izzy thought to himself as he became entranced by the powerful hypnotic motion of Jean's buttocks and thighs.

Jean came to a stop as she reached the intersection at the end of the block. Izzy, however, had sealed himself inside a fantasy world dominated by twenty-year-old thighs. Therefore, when Jean stopped walking Izzy crashed into her. The collision caused Jean to drop the book she had been reading.

"I'm so sorry," Izzy apologized as he knelt and picked up the book. He glanced at the title which caused an involuntary shiver to run down his spine. *Hitler's Willing Executioners, Ordinary Germans and The Holocaust* by Daniel Jonah Goldhagen. It was one of the books that Izzy had promised himself that he would read someday. However, he had put it off, not wanting to confront the emotions that the book often gave rise to. Goldhagen produced a firestorm of controversy when the book was first released. This was especially true among Holocaust survivors and their descendants. Perhaps Izzy should have seen the connection between the book and the fact that he had come to Yale to investigate German research during World War II. As it was, he didn't even note it as a coincidence as he handed to the book back to Jean. She took it and continued on across the street without saying a word.

The name on the door read, 'Doctor Ithamar M. Polansky,' and memories flooded Izzy's head. Doctor Polansky had been Izzy's advisor during graduate school. Ithamar Polansky was in his early forties when Izzy arrived at Yale in 1969. As an Orthodox Jew, he always seemed to have his nose buried in the Bible. He was only ten when his tiny Polish village was overrun by the Nazis. The horrors of the Dachau concentration camp left permanent scars, both physically and psychologically. It also gave the learned and observant professor a fierce attachment to the Jewish people, and to God.

"Why did I survive, when so many perished?" Izzy could remember that Doctor Polansky wrestled with that question often. Of course, there was no answer. Accepting it merely as God's will brought Doctor Polansky no solace. The atrocities he witnessed convinced him of both humanity's barbarism and the depth of its compassion. He had seen many sacrifice everything, including their own lives, so that others could live. Politically he was far more hawk than dove, believing that the Jewish people must be ever vigilant against what seemed like never ending anti-Semitism. Even though he believed that a second Holocaust was very possible, he remained committed to *tikun olum*, a rebuilding of the world through acts of kindness and peace. Every day he tried to follow the counsel of one of the wisest of the Jewish sages, Rabbi Hillel. The great rabbi instructed, "The more Torah, the more life, the more counsel, the more understanding; the more justice, the more peace."

Izzy clearly remembered Friday nights at the Polansky home. It was a small, blue 1920's cape, in the Orthodox section of New Haven called Westville. Directly across from the house was the Orthodox synagogue, and there was a large kosher market less than a block away. Ithamar's wife Eda treated Izzy like an adopted son. She always set a place for him on the Sabbath. Her chicken soup with homemade matzo balls was served in a bowl that was large enough to have fed King Solomon and all of his wives. Nothing made Eda Polansky happier than watching Izzy eat. On the Fridays when Izzy arrived late, he would find the Sabbath candles already lit. Ithamar was never in the house on those Fridays, having already left for services at the synagogue.

Izzy knocked on the door and a familiar, "Come in," beckoned him inward. He opened the door and found himself staring at an old man. For a moment Izzy was taken aback, wondering if he had entered the wrong office. His eyes even glanced at the name on the door for confirmation. The face looked familiar, Izzy realized, excepting for the fact that it was creased with the lines of old age. What hair was left had turned gray, and a pair of very thick looking glasses covered the eyes. Doubts that lingered, vanished completely when Ithamar looked up from the book he was reading. Of course, it was his Bible.

Ithamar stood slowly from his chair as a smile spread across his face. "Isaiah, my friend. What a pleasant surprise. What brings a *macha* like you to my little office?" A tinge of sarcasm could be heard in Ithamar's voice as he used the yiddish word for 'big shot.'

Izzy held up his hands defensively. "A *macha*? I think you meant to say *piske*." A *piske* was the yiddish word for "very little man." "The truth of it is I came to New Haven to see you."

"To see me?" Ithamar gushed. "For that you get a hug." Izzy felt crushed as two broad arms encircled him. For a gray-haired, bespectacled man of seventy, Itahmar was still strong as a bull.

"If you're here for only one day, I can have a graduate student cover my genetics class."

Izzy shook his head. "That won't be necessary. I'll be staying at least until tomorrow. I'm going to need to use the science library. I can meet with you any time that you find it convenient."

"Where are you staying?"

"I noticed a Residence Suites Hotel down by the water at Long Wharf. I'll head over after I start my research. However, if you'd like to get together later today, I'll go check in after dinner."

Ithamar looked at Izzy disapprovingly. "Absolutely not. I will not hear of such a thing. I'll call Eda and you'll be having dinner with us. And we'll be putting you up in the guest room as well. After a nice meal, and a little glass of schnapps, we'll have our chat."

Izzy knew there was no point in arguing. He shrugged his

shoulders in resignation and graciously accepted. He walked to Ithamar and draped an arm around his old professor's shoulder. When he spoke, he did so with an eastern European accent, even thicker than Ithamar's. "Of course, I would normally not accept such an offer of hospitality. However, for your sake I will accept."

Ithamar laughed. "For my sake? Eda will be very glad to hear that her 'little Izzy' has not become so famous that he can no longer stay with us."

"And how is Mrs. Polansky?" Izzy asked.

Ithamar looked toward heaven and let out a big sigh. "Eda is a difficult woman." He dropped his eyes and let them rest on the picture of his wife that sat squarely in the middle of his desk. It was a picture he had taken himself back in 1957, in black and white. His wife, still an attractive woman in her thirties, stood in front of the main gate of Yankee stadium. On her head was a Yankee hat. If the Nazis had finished 'The Final Solution', Eda would have been exterminated at Dachau, just another worthless Jewish Pole. But somehow, like Ithamar, she survived. She came to America as an orphan from family and country in 1946. The trauma of the Holocaust never went away, but eventually, she was able to manage her sorrow by hiding it down deep. She met Ithamar at a wedding for a mutual friend. They spent their first date walking on the boardwalk in Coney Island. Ithamar could remember trying to converse in Polish, Eda would have none of it. She disavowed any connection to her former country and would only speak English. Eda embraced America with arms wide. The picture of her with the Yankee's hat, and that big smile, always reminded Ithamar of how important America was to his wife.

After leaving Ithamar's office, Izzy found his way to the science library in the basement of the Kline Tower. The library had been updated since Izzy had last seen it. Rows and rows of colorful Apple computers filled the main research room. When Izzy had been a student, everything was in paper form. The room that he now stood in once contained over 50,000 bound journals, and it wasn't nearly as well lit. There were only a dozen or so students dispersed at computer stations around the room. Izzy stopped at the circulation desk and asked for directions to the lower stacks, just in case those had been moved as well. Fortunately, the lower stacks were the same as they always were. They contained the most technical and obscure journals. With the exception of Ph.D. candidates, hardly anyone ever went down into the bowels of the Kline Biology Library.

Izzy found the article he was searching for in the current edition of *Virus*. A research team at John Hopkins had discovered a frightening new twist pertaining to HIV, the virus thought to be responsible for AIDS. The medical community had been fighting the virus with powerful combinations of anti-virals. These powerful 'drug cocktails' had been shown to be very effective in eliminating any trace of HIV in an infected person's blood. The Hopkins team found that the HIV didn't vanish, it merely broke down into its molecular proteins, which in turn hid inside parts of cells where the virus proteins could no longer be attacked. This new data doomed patients to a life that would never be free of powerful, costly medicines. Worse, the data suggested that the viral proteins had the ability to reorder themselves, emerging from the host cell with an immunity to the original drug cocktail. If the study was accurate, and Izzy thought the data looked pretty damn convincing, the war on AIDS was going to get considerably harder, and many more people were going to die.

It was the conclusion of the Johns Hopkins team that left Izzy the most unsettled. "After much study we have concluded that the current batch of protease inhibitors does little or nothing to eliminate HIV from hosts. The inhibitors merely force the virus to splinter into protein fragments, and these fragments have the potential to reemerge as more virulent cellular invaders. We are forced to conclude that current science is not curing the disease, but merely treating a symptom. If and when the medical community has the ability to reorder the protein sequence, it will also have the ability to render the human immuno virus impotent."

"Reorder the protein sequence, reorder the protein sequence," the words played in Izzy's mind over and over again. The exact phrase used by Doctor Van Bassen before he placed the gun in his mouth and pulled the trigger. Now, here it was again, a reference to a type of therapy that was at best science fiction. Izzy found his way back to the circulation desk, purchased a magnetic strip access card for use on a copy machine, and proceeded to copy the entire eighteen page journal article. It was a little after five when Izzy left the Yale parking lot. He remembered how much Mrs. Polansky hated it when he arrived late for dinner.

"Is zat my leetle Izzy?" cried Eda Polansky as she swung open the door to her home. Her Polish accent hadn't been the least bit diminished. Izzy's couldn't believe his eyes. Eda looked worse than her husband, much worse. She had become quite *zaftig*, with a noticeable bend in her spine. Both her wrists and ankles were swollen with edema, and her coloring was quite pale.

When she stepped back so that Izzy could enter, he noticed she needed to balance herself with a white cane. "Ithamar's in the study. Go on in and I will call the two of you when dinner is ready."

Izzy entered the office, which was really a converted sun-porch. Ithamar stood in the far corner, looking towards the wall. His shoulder and arms were draped in a talis, a Jewish prayer shawl. Around his head a Tefillin box was tied with leather straps. The box contained a parchment on which part of the Torah was written. Though Ithamar held an open Bible in both hands, his eyes were shut tightly. He rocked back and forth on the balls of his feet, praying silently to God. When at last he opened his eyes, a peaceful, rested look settled on his face.

As Ithamar slowly and lovingly folded his talis, and replaced it in its worn velvet carrying bag, Izzy made an observation, "In all the years that I have known you, I have never once seen you reading anything but the Bible. Not even journals. I don't think I've ever seen you more than glance at a textbook, and then only during a lecture. How is it that you stay on top of everything? There are new biological discoveries every day."

Ithamar nodded and held out his Bible lovingly. "There is much biology in the Bible, Isaiah. Much biology!" That's what Ithamar said about everything. That there was "much of everything" in God's Bible.

Eda called the men to dinner, and they assembled at the table in the kitchen. A quick motzi was said over the bread, and chicken soup with matzo balls was served.

"So what brought you to see me?" Ithamar asked between spoonfuls of soup.

Izzy took a moment to frame his question. "I've been looking into the work of Pieter Heneke. His current work suggests that the Germans were experimenting on manipulations of mRNA during World War II. Do you know anything about that?"

Ithamar stopped eating and looked up at Izzy. "I know Pieter's work. He's a good scientist."

"He suggests that they were doing experimentation on living people."

Eda shivered but remained silent. She did her best to force the images of the Holocaust from her mind. How many Jewish children did she see disappear into the clinics, never to reappear.

"I think the record is quite clear on German medical atrocities. Anything Pieter said happened, probably did."

"His current research is on black populations. Do you remember any blacks in the camps?"

Ithamar let his mind drift back. "Blacks? When I was at Dachau there were only Jews and gypsies. I think France was the only European country with an established Negro population. Ask Eda, she might remember differently."

Izzy turned towards Mrs. Polansky who was having trouble keeping her lower lip from trembling. Her anger burst out as she began speaking rapidly with her hands. "*Schvatzas*, you want me to remember *schvatzas*? I lost my bubbie and my zadie, not to mention my parents and my sisters, and you're asking me about *schvatzas*? No, Izzy, there were no *schvatzas* in the camps!" When Eda finished she had troubling catching her breath.

Ithamar noticed the trembling in his wife's hands. "Eda, did you take your medicine?"

Eda was having trouble thinking clearly. Her agitated state-of-mind caused the glucose levels in her blood to rise. She was beginning to show the signs of a diabetic episode. Ithamar immediately left the table and retrieved his wife's prescription of glyburide, an anti-diabetic drug. He removed a pill from the container and placed it in her right hand. With effort, she guided the pill into her mouth, and swallowed. As with all medicines that treat diabetes mellitus, it took several minutes for the glyburide to stimulate insulin production in the pancreas. Izzy watched nervously as the woman who had been like a second mother to him started to return to normal.

"Eda, perhaps you should go lie down for a little while," Ithamar suggested. Eda agreed. She stood, stepped gingerly from the table and her husband helped her slowly walk to the bedroom. Several moments later he returned to the kitchen table. Izzy's face was etched with lines of tension and worry.

"As you can see, Eda has diabetes. She developed the condition about eight years ago. It's not so bad. As long as she takes her medicine, she's fine." Ithamar went on with his explanation, more for his own sake than for Izzy's. "It's mostly at this time of year. What with schlepping to the cemetery and cleaning the whole house for Rosh Hashanah. It would make anyone sick."

"Since when do black people make her so crazy?"

Ithamar's voice became very firm. "Shame on you, Isaiah. Shame on you. Eda Polansky is no bigot."

"I didn't say that she was."

Ithamar took a big breath and tried to calm himself. "Over the past decade the black community has surrounded this little neighborhood. Eda's been accosted on the street numerous times, in broad daylight."

"You can't blame that on the black community?"

"Why not?" Ithamar questioned as he drew close to Izzy. "When I first came to this country I had nothing. One tiny room in Flatbush. No one had anything. But what we had, we cherished. Harlem was filled with black men who pulled themselves up, through education."

"Things are a lot different today. A big part of the educational system has failed to meet the needs of inner city kids."

Ithamar disagreed. "Maybe it's inner city kids who fail to meet the needs of the educational system. It's hard to get an education when you're roaming the streets at eleven in the morning. If you want to blame it on the family, I will agree with you. These inner city parents have failed, and failed miserably. You want out of the jungle? The only way out is through education."

Before Izzy could reply, the phone rang. Ithamar listened for a moment and replied with a "I'll be right there."

"Is something wrong?" Izzy asked.

Ithamar shook his head. "They need a minyan at the synagogue so they can say kaddish. I should be back in about an hour. Eda made a bed for you in the guest room. Feel free to watch television, or you can read in my study?"

"I hope I haven't caused too many problems."

Ithamar shook his head as he pulled on his heavy, woolen overcoat. "Don't be silly. This is how Jews discuss everything." Ithamar took a step towards the door, hesitated, and looked back towards Izzy. "Racism and anti-Semitism are two sides of the same coin. *Shver tzu zein ein yid*." Ithamar departed by reminding, in Yiddish, that it was "very hard to be a Jew."

Doctor Polansky's study was crammed with research books

and journals. The bookshelves were the type that were attached right to the walls with brackets. Izzy noticed the weight of the shelves had started to cause the bracket screws to pull out of the plaster of the walls. On one of the shelves was copy of Dave Dunlevy's book on AIDS entitled *The Dunlevy Dilemma*. Izzy removed the book and settled himself behind Ithamar's tiny wooden desk. It reminded Izzy of the type of desk that was often found in public schools, those whitewashed oak desks that hadn't been made in forty years. Izzy was certain that Ithamar must have found it at a neighborhood tag sale.

It had been several years since Izzy had looked at the Dunlevy book. Dave had fired up a controversy within the scientific community. According to his findings, the connection between HIV and AIDS was anecdotal at best. The Dunlevy hypothesis contended that most AIDS related diseases could be related to drug use, especially among America's gay community. He pointed out that alkyl nitrates, commonly called 'poppers', were used as aphrodisiacs by gay men. The drug also helped to loosen anal muscles, thereby allowing easier penile insertion.

Alkyl nitrates were highly toxic. So toxic, that most human cells died within minutes of direct contact. Many of the nitrates had been shown to cause cancer in laboratory animals, many of the same cancers that were thought to be AIDS related. Dave went on to show that many patients with HIV, who weren't drug users, never developed an AIDS disease. He also showed case histories of HIV negative drug users who suffered from bacterial infections, cytomegalovirus infections, and Kaposi's sarcoma, all considered to be consequences of HIV.

Unfortunately, Dunlevy's hypothesis fell apart when he looked at African data. HIV was an epidemic in Africa, with over 40 million cases reported. Those numbers were roughly forty times greater than the numbers in America, forty times. Dunlevy couldn't explain why forty million African's were on their death beds?

Lack of condom use and multiple sexual partners couldn't account for the widespread proliferation of a slow developing medical condition. He also couldn't explain why Africa has more HIV positive women than men?

Izzy flipped through Dave's book and thought back to Heneke's journal article. His findings on genotypic differences in African populations was in keeping with current American studies. Scientists at Harvard and Yale had shown that twenty-four percent of white people carry an HIV resistant gene, in comparison with less than two percent for blacks. Those findings did a lot to answer Dunlevy's question about Africans. They lived in a society that had little access or use for condoms or 'safe sex', and they had little natural immunity to the virus. Dunlevy had no argument with the fact that the HIV virus was transmitted sexually.

Izzy put the book down and noticed a heavily dog-eared issue of Scientific America sitting on Ithamar's desk. He flipped through the pages of the journal and came upon an article entitled "How HIV Defeats the Immune System." Its authors were Martin Nowak and Andrew McMichael, two Brits that Izzy respected. They were both at the University of Oxford. Izzy hadn't seen either in years, but he remembered them both to be excellent and detailed. He read their article with interest and fascination.

"Research indicates that HIV replicates prodigiously and destroys many cells of the immune system each day. But this growth is met, usually for many years, by a vigorous defensive response that blocks the virus from multiplying out of control. Commonly, however, the balance of power shifts so that HIV gains the upper hand and causes sever immune impairment that defines full blown AIDS."

Clearly, the Brits were not in Dunlevy's camp. They could see a connection between a HIV weakened immune system and the AIDS diseases. They pointed out that the white blood cells which could attack and destroy HIV were peptide specific. Like any virus,

HIV can only replicate inside a host cell. The host cell fragments the virus into peptides, or protein fragments, which are then in turn displayed on the cell's surface. If the appropriate killer lymphocyte for that specific peptide passes by, the host cell is destroyed. Unfortunately, while white blood cells can only destroy one peptide specific type of HIV, the virus can kill any type of white blood cell. The Brits compared it to a battle, one in which the human body's defenses were outnumbered at the start.

They took the battle analogy a step further, showing that the body's t-cell defenses were attacked differently. The t-cells could be split into killer t-cells and helper t-cells. The killers couldn't be effective without the aid of the helpers. If HIV attacked a killer t-cell, there was a high likelihood that the virus itself would be destroyed. However, if HIV attacked the helper cell, there was little damage to itself. What's more, with the helpers gone, the virus had little to fear from the killer t-cells. It was almost as if the virus had been programmed in its mode of attack.

"A smart virus." The thought made Izzy shudder just as Ithamar walked into the study. Ithamar noticed the journal in Izzy's hand and Dunlevy's book on the desk. Ithamar took off his woolen coat and placed it gently on the hook behind the door.

"Come into the kitchen and I'll fix us both a nice cup of tea. I'll also explain why your friend David is such an idiot. I still can't believe he was once one of my students."

Izzy followed dutifully into the kitchen. Ithamar lifted the tarnished copper kettle from the stove, filled it with water at the tap, and placed it atop a burner on the gas stove. He placed a ceramic cookie jar, built in the shape of Noah's Arc, in the center of the table. Once he had retrieved two cups from the cabinet, he took off the top of the cookie jar and grabbed a homebaked, chocolate chip cookie. Between bites he began to explain his position. "Dunlevy contends that HIV doesn't cause disease. He points to cancers and sarcomas. He's correct in asserting that a healthy immune system does not protect against cellular mutation, nor does a defective immune system allow for greater cellular mutation. However, a deficient immune system certainly does allow for bacterial and secondary viral infection. Nowak and McMichael make it quite clear that HIV destroys the helper t-cells."

"How?"

"Let me grab the kettle and I'll tell you." Ithamar dropped a tea bag into each cup and then poured the hot water. Izzy reached for a cup but Ithamar wouldn't let him take it. "The Brits would tell you that it has to steep. Leave it and I will give it to you when it is ready."

"You've been spending too much time around Mrs. Polansky, do you know that?"

Ithamar nodded happily. "Thirty-four years. Be thankful that Yale still allows me to teach, and to do research. I'd really be a nudge if I had to stay home all the time. And Eda would divorce me." Ithamar pulled the tea bags from the cups and dropped them in the sink.

"They'll stain if you leave them in there," Izzy admonished.

"Do you want me to continue or not?" Ithamar asked as he pulled the tea bags from the sink and dropped them in the trash barrel.

"Please do," Izzy responded as he stirred a teaspoonful of sugar into his mug. "Explain to me why the body loses its ability to counter HIV attack? Even if killer cells are protein fragment specific, the body should be able to produce them, ad infinitum."

Ithamar looked at Izzy with an expression of pride. "Now you can see why that you, among all the others who have ever been in my classes, were my favorite. Somehow, Isaiah, you have the ability to see the forest from the trees. We know that HIV uses reverse transcriptase to copy its RNA genome into double stranded DNA. The virus mutates rapidly during this process because reverse transcriptase is rather error prone. I've read studies that show that each new generation of HIV is slightly different than the one that came before. That would make it the most genetically variably virus ever discovered. For our bodily defenses, it means trying to capture and destroy a moving target."

Izzy nodded his agreement. "So the virus kills a billion white blood cells or so. Why aren't there another billion or so to instantly take their place?"

Ithamar took a seat and pulled his chair close. He looked Izzy directly in the eyes before answering. "I believe the virus learns how to attack the cells of the thymus."

"Cellular attack of an organ? Maybe by something like Ebola, but not HIV."

"The virus does not destroy the thymus. It merely invades thymus cellular structure, actually overwhelms is a better word. As a consequence, t-cells recognize the peptides that they are looking for in cellular tissue and begin an attack. Eventually the attack is so great, the thymus loses its ability to operate. This causes complete collapse of the immune system."

"Have you any proof of this?"

Ithamar laughed. "Proof? Except for the presence of anti-bodies, and dropping t-cells counts, I can't even prove that HIV really exists inside people."

Both men finished their tea in silence. Izzy could see the implications. Maybe it would take years for an immune system to collapse, but eventually an all-infected immune system would cease to function. With a virus that was still spreading in all corners of the globe, deaths would be in the hundreds of millions. If the latent period for the virus stretched itself out long enough, perhaps over decades, the majority of the world's population could become infected. HIV would become a fatal pandemic of a type mankind had never before experienced.

Chapter 5

Wolfgang Hauer, president of Kaiser pharmaceutics, glanced out his office window. A thin blanket of fresh snow had fallen earlier, blanketing the Kaiser complex in a coating of white. The snow caused Mr. Hauer to think about the upcoming Christmas season, and thinking about Christmas allowed for some reflection on the past year. Construction of this new world headquarters and research complex had been completed in the spring, three months ahead of schedule. The two-wing, v-shaped, four-story building was small by pharmaceutical standards. However, what it lacked in size, it made up for in complexity of its organization.

Two-thirds of the building consisted of research laboratories. There were a total of fifteen separate research teams at work in the building. Each team was assigned one specific drug to develop and evaluate. Teams did not co-mingle with one another, share research breakthroughs or resources. Mr. Hauer believed such a system allowed for discipline and no distractions. His proof was in the financial success of the company. Six new Kaiser drugs were approved worldwide in the past year, and two had staked out dominant positions in the important North American territory.

Mr. Hauer was the first non-Kaiser to run Kaiser pharmaceutics.

He was a German's German—tall, with golden-blond neatly cropped hair, and the requisite blue eyes. His demeanor was precise and analytical. While there could be no arguing that his methods produced results, many Kaiser scientists believed him to be too much of a slave of the bottom line. Drugs intended to help rare conditions were never funded because there was no profit in them. Profits were Mr. Hauer's only motivation. Synthesis of artificial clotting factors had placed Kaiser products in every hospital in the world. However, Doctor Heneke's AIDS drug named PIRT-I9 or "Protease Inhibitor Reverse Transcriptase-I9," would catapult Kaiser to the top-tier of pharmaceutical companies.

Mr. Hauer had the financial projections sitting on his desk and they were astronomical. PIRT-I9 was the first single dose medicine which effectively eliminated the HIV virus from the human blood stream. Most HIV positive patients required a drug-cocktail mixture made up of four to six medications, all extremely expensive. Clinical trials had shown the best of cocktails to be effective on 68 percent of HIV positives. PIRT-I9 showed better than 95 percent effectiveness, with none of the toxic side effects that could be encountered with cocktails.

PIRT-I9 was not a project that Mr. Hauer had approved. Doctor Heneke's team was working on the drug long before Mr. Hauer arrived. From what Mr. Hauer knew, the research had been going on for better than twenty years, and Heneke's team didn't report to him. Everything that Heneke produced went directly to Adolf Kaiser, chairman of Kaiser's board of directors. It was Adolf who had propelled PIRT-I9 through the European approval process, gaining acceptance in less than a quarter of the time required for a typical drug.

Adolf was also responsible for coordinating the investigation into Doctor Heneke's death. In fact, he had been the first one to suggest to police that the explosion of Heneke's car had been deliberate. In the two weeks since the car fire, Adolf had pressed harder to win a quick approval for PIRT-I9 in America. He forced Heneke's team to work around the clock to prepare the New Drug Application (NDA) required by the Food and Drug Administration. Every time Mr. Hauer questioned the need for expediency, he was rebuffed. Kaiser was a privately held company, with Adolf its largest share holder. Therefore, Mr. Hauer could do little to press the issue.

Doctor Heneke and Adolf Kaiser had a long history. Adolf was born November 22nd, 1954. His father was a Nazi and Adolf had been named after the Fuhrer. Kaiser pharmaceutics supplied Germany with plasma products during World War II. When pseudo-geneticist, Doctor Joseph Mengele, first presented his final solution for Africa, he was laughed at. However, Hitler had much regard for Mengele. The Fuhrer introduced Mengele to the Kaisers, who embraced the idea of a genetically engineered Holocaust. The research was marked top secret. When it was clear that Germany was going to lose the war, the research was forgotten. . . forgotten by everyone except the Kaiser family.

Pieter Heneke was fresh out of residency in Berlin when he decided upon a research career. He was just a few weeks shy of his 24th birthday when he accepted the job offer from Kaiser. He could have gone anywhere. Many young scientists were called up by the war effort. German giants like Bayer were scooping up every scientist they could find. Heneke's specialty was protein chemistry, and Kaiser's work in plasmas seemed to be a good fit. Therefore, Heneke had witnessed the genesis of Mengele's work.

Mengele spent most of his time away from the Kaiser facility. He preferred the privacy of his clinics within the concentration camps. Within those walls he was free to absorb himself in atrocities. It was the children that presented the perfect laboratory, especially if they were twins.

One child would be used for experimentation, the other control. Usually both children died horrible, excruciating deaths. Most of

Mengele's experimentation went nowhere. Much as he tried to genetically change eye color, he failed. Much of his failure could be attributed to a rather poor understanding of genetics. Mengele was not a good scientist. However, because he experimented on living human beings, something ethical scientists would never dream of, he did make some discoveries which were well in advance of the traditional research of the day.

His biggest breakthrough came when he discovered genetic similarities between Tay-Sachs disease and sickle-cell anemia. While there were very few blacks available for experimentation, Jews were abundant. Jews with Tay-Sachs were studied in great detail. The gene controlling the disease was identified, and broken down into its proteins. Those proteins were then randomly reordered and reinserted in the cell. Those cells, in turn, were injected back into living hosts. In most cases nothing happened. Mengele had no idea what he was looking for, but if something didn't develop within six weeks, the trial was considered a failure.

Heneke was never allowed inside the camps. He was never allowed to review Mengele's scientific method or his procedures. His only role was to review the data. Being detached from the actual research left Heneke with a clear conscience. He was the one who had first proposed an alteration of mRNA along the DNA template. It had to be a small mutation; anything greater was beyond their science. And it had to be something that was self-replicating. After thousands of trials, Heneke was able to sustain a colony of cells with genetically altered mRNA.

Holocaust victims developed symptoms of illness within weeks of being injected with the cells. Many died of high fevers and other flu-like conditions. Mengele could see the results in infected people, but he was never able to actually identify a virus in their blood or tissues. The few patients who did not die, fully recovered, showing no trace of illness. However, the high mortality rate gave Mengele high hopes. If the cells also made Africans ill, Hitler could destroy the entire continent and it would be attributed to an epidemic. Mengele brought his findings to Hitler who ordered German troops to inoculate African populations. Between April and June of 1944, 20,000 Africans were inoculated. Most of those infected were in The Congo river area, the deepest, darkest part of the continent. Mengele and Hitler waited and nothing happened. Hitler concluded that Mengele's cell had no affect on African populations, and Germany abandoned the program. Mengele, however, was certain that something would happen. He hypothesized that Africans had a natural immunity which would eventually break down.

After Hitler committed suicide, Mengele fled to Argentina. He took with him all of his research and began his trials in South America. Over the remainder of his life, Mengele stayed in contact with Adolf Kaiser. Together they tracked the development of what would be termed the 'Mengele cell.' By the time Mengele died, manifestations of his cell had broken out in populations around the world. Usually they were seen as rare malignant cancers, accompanied by an impaired immune reaction.

Sometimes the manifestations were much worse. The Congo had seen many unexplained cases of hemorrhagic fever. Entire villages of people often died, with the deaths stretched out over years. Most hemorrhagic diseases, like those caused by the Ebola virus, spread and killed rapidly. All the available data from the Congo made its way to Adolf Kaiser, who turned it over to Heneke for analysis. The distance and lag times between flare-ups forced Heneke to come up with a unique hypothesis. He believed that the Mengele cell gave rise to a new kind of virus, a virus that could be passed by heredity to future generations. When the mortality numbers started to climb, Heneke realized that a virus could also be transmitted sexually between people.

By the early 1980's, Heneke could see that the problem was far more complex than he had imagined. Acquired Immune Deficiency Syndrome had exploded on the world. Each day there were new findings about a virus that attacked the immune system. This new virus had emerged mysteriously. In Europe and America it attacked the homosexual community first, and then moved into the general population. In Africa, it attacked just about everyone. The virus took the scientific community off-guard. It was the first invading microbe that couldn't even be detected in human blood for a decade or longer. Some patients developed sarcomas, most didn't. Some patients developed secondary infections, some didn't. While most scientists believed that this new virus, which they named HIV, destroyed immune function, none of them could explain why so many HIV positives never became sick. A fraction attributed it to natural immunity, most said they simply didn't know.

But as the decade of the eighties came to a close, Heneke knew. This new virus was actually a flag that waved over a Mengele cell. These cells were the breeding site for the virus. Eventually the virus would invade cells of the thymus. The thymus would be attacked by the body's own defenses, and the immune system would fail. It was exactly as Ithamar Polansky had described. Heneke also found that Mengele cells had a higher incidence of carcinogenic activity than normal cells. That explained the high rate of unusual cancers in HIV patients.

Mengele had succeeded in giving the world its first viral paradox. Not only were humans the target species for the virus, specific cells within humans were the host for the virus. That was supposed to be scientifically impossible. Hanta virus, for example, could be traced back to nearby rodent populations. That's the way viruses worked. One species was a host which harbored the virus but was unaffected by it. Another species was a target. The target species often died from the virus, with the virus hoping to infect another target before the first died. HIV changed the rules. With host and target being one and the same, there could be only one inevitable conclusion—death.

Heneke had to devise a two-tiered therapy. First, he had to

eliminate any trace of the virus from the human body. PIRT-I9 was very effective at completing the first stage of the treatment.

Unfortunately, Heneke also needed to be able to recreate the very first mutation from healthy cell to first generation Mengele cell. If that very first mutation could be undone using gene therapy, it was hypothetically possible to repair damaged cells within a patient. The reservoir for the virus would be destroyed.

After almost sixty years, millions of infected humans, and trillions of mutations, there was no way to use trial and error to trace back to the original mutation. The only way back was through Mengele's original notes. When Mengele fled a crumbling Nazi Germany, he took his research with him. Heneke was the last person to have seen the well documented research, and that was over fifty-five years ago. Heneke realized that it was beyond his ability to retrace Mengele's steps. As an arthritic eighty-one year-old, he could hardly put his shoes on in the morning. He needed a younger man, someone who had a prerequisite understanding of protein chemistry. This younger scientist would need to retrace Mengele's steps, quickly sift through what was relevant, and bring back his findings. The scientist that Heneke settled on was Isaiah Slesinger.

Adolf Kaiser followed the progression of Mengele's creation with great interest. Even after Mengele died, he did his best to track each eruption of disease and death. It was difficult getting information from undeveloped countries in Africa. He was also never certain if incidences of high mortality were caused by Mengele cells, or the myriad of diseases that were connected to poor sanitation and malnutrition. Sorting through the volumes of data was almost a full time job itself, and Adolf trusted no one well enough to share the task. By the end of 1989, Adolf had been able to attribute more than thirty million African mortalities to Mengele cells. Those deaths were stretched out over forty years.

Just as Adolf finished his analysis, East and West Germany tore down the Berlin Wall and reunited with one another. The influx of

East Germans and Poles inflamed members of neo-Nazi groups. These groups started calling for Aryan purity, no one louder than Adolf Kaiser. Germany had established the toughest anti-hate laws in the world and cracked down on skinheads and other Hitler motivated organizations. The crackdowns merely caused the groups to be more covert. Many relocated their operations to Austria in the North. Austria boasted about a population that was willing to look at Hitler less harshly. Many were willing to accept him as a national hero.

It was in the mid 1990's that Adolf came to realize the full implications of the Mengele cell. Hitler had searched for a final solution and Mengele had given birth to one, for all of humanity. However, Germans loyal to Hitler's ideals could still triumph over the world. All they needed to do was isolate themselves from other populations. Sexual contact between loyal Aryans and anyone else needed to be forbidden. There also needed to be an isolation from outside blood products. If they could accomplish something that seemed so simple, eventually they would rule the world.

Adolf encouraged Heneke's work on PIRT-I9. Elimination of the virus was a key element in the plan. With the specter of HIV lifted from the world, self-imposed sexual restraint would vanish. There would be a return to the free sex lifestyle of the 1970's, especially in America. It was exactly the social atmosphere required to spread Mengele cells freely. Adolf developed a computer program that projected an eighty-one percent worldwide infection by the year 2039. By then, a core group of loyal Aryans would grow to a population of several million. While he wouldn't see it with his own eyes, Adolf knew that a pure Aryan population would soon rule the planet.

Heneke's demise removed one less obstacle. With the PIRT-I9 vaccine proven, Heneke was considered a liability. Adolf was relatively certain that Heneke would fail in his quest to genetically repair Mengele cells. His greater fear was that Heneke would go to the government in Berlin with all his data. If the government realized what was happening, the plan would fail. Had Heneke not perished in the car fire, Adolf would have had the elderly scientist assassinated. With Heneke gone, Adolf simply had to push the PIRT-I9 vaccine through the various medical reviews around the world. Once it was accepted in America, he would consider most of his problems over.

Chaper 6

Izzy returned to Manhattan on Monday morning. He had spent the weekend researching in New Haven. As the little blue BMW passed under the George Washington Bridge, a light snow began to fall on the road. Almost immediately, the car began to slip. The beemers rear wheel drive offered little in the way of grip on icy surfaces, and Izzy backed his speed down to fifty.

"Snow," he thought to himself wonderingly as he made a left turn on 47th Street. "Two days ago it felt like spring." It was just one of nature's little reminders of how quickly things can change.

A cold shiver gripped Izzy the moment he walked in his door. He stood motionless, his eyes darting around the apartment. There was something different about the place, even though every thing looked the same. He immediately went to the filing cabinet beside his computer desk. The notebooks and journals were neatly piled, exactly in order. It was too neat and orderly; as if someone had broken in, stole nothing, and then straightened the place up. The flashing light on his answering machine caught his attention. He activated the playback and listened to four messages. Each was from Doctor Oksana Zibrova, and each sounded more frantic than the last.

"Izzy, this is Oksana, Oksana Zibrova. It is early Sunday and I have just been visited by American CIA. I am worried about you."

The last message, left late Sunday night, was the most panicked. "Izzy, it is Oksana again! Why haven't you called me? I am trying not to think the worst. I fear I am being followed by KGB." Izzy could plainly hear the distinctive, repeated clicks on the answering machine. He knew that meant someone had tapped into Oksana's phone line.

"This is crazy," he thought to himself as he grabbed his car keys and raced back out the door.

"What has Heneke gotten me into?" His heart pounded rapidly in his chest as he resettled himself behind the steering wheel. A loud screech reverberated through the building's underground parking garage. Izzy darted through mid morning traffic, narrowly missing a double parked car on 32nd and Third. By the time he reached the Brooklyn Battery Tunnel his mind was like a runaway freight train. He imagined terrorists abducting Oksana and spiriting her away.

The snow that had been falling in Manhattan was rain in Brooklyn. Izzy drove slowly through the Brighton Beach neighborhood that was home to a large cluster of immigrant Russian Jews. Despite having taken Oksana home after Rosh Hashanah dinner, he had trouble picking out her home. He remembered that it was a turn-of-the-century brick duplex. Unfortunately, that described most of the tenements on East Shore Road. The second to last duplex on the left seemed to jog his memory and he pulled over by the curb. The name under the second floor door bell spelled Zibrova and Izzy pressed into it several times. There was no response. However, an elderly woman pulled back the curtain of the first floor apartment, quickly peered at Izzy, and then pulled the curtain closed. Having no other recourse, Izzy rang the first floor bell. A moment later the door unbolted, and a small, gray-haired woman looked up at Izzy cautiously.

"Yes?"

"I am looking for Oksana Zibrova. Have you seen her?"

The woman instantly began trembling. "We vant no trouble. Go away!" The door slammed shut, leaving Izzy wet and cold out on the stoop.

Izzy's anxiety jumped to a new level. He stood motionlessly, staring at the front door and weighing his options. He was so lost in thought, he didn't hear Oksana's approach. When she tapped him on the shoulder he nearly jumped out his skin. He was so overjoyed at seeing her, he nearly crushed her with a huge bear hug.

"Izzy, let go of me," Oksana cried. Izzy dropped his arms and she backed away several steps. "I am very cross with you. You did not return my calls."

"I was out-of-town," Izzy replied. "As soon as I heard your messages I came right over. What the hell is going on?"

"I have been visited by an agent Hafler from the CIA. He wanted to know what you had told me about Doctor Heneke's research. I told him I did not know anything. I do not think he believed me...and I believe that I am being followed by the KGB."

Izzy looked over Oksana's shoulder for any signs of surveillance. The street was completely deserted. "Followed? The KGB? You're certain?"

Oksana nodded. "We should go inside and I will tell you about it." Oksana slipped her key into the door. She stepped into the hallway but Izzy hesitated.

"I need to get my research notes from New Haven. You won't believe the things I found out. I am starting to develop a theory that is so incredible. . . " Izzy stopped himself, deciding that it might be better to discuss it inside, especially if there were really others watching. He grabbed his files from the front seat of the BMW and locked the car tightly. As he turned towards the duplex apartment, he thought he could see a face move in a car that was parked half way down the block. The thought sent a shiver down his spine and he quickened his pace as he entered Oksana's building. Once inside he locked and double-bolted the door. After checking to make sure that it was secure, he climbed the stairs to Oksana's apartment.

Oksana was in the kitchen filling a teapot with tap water when Izzy walked in and placed a huge pile of material on her tiny, round kitchen table. She turned the tap off and placed the kettle on the stove. It took several seconds for the gas burner to catch. Oksana retrieved two cups from a cabinet and dropped a tea bag into each. "You were going to tell me about a new theory?"

Izzy took a moment to frame his words carefully. "I believe that the HIV virus has the ability to bring about somatic mutation in cells."

"Somatic mutation? Impossible. Viruses are incapable of changing the genetic make-up of cells."

Izzy nodded in agreement. "I know it sounds nuts. But it's the only way I can explain the cancers. You want to tell me that a patient with an impaired immune system can't fight off infection, no problem. But these bizarre cancers are something else. There is another mechanism at work, and I believe the virus somehow has the ability to change the genetic code."

Oksana grabbed the tea pot just before it whistled. She voiced her objection as she poured hot water into the two cups. "Only thirteen percent of AIDS patients die of sarcomas or carcinomas. We have just scratched the surface in understanding how the immune system battles cancerous and pre-cancerous cells. I will agree that many of the cancers are unusual, but viral induced somatic mutation, not possible!" Oksana lifted the tea bags from the cups and tossed them into her sink. "Would you like sugar?"

"What I'd like is an aspirin and a fifteen minute nap. I haven't slept well the last couple of nights and I have a headache the size of Texas."

Oksana left the room and came back with a bottle of aspirin. Izzy took two pills and retreated to the sofa in Oksana's living room. Within moments of settling himself he was sound asleep. Oksana retrieved an Afghan blanket from her bedroom and covered Izzy with it. When Izzy opened his eyes next it was a little after six in the evening. He had been asleep for almost two hours. Half-awake, Izzy stood and stared around the living room, trying to remember exactly where he was. There were photographs sitting in frames on top of an old, console-style television set. Izzy drifted to the photographs.

They were pictures of Oksana's family. Just as Izzy looked close, Oksana walked into the living room clutching one of Izzy's journal articles.

"Have you seen this paper by Heneke?"

Izzy turned from the pictures and looked at the journal as Oksana held it out in his direction. "That's the last paper Heneke wrote. It's about mRNA anomalies in African populations."

"Did you look at his references?" Oksana flipped through the article and exposed the back page. She pointed towards the initials next to the research that was conducted in the 1930's. "You realize who this is? Who Heneke collaborated with?"

"Haven't been able to figure that out," Izzy shrugged.

"Mengele, Joseph Mengele!"

"Mengele?" Like shifting shapes in a kaleidoscope, Izzy's world instantly fell away from him. He was now in a place that no one, especially no one who is Jewish, should enter.

"Mengele," Izzy thought to himself. The only butcher who was even more horrible than Hitler. So horrible, Izzy refused to believe it. "You must be mistaken," he replied with rising apprehension.

Oksana held firm to her assertion. "I have seen that citation many times. Much of Mengele's research fell into Russian hands after the war. His work is a chronology of atrocities beyond the imagining."

"Mengele?" Izzy repeated the name in a soft, dull monotone. "Auschwitz Mengele?" The name conjured images of walking skeletons. Images that were burned in Izzy's mind, from the countless black and white newsreels that he had watched as a boy during Hebrew school. Those images of horror had been compartmentalized deep into Izzy's subconscious. Over the past thirty years they were confronted infrequently. The last time was when the Swiss were accused of stealing Jewish assets. Before that, when Spielberg released 'Schindler's List.' That film was too large to ignore. Mostly, Izzy dealt with the hurt, anger, and confusion by not dealing with it.

Hitler was a very real evil in the Jewish section of Flatbush. Every family had a relative, a cousin, an uncle, grandparents who remained in the old country. Izzy's father, Ira, had many relatives who lived in the villages of southern Germany. The atrocities that were reported through an underground network seemed too brutal to comprehend. At first it was easy to dismiss the stories. As months turned into years and the war rolled on, the reports were no longer possible to ignore. In April of 1943, Ira Slesinger enlisted in the U.S. Army. Six weeks later he bid a sad goodbye to his pregnant wife and three year old daughter.

It was Ira Slesinger's battalion that was the first to enter Dachau. They could smell the putrid odor of rotting corpses long before they could see the barbed wire encased camp. The surviving prisoners were beyond emaciation, skeletons, barely alive. After a long, brutal war, it was more than many of the American soldiers could bear. A private in Ira's battalion snapped completely. He aimed his automatic assault rifle at a group of German POW's and dispatched them without uttering a sound. When the last body fell, he turned the weapon on himself.

By the time Ira Slesinger returned to America, Izzy was already eight-months-old. From his first day home a deep seated guilt ate at him for not having done something earlier. There was very little conversation in the Slesinger household about the concentration camp. What little was said fell into Shana's purvey. She was the oldest and, therefore, became the recipient of the stories that Ira was able to share. It would have been hard for Izzy to say that he felt left out. He was too young to understand the hushed words that his father shared with his older sister. Ira Slesinger shouldered most of his embarrassment silently, yet it was as plain as an albatross around his neck. The feelings of guilt and remorse stayed with him until the day he died at age fifty-six. Unfortunately, the shame did not die with him. He passed it along to Izzy.

"If Doctor Heneke based his work on Mengele's research, no good will come of it! I can assure you that!" Oksana's words were sharp, yet Izzy barely heard them. He was lost in memories of his old house. Of sitting outside of Shana's door and listening to his father speaking in hushed tones, and weeping. "Izzy, are you all right?"

"Uh, yeah, I guess. It's just a bit much to wrap my brain around."

"You look a little pale. It's almost dinner time. I'll go into the kitchen and fix us something to eat."

While Oksana worked on dinner, Izzy reread Heneke's paper again. He was seated on the sofa when a hand from another time reached out across half a century. The fingers tore deeply into Izzy's shoulder and the hand shook him. He shivered with a sudden cold chill and placed the paper aside. By the time he reached the kitchen his teeth were actually chattering.

Oksana took one look at Izzy and directed him to a seat at the table. A moment later she served a steaming hot bowl of chicken soup. The soup was almost too hot to eat, but Izzy relished the warmth. It wasn't long before the feeling of coldness abated. The dinner was consumed in near silence. Izzy was lost in thought, and Oksana realized that there was no point in conversation.

Immediately after dinner, Izzy went back to the living room and began reading Heneke's article again. There was something more to this mRNA anomaly in black populations, something much more. It was commonly believed that HIV had made the leap from a primate host to man. The first HIV cases were traced back to Africa, and since the other thread viruses were simian based, that was the natural assumption for HIV as well. However, no one had ever found the host species. Scientists around the world had tested tens of thousands of different types of primates with no luck.

"What if Mengele somehow designed this virus?" The thought made Izzy shudder. "Could it have been designed as a type of weapon?" Izzy dismissed that idea immediately. HIV was a poor device for targeted destruction. The virus had an enormously long gestation period, it wasn't always lethal, and it couldn't be targeted at any individual population. Germany had as many AIDS patients as the rest of Europe, maybe more. "What if Mengele engineered the virus as a doomsday weapon, targeted at the entire world?" That question was not quite so easy to dismiss. Izzy could imagine the Nazis attempting one last desperate act before they were defeated. If Germany were to fall, so too would the rest of humanity. Even if such a fall would take time.

Oksana placed her hands on the back of Izzy's shoulders and tried to massage the tension out of his muscles. Izzy rotated his torso and looked up at Oksana. "What if AIDS is a manufactured virus? What if the Nazis had created it as a weapon of last recourse?" Izzy's question brought a sudden shift in Oksana's demeanor. Her hands slipped from Izzy's shoulders and a somber expression creased her face.

"A weapon? I do not think so. A weapon must kill quickly. A bacterial poison such as botulinal extract would be much more effective." Oksana made a space between her right thumb and forefinger. "A vile this large could contain enough toxin to kill millions."

Izzy stood from the sofa and began to pace. "Yes, if you want the deaths quick and sudden. The problem with biological attack is the destruction is localized. One battalion, one town, maybe a county or a drinking reservoir. But that's it."

Oksana looked perplexed. "Isn't that enough?"

Izzy shook his head. "Not if your target is the whole world. Think about the plague in the 1400's. One-third of Europe died, one-third! And the whole continent might have expired if they didn't get rid of the rats and fleas. For a biological to be an effective weapon, you need both target and host species in close proximity."

"That is exactly why HIV could not be a weapon. Transmission is via bodily fluids. One person at a time. I have seen many infected HIV patients. Onset of disease and complicating factors can be many years, even decades."

"Which, if you were targeting the whole world, would be precisely how you would want it to be. The virus would spread slowly, mostly through sexual contact. Not only does the virus infect other people, but also conceived fetuses. Therefore, each new infected generation is larger than the one that came before it."

Oksana rejected Izzy's theory. "Actual cases of AIDS-related diseases are rising fastest in the old Soviet republics. I've seen these people with my own eyes. They aren't having intercourse! Most have all they can do just to keep death away on a daily basis. They die horrible, long-suffering deaths."

Izzy picked up a yellow lined pad and began to scratch out a rough time-line. He placed 1943 at one end and left the other open. "Africa is the conundrum!" he stated as he tapped the end of his pencil against the pad. "I'm going to assume that millions of Africans have died from AIDS over the past fifty years. Most deaths have been attributed to other causes because of the lack of advanced medical care. However, it doesn't explain why there are at least ten or fifteen million HIV positives who show no signs of illness. What good is a doomsday virus if it leaves a large segment of the population unharmed?" While Izzy's unanswered questions pointed him in the right direction, he had forgotten about Ice-9. That oversight caused him to put everything else backwards.

Chapter 7

Thick, gray clouds hung tightly over Brighton Beach on Thursday morning. The rain had stopped, but there was a rawness in the air that made Izzy shiver as he settled himself in the passenger's seat of Oksana's red Saab 900. The car was ancient, with seats that were worn and tattered. The rubber seals around the sunroof were cracked and droplets of water dripped into the backseat. A droplet splashed onto Izzy's forehead as Oksana turned onto the Grand Central Parkway which connected Brooklyn to the Queens. Izzy wiped the water from his brow and pressed his face to the passenger side window. He could barely see the outline of Shea Stadium off in the distance. As Oksana got closer to the stadium the rains began to fall again.

"I should go with you," Oksana repeated for about the twentieth time. Izzy hadn't been able to get much sleep on Oksana's sofa, his brain just wouldn't shut off. Shortly before midnight he decided that he needed to see Dave Dunlevy in California. His phone call to airline reservations woke Oksana, who wasn't sleeping all that well herself.

Izzy turned in his seat towards her. "We've been through this. You have patients to see, and a practice to maintain. I'm only going to be in L.A. for two days. Dave's going to pick me up at the airport and I'll be staying with him."

Oksana glanced towards Izzy as she exited the Parkway at LaGuardia airport. "I will be worried about you, Izzy."

A lump formed in Izzy's throat. He had known Oksana for less than a week, and yet, he felt closer to her than any other woman he had known in a very long time. As worried as she was about him, he was doubly worried about her. What if she was right and the KGB was really following her. Her lack of information would prove to be little defense if she was abducted and interrogated.

"I'll be home in time for Kol Nidre services on Sunday. This whole week has passed in a blur. One second I'm in temple for Rosh Hashanah, then poof, I'm smack dab in the middle of a medical mystery that Robin Cook couldn't dream up on his best day."

Oksana stopped the car in front of the United Airlines terminal. She put the car in neutral and released her seatbelt. "You will be careful," Oksana admonished as she leaned over and gave Izzy a quick kiss on the cheek.

Izzy reached into his pocket and removed his keys. He placed them on top of the dashboard.

"I'd feel better if you stayed at my place until I got back. At least I've got a doorman. And there are a lot of other people in the building. If you take the BMW you can use the opener in the glove compartment to get into the parking garage." Izzy grabbed his suitcase from the backseat and opened his door. He stepped to the curb and lingered before closing the door. Izzy motioned for Oksana to roll down the window which she did. He placed both hands on the window frame and leaned his head back into the car. "I have heard that Latvian women have no sexual stamina."

Before Oksana could respond, Izzy was on his way inside the terminal. As the automatic doors slid shut, paranoia set in. Izzy rocked nervously from foot to foot as he waited at the ticket counter. Each time someone walked by, he jumped. He imagined KGB agents around him everywhere. Not only KGB, but CIA. It wasn't until Izzy stepped on the Boeing 757 that he calmed down. At least on the plane no one would be bold enough to confront him.

The direct flight from New York to Los Angeles International Airport took four hours and thirty-seven minutes. Izzy spent the entire flight working through his thoughts on a pad of paper. He wrote thirty pages and crossed out twenty-nine. The only thing that he didn't cross out was a summary of 'Koch's postulates.'

Doctor Robert Koch was a German physician who studied both anthrax and tuberculosis in the late nineteenth century. In 1884 he published a key paper on tuberculosis which spelled out the three criteria required to tie a microorganism to a disease. Izzy reviewed the criteria over and over again:

*The organism must be found in abundance in every patient and in every diseased tissue.

*The organism must be isolated and cultured in a test tube.

*The organism must produce the disease when injected into another host.

Izzy thought about all the diseases that had failed the scrutiny of Koch's postulates. Pellagra was a good example. At first the deadly vitamin deficiency was thought to be microbial in origin. Its symptoms paralleled those of AIDS: nervous disorders, dementia, muscle wasting, slime disease, diarrhea, and death. Epidemics were all too common in Europe in the late eighteenth and early nineteenth centuries. In the early twentieth century, pellagra made its way to the United States. Scientists could not identify a particular microbe, nor could they produce pellagra in another species. In the 1930s, scientists discovered the vitamin niacin, and its importance in diets. Since the discovery, pellagra has almost completely disappeared.

Izzy subjected HIV to the postulates, and like pellagra, it failed to meet the criteria. To the best of Izzy's knowledge, there were thousands of HIV positives who never became ill. "Perhaps this is the one microbe that doesn't fit the postulates?" Izzy thought as the wheels of the jet kissed the tarmac. Izzy gathered his belongings. He pulled his small suitcase from underneath the seat and retrieved his monogrammed soft-sided briefcase from the overhead compartment. As Izzy waited for the plane to empty, he hoped that Dave Dunlevy would be able to provide some answers.

Hazy sunshine cascaded through the windows of the United terminal. True to his word, Dave Dunlevy was waiting by the gate. Izzy was immediately struck by how gray Dave's hair had gotten. It had been less than three years since they had seen each other and Dave had gone from salt and pepper to almost solid gray. However, he still looked as trim as he did in college.

"Dizzy, Izzy Slesinger finally visits L.A. Emily's put together a list of girlfriends she'd like to fix you up with."

Izzy rolled his eyes contemptuously. "I'm here ten seconds and I'm already thinking of heading back to New York." Actually, Izzy was a bit nervous about seeing Emily again. Every time they got together, he remembered how much of a crush he had on her in college. On this visit he was certain that it would be different, certain that he finally had Emily out of his system.

"I've been telling you for twenty years that this place is paradise. God, with your C.V. you could make ten times out here what they pay you at The Institute. You could buy a nice house. . . "

Izzy held up his hand to silence Dave. "If I want suburbs I'll move to Westchester. When someone in California invents a real city, I'll be the first to move in." The automatic doors of the airport terminal slid open and the heat of the California sun made Izzy blanche. He immediately removed his long, black winter coat, folded it twice, and tucked it under his arm. The brightness made him squint and as he raised his right arm in an attempt to shield his eyes, he dropped his briefcase. He bent over to pick it up and got the sensation that he was being watched. He stood slowly as he let his eyes dart from side to side. He didn't see anyone, but that did nothing to calm his nerves.

Izzy was still tense as Dave pulled his brand new Honda sport utility vehicle out of the airport parking lot. The sudden burst of adrenalin gave Izzy a headache and he tried to calm it by closing his eyes.

"You still getting those tension migraines?" Dave asked the question as he fought his way through three lanes of speeding traffic and got off at the first Glendale exit.

Izzy opened his eyes and forced himself to concentrate on Dave's profile. He had to admit to himself that the fully gray beard and new gun metal colored bifocals gave his old college roommate a rather scholarly appearance. "I think the older I get, the worse the headaches get. Fortunately, I only get them every couple of months."

"Someday, we're going to be able to cure that," Dave responded as he pulled onto a street lined with white and red stucco homes. "We are going to have the ability to identify the gene that controls those migraines and shut them off. And it is going to happen sooner, as opposed to later." Dave stopped the SUV in front of a large, Spanish style house. The house seemed out-of-place on its lot, stretching almost the full distance from one property border to the other. Izzy guessed that there couldn't be more than half a dozen feet separating Dave's house from his neighbor's. The full size John Deere riding mower by the garage was an interesting juxtapose, con- sidering that the front lawn couldn't have been bigger than 12' x 30'.

As soon as Izzy stepped out of the SUV, the front door of the house opened and Emily ran out onto the lawn. "How y'all doing, Izzy?" Fifteen years among the Angelinos had done little to weaken Emily's Atlanta accent. However, everything else about her was quite different. The long, flowing blond hair had been cropped short, just about ear length. She was dressed in navy blue tailored slacks and white silk blouse. Izzy let his eyes drop to Emily's chest. She was definitely a lot larger than he remembered. She even felt larger when she gave him a big hug.

"It's so good to see y'all. The girls will be so thrilled to finally meet crazy uncle Izzy."

"Where are Sarah and Susan?" Izzy knew the names of the twin seven-year-old girls from the Hanukkah card Emily sent every year.

Emily tapped her watch. "Why they're in school of course. It's just a bit past lunch time. Did y'all forget to set back your watch?"

Izzy had forgotten all about the time difference. His thoughts on the plane had been consumed by Koch's postulates. He reached down and pulled out the stem of his watch and set the time back three hours. Dave came up beside Izzy and handed his wife the keys to the Honda.

"I put gas in the tank before I went to the airport. The Honda dealer is going to call when the car is ready. They said they would deliver the car to the house."

Emily nodded and gave Dave a quick kiss on the cheek. "Dharma's coming into the office to talk about career strategy. She wants me to get her a movie, a big movie. I keep telling her how hard it is to go from television. . . but will she listen?"

Dave just nodded as Emily walked to the SUV and got in. He turned toward Izzy as Emily drove away from the house. "Emily opened a management practice for film and television actors. Talk about a different world."

Izzy chuckled. "Emily? You've got to be kidding. I remember how much pride she took in being in Yale's first graduating class of environmental lawyers. She was single handedly going to change the world."

"People change," was Dave's only response. That, and a shrug of the shoulders. He led Izzy inside the house and gave him a quick tour. After Izzy placed his suitcase on top of the bed in the guest room, he followed Dave into the kitchen. It was an earthy, yet not totally inviting space. The walls were sponge painted with a mixture of greens and browns. Large glass windows dominated the back kitchen wall, and those windows looked down on hills dotted with sagebrush and other homes. Izzy hadn't realized it, but Dave's neighborhood was built high on a hill.

Dave pulled a can of tuna from a kitchen shelf and retrieved mayonnaise and a loaf of bread from the refrigerator. "So what was this big secret you wanted to talk to me about?" Dave asked the question as he dropped a big glob of mayonnaise into a glass mixing bowl and then scooped the tuna out of the can.

"I believe HIV has been around longer than the scientific community realizes."

Dave stopped mixing the tuna and turned towards his friend with a curious expression on his face. "You couldn't have told me that over the phone?"

"Look at the numbers in Africa. Over 28 million positives, almost all of them heterosexuals who don't use drugs. Africa has a 50/50 distribution of infection between men and women. Now conventional wisdom wants us to believe that Africa has such a high rate of infection because of polygamous mating. I don't buy it."

Dave laughed. "You don't buy it? So how, pray tell, did these 28 million infections occur? Osmosis?"

Izzy shrugged his shoulders and cast his gaze towards the kitchen floor. "I'm not sure. What I believe is that there is a huge host reservoir of this bug, and that this reservoir has been in close proximity to people for a long time, maybe as much as half a century. Further, I believe that we've already had millions of deaths from HIV around the world, dating back three, maybe four decades."

Dave did the math in his head quickly. "You think this goes back to the sixties?"

"The late fifties," Izzy replied and then became silent.

Dave spread some tuna on two slices of bread, added some tomato, lettuce and a slice of American cheese. He then added a second slice of bread to top each sandwich. "You could be right," Dave replied nonchalantly, not finding anything particularly earth shattering in Izzy's theory. "We know the host is some type of monkey. Lots of monkeys in Africa. There were even more of them thirty or forty years ago."

Izzy shook his head as he took a seat at the kitchen table and Dave placed the sandwich in front of him. "It's not a monkey."

Dave took a seat next to Izzy. "Of course it's a monkey."

"It's not!" Izzy replied firmly. "That much I know."

Dave could tell there was something that Izzy wasn't telling him. "Okay Slesinger, out with it. What is it that you aren't telling me?"

"I realize that you are skeptical about the correlation between the virus and AIDS."

"Damn right," Dave interjected. "Beyond the secondary infections I see no correlation. Viruses do not in and of themselves cause cellular disruption."

"Not unless that is what they were engineered to do."

"Excuse me? Did I just hear you say engineered?"

Izzy nodded slowly. "I believe HIV is man-made."

"Man-made?" Dave laughed. "You think it was man-made, and that it goes back fifty years. Impossible!"

Izzy reached out and grabbed a hold of Dave's right hand. "Doctor Joseph Mengele."

Dave immediately burst out laughing. "You think HIV was some type of Nazi weapon?"

Izzy nodded again. "I do."

Dave slapped Izzy across the shoulders. "Tell you what. You write the screenplay, I'll give it to Emily, she in turn will call her buddies at the studios, and we'll make a ton of money from the movie."

Izzy glared at his friend. "I'm being serious about this. I believe Mengele engineered this virus, and then this new virus found a host...not a monkey. . . that is in close proximity to human populations. Maybe a rodent."

"Izzy, I think you're way off base on this one," Dave replied. "And how would Mengele engineer a virus that we can't engineer today? It just doesn't make sense."

"If it made sense I wouldn't have flown all the way to California." Izzy paused, stood on his feet, and began pacing. "If it made sense, a

Dutch Doctor would not have blown his brains out in my office!" Izzy's voice became louder and his pacing became frantic. "If it made sense, the KGB would not be following my girlfriend."

Dave tried to calm Izzy down. "Okay. Okay. Let's assume you're right. Viruses aren't missiles, you can't aim them. And why engineer a virus with an extremely long latency?"

"Here's the really crazy part. I think the original virus was designed to be population specific. Mengele intended it to destroy Africa. Destroy Africa not immediately, but over generations."

"You seriously want me to believe that not only was HIV engineered to be virulent, but it was also supposed to be race specific."

"That's what I believe," Izzy replied.

Dave just shook his head. "It's got to be the nuttiest thing I have ever heard. Get a grip, Izzy. What you're saying is not only not possible, it's science fiction. Plain and simple."

"So you're saying you don't believe me?"

"Uh, duh!" Dave replied with a touch of valley girl sarcasm. "Show me one shred of evidence proving this cockamamie story and I'll call the press conference myself."

"Can I use your phone?"

Dave pointed to the cordless phone on the wall. Izzy picked up the handset and then reached into his back pocket and fished out his wallet. He looked inside the wallet and searched for a phone number.

"Who do you want to call?" Dave asked.

"American Airlines. I'm going to get you proof!"

Dave chuckled. "And you need an airline ticket for that? Going someplace particular?"

"Buenos Aires," Izzy replied as he began to dial.

Chapter 8

"Can you believe that Dunlevy didn't believe a word I said?" Izzy had grown extremely angry on his flight back to New York. He couldn't believe that his best friend thought he was crazy. He was so angry that he had trouble tying his tie correctly and Oksana had to help him. "Dave Dunlevy, the man whose book the *New York Times* called 'Dunlevy's Dogma,' thinks I'm crazy."

Oksana wasn't certain how she should respond. Even though she was well acquainted with the horrors of Doctor Mengele, Izzy's theory was a lot to take in. Whoever had been following her disappeared when Izzy left for California. She had been concerned that Izzy was now the one being followed. When he stepped safely from the plane at LaGuardia, she felt greatly relieved. He had not yet told her he planned to leave for Argentina's capital the day after Yom Kippur.

"We must leave now if we are to get seats for Kol Nidre," Oksana admonished as she helped Izzy pull his tie straight.

Izzy held up three fingers. "Three times they say Kol Nidre. Three times. I hardly doubt that we could possibly miss all of them." Izzy's words were laced with sarcasm. He had big problems with Yom Kippur, the Day of Atonement. How many pious Jews had Izzy watched over the years slip away in infirmity. How many had poured out their souls during Kol Nidre, begging to be released from past transgressions. Many were rewarded for their piety with debilitating diseases, slipping away painfully, never to utter the words of the Kol Nidre prayer again. The whole 'once-a-year atonement' didn't sit well with Izzy. However, the tradition of going to synagogue on Yom Kippur was too deeply ingrained to be ignored. Therefore, he reluctantly put on his jacket, grabbed his tallis, and followed Oksana out the door.

The Kol Nidre service lasted for just a bit more than 90 minutes. For Izzy, the service passed in a blur. He stood when he needed to stand, sat when the rabbi motioned to sit, but otherwise, his mind was half a world a way. He tried to mentally catalog all the things he would need to search for in Argentina. Unfortunately, with so much of Mengele's life being unknown, Izzy had no idea what to search for or where to begin. During the last chanting of the Kol Nidre prayer, Izzy dropped his prayer book. Instantly, he stooped to pick it up. Izzy lifted the text and brought it to his lips. The book was opened to a reading from one of the Jewish sages, Rabbi Hillel.

"If I am not for myself, who will be for me? If I am only for myself, what am I? And if not now? When?" The reading gave Izzy cause for pause. Rabbi Hillel could see that every person was in some way connected to every other person. Izzy thought for a moment about the millions who had died in the Holocaust, and those who did nothing to help them. How many had died at Mengele's hand? Not nearly the number that would die if Izzy's theory proved correct. The world had no precedent for the scope of this disease. Even bubonic plague, which destroyed one-third of Europe's population, paled by comparison. In Izzy's mind it was clear that HIV could do for humanity what the asteroids did for the dinosaurs.

After Yom Kippur ended, Izzy broke the fast at Oksana's apartment. Oksana had purchased an array of smoked fish, some cream cheese and fresh baked bagels. At least they were fresh when Yom Kippur began a day ago. Now they resembled hard, little wheels made out of dough. Izzy picked one up and nodded approvingly.

"Now this is a real bagel. This is hard enough to be a lethal weapon, but ten seconds in the microwave and it will be soft, warm and toasty." Izzy quickly freshened all the bagels, he sliced them in half, and placed them back on a plate which he placed in the center of the table. Oksana had busied herself with squeezing fresh orange juice. She placed a glass in front of Izzy's place just as he took a seat at the table.

"Brain food," he commented as he spread cream cheese on both halves of his bagel. "This is why Dunlevy can't see the forest from the trees. No real bagels out there and his brain has atrophied."

Oksana chuckled as she took her seat. "Maybe you should send him some."

Izzy thought about it. "Mail some bagels? By the time they got there they would be harder than a rock. Even a microwave wouldn't help. Besides, I think Dave Dunlevy is past saving anyway. I told him I was going to get the proof and he refused to come with me."

Oksana's head shot up. "Proof? You are going to Europe?" Her voice was filled with concern.

Izzy shook his head and Oksana relaxed a bit. "Actually I'm going down to Buenos Aires."

Oksana glared at Izzy as if he had lost his mind. "Argentina? What are you thinking?"

"I'm thinking that Jesse Owens is alive and well in Argentina. I need to know what that means. And I've discovered something that's more than a bit frightening. New cases of HIV are growing exponentially in Latin America. Within a decade things will be as bad as they are in Africa."

Oksana remained silent for a long moment. "You may drive James Bond's car, but you are not James Bond."

"Really?" Izzy replied sarcastically. "And I always thought I'd be a great Bond, not as good as Connery mind you, but better than Roger Moore."

"The KGB does not fire fake bullets. Of that I can assure you."

"I thought they were called the Russian Security Force now."

"Call them what you will," Oksana admonished. "You should still stay home."

Izzy disagreed. "I've got to go. Heneke has propelled me into the middle of this and now I need to see it through. That's just the way it is." The meal was finished in silence. When Oksana offered to have Izzy stay the night, he declined. "I've got an early flight in the morning."

Oksana hugged Izzy tightly. "If you get yourself killed, I will hate you for the rest of my life."

Izzy laughed. "I'll try to keep that in mind." He paused, blushed a tiny bit, and then took Oksana completely off-guard. "Remind me to tell you that I think I'm falling in love with you when I get back." Izzy gave Oksana a quick kiss and then left. She stood silent, stunned by Izzy's proclamation.

Packing was a nightmare. Izzy tried to fit five-days worth of clothes, and his research notes, inside his portable suitcase on wheels, but it just wouldn't all fit. He packed his bag several times, finally deciding that he would need to take along a large briefcase for his notes. It was well after two in the morning when he finally turned out the lights. The alarm clock woke him at 4:45 a.m. Even after a hot shower and two cups of coffee, he still looked half asleep. He walked in a daze out the front of his building, passing on his usual small talk with the building's doorman. A privately chartered Lincoln Continental was waiting by the curb. The driver took Izzy's suitcase and placed it in the trunk. Izzy insisted on keeping his briefcase in the back seat so that he could review his notes on the way to the airport. However, within minutes of settling in the car, he was sound asleep.

The flight from New York to Buenos Aires was quite long, with a change of planes in Miami. Izzy was already feeling worn down as the plane's wheels touched down on the runway in Argentina's Ezeiza airport. Izzy quickly retrieved his bag and moved to the customs area.

"What is your business in Argentina?" The question came from a stern looking security guard.

"Medical research," Izzy replied as the guard picked his way through Izzy's belongings. The guard paused when he came across the hardcover book that Izzy had brought along. The book was entitled, *Mengele, The Complete Story*. The guard gave Izzy a furtive glance, studied him for a moment, and then closed Izzy's suitcase.

"Enjoy your visit to Argentina," the guard said with little emotion as he handed Izzy's suitcase back to him.

A moment later Izzy was outside the terminal, considering his transportation options. The biography on Mengele gave little information that was useful. Izzy knew that Mengele had lived in Argentina under the assumed name of Helmut Gregor. He operated a small machine shop and was considered a good business man. There was a small reference to a start-up pharmaceutical company called Fadro Farm KGSA. According to the book, Mengele was an investor and helped study tuberculosis treatments. However, he was associated with the company for only one year. By the beginning of 1958, the Buenos Aires police suspected that Mengele was practicing medicine without a license. A month after the police began their investigation, Mengele was on his way to Paraguay.

Izzy believed that Mengele had continued research on the genetically mutated cell when he arrived in Argentina. The biography made it quite clear that Mengele held little regard for his South American hosts. He considered them inferior, much the way Hitler had considered Africans inferior. It was not difficult for Izzy to imagine Mengele inoculating the poor port dwellers referred to as portenos. These people lived in slums called *villas miserias*, or villages of misery. Health conditions within the slums were bad, with residents often being neglected by the established medical community.

Unfortunately for Izzy, the Argentine Ministry of Health records were useless. Argentina in the 1940s was very much a creation of her president, Juan Peron. President Peron tried to isolate his country from the rest of the world. Argentina was a very secretive place and medical records from the period were almost nonexistent. What did exist were woefully incomplete. Izzy visited every major hospital in the city and found their records also lacking. With nowhere else to turn, Izzy headed for the German section of Buenos Aires.

Many Germans who fled their mother country during World War II ended up in Buenos Aires. Many of them brought with them an empathy for Nazism. It so concerned President Peron that he set up a commission to determine whether the German community posed any threat to Argentina. The Investigating Commission on Anti-Argentine Activities concluded that thousands of Germans were controlled by the Reich, and that many received financial assistance in order to foment a Third Reich in Argentina.

When the Germans flooded into Buenos Aires, they also brought their social preferences. One of these was a love of the cabaret, where burlesque was the entertainment of choice. In the fifty-odd years since the war, many of them had been shut down. The German section was much like the rest of Buenos Aires, having thrown off protectionism in favor of a free-market economy. The cabaret that Izzy wandered into was very much like a modern day German nightclub. People were gathered at the bar and around the room. Izzy took a seat at the bar and sighed in disappointment. He had hoped to find the cabaret still filled with burlesque. Burlesque was often accompanied by prostitution, and prostitutes are often the best source of information when it pertains to sexually transmitted disease within a city.

Little did Izzy realize that he was being followed and watched.

Two blond men, both about average in height slipped into the club. They wore black trousers, Hollywood style collarless shirts, and black blazers. The jackets were enough to make them stand out, considering how hot it was. However, Izzy's mind was focused on Heneke and Ice-9. Therefore, he didn't even notice them. Once inside they split up and watched Izzy from opposite sides of the floor.

A jazz quartet settled in one corner of the room and started playing. Izzy nursed a Heineken as the musicians segued from Duke Ellington to modern-day, experimental pieces. After an hour Izzy was ready to leave and head back to his hotel. Just as he stood, a young woman brushed up against him.

"Excuse me," the woman offered in perfect English.

"No problem," Izzy replied with a bit of surprise in his voice. He hadn't heard many people speak English since he arrived in Buenos Aires, certainly not clear, properly enunciated English. Without staring, he appraised the woman who had just taken a seat. She was young, he guessed in her early twenties. Long blond hair cascaded down to her shoulders, but somehow she didn't look like a blond. Maybe it was the dark eyebrows, or the deep brown eyes. There was also something about her that was strangely familiar. She had a face that Izzy was certain that he had seen before but couldn't place.

"You looked lonely," the woman said nonchalantly as the bartender brought her a glass of rum. "I'm guessing an American businessman away from home."

Izzy nodded. "Something like that."

The woman patted the cushion of a bar stool. "Stay awhile. I don't get much of a chance to talk to Americans."

Izzy shook his head. "I'm going back to my hotel."

The woman reached out and touched Izzy's hand gently. "Just one drink. I'll buy."

Izzy nodded in agreement and retook his place on the stool. He stayed partly because of the invitation, and partly because he was even more certain that he had seen this woman before. Perhaps he had seen her at the airport or on the street. Not only did she look familiar, there was also something about her voice. Her accent seemed out-of-place. It was European, but Izzy couldn't place its origin.

The bartender brought Izzy another steinful of beer and placed it in front him. The woman handed the bartender some money, which Izzy protested.

"So what brings you to Argentina, Mr. . . ?"

"Slesinger, Doctor Izzy Slesinger."

"A doctor?"

"Yes. You might say that I'm here doing a little research."

The young woman leaned in close and kissed Izzy full on the lips. Kiss is probably not the correct term, actually she drove her tongue deeply into his mouth. She then pulled back as if it was nothing out of the usual. Izzy, however, was a bit shocked. The woman shrugged her shoulders.

"I wanted to see if you could kiss."

Izzy chuckled. "You always do what you want?"

The woman nodded as she took a sip of rum. "Usually."

"So can I?"

"What?"

"Kiss?"

"Not bad. You have a nice tongue." The woman took another sip of rum. "So you want to take me back to your hotel room and show me what else you can do with that tongue?"

A smile slid across Izzy's face. Could it be that a prostitute had found him? "I might know a couple of tricks." It hit him slowly. At first it was just a bit of dizziness. Izzy stood from his stool and had to steady himself.

"Are you all right?" his new companion inquired.

"One too many beers, I guess," Izzy replied as his vision began to blur. "Stronger here than at home." Izzy's words were now slurred. He took a small step and then collapsed on the floor. Fifteen seconds later he was turning blue.

The woman who was with Izzy began screaming for a doctor. The two blond men who had entered earlier rushed over with several others. One of the men put a hand on Izzy's jugular and his eyes opened wide in both fear and surprise. "Nein."

A moment later two paramedics rushed into the club. They quickly loaded Izzy onto a stretcher and raced him out to a waiting ambulance. The young woman and the two blond men watched as the paramedics loaded Izzy into the ambulance. A paramedic immediately administered an IV drip. The other grabbed a pair of heart paddles and applied them to Izzy's chest. Four strong electrical jolts caused Izzy's body to convulse. A paramedic placed a finger to Izzy's neck and then shook his head. Meanwhile, the two blond men were silent. They watched as the paramedics got into of the ambulance, they watched as the ambulance door was closed, and then they watched as the ambulance roared away.

Chapter 9

When Izzy awoke there was a fire burning in his right arm and his head felt like exploding. He tried to sit up, but found that he was strapped down. His mind cleared slowly. He could hear the high pitched whine of jet engines as his eyes darted from side to side. His pulse quickened as he discovered that he was looking at the ceiling of a private jet. For some reason he had been drugged and abducted.

"Doctor Slesinger," Izzy instantly recognized the voice. It was of the young woman who had kissed him in the night club. She walked over and undid his restraints. "We needed the straps to hold you in place while the plane departed. I'm sure that you have many questions."

Izzy sat up and looked dumbfounded. This was not the blond who had kissed him in the nightclub, but the young brunette coed that he had encountered on the street in New Haven. He knew she looked familiar. She was now dressed in a red and black lycra unitard that hugged every curve of her tightly muscled body. The initials 'BP' were embossed over her right breast.

The young woman extended a hand and helped Izzy stand from the stretcher. His legs were a bit wobbly and she helped him to a leather chair that swiveled 360 degrees. Izzy almost collapsed in the seat, but his gaze was locked on the woman. His eyes didn't even blink. She took a step back across the isle and settled into a leather chair of her own.

"It was the kiss. My tongue was coated with a rare herb found in the deepest part of the Congo. The herb slows bodily function almost to complete stasis. We went into your right arm with the antidote. You may feel a burning sensation for a little while."

"Who the hell are you?" The words exploded out of Izzy mouth as he jumped up from his chair. Immediately he felt dizzy but stayed on his feet.

The young woman stood and looked directly into Izzy's eyes. "I told you in New Haven, Jean Dulac. I work for Doctor Heneke."

Izzy blinked several times as he let it sink in. "Heneke? This is his doing?"

Jean nodded. "He sent me to the states as a messenger, and to keep an eye on you. I was hoping to introduce myself on my schedule, but your little trip to Argentina changed all that."

"I won't even pretend to understand."

"We thought that you would come to Germany, perhaps visit the Congo, or maybe South Africa. We were not prepared for Argentina."

"You've been watching me?"

Jean took a step closer. "Round the clock. All the notes you received were from me. I sent the email from a secured location. Doctor Heneke believes that you are alone in your ability to unravel the mystery of the Mengele cell. Unfortunately, the suicide in your office has focused many eyes in your direction. You did not realize it, but two members of Argentina's Reich were about to make things very unpleasant for you. I hope they found your death convincing."

"My death? I'm supposed to be dead?"

"As far as the rest of the world is concerned, you are officially deceased. However, rest assured that I will do everything within my power to keep you very much alive."

Izzy felt like he had just stepped into the middle of a very bad, bad dream. Here he was, flying to God knows where, and this pixie sized brunette dressed in spandex was promising to protect him. It was beyond surreal, it was insane. "I don't suppose you could tell me where we're headed?"

"You will be fully briefed when we get there!"

"I see," Izzy replied as the small jet began its descent. He had to move his jaw from side to side to equalize the pressure inside his ears. Jean reached into a storage pocket on the back of her leather chair and pulled out a pack of gum. She tossed a piece to Izzy who looked at it cautiously.

Jean spoke to his hesitation. "I assure you, we are the good guys. And if I wanted to hurt you, I wouldn't need to resort to tainted chewing gum. Now please return to your seat until the plane lands."

As soon as the plane stopped rolling, the passenger door was opened from the outside. Two stocky young men, dressed in black unitards entered. They both gripped automatic weapons and their eyes darted around every inch of the plane. Jean moved to them and had a brief, muffled conversation. To Izzy it sounded as if she was speaking French. Jean held up two fingers and pointed at Izzy. One of the men nodded in apparent agreement, and then he and his colleague exited the plane. Jean turned her attention back to Izzy.

"We are going to have to wait for several moments. Doctor Heneke wants you to have a level two security clearance and the computers won't accept it for some reason. We are working on a solution to the problem."

Izzy walked to the open door and looked out. The runway was built beside what looked like the ocean. But which ocean? Large, frothy waves were the only thing that Izzy could see from his vantage point. Jean walked to his side and pointed at the water.

"It's the English Channel. I can tell you that you are in France, the province of Brittany."

One of the young men returned and nodded his head. Jean led Izzy off the plane and he had his first glimpse of his surroundings. The runway couldn't have been more than several dozen yards from the water. Izzy turned landward and saw very little. There was one small building, about the size of the typical airport car rental return. The building, built from masonry, was painted white. Dark, tinted glass kept Izzy from seeing inside the structure. From where Izzy stood it looked as if the building had no entrance. Aside from the small structure there was nothing. Undeveloped marshland extended out for as far as Izzy could see. Off in this distance there were some rolling hills, but nothing else.

Jean touched Izzy on the arm. "I think they've figured out the override. We can go inside now."

Izzy looked at Jean skeptically. "Inside where?"

Jean turned toward the white building and started walking. Izzy followed after her. The two young men with the automatic weapons stayed with the plane. Jean stopped directly in front of the building and a portion of the glass illuminated. Izzy was amazed to see a computer touch screen instantly appear before his eyes. Jean held her right hand open and placed it on the screen. A glass panel that served as the door retracted into the ground. Izzy swallowed hard and allowed Jean to lead him into the building. As soon as he stepped inside, the glass panel closed.

The little building was as odd on the inside as on the out. With the glass door shut, it was quite dark. The only light came from long, purple tubes that ran the entire length of the ceiling. There were two openings in the back wall of the building. The international symbol for male was above one door, female above the other. The signs seemed to glow, reminding Izzy of the felt blacklight posters of his youth. Jean came up beside Izzy and offered an explanation.

"Viruses degrade quickly when exposed to ultraviolet radiation.

When you go into the changing room you will be instructed to remove your clothing. Place your wallet, keys, and other belongings into a decontamination tube and put it in the port."

"You want me to take off my clothing and give you my belongings? Now why on Earth should I agree to do that?"

"Because we cannot allow you access to the facility if you don't. I assure you that we will take good care of your belongings and they will be returned to you in short order."

Izzy glanced around at the darkened room. Even if he could find his way back to the glass panel door, he was certain that there would be no way for him to open it. "Looks like I have no choice. Where to next?"

Jean pointed to the open door displaying the male symbol. "The entrance is positive pressure. Once inside you will receive directions."

Izzy hesitated for a moment and then entered into the changing room. Jean waited to make sure that he did not suddenly change his mind, and then she entered the room marked for women. Izzy's movement activated a bank of blinding white lights which caused Izzy to squint. It took him a moment to adjust to the brightness. There really wasn't much to the changing room. There was a shower, with a shower head that extended straight down through the ceiling. There was also a series of lamps built into the ceiling of the shower. Next to the shower stall was a black plastic tube that disappeared into the floor. Resting on top of the tube was a clear plastic container, the type banks use for making deposits at the automatic teller windows. The only other thing in the room were several lockers, all painted white. And a white metal door that had no handle on it.

"Good afternoon, Doctor Slesinger." A deep metallic female voice emanated from a flush mounted speaker in the ceiling. "Please take your belongings from your pocket and place them in the cylinder. Screw the cylinder shut and place it in the black tube." Izzy did as he was told.

Immediately after he placed the cylinder in the tube there was a sucking sound. "Now please remove your clothing and place it in the locker farthest to the right. Once you have removed all your clothes, please proceed to the shower. However, before you do, remove the goggles from the shelf of the locker and take them with you into the shower."

Izzy nervously undressed. The tips of his fingers began to perspire as he undid the buckle on his pants. He was certain the room was monitored on close circuit cameras, and he didn't relish the thought of being naked in front of God knows how many strangers. With a sigh he placed both hands inside the waistband of his underwear and slid it to the floor. He picked the underwear up, folded it in half, and placed it on top of his shoes in the locker. He grabbed hold of the goggles, closed the locker door, and headed for the shower. Once inside the shower Izzy noticed there were no knobs or handles. He waited anxiously for something to happen, his hands covering his privates from public view. The goggles were clutched tightly in his right hand.

"Doctor Slesinger, this shower is intended to disinfect. You will be sprayed with antiseptic wash, followed by an antiviral solution which will kill all airborne pathogens. We will then irradiate your body with high intensity lighting. This lighting will cover the entire UV/IR spectrum. We are going to have to ask you to wear the goggles to protect your eyes. You are also going to have to spread your legs and open your hands as you reach both hands towards the ceiling."

"Why?" Izzy asked as he placed the goggles over his eyes. However, he kept his legs firmly shut and once the goggles were in place he put his hands back down in front of genitals.

"Nozzles are built into both the floor and walls of this shower. We need to completely immerse your body. If your hands are down, we cannot disinfect your underarms. If your legs are not spread, we can not disinfect your scrotum."

Izzy hesitated for just another moment and then did as he was requested. He opened his palms and spread his legs. As soon as he put both arms into the air, the spray jets activated. Izzy had been expecting a hard blasting shower. However, the antiseptic rained down, and up, in a fine mist. This was followed by a thick, milky paste that seemed to miraculously vanish as soon as it touched his skin. Another bout of misting solution, and then the lights in the ceiling came on. It took about a minute to channel through the entire spectrum. Lastly, high-intensity, hot air jets blasted from all sides. It wasn't long before Izzy was completely dry. The hot air turned off and the room fell silent.

Izzy stepped out of the shower and waited. He made no attempt to recover his genitals, even though he was certain that his every move was being watched by a closed-circuit camera. The white metal door in the back wall slid open to reveal an elevator. Izzy walked to the opening and instantly spotted the lycra unitard that was neatly folded and placed on small metal table at the back of the elevator.

"Doctor Slesinger," the same female voice as before came out the speaker in the elevator. "Please come into the elevator and put on the clothing provided."

Izzy stepped into the elevator and lifted the unitard. A white cotton jock strap lay underneath. Izzy struggled into the jock and then squirmed his way into the unitard. The door of the elevator closed and Izzy could feel the car that he was in begin to move. On the back of the elevator door was a full length mirror. Obviously installed to show occupants how ridiculous they looked in athletic apparel designed for kids in their twenties. Izzy looked at his reflection and for the first time noticed that Doctor I. Slesinger had been embossed above his heart. He glanced down towards his crotch and was alarmed by the way the jock seemed to make him bulge out against the nylon. Perhaps it would be appropriate for a beach somewhere in Brazil, but certainly not for a medical research facility.

The door of the elevator opened and Jean Dulac was waiting in the corridor outside. Her eyes quickly assessed Izzy in his new outfit. The thinnest of smiles appeared when her eyes dropped below his waist. Izzy couldn't tell if she found it erotically appealing, or absurdly amusing, and he didn't care. At the moment he was just interested in getting to see Heneke. He took a step off the elevator and Jean motioned towards the right.

"If you will follow me, I will take you to see Doctor Heneke." Jean led Izzy down the corridor. She came upon a closed door and knocked.

"*Betreten*," a raspy German voice replied, inviting entry. Jean opened the door and there was Heneke. Or at least Izzy thought it was Heneke. The man he remembered was rather stocky and had a full head of curly, graying hair. The person in front of him was gaunt, almost skeletal. Just the fewest of hairs remained, and his scalp was curiously discolored with angry red splotches. He was dressed in a long white sleeve shirt and white pants. Heneke appraised Izzy's outfit and shook his head as he extended his hand.

"Nein, I told them regular clothing and they give you that ridiculous looking thing? I will take care of this immediately." The handshake was brief, and then Heneke walked over to his gray, high-tech melamine desk. He tapped a button on his phone and began barking orders in German. He then returned to Izzy. "Argentina? Why?"

"Mengele fled to Buenos Aires."

Heneke nodded and led Izzy to his desk. "You and I have much to discuss."

"Got that right," Izzy replied in agreement. "Let's start with why I'm here? Or better yet, how does any of this have anything to do with me?"

Heneke turned and looked Izzy directly in the eye. "Remember how your professors taught you that an asteroid hit the Earth, altered its orbit, and brought about the extinction of the dinosaurs?" It was a rhetorical question and Heneke continued on. "The cataclysm that Mengele unleashed on the world is unlike anything ever seen before. It is very possible that history is wrong and that Hitler actually won the war. As to why you're here? You are mankind's only hope." Heneke's pronouncement was so direct that Izzy actually felt terrified for the first time.

"Maybe you should start at the beginning."

Heneke nodded and had Izzy take a seat beside him at his desk.

"In one blinding burst of speed, Hitler watched Jesse Owens shatter the myth of Aryan superiority. Elimination of the Jews was necessary. However, destruction of the Negro race was mandatory. Mengele supplied him with the means."

"How exactly do you supply the means to destroy a whole race of people?"

Heneke tossed open his journal and pointed to several notations. "Ice-9."

"Your metaphor for change. Mengele engineered the virus?"

Heneke laughed, and the laugh turned into a deep hacking cough. For a moment it was hard for him to catch his breath. After a moment he was able to continue. "Engineering viruses was well beyond our science. Mengele and I were both at the Third Reich Institute for Heredity, Biology and Racial Purity at the University of Frankfort. We studied with von Verscher, who was maybe twenty or thirty years ahead of every geneticist of his age."

"I don't recognize the name," Izzy interjected. "How is it that I have not heard of him?"

"He was a Nazi! How many Nazi research scientists have you heard of?"

"I've heard of Mengele."

"Only because Mengele was a barbaric madman. It was von Verscher who gave him his appetite for Jewish twins. Mengele would use one child for experimentation, and one as a control." Heneke paused as a tears began to well up in his eyes. It was as if he could see it all clearly in his mind. "The similarities between Tay-Sachs and sickle-cell anemia suggested genetic similarities between Jews and Negroes. Mengele reached into the cellular protein sequence of DNA and changed it. That was just within our science. However, we had no idea what results a change would bring about. Most changes did nothing, either the cells weren't viable, or they were destroyed by bodily defenses when injected into hosts."

Izzy blanched at having first hand confirmation that experiments were actually conducted on human beings. It was made all the more horrible to learn that the experiments were focused on children. "Why the children?" Izzy asked the question in a voice that was barely a whisper, hoping that he would not hear the answer that he feared.

"Children have an underdeveloped immune system." Heneke looked pale but pressed on. "Most of Mengele's research was nonsense. He was never the scientist that von Verscher was. However, when Mengele changed his focus from entire proteins to singular amino acids, he began to get results."

"Results?"

"Cellular cancers. Many died. . . horribly. . . painfully. I couldn't watch any longer." Heneke's head dropped and he fell silent. Izzy could do nothing except wait for Heneke to regain his composure. Heneke's head shot up and he looked directly into Izzy's eyes. "Imagine a cell that is cancerous, but appears normal. A cell that has the ability to lie dormant, or spring to life, instantly corrupting other cells."

"How does this relate to AIDS?"

"This nearly identical cell is the host for the virus."

Izzy felt the entire scientific world shift. Humans could not be hosts and targets for the same virus. "Impossible."

Heneke handed Izzy his journals. "Read it. You will see that what I am saying is scientifically possible. This cell is an invader, brilliantly camouflaged to blend in, escaping bodily defenses until it is too late."

"And this cell is a host for HIV?"

Heneke nodded sadly. "Why hasn't the scientific community been able to identify a carrier for this virus? They've been testing apes and monkeys for two decades. It is because this virus could have come from anywhere, maybe from inside the human body. Originally it was non-virulent. However, this new host cell, that had never existed before, changed the virus into something that is very virulent."

Izzy was in too deep a state of shock of say anything. It sounded like fiction, but Heneke also made it sound very believable. Therefore, he said nothing, staring blankly into Heneke's face.

Heneke nodded, as if confirming that all of it was true. "You and I cannot detect a Mengele cell, that is what I named it, a Mengele cell. However, the HIV virus can only exist inside them. Attack HIV with all the protease inhibitors you like. Attack it with the new drug that I developed, the one Kaiser is shouting to the world about. The virus will disassociate and its protein will take refuge inside Mengele cells. Inside the cell they mutate, eventually emerging with an immunity to the vaccine."

"Is it your belief that there is no way to cure it?" Izzy's face drained of color as he realized what Heneke was trying to say. That it was not possible to eliminate the virus from infected people. Eventually all infected people would die. The pharmaceutical companies were buying patients' time, nothing more.

"Drug therapies are not the answer. A small percentage of people show a naturally immunity. This indicates that a solution can be engineered through gene therapy."

Izzy shook his head. "The permutations are endless. How would someone even find a starting place?"

"Mengele's original notes. They hold the first step. The key to unraveling this whole mystery."

"So let's see them," Izzy replied anxiously.

Heneke shrugged. "We have no idea where they are.

Disappeared at the end of the war. Now you must find them."

"Me? You have got to be kidding?"

"It has to be you. There are many who don't want the papers found. They will lay false trails. You are perhaps the only scientist in the world who will understand the amino acid chains contained in the notes."

Izzy shook his head. "Oh no, you got the wrong guy. No way I'm chasing around Europe. What if the notes were completely lost, or destroyed? What then?"

Heneke frowned as he thought about the implications. "Then, we are all doomed."

Chapter 10

The Brittany Pharmalogics research facility was the most amazing thing that Izzy had ever seen. The entire complex had been built 40 meters underground. Heneke explained that it was a Class One facility, meaning that there was no more than one particle of dust in every cubic meter of air. Typical semi-conductor clean rooms were no better than class 100, and even Intel couldn't boast of a clean room that was over 60,000 square feet in size. The clothing that Izzy wore was made from a special fabric that didn't allow for the escape of exfoliated skin cells. The same could be said of the tight fitting lycra that most of the staff wore.

"Europe's best and brightest young research minds work in this facility, and yet, its existence is almost unknown in the outside world." There was real pride in Heneke's voice as he stopped at the door that led into the live virus research area. He pointed through a window at several scientists who were dressed in self-contained bubble suits. "The live virus area is restricted. Those scientists are actively forcing HIV to mutate. While we try to control the changes, there is also the very real possibility that we could create an even more deadly virus."

"Isn't that a cheery thought," Izzy replied sarcastically. "You're sure that all of this is necessary?"

"Fourteen years ago I came across a young man in a hospital in Munich. Each day his conditioned worsened, and yet all of the test results came back negative. His immune system was intact, no elevated white blood cell count, and no cancers. After just one week in the hospital, one of Germany's most advanced facilities I might add, he was dead."

"Did they do an autopsy?"

Heneke nodded. "They listed the cause of death as systemic failure."

"Systemic failure? What does that mean?"

"It means they had no clue. He just died." Heneke took his right hand and pointed to his stomach. "Deep in my gut I knew what had killed him. It was Mengele cells, so brilliantly camouflaged that Germany's best scientists couldn't see them. They had invaded, multiplied, and when there were enough of them the body just shut down. It could no longer function. Therefore, just eliminating the virus from the host does not mean the patient will be saved."

Izzy shook his head. "Wildest theory I've ever heard. If you can't tell a Mengele cell from a healthy cell, how do you know they exist?"

Heneke turned toward Izzy and let out a sigh. "Because I am dying."

Izzy's mouth dropped open. "Dying? Of what? I don't understand?"

"I took a sample of that young man's blood and spun it down. Two years ago I injected myself with the sample. Six months ago I tested positive for HIV, even though there was no trace of it in his blood. That's when I concluded that the virus is indigenous to either the human body, or to our environment. It is the cell that turns it virulent."

Izzy hardly heard a word that Heneke had said. His mind was still wrapped around the fact that Heneke had injected himself with blood products from his patient. "You did what?" Izzy gasped in horror. "Are you completely insane?"

Heneke spun towards Izzy and his anger burst out. "There was nothing else for me to do."

"Really? Nothing else? I can think of only about a thousand other things to do, Herr Doctor." The revulsion in Izzy's voice was clear and it made Heneke even madder. So mad that he started yelling at Izzy at the top of his lungs.

"Joseph Mengele did not operate in your universe, Doctor Slesinger. He did not use test tubes, petri dishes, and computers. His experiments were conducted in living human beings. We could model for a millennium and not figure out what his madness has wrought. And I can assure you that mankind does not have a millennia left." All of a sudden Heneke began to tremble, and then convulse. He took one step forward and collapsed.

"I need help," Izzy screamed as he knelt by Heneke's side. Heneke's seizure looked like an epileptic episode. Therefore, Izzy pried his mouth open and grabbed a hold of the elderly doctor's tongue to prevent it from being bitten or swallowed. Jean Dulac was the first one to reach Izzy. However, right in back of her was a whole emergency medical team. People surrounded Heneke, but no one was quite certain the course of action. One technician took out a chemical ice pack and squeezed it with his hands. The inner compartment burst, mixing the two chemicals which created an endothermic reaction. The pack got cold and technician placed it on Heneke's forehead.

"An ice pack?" Izzy asked incredulously.

"We do not know why he has these episodes," Jean replied softly.

"Obviously it's grand mal seizure. Dilantin will at least bring him out of the convulsions."

Just then Heneke stopped shaking, his eyes opened, and he sat up right. He tried to stand, assuring every one that he was perfectly fine. Within seconds he was back to himself, shooing everyone away so that he could again be alone with Izzy.

"Come with me to the research center. There is someone there who would like to speak with you."

The research center was at the heart of the facility. Laboratories were constructed in a circular pattern. Glass partitions separated the labs. Heneke led Izzy into a lab labeled 'Simian Virology.' The walls vibrated with the howls of dozens of monkeys that filled cages in the room. A group of scientists huddled around a Japanese macaque, a rare and expensive primate used in research. Izzy was quite familiar with the macaque from his work in graduate school. It was a primate high on the evolutionary chain, and far more pleasant in attitude than rhesus or howler monkeys. The particular macaque being watched was named Picasso, so named because he showed a real flair for painting. Unfortunately, like the real Picasso he was moody as hell and often refused to cooperate.

The scientists all stood silently watching while Picasso sat in a corner of the room, his back to the scientists. When Izzy closed the door to the lab behind him, Picasso sprang to life. He crossed the room in two leaps and jumped directly into Izzy's arms. The other scientists were utterly stunned. While Picasso was never violent, no one would have ever called him a hugger.

Yet here he was, arms draped around Izzy's neck. Izzy supported him with one arm and patted him on the back with his other hand.

Doctor Claude Thomae, world expert on retroviruses, and an old friend of Izzy's, separated himself from his three colleagues and approached. Picasso rotated his head around and gave Thomae a menacing hiss. So menacing that it caused the French researcher to pause.

"Izzy, mon ami," Thomae cried. "How good it is to see you again."

Izzy just frowned. "God, this gets better all the time. Haven't seen you since the Yale reunion in 1999."

Claude reached up to adjust his wire-rimmed bifocals so that they would sit higher on his nose. "Has it been that long?"

Izzy nodded. "Not long enough. If memory serves correctly, you and Dunlevy almost got in a fistfight in front of Toad's Place.

Bouncers ran out of the nightclub and had to separate the two of you. It was clearly one of the most embarrassing nights of my life."

"Dunlevy is an imbecile. He knows so little that it still amazes me that Yale allowed him to graduate."

Izzy nodded and replied sarcastically, "Right, this is from Claude, the cloddish frog."

Heneke walked over and took Picasso from Izzy. "Nice to see the two of you are so intimate."

"Not exactly the word I would have picked," Izzy shot back. "I thought you said only Europe's best scientists."

The other three researchers who had been silent began to chuckle. Their laughter only made the insult worse, and Claude stormed out of the research room. Heneke placed Picasso back in his cage and made the introductions. He started with Anna Brovsky, a petite, middle-aged, micro paleontologist from Kiev. Anna's specialty was investigating and documenting viral matter contained in fossils from ancient civilizations. He next introduced Rodney Bassett, a curly-haired Brit who reminded Izzy of tennis star John McEnroe. Rodney was the senior primatologist at Brittany Pharmalogics, and the one who was the most surprised by Picasso's behavior.

"I have never seen Picasso run to anyone before, and certainly never embrace them."

Izzy shrugged, "Animals feel safe with me. Been that way my whole life."

"Amazing, truly amazing."

Heneke lastly introduced Brian Crighton. One of the few Americans at the facility, and perhaps the world's leading authority on mathematic probability modeling.

"Nice to see someone put that pompous ass in his place," Brian offered as he extended his hand. Izzy had to look a long way up, considering that Brian was almost 6'10" tall.

"I know you," Izzy said as recognition lit up in his eyes. "UCLA center when the Bruins won the NCAA. If I remember correctly, you were undefeated. They said you were going to be the next Bill Walton."

Brian nodded. "Yup, that's me. Passed up a contract with the Lakers and went on to grad school at Cal Poly."

Izzy looked at Brian in awe. "And thank God for the Knicks that you did."

Brian laughed. "Basketball is a mathematically simplistic game. Very little challenge. Now the epidemiologic analysis and implications of HIV, that's another story entirely."

"I need the three of you to bring Doctor Slesinger up to speed. I'll go see if I can locate Claude and assuage his feelings. We are going to need his input. Therefore, I want you all to promise me that you will not antagonize him." Izzy reluctantly agreed, as did the others. Heneke left the room and Brian Crighton began to explain the things that he was able to document.

Brian walked to a computer control panel and flipped a silver colored rocker switch. The research lab instantly went dark, with the glass partitions becoming black, almost by magic. A panel in the ceiling slid back and a video projector dropped down through the opening. A map of the globe was projected onto one of the black, glass walls. Brian picked up a laser pointer and projected a round, red dot onto the map. He moved the pointer so that the dot was focused on the Congo.

"Almost thirty million cases of HIV in the sub-Sahara region, and another twelve million cases in Asia." Brian moved the pointer from the Congo to Bangkok in Thailand. "We believe that the Nazis injected 25,000 Africans and 25,000 Asians between 1941 and 1943."

"Asians?" Izzy had only been told about Hitler's hatred of Negroes.

"Hitler assumed that his military forces would crush the Russians, and eventually America. However, the enormous population of China could not be toppled using military force."

Anna Brovsky walked to Brian and took the pointer from him. She placed the red dot on the heart of Moscow.

"It is only recently that we have seen a rapid rise of HIV in the republics. I attribute this to more interaction between people since the fall of communism. The same can be said of infections in the rest of Europe. Outbreaks can be attributed to sexual contact with outsiders."

Rodney Bassett placed a hand on Izzy's shoulder and pulled him close. "But you solved the South American conundrum, my good fellow."

"The South American conundrum? I'm almost afraid to ask."

Anna placed her pointer on Brazil and Rodney explained. "Two million cases of HIV in Brazil, twice the number as in America. How can you explain that many cases in a country that has less than half the population of the United States?"

Izzy turned away from the map projected on the glass and stared at Rodney through the darkness. "Could be a lot of things. The American pharmaceutical companies have been on top of this thing from the start. Brazil doesn't have nearly the access to medical care that we do."

Rodney agreed with Izzy, and then disagreed. "There must have been inoculations in Brazil. You followed Mengele to Argentina. He must have continued the program on his own, or with help from other loyal Nazis. Until you went down there we couldn't see it. It was right there and we couldn't see it."

Izzy looked back at the map on the wall. "You say the inoculations took place in Africa between '43 and '44? Then why haven't we seen millions of deaths before now?"

"We have," Brian countered. "Perhaps tens of millions of them. How many Africans have perished over the past four decades from this? God only knows! Maybe it was only thousands in the 1950's, and didn't reach millions until the 1980's .

"This is an inter-generational killer," Anna interjected. "The cells can pass between people, or be passed to the fetus."

Heneke walked into the room with Claude by his side. Doctor Thomae picked up the discussions as if he had been in the room for entire time. "It is a two-pronged problem. First, you must control the virus, then you must eliminate the host cells. One without the other means nothing."

Heneke walked to the control panel and touched it. The map was replaced with a picture of HIV taken with a scanning electron microscope. "PIRT-I9 is very effective at controlling the virus at the present time. Our estimates are that we have a decade to solve this problem, maybe a bit longer."

"And then what?" Izzy questioned as walked to the glass and studied the picture of the virus. Brian walked beside him and pointed to several spots on the picture.

"Protease inhibitors force HIV to break down to its DNA and hide. The Mengele cell provides refuge. It is a period of latency, in which time the DNA reorders itself to a form that is resistant to treatment. The good news is that the inhibitors also slow the division rate of infected cells."

Heneke tapped the control panel again, the projector turned off and the lights came on in the room. "You see, Doctor Slesinger. The virus can kill, but so too can the host cell, independent of the virus. And it is a true symbiotic relationship. HIV is perhaps the most mutagenic virus we have ever seen. Each copy is slightly different from the original. As the virus changes, so does the cell."

"And each of these changes. . ." Izzy didn't finish the sentence so Anna finished it for him.

"Many of them become cancers."

"How many?" Izzy demanded.

"Can't model it," Brian replied. "Too complex. The only thing I have been able to extrapolate is a date. 2043."

"2043?" Izzy repeated. "What exactly happens then?"

"Our extinction." Brian's comment was made plainly, calmly, and devoid of emotion. "Infections rates will be near eighty-seven percent worldwide with billions already dead."

Izzy was dumbfounded. He felt like a freshman chemistry

student who had just been immersed in organic chemistry for the first time. This was a strange new language and Izzy didn't understand it, his mind wouldn't comprehend it. "Surely you can't all believe this?" Izzy's gaze moved from scientist to scientist. They all nodded solemnly in agreement. "If you know all this why don't you go public? The scientific community will be able to find answers!"

Heneke shook his head, "It would create worldwide hysteria. Or worse, the established medical community would reject the data for years, and the problem would be ignored."

Claude Thomae walked to Izzy's side. "We know what a healthy cell looks like, mon ami. And we know the genetics of the current Mengele cell. What we don't know is how we got here. What was the original mutation that Mengele forced? If we can determine that, we have a chance to use gene therapy to repair the damage. If we eliminate the host, the virus will follow. It is our only hope."

"How do we find the original mutation?" Izzy asked weakly. He was beginning to feel the start of a migraine and his temples began to throb.

"It is as I explained before," replied Heneke. "We are going to send you out to find Mengele's original notes. I remember him documenting the steps. We know most of Mengele's movements at the end of the war. Hopefully, you will be able to follow the trail and find what we need."

Izzy reached up with both hands and tried to massage the sides of his head. "Why aren't any of you going?"

Claude offered the answer. "Because we do not understand protein linkage as well as you do. I would go, but I must admit, you are better suited for it." It was a stunning admission and display of humility. So much so that it left Izzy speechless.

"Jean Dulac will go with you," Heneke offered. "She will be your protection."

"Doesn't that make me feel warm and fuzzy," Izzy replied half under his voice.

Heneke came up to him directly and stared into his eyes. "Do not underestimate her, and do not underestimate the German Reich. There are powerful, dangerous men who believe that pure Aryans can isolate themselves from this, eventually inheriting the world. It is their goal to keep this a secret, until it is too late."

Izzy settled himself into bed in the room that was provided to him. Everything was white in color, the walls, the ceiling, even the floors. The satin-acetate comforter was white and so were the matching sheets. Izzy tried to get comfortable in the bed, but couldn't. He tossed and turned, sliding on the slick sheets from one side of the bed to the other. Sleep was out of the question, his mind was racing and wouldn't shut off. He tried just closing his eyes but found Mengele waiting for him there in the dark. He had seen his picture on the back of the biography and now that face was staring at him. The eyes remained focused, projecting an air of Aryan superiority. Izzy jumped and opened his eyes. After the first encounter Izzy decided not to risk another and got out of bed completely. By the time morning arrived he was sleep deprived, and a mess.

Izzy managed to get most of his hair combed by the time an escort showed up to take him to the cafeteria. He stared at the unshaven stubble on his face, thought about shaving, and decided that he was way too tired to hold a razor in his hand. Heneke and Claude Thomae were already eating when Izzy arrived. Claude patted a spot on the bench by his side and Izzy sat down.

"Looks like you had a rough night," Claude commented as he pushed a pitcher of coffee in Izzy's direction. "We threw a bit much at you yesterday."

Izzy poured a cup of coffee and took a sip. He placed the cup down on the table and focused his gaze on Heneke.

"Pieter, do you know the phrase *Die Endlosung*?"

Heneke nodded. "Hitler's final solution for the Jews."

"And there you were at the beginning, right by Mengele's side. How many Jewish children did you murder in the name of racial purity?"

At first Heneke looked enraged. A moment later he was crying, his hands covering his eyes.

"Funny you should need someone like me," Izzy continued. "Me! Not Vinter in Switzerland, or our distinguished Doctor Thomae. And if it were another age, how fast would they have sent me to the chambers, or the crematoria?"

Heneke pulled his hands from his eyes and held up his palms. Tears dripped onto his wrists, and then onto the table. "My hands are empty. I cannot change history. What was. . . was. All I can try to do is protect the future."

"Lucky for you that I've decided to join this little adventure." Izzy paused to glance down at his newly disinfected watch. "I'm guessing it's about 2 a.m. in New York. I'm going to have to call The Institute later this morning and tell them I'm taking a leave of absence for several weeks. I also need to make some personal calls."

Heneke stared at Claude, then at Izzy, and then back at Claude. He didn't say a word. Izzy felt the tension in the room rise immediately.

"Something the two of you aren't telling me?" Izzy's question was edged and his voice was just beginning to show traces of hostility.

After hesitating for a moment, Heneke explained the truth. "The world thinks you are dead. Coronary in Argentina. Somehow the authorities have misplaced your body."

Izzy could feel the start of one hell of a migraine. "Dead? What the hell are you talking about?"

"We needed to throw the Reich off of your trail. After your funeral, you will have the ability to move around without raising suspicion. At least for a little while."

Izzy threw his hands up in disgust. He jumped up from the table and stormed out of the cafeteria.

"I'll go after him," Claude said. He finally found Izzy in the primate area. Izzy had taken Picasso from his cage and was feeding him pieces of sliced papaya. As Claude approached, Picasso bared his teeth and hissed.

"He really doesn't like you, Claude. Funny how monkeys are such a wonderful judge of character."

"Heneke had no choice. You were the one who decided to go to Argentina."

"And he was the one who decided to get me involved in the first place. What did I do to deserve this? I do not need this shit!"

"He wasn't the one," Claude offered. "I was the one who suggested you. Heneke resisted. He didn't think an American could get worked up over a problem that doesn't seem so bad in America. For all your awareness and campaigns and research, AIDS is a problem that America would like to leave to the rest of the world. However, I think you can now see how connected we all are."

"It was you? You suggested me?" Izzy asked the question with real surprise in his voice.

Claude nodded. "From our very first day at Yale I knew that you were the very best. You have a once-in-a-generation mind. Doctor Polansky often said, 'Slesinger has the intellect to change this world. Try to be like him and you'll do just fine.

Izzy didn't know what to say. In silence he lifted Picasso and placed him back into his cage. Once the cage door was secured he turned back towards Claude. "What exactly am I looking for?"

Claude walked to a cabinet that sat beside a computer work station. He opened it and removed a gold plated CD-ROM storage disc. He then removed a portable, hand-held CD-ROM player and placed the disc into the reader's slot. "We took biopsies of Heneke's tissues and broke them down to amino-acid chains. We've compared his amino acids with those in healthy, normal cells and have been able to narrow the potential acid changes to two or three possibilities. However, we don't know the ordering of amino acids that Mengele forced in the first mutation. That's what we need." Claude handed the CD-player to Izzy.

Izzy shook his head back and forth as he studied the player.

"I can think of only about a billion things wrong with that kind of scientific model. Is that the best theory you have?"

"The only thing we are absolutely certain of is that we cannot get to where we need to be from here. Therefore, our only hope is to start at the beginning and follow the mutations from that end."

"It will be like looking for a needle in a haystack. And have you considered that I don't speak or read one word of German?"

"Jean will be going with you. She is fluent in German and Russian, as well as French."

Heneke walked into the lab with the rest of the research team. Jean Dulac was with them. She was dressed in a plain cotton white blouse and blue slacks. In his short time in the facility, Izzy had become accustomed to seeing people dressed in clothing made from synthetics. A feeling inside his gut told him that her outfit was a harbinger of bad things to come. Jean walked to Izzy's side and handed him a plane ticket. The ticket was printed in French and Izzy was only able to make out one word: Leningrad.

"Russia?"

Heneke nodded. "We have reliable information that Mengele gave his papers to a young German nurse who was stationed with a unit in the Sudetenland. If you find her, providing that she is still alive, perhaps you will find the papers."

Izzy did the mental math in his head. "This just keeps getting better all the time! You want us to find a nurse, who if still alive is well into her eighties. Do you have a name?"

Heneke shook his head. "No, but we do have a photograph of her. Jean will show it to you when you are in transit." Heneke turned towards the research team and asked them to leave the room so that he could speak with Izzy privately. When they were gone he closed the door to the lab and walked to Izzy's side. "Your words before. . . I want you to know I never experimented on children."

Izzy nodded slightly but remained silent.

"But you were right about the crematoria. Jewish scientists were the first to go." Heneke paused, searching for the right phrases. "In 1935 Hitler created the German purity laws which forbade relations between Germans and Jews. Mengele shared his dream of Aryan purity, as did many others."

"And for all the death and misery, Germany has become a multiethnic melting pot."

Heneke nodded in agreement. "Very true. But there are many others like Hitler and Mengele. The dream of Aryan purity is very much alive. There are men, powerful men, who would like to see this infection spread to every corner of the planet."

Izzy reached out and grabbed Heneke by the hand. "Why are you telling me this?"

"So you are aware that you have enemies. Adolf Kaiser, Chairman of Kaiser pharmaceutics has pushed PIRT-I9 for only one reason. He hopes that the medicine will make the world believe the battle with HIV is won. Humanity will lower its guard, eliminating the need for safe sex. Meanwhile, the Mengele cell will be passed from person to person, nation to nation, mother to child."

"And only the purest of Aryans will survive?" Izzy asked in disbelief.

Heneke nodded. "That is what they are striving for. They feared that I was about to go to the government. I began to receive death threats. That's when my friends decided it was time for me to leave Kaiser and disappear. For all the advances that this facility holds, I had cultures at Kaiser which would have proved invaluable. Claude convinced me that they meant nothing if I was dead."

Izzy understood what Heneke was trying to say. "I believe you are telling me to be careful."

Heneke nodded. "You are believed dead. That will give you an advantage, but only for a short while. There are many people who would like to find Mengele's journals, and some who hope they are never found."

Chapter 11

The key turned in the lock of Izzy's apartment and a very weary Shana and Mitchell Stern entered slowly. The State Department had sent a representative to inform Shana that her little brother had died in Argentina. Shana spent the better part of an hour battling for information that was not available. The man in the long, black trench coat couldn't tell her much of anything, except that Izzy was dead. He also mentioned that the government had no idea of what happened to Izzy's body, but they were confident it would be found and retrieved quickly.

The news had left Shana in a state of shock. She had spoken with Izzy just before Rosh Hashanah, just a little more than two weeks ago. The Stern family was in their backyard Succah, celebrating the Jewish festival of harvest when the man from the State Department rang the front door bell. A beautiful, crisp autumn evening of celebration was instantly transformed into tears and disbelief. It was Mitchell who suggested that they go to Izzy's apartment in Manhattan and Shana agreed. While she silently hoped that the State Department was wrong, Mitchell was more interested in seeing if Izzy had left any notes or documentation on his travel plans. The Sterns quickly found a babysitter for the kids and headed for New York.

"I will not call the family," Shana argued angrily as she looked around Izzy's apartment for the second time. "Not until I am absolutely sure."

Mitchell nodded solemnly, more out of wanting to avoid a fight, than from agreement. "Izzy had friends. One of them must have known what was going on."

Shana moved to Izzy's computer desk and found a yellow self-stick note on the side of his computer which read, "Oksana to Vermont?" The note made Shana hopeful. Maybe the CIA had gotten it wrong. Maybe Izzy had gone to his condominium near Mount Snow? Maybe he was there right now, with this Oksana woman. Shana reached for her purse and pulled out her address book. She found the number to Izzy's condo and dialed with heart racing. After ten rings she put the receiver down reluctantly. However, she still wasn't ready to accept the fact that her little brother could really be dead.

The ringing of the phone froze Shana in her place. Izzy's computer answered the call, and Shana listened to the incoming message. "Izzy, it is Oksana. It is very late and I know that you are not home until tomorrow. I needed to tell you that I am also now feeling love for you. I hope you are safe. Call me. . . "

Shana grabbed the phone receiver which disabled the answering machine in the computer. "Hello? This is Izzy's sister. Do you know where my brother is?"

There was a brief pause before Oksana replied. "Izzy's sister? But you are in Pennsylvania. Izzy told me Philadelphia."

"Yes, yes! But I need to find my brother!" The anxiety in Shana's voice grew with each syllable.

"Izzy went to Argentina three days ago. Is there a problem?"

Oksana's confirmation pushed Shana over the edge. "Izzy!" she cried as tears began to flow in earnest. "Not Izzy, Not IZZY, NOT IZZY..." She wailed over and over again, her breath coming in ragged gasps. Mitchell moved to his wife and tried to comfort her with a hug. She squirmed out of his arms and ran off into the bathroom, slamming the door behind herself. Mitchell picked up the receiver that she had let drop and found that the line was still open.

"Hello? Are you still there?"

"Who is this?"

"Mitchell Stern, I'm Izzy's brother-in-law." Mitchell picked his words carefully. "I'm afraid there has been an accident"

"Izzy is dead." Oksana said it as a statement rather than a question.

"Yes, how did you know?"

"I will get dressed and come to see you. The story is very complicated."

"Okay," Mitchell agreed. "We will wait for you here."

By the time Oksana reached the apartment, Shana had calmed down. Oksana's knock brought Mitchell to the front door. He pulled it back and stared at Oksana awkwardly, not knowing exactly the right salutation for such a first meeting. "Please come in," he stammered in a hushed voice.

Shana had always held a mental picture of the type of woman that her little brother would find attractive. Oksana was very close to what she had imagined. Oksana's dark olive skin and long, deep black hair made her look like a sabra, a native born Israeli. Shana stood from the sofa in a daze. In a faraway corner of her mind she could picture this woman standing with Izzy under a hupa. She forced the thought from her mind. There would be no wedding canopy for Izzy. He would never have the joy of signing his name below the Mogan-David on a Ketubah, the Jewish wedding contract. Tears began to flow again as she realized that the only Star of David that Izzy would know would be on his coffin.

Without even saying hello, Oksana pulled Shana close and hugged her tightly.

"Why Izzy?" Shana wailed. "It isn't fair!"

"I do not know," Oksana replied softly. "I did not know Izzy long, but. . . " Oksana had to stop to compose herself or she would have started to cry as well. "Who told you that Izzy was dead?"

Mitchell stepped beside the two women. "We were visited by a man from the government. They said the government of Argentina could not find Izzy's body, but they were looking for it."

"Governments do not find bodies," Oksana replied with open contempt. "They make them disappear."

Instantly, Shana stopped crying. She looked at Oksana curiously. "Do you know why Izzy went to Argentina?"

Oksana nodded. "Izzy believed he had discovered the source of the HIV virus. He went to Buenos Aires to see if he could find proof."

Mitchell began to pace around the room. "The CIA said they believe that Izzy died of heart failure. Just keeled over in a night-club. There were lots of witnesses. Izzy never once mentioned anything about a heart condition."

Shana sighed heavily. "I guess I should start making calls to the family. But I don't think we can do a funeral, not without. . . without." Tears began to flow again. Shana couldn't say body, and she couldn't accept the fact that she would never see her little brother again.

Neither would Oksana.

Chapter 12

The flight to Paris aboard Brittany Pharmalogics private jet lasted little more than half an hour. Izzy had been provided with a new wardrobe and a new identity. He was now Sheldon Kramer, a salesman of medical diagnostic equipment from Camden, New Jersey. Heneke had insisted that Izzy shave off his beard and mustache to alter his look as much as possible. Izzy resisted at first. He had grown the beard at the age of twenty-four. After twenty some years he had grown comfortable with who he was and how he looked. However, Heneke explained in graphic detail what the modern day Reich did to people that it captured. With the need for stealth laid out in black and white, Izzy spent the better part of an hour, and three razor cartridges, shaving.

Izzy looked at the picture that had been placed on his new passport, and the one that was on his replicated New Jersey driver's license. Without the beard, Izzy hardly recognized himself. The photographer had made him change shirts for each picture. Wearing the same shirt in both a passport and driver's license photograph might seem like too much of a coincidence. Inquiry by a suspicious customs agent could bring unwanted attention. Every effort was made to invent a person who seamlessly blended in.

"Should I call you Sheldon, or Shelly?" Jean inquired as the landing gear dropped into position. She was now Mrs. Sheldon Kramer. According to her new dossier, she worked as a booking agent for professional conferences. It was at one of these conferences that she met Sheldon. At first she didn't want to go out with him because of the age difference. However, Sheldon pursued her relentlessly. They dated for almost a year and then got married. This was her first trip to Europe and the first time she was accompanying her husband on one of his frequent business trips.

Izzy looked at Jean and just shook his head from side to side. He folded the leather wallet that he had been given and it slipped from his hand. He bent forward to pick it up, which was quite difficult with his seat belt fastened. He was just able to reach it with two fingers when the wheels of the plane touched the ground. The jolt caused Izzy to lose his grip on the wallet and it fell to the floor again, only this time the momentum carried it several feet farther away.

"Sheldon, you must try to calm down. You look as nervous as a turkey before Thanksgiving." Jean said the words with a thick Jersey accent, every remnant of her French heritage buried beyond detection.

Izzy glared at her as he released the seatbelt mechanism. "Nervous? I look nervous?"

Jean stood from her seat. She was dressed simply in baggy blue jeans and a light blue turtleneck. On her feet were a battered pair of Reebok sneakers. She lifted a foot and placed it down on Izzy's right thigh before he had a chance to stand. "Tonight I will do my best to completely relax you."

Izzy looked into Jean's face and burst out laughing. He pushed Jean's foot off and got out of his seat. Izzy's rebuff left Jean startled. However, she continued to press the seduction. "You do not want to sleep with me?"

Izzy spun towards Jean aggressively. "If you are going to walk the walk, talk the talk. Jersey girls are in-your-face tough." Izzy moved closer to Jean and she backed away from him. He pushed her up against a wall of the plane and gave her one of his tough looks, the kind that he had practiced riding the Brooklyn subways when he was in high school. "A Jersey girl would say, 'I'm going to fuck your brains out tonight.' And they don't just say it, they do it."

A flush came to Jean's cheeks and her breathing deepened. This aggressive side to Izzy's personality frightened and excited her at the same time.

"One other thing," Izzy added as he turned toward the now open door of the plane. "Don't ever call me Sheldon!"

The scene inside the main terminal building at Paris International Airport was anything but ordinary. Soldiers from the Army combined with French gendarmes as they swept carefully through the terminal with bomb sniffing dogs. The building was filled with the multi-lingual chatter of tourists who seemed curiously on edge. Inspectors were going through each piece of luggage individually. The inspections were time consuming and lines at the Air France and American Airlines counters were several hundred people deep. Jean and Izzy fought their way toward the Aeroflot counter.

Izzy passed the American Airlines area and noticed a group of people had gathered around a information monitor that hung down from the ceiling. It was a typical airport screen, the type that announced flight departures. However, for some reason the monitor had been converted to a television. The people gathered round the set stood there in stunned silence, all eyes glued to the screen. Izzy motioned to Jean and they fought their way over to the group. The television was turned to an English language broadcast from CNN.

On the screen were pictures of ambulances, fire trucks, police cars, and military vehicles. They were off in the distance, maybe half a mile from where the CNN cameraman was filming. A shaken Margorie Harris, CNN's London correspondent, grasped a microphone and stared into the camera.

"For those of you just joining us, I am standing near what thirty minutes ago was the Brittany Pharmalogics research facility. A massive explosion ripped through this state-of-the-art underground complex, causing large sections of the facility to cave in. There is no word yet on casualties. As you can see from our pictures, the authorities are not letting us near the actual site of the explosion.

The blood instantly drained from Jean's face and Izzy's mouth fell open. They glanced at each other and then retrained their attention on the reporter on the screen.

"This just in," Marjorie added as she relayed the information that came to her through an earpiece. "The French government has confirmed that they believe this to be an act of terrorism. Officials in Paris say they are on high alert. They have increased security at airports, train stations, and all border crossings." Marjorie stopped and turned to look at the scene in the distance as several ambulances sped away from the scene. She placed her hand to her ear, trying to shield out noise and listen carefully to the news coming over the tiny speaker. When she turned back towards the camera she had the slightest tear in her eye. "We have confirmed reports that French scientist Claude Thomae, the Nobel prize winner for the discovery of the AIDS virus, is among the dead. I repeat, we have confirmation that Nobel prize winner, Doctor Claude Thomae, is dead."

Jean felt the room spin and her knees buckled. When she awoke she was inside the private, members-only Swiss Air travel lounge. Izzy was by her side, as were several doctors and gendarmes.

"Don't sit up too quickly," Izzy admonished. Jean ignored his request, jumped up, and moved to a television that was in the corner of the lounge. This was an actual receiver, with a twenty-seven inch screen. It was also tuned to CNN. Jean had yet to say a word to anyone. She watched in an almost trance-like state as a steady stream of ambulances pulled up to a seaside hotel. The camera panned back and tiny fishing boats could be seen bobbing in the harbor of a sleeping fishing village. Marjorie Harris's voice-over shattered the tranquility of the scene.

"You are looking at the Hotel Bellevue in Roscoff, France. Authorities have transformed the hotel into a temporary triage site. After immediate care, survivors will be flown by helicopter to a hospital in the capital city of Quimper. Burn victims are being taken directly to Paris."

The camera zoomed in close as an ambulance stopped in front of the hotel. Paramedics opened the doors of the vehicle and lifted out a survivor. The camera zoomed in closer, close enough to see that the victim was male, and that his white lycra unitard had melted into his skin. What was left of it resembled shriveled plastic wrap. The camera pulled back to reveal a helicopter hovering overhead. The paramedics motioned for the helicopter and it settled on the hotel's small, gravel parking lot. The young man was wrapped with ice packs and then loaded into the helicopter. In Paris, doctors with diamond tipped scalpels would cut away the burned nylon and dead skin.

Jean turned from the television just as the helicopter lifted off. She spoke for the first time since passing out. Despite her traumatized state she was able to maintain her accent. "Izzy, we need to hurry or we will miss our flight to Moscow."

Neither the police or the assembled doctors objected and Jean and Izzy continued on their way. It wasn't until the big Russian plane was high in the sky that Jean allowed the tears to flow. She gasped uncontrollably, her whole body shaking in spasms. Izzy looked towards her but said nothing. He had no words for the situation and was in a state of shock himself. It had not yet dawned on him that he and Jean might be the only two people left alive who knew anything about Mengele cells.

A young, ill-equipped stewardess approached with a box of tissues in her hand. She offered assistance while other passengers glanced at Jean repeatedly. The stewardess spoke a bit of broken English. Therefore, communicating was difficult. After repeated attempts, Izzy finally got her to bring Jean a cup of tea. While the stewardess was gone, Jean's crying had stopped. She graciously accepted the tea, assuring the young woman in Russian that she would be all right. The stewardess smiled, nodded, and walked away. Jean left the tea on her seat tray untouched. She turned away from Izzy and stared blankly out the window. After a long period of silence she finally spoke.

"If it takes me the rest of my life I will hunt them down." Jean's words were spoken softly, but with intensity and purpose. They raised Izzy's already paranoid state to a new high. He started darting his eyes around the cabin. Even the slightest twitch from fellow passengers alerted his attention. If the Nazis could access the research facility and blow it up, they certainly would have no problem with a plane. Jean noticed Izzy's eyes darting about and spoke to it. "What are you doing?"

"Staying alert," Izzy replied as he whipped his head around to watch a woman leave her seat. His eyes stayed fix on her as she entered the plane's bathroom.

"Stop it!" Jean implored. "We do not want to draw attention."

"Attention?" Izzy replied in a voice that was way too loud.

"Sssh!" Jean admonished. "The world thinks you are dead. At least for now there is no threat. Be happy that you are not my father."

"Your father?" Izzy asked in confusion as he turned to look squarely at Jean.

"Claude was my father. He saved me from an orphanage when I was little." Jean had to pause and compose herself. Izzy was shocked. He had no idea that Jean was the child that Thomae boasted of during the viral medical conferences. Izzy reached out and grabbed Jean's hand.

"He was a good man."

Jean nodded. "I was very sick as a child. No one else wanted me. But my father loved me from the first second."

"You had a pony," Izzy remembered.

A melancholy smile spread across Jean's face. "Lancelot, my

father bought him when I was nine. Dulac was my original Christian name, and my father insisted that I retain it. We both laughed when I picked the name for the horse. 'But of course...' he said. 'What other name could a Dulac have.'" Jean paused and looked at Izzy curiously. "How did you know that I had a pony?"

Izzy squeezed Jean's hand tightly. "Let's just say your father loved you very much." For a long time after Izzy spoke there was silence. The two companions were lost in thought, each wondering how their lives would now be changed forever. One had lost a father, the other, a good friend. At last Jean broke the silence with a question.

"How will you convince them?"

"What?"

"How will you convince the rest of the world? How will you get them to believe?"

Izzy shook his head back and forth as he contemplated the question. Assuming that they found Mengele's notes, Henekc was the only one who had the ability to piece the puzzle together. Izzy assumed the worst and presumed that Heneke was also now dead. Establishing a viral host cell theory would bring universal laughter from the global medical community. At last, Izzy gave up on the problem. "Not knowing the truth does not stop the truth from being true."

Izzy thought about the early pioneers of biology. Dutch scientist Anton Von Leeuwenhook was derided publicly in 1677 for describing sperm cells as animalcules. It was much worse for Darwin, mocked and laughed at for his theory of evolution in *Origin of The Species*. Getting the skeptics to believe was the least of his problems. Secretly he was praying just to stay alive.

Chapter 13

The architectural splendor of Moscow's Red Square caused Izzy to gape in awe. The seven brightly colored cathedral domes spoke loudly of an age gone by. An age in which Russia was truly the mother country. Jean nudged Izzy towards the steps of Saint Basil's cathedral. They were surrounded by a sea of tourists, all transfixed by the enormity of the structure. Izzy had traveled the world. He had seen the famous churches in New York, Montreal, Paris, and London. None could compare with the building that stood in front of him. He reached his hand out to touch the hand carved marble and realized that Moscow was a capital unlike any other. While other cities rocketed towards modern technology, this place was a testament to tradition, and spirits long past gone.

Jean had been the one who suggested the cathedral as a meeting place. It was best to stay out in the open. Lurking in shadows would only attract attention, attention that they could not afford. Jean placed a foot on the first step of the cathedral and she could feel eyes focused on her from behind. Casually she turned back to look at Izzy, who had not yet touched the stairs. Her eyes narrowed to slits as she stared over Izzy's shoulder at the stranger who approached. Izzy could sense her apprehension, and lacking her sense of stealth, spun around. He found himself face-to-face with a hard looking, dark-haired man. The face was world-worn, with deep set eyes. A dark mustache with streaks of gray reminded Izzy of Charles Bronson, the actor. The man ignored Izzy and focused his attention on Jean.

"Una o'chen usta' la"

Jean nodded as she lowered her voice and translated for Izzy. "He says that I look tired. I will ask him where the hospital is. *Gdye zzdyes balni tsa?"*

"Vy plo' kho sybya choo' stvuyu?"

Jean shook her head from side to side. "I do not feel ill. *Nyet. My ye dem is chor noye."*

Jean had just told the man, "We have come from the Black Sea." It was the password that Heneke had instructed her to use.

The man turned toward Izzy and extended his hand. "Doctor Slesinger, I am Ilya Babekov. Doctor Chazov is very anxious to have you see first hand the results of *leker stva."*

Izzy's face remained blank. "I'm sorry," he said. "I do not speak Russian. Liquor sta? What is that?"

"Leker stva," the man corrected as he led Izzy and Jean away from the square. "It is the medicine."

"Medicine?"

"PIRT-I9," Jean explained as she interjected herself into the conversation. "Doctor Heneke finished laboratory testing five years ago. It was easier to conduct clinical trials in Russia without being detected. We could never have accomplished this in France or Germany."

Izzy's stomach rumbled with acid as he silently made note of how Heneke was still using living human beings for experimentation, without first going through the proper protocol or channels. In America, such experimentation wouldn't even be considered. Even radical researchers, the ones who railed against the Food and Drug Administration on a daily basis, would never attempt such trials. It made Izzy wonder how Heneke could claim to be trying to save humanity, when it was clear that he had so little regard for the welfare of humans.

Ilya Babekov stopped in front of a white and red brick building on Serova Street. It was an old building, with the mortar between the bricks crumbling to dust. There was no identification of any kind on the outside of the building, or over the heavy, weathered brass door. Ilya nodded towards the entrance. "Doctor Chazov's clinic is through door. Walk corridor to end. You will find it."

"Aren't you coming in?" Izzy asked.

Ilya shook his head. "I need to make arrangements for transportation. I will be back soon."

Ilya turned and walked down the crowded street, leaving Izzy and Jean alone. Izzy was anxious to find out what awaited him inside the clinic. Therefore, he took the lead, pushing open the big door. The interior was a surprise. The corridor he and Jean stepped into was modern, with overhead fluorescent lighting for illumination. The walls, which were a saffron yellow, looked freshly painted. The floors, which were a gray epoxy material, were spotless.

The clinic was also somewhat of a surprise. There was a small waiting room which could have been in any private physician's office in America. There was just one patient in the waiting room. He was a boy of about thirteen, Izzy guessed. He sat quietly beside his mother. He could have been a typical American teenager, dressed in his American-made blue jeans. However, there was something wrong with the proportions of his extremities. Izzy's eyes focused on the boy's hands which were swollen and grotesque. The arms, covered by long sleeves, were also swollen.

"Lymphademia?" Izzy mouthed the word softly as he considered the swelling. Lymphademia was a rare condition in which a person is born with missing lymph nodes and there is no way for the body to remove lymph from tissues. Therefore the fluid accumulates and swells the skin painfully.

"Similar," the response came from a short matronly, middle-aged woman dressed in a white medical jacket. The woman extended her hand to Izzy. "Lidia Chazov. I am very glad to meet you."

Izzy shook her hand and then turned back towards the boy. "Not lymphademia? You're certain?"

Lidia nodded. "It is a complication we have seen with a new type of non-Hodgkin's lymphomas. For some reason the condition is mostly seen in male patients, but age does not seem to be a limiting factor. Let me show you the others," Lidia suggested as she walked toward a closed door. Izzy followed after her as did Jean.

Inside, the clinic could have been taken for an American hospital, except that it was a large open space. There were almost eighty beds spaced around the room. All the beds were filled, with men and boys to the right, women and girls to the left. Not all the patients were bed-ridden. Some walked around the room, pushing portable intravenous systems. Others looked out the windows at people passing by in the street. They too were tethered to intravenous lines, as were the patients who sat up on their beds, and the ones who were too weak to sit up. The one thing that every patient had in common was the little blue bottle of medicine that dripped into the line and mixed with the saline solution.

Lidia came to a stop by a young woman who sat by the side of her bed. "This is Elaina. She came to us with a vaginal cancer we are just now starting to understand. She is but one of several thousand we have seen."

"Several thousand?" Izzy asked in amazement. His eyes studied the girl carefully. She couldn't be more than eighteen. Vaginal cancer was extremely rare, and usually confined to older women. "You are certain of the diagnosis?"

Lydia nodded. "But it is difficult to diagnose. Elaina came to us with extreme bleeding and pain. Many doctors dismiss this as a normal menses with a heavy blood flow. Several hundred women in Leningrad died because they were improperly treated. We have seen patients who have died of blood loss, years after having had a complete hysterectomy. "Lidia walked to a supply closet and retrieved an intravenous drip bag which was filled with light green fluid. She handed the bag to Izzy. He studied it carefully. The label was written in Russian.

"What is it?" Izzy asked.

"AKCF. Artificial Clotting Factor from Kaiser. No one can explain why this stops the cancers from bleeding. We have had it analyzed and it seems similar to many other products we import from the west. But only this one works."

"Heneke," Izzy muttered under his breath. Surely this clotting factor was another one of his inventions. He must have surmised that hemorrhage could be induced in vaginal tissue that had been compromised by Mengele cells. It only made sense that a virus conducted sexually would eventually compromise the sexual organs. Syphilis and herpes were examples that were on a long, long list.

Lidia anticipated Izzy's next question. "All these patients were at one time HIV positive. They all receive PIRT-I9." Lydia touched a finger to the little blue bottle that mixed with Elaina's intravenous fluid. "Over ninety percent are now HIV negative. We can no longer even detect antibodies. And yet most have medical conditions that continue to worsen."

Izzy spent several hours pouring over case histories with Lidia beside him. In America, most AIDS deaths were from complicating factors such as pneumonia. Secondary infections were the commonest cause of fatalities in the HIV community. A compromised immune system offers little protection against a host of nasty bacteria and viruses. However, in Russia, it was a completely different picture. Patients at the clinic had almost as much chance of dying from cancers as they did from secondary infections. Over a quarter of all patients in the past five years had contracted Kaposi's sarcoma. Those kind of numbers were hard to argue with, especially for cancers which were hardly seen in other parts of the world. Izzy needed no further proof that there was a causative link between HIV and Mengele cells. Therefore, Heneke was probably right in hypothesizing that eliminating the virus alone would not be enough. PIRT-I9 was very effective at eliminating the virus in the patients in the clinic and they were still very sick.

While Izzy poured through the data, Jean chatted with Elaina. Every once in a while Izzy would glance in their direction. They could have been sisters. Elaina complained of tiredness and Jean nodded in understanding. She gave her new friend a hug and made her way back to Izzy's side. It was getting late and Izzy had seen more than enough deaths recorded in detail for one day. He thanked Lidia for sharing the information and then departed with Jean beside him. Neither said a word as they walked out of the heavy brass door and stepped onto the street. Ilya Babekov was waiting for them. Jean walked directly to him and pointed towards the Moscow train station.

"My ye dyem v gorod' Sosnovka!"

"You are going to Sosnovka?" Ilya asked incredulously. "Nyet. I cannot allow it!"

Jean ignored Ilya and started walking towards the train station. Both Ilya and Izzy went after her. Ilya reached out and grabbed a hold of Jean by the arm. She tried to pull free but Ilya would not let go.

"You will not find the papers in Sosnovka," Ilya implored. "But it is very possible you will find the Reich and that means trouble. We cannot risk it."

Realizing that she wasn't strong enough to pull free, Jean instead threw herself against Ilya.

They both crashed to the ground. Jean jumped to her feet and started sprinting towards the train station. Ilya stood slowly. He walked to Izzy who had become a forgotten bystander.

"Fine," Ilya called after her. "But Doctor Slesinger is staying here with me."

Ilya's words froze Jean in her tracks. Her conversation with Elaina had made her sad. To hear about the pain and humiliation of her condition angered Jean. It wasn't fair. Elaina put a face on the disease they were up against. Jean became even more resolute in her commitment to find the missing pieces of the puzzle. However, it was very clear to her that she would never find what she was looking for on her own. Therefore, she returned to Ilya and tried to reason with him.

"The nurse was last seen in Sosnovka. We must go there!"

Ilya shook his head. . . "That was sixty-years ago. The woman would be in her eighties, assuming that she isn't dead. We do not know that she remained in that area."

"We must start there," Jean argued. "We must!"

"Why?" Ilya begged. "Why there?"

"Because we have nothing else."

Ilya stood silently for a long time considering options. "I will make the arrangements," he said at last. "Go back to your hotel. I will come for you in the morning."

The train ride from Moscow to Cherkassy was long. Izzy took a window seat on the train, with Jean beside him on the aisle. Ilya Babakov saw them to the train station and told them he would meet up with them in Sosnovka. Izzy decided against reviewing his notes on the train, his head was already overloaded with theory and hypothesis. Instead, he pressed his face against the glass of the window and watched as the train worked its way past hundreds of small farms. Izzy thought that it was ironic that this country, once called The Evil Empire by an American President, so resembled the heartland of America. The farms whizzing by could have easily been in Kansas or Iowa.

The train came to a stop at a road crossing. Out the window Izzy glimpsed several young people, teenagers actually, dashing about in a corn field. "How different their world will be if we don't get a handle on this," Izzy thought to himself. He forced the images from his mind. He was not about to get caught up in Brian Crighton's mathematical models of doom. A tear formed in the corner of his eye as he thought about the young, tall statistician. A life of brilliance, still waiting to be led, had probably been extinguished along with Claude Thomae in the explosion. Izzy shut his eyes to the image and focused his mind on the clickety-clack of the train. Slowly, his mind gave into his body's fatigue and he drifted off to a restless sleep.

Little whimpering noises emitted from Izzy as he moved from one nightmare to the next. His head tossed from side-to-side in his seat, not finding a true spot of comfort. The noises caused several people to stare in Izzy's direction. They also awoke Jean from her own slumbers. She placed a hand on Izzy's shoulder and shook him lightly.

"What? What?" Izzy cried as his eyes shot open. There was a look of panic on his face.

"You were whimpering," Jean said softly.

"Whimpering?"

Jean nodded and pointed a finger over Izzy's shoulder. Izzy turned around in his seat and looked back outside the window. The farms had disappeared, the tracks now ran beside an industrialized river. "It is the Dnieper. We will be in Cherkassy soon."

"Cherkassy? You said we were going to Sos. . . nov. . . ka."

"We are," Jean agreed. "But first we must go through Cherkassy. It is here we must be very careful."

Izzy twisted in his seat so that he was facing Jean. "Where exactly are you taking me?"

"Cherkassy is in the West. Or for Germany, on the Eastern Front. The city was among the first to fall to the Reich. The Russian's liberated the city in December of '43. According to the KGB, many German officers defected as the Russian army advanced. It is believed they escaped by blending in with Cherkessy's civilian population. We know that there are groups who are sympathetic to Nazi doctrines within the city."

Izzy reflected on the new information. "That's why Mr. Babakov didn't want us to come. He feared neo-Nazis will try and kill us."

"I don't think so," Jean replied. "You are believed dead. Ilya was nervous that we would attract the attention of Russian security. Cherkessy makes Moscow nervous."

"Nervous?"

"It is a city of 300,000. Most of it is a modern trade city, more connected with Europe than even Leningrad. It is also quite liberal by Russian standards. Therefore, security forces watch the population closely."

The train slowed, lurched forward, and stopped. The doors slid open and people began getting off. Jean and Izzy waited until the car was completely empty before exiting. Directly across from the train station was a modern high-rise Hilton hotel. Izzy and Jean made their way into the lobby and waited by the front desk. A middle-aged man in a dark suit approached from behind the desk. He said something in Russian and waited for a reply. Izzy glanced at Jean but she said nothing. The man repeated the phrase and Izzy grew increasingly nervous. This was a very strange time Jean picked to play a mute.

"Sheldon," Jean intoned in her thickest Jersey accent. "Tell 'em we don't speak Russian."

"No need," the man replied. "I am fluent in English. If I could get you to sign our guest book, and hand me a credit card, I will arrange a room."

Nervously Izzy watched as the man ran his credit card through the system. While it was being processed, Izzy signed 'Mr. and Mrs. Sheldon Kramer' to the register. The man came back with Izzy's card and handed it to him. "You are in room 321, Mr. Kramer. I hope you will find your stay with us enjoyable. Should you need anything, ask. We do request that you give us twelve hours notice before checking out."

"Thank you," Izzy responded as he put the credit card back into his wallet. He and Jean turned away from the desk and found the elevator. It was only after the silver metal doors had slid shut that Izzy allowed himself a deep breath.

As soon as they were settled in their hotel room, Jean announced that she was going to take a shower before dinner. Izzy nodded casually, pretending not to be interested. However, Izzy listened close for the sound of the shower. When he heard the spray of water he moved to the telephone beside the bed. He retrieved his telephone log from his briefcase and quietly picked up the receiver.

"Operator, I'd like to place a call to the USA, reverse charges. The number is 718-793-2651."

It was a little past two in the morning when the phone woke Oksana from a deep sleep. She groggily reached for the phone, expecting that it must be the hospital calling about a sick patient. When the operator explained that it was a reverse-charge call from Russia, Oksana became wide awake. Only a handful of people back home had her American phone number. None of them would call in the middle of the night unless it was a real emergency.

"Yes, go ahead. I will accept the charges."

There was a tiny pause from satellite delay and then Izzy was on the line.

"Oksana, is that you?"

Oksana had been expecting a voice in Russian. Therefore, it took her a moment before responding. "Who is this?"

"It's Izzy."

"Izzy?" Oksana repeated weakly as most of the color drained from her face. "You are dead."

"I'm not dead."

Oksana had to strain to hear Izzy's whispered words.

"Where are you?"

"I'm staying at the Hilton in Cherkassy."

Oksana gasped. "Cherkassy? In Russia? How did you get there from Argentina?"

"Can't explain. I need you here. Take the next flight out."

"You want me to come to Cherkassy?" The line went dead

before Oksana could finish her question. "Izzy, Izzy? Are you still there?" The only sound Oksana heard was the dial tone.

Izzy let the phone drop from his fingers as Jean emerged from the bathroom. She walked into the room half-naked, her towel wrapped around her waist. Izzy couldn't help but appraise the firmness of her breasts. Jean noticed his glance and smiled. She walked to him, making no effort to hide the fact that her nipples were hardening. Izzy tried to avert his gaze, but it was a hard thing to do with a half-naked woman just inches away. Jean made it even harder when she let the towel drop. Izzy allowed his eyes to fall for only a nanosecond. Just long enough to admire Jean's neatly cropped bush. As Jean inched forward, Izzy broke out in a sweat. The look of lust in her eyes was unmistakable, and difficult to refuse. Jean placed a hand under her right breast and lifted it gently.

"You look so hungry." She cooed with her native Parisian accent.

It took all of Izzy's reserves, but he stepped by her and placed his hand on the knob of the hotel room door. "I am starving," he replied, pretending to be oblivious to such a blatant sexual offering. "When you're dressed, come down to the restaurant."

Jean shook her head in dismay as Izzy disappeared and the door shut. No man had ever refused her sex. Izzy was turning out to be much more difficult to read than she had expected.

However, instead of being put off, Jean became even more aroused. How much better the sex would be if she had to play lioness, hunting her prey.

The restaurant within the Hilton was filled to capacity. Izzy was still waiting for a table when Jean stepped through the door of the restaurant. When she was next to Izzy she leaned close and whispered into his ear.

"You are a very complicated man, Doctor Slesinger."

Izzy smiled in agreement. "Thank you, Mrs. Kramer." With Jean close, Izzy turned his head to the side and gave her a quick peck on the lips. He was teasing her, and damn well enjoying it.

Dinner was an interesting affair. The room was alive with the sound of many different languages and dialects, proving that Cherkassy was indeed an international city of business. Izzy and Jean were seated at a small booth, built for two people. The table had been draped with a white table cloth that hung almost to the floor. It was obviously made for one of the larger tables. It formed the perfect cover for Jean. During dessert she slipped off the shoe on her right foot. Casually she lifted her leg at the knee and placed her foot directly on Izzy's crotch. Izzy's eyes opened wide in surprise.

Jean seductively licked a spot of chocolate sauce from the corner of her mouth. She was so caught up in the idea of seduction, she didn't notice the gorgeous blond woman who was dining alone, several tables away. However, Izzy noticed her. Mostly because she kept looking directly at him, like she was studying him. It made Izzy nervous and he deftly used a hand to remove Jean's foot from his crotch. He leaned forward slightly in his seat and lowered his voice.

"I think I'm being watched."

Jean's demeanor instantly changed. Izzy could see it in her eyes. The seductive quality vanished, replaced with a hard, steely edge. Jean excused herself to go to the bathroom. She walked directly past the blond and appraised her as she walked by. The woman was tall. Jean guessed around 5'11". Her well developed frame was that of a body builder. Jean glanced at the woman's face, definitely Aryan. Her eyes were deeply set and difficult to read on only a glance.

As soon as Jean disappeared down the corridor to the restroom, the blond woman stood and walked to Izzy. She looked down at him and smiled.

"I noticed you from across the room. I am in Cherkassy for one night." The woman opened her purse, removed a slip of paper, and wrote her room number on it. She placed the slip of paper directly in front of Izzy. "You do not seem to be the type of man who would settle for a child, when he could have a woman instead." Then she was gone, leaving most of the food on her plate uneaten. She had offered herself without so much as an introduction. It left Izzy unsettled. He stared at the slip of paper. He picked it up and crumpled it into a ball. However, instead of putting it in the ashtray, he slipped it into his pocket.

Izzy scribbled 'Sheldon Kramer' on the check and met Jean as she came out of the bathroom.

"I think maybe I'm just being paranoid. The woman got up and left."

"Maybe not," Jean countered. "We must be very careful. My behavior was not appropriate. I apologize."

Izzy extended his hand and Jean shook it. "Apology excepted." Izzy paused for a moment and smiled. "But who could refuse a pharmaceutical salesman from New Jersey?" There was more than a trace of sarcasm in his voice.

Izzy laid awake in bed for a long time. Jean fell asleep as soon as her head hit the pillow. Izzy couldn't sleep. He toyed with the idea of heading to the blond woman's room. It would be a quick rendezvous. Brief, intense, zipless sex. No names, no addresses. The thought aroused him and then he remembered where he was, and what he was doing. What if the woman was a member of the Reich? She could be waiting for him with a gun, or a knife. She might wait until he was in the throes of a powerful orgasm and simultaneously slit his throat. It was not the way he wanted to die, or be remembered.

Finally he got out of bed and decided to study his notes. As he reached for his briefcase, he instead picked up his pants which were draped over a chair. Izzy retrieved the crumpled ball of paper from his pocket. He uncrumpled it and stared at the room number. He shook his head, crumpled the paper again, and tossed it in the waste basket.

Izzy was up early the next morning. He quietly got dressed, moving slowly around the room so as not to make noise and wake Jean. He cautiously opened a desk drawer and removed an envelope from the small pile of stationary supplies. He placed his card key in the envelope, scribbled Oksana's name on it, and then licked it shut. Izzy tip-toed to the room door. He lifted up on the door while opening it, insuring that the hinges wouldn't squeak. Izzy left the door slightly ajar, insuring that he would be able to reenter the room without the card key that he had just put into the envelope.

When Jean awoke she found herself staring directly down the barrel of a 9mm Glock semi-automatic handgun. The blond woman that Jean had seen at dinner had pulled a chair beside the bed. She was now seated in the chair and had the gun pointed directly at Jean's heart. The woman was now dressed in black jeans, and long sleeve black polo shirt. Her long blond hair was pulled up into a bun.

"Where is Doctor Slesinger?"

Jean sat up in bed, her eyes darting around the room. She had no idea where Izzy was. Therefore, she decided to play dumb. "Excuse me, sweetheart," she whined with the persona of a homemaker from Orange County. "I'm afraid you're in the wrong room. My husband and I are here from Jersey. I've never heard of a Doctor Slesinger."

The woman released the safety on the pistol. "One more lie and I will put a bullet through your heart."

Jean thought about jumping up and grabbing for the gun. She concluded that the odds were very good that she'd be dead before she even left the bed. "I'm afraid I don't know where he is," Jean confessed. Her voice now stripped of the false accent.

The woman shook her head as she stood from the chair. She grasped the handle of the gun firmly and slapped the barrel across Jean's face. The metal ripped a gash into Jean's cheek and blood poured out. The force of the blow caused Jean to topple over in bed, her torn flesh falling onto a pillow. "Liar," she screamed. "I will kill you."

Jean moved her right hand under the pillow and swiftly pulled out a gun of her own, taking aim at the woman's head. "You might hit my heart, I will definitely hit your brain." Jean slowly propped herself up. She got out of bed on the side opposite of her assailant, all the while keeping her gun trained on the woman. Jean kept a focus on her as she backed her way towards the open door. A roughened hand reached out and pulled Jean backward, by the throat. Before she could respond, a second hand covered her mouth and nose with a cloth. As she struggled against the second assailant her lungs filled with ether. Several seconds later she passed out. When her body went limp, the second attacker released her and she crumpled to the floor. The blond woman walked to her, rolled a large wad of saliva in her cheek, and spit down on Jean's bloody face.

"You did not have to do that."

The woman laughed. "Come now, Comrade Babakov. You have no stomach for this? Perhaps I should rip off her panties and let you rape her. I'm sure a Cossack like you would enjoy it."

Ilya ignored the remark and kept his anger under control. "Dress her. We will hold her as insurance. However, with Dulac out of the way, Slesinger will fail."

Izzy dropped the room card key, in the envelope marked for Oksana, at the front desk. He told the man behind the concierge that he was expecting a Doctor Oksana Zibrova, and the envelope was for her. When he was certain that the man understood, he headed back towards the elevators. Izzy was surprised to find the door to his room closed all the way. He knocked on the door, but there was no answer. At the far end of the hotel corridor, a chamber maid was just coming in for morning duty. Izzy did his best to keep his anxiety under control as he approached the woman.

"Do you speak English?"

"A little," the young woman replied as she removed her heavy woolen coat. Underneath she wore a navy blue housekeeping dress that the hotel had provided.

"Uh, I seem to have left my key inside my room. Could you unlock my door?"

The woman nodded and proceeded to walk with Izzy to the

room. She inserted the master key into the lock and pulled down the handle. She pushed the door open, but only an inch.

"Thank you," Izzy offered as the woman turned back towards her work room. Izzy watched as she walked away. He opened the door to his room and entered, his stomach doing flip-flops from the anxiety. He quickly closed the door behind himself and stared in disbelief at the bed. There was no sign of Jean, and one pillow was soaked with blood. A wave of cold chills gripped Izzy and he literally began to tremble a bit. He was ill-equipped for this type of situation. Trying to calm himself, he breathed in deeply. The residual smell of ether made him gag. A wave of nausea gripped him and he made a dash to the bathroom. A moment later he vomited in the toilet.

Izzy's mind raced, searching for possible courses of action. "Perhaps he should go to the police?" He thought to himself. Immediately, he dismissed the idea. Going to the Russian police in Cherkassy would create more problems. They would surely detain him, asking him questions for which he had no answers. There was no denying that Jean's disappearance, and the blood, meant that she was dead. Therefore, Izzy concluded the Reich knew that he was still alive. It meant that he needed to get moving. He realized that his only chance for survival was to find Mengele's documents. Then, if he were captured, he could use them as a bargaining chip.

Izzy spent the next fifteen minutes packing. He gathered up Jean's clothes and stuffed them into his suitcase. Since Jean's valise was now empty, Izzy used it to store and hide the bloody pillow. Fortunately, no blood had gotten on the sheets. Izzy put Jean's suitcase under his right arm and picked his own up with his right hand. He used his left hand to lift his soft-sided briefcase. He stood staring at the closed door for several moments. The puzzle of opening it with full hands was more than his overworked mind could handle. Instead of simply putting the bags down, he attempted to push down on the door handle with his elbow. When that failed, he bent over and pushed the handle down with his forehead. The dead bolt clicked back from the door frame and Izzy grabbed the handle with his teeth. With a quick jerk he pulled back and the door opened. The quick motion ripped the metal handle from Izzy's teeth painfully. He let out a loud sigh when he realized that there was no way to close the door shut without putting his bags down, which he did.

It was during checkout that Izzy remembered Oksana. The concierge asked for both room keys and Izzy could only produce the one that was with Jean's belongings. He asked for the envelope that he had left earlier. When the concierge handed it to him he ripped it open, removed his own room key, and returned it. "Oksana, what to do about Oksana?" Izzy pondered silently. He couldn't let her come to the hotel. There was no telling how much the Reich knew?

If they had been watching him in America, they might know about Oksana. The thought forced Izzy to shudder. It also forced him to change his plans. He guessed Oksana would have immediately called Aeroflot for the next available flight to Moscow. That meant she would be on a 6:30 a.m. plane, arriving in what would be late evening, Moscow time. Instead of renting a car and heading to Sosnovka, Izzy headed for the train station for the long trip back to Moscow.

Izzy wasn't the only one in transit. Jean awoke to the high pitched roar of aircraft turbine engines spooling up for take-off. She had been strapped into a deeply padded leather seat, but her hands were suspiciously unbound and free from encumbrance. She reached for the clasp on the seatbelt and discovered that there wasn't any. Jean felt eyes watching from behind. She turned her head as much as possible and looked back over the back of her chair. The turning motion caused the lines of her face to go taut, which in turn pulled at the tape and gauze bandage that had been placed on her cheek.

It was the blond woman who was watching her. The one who had struck her with the gun. Jean's movement brought a wicked smile to the woman's face. The woman unfastened her own seat-belt, stood, and walked to Jean. Without saying anything she reached into a back pocket of her tight black denim pants and removed a switchblade. She tapped the button on the handle and a 7 inch, pointed and razor sharp blade sprang out. The woman held the blade several inches in front of Jean's eyes. It was close enough for Jean to see the dried blood.

"Babakov would not let me kill you," the woman hissed. If you even think about trying to escape, I will unleash a crimson fountain from your neck. Do we understand each other?"

Jean nodded slightly and the woman pulled the knife back. She held it up and inspected the blade closely.

"I was very disappointed when Doctor Slesinger passed on my offer of carnal pleasures. I would have allowed him to stick his rancid Juden penis in me, and then I would have stuck him."

The woman made a thrusting move with the knife, laughed, and then refolded the blade.

Jean asked the only thing that she could think of. "Who are you?"

"Anna Kaiser."

"Kaiser?" Jean screamed as she struggled against her belt, trying to worm her way out. "Your fucking brother blew up the facility!"

Anna's eyes opened wide in alarm as she spun towards Jean. "Who told you that?" she demanded.

Jean kept her lips tightly shut as she continued to struggle against her restraint. Anna lashed out with the back of her hand, slapping Jean hard against the cheek that was not torn. The force of the blow sent Jean's head crashing back into her seat. Anna disappeared into the back of the plane. She returned a moment later with a brute of a man by her side. While not particularly tall, he was powerfully built, with a bulging chest and huge biceps. The man was unshaven and his hair looked greasy. Anna whispered something to him in German and the man laughed while shaking his head in agreement. He moved in back of Jean's chair, squatted, and wrap both arms around her from behind. He placed his right hand on Jean's forehead and pulled her tautly back against the seat.

Meanwhile, Anna climbed onto Jean's chair. She stood with a foot on each armrest and bent over, her right hand planted on the back of Jean's chair. With her left hand she undid the clasp of her black jeans and squirmed them down her legs. She wasn't wearing any panties and Jean found her eyes glued to the neatly cropped, blond pubic bush that was just inches from her face.

The urine burst forth in a torrent. It splashed into Jean's eyes, burning them, and forcing them shut. She wanted to scream, but that would have allowed the yellow liquid to enter her mouth. Therefore, she pursed her lips tightly. The man behind the chair was laughing hysterically. When Anna finally finished, she jumped down from the chair. Instead of pulling her pants back up, she removed them completely.

Jean was soaked in urine. There wasn't a part of her that wasn't wet. She opened her eyes just as Anna pulled off her top and released her large, firm breasts from her bra. The big blond Aryan was now completely naked.

Anna tossed her hair back over her shoulders and laughed at Jean. "Now that your refreshed, I am going to leave you for a while. Boris and I are going to go in the back for some exercise. I trust you will be a good girl while I'm gone." Anna stepped into the aisle and hesitated before walking to the back of the plane. She leaned over and hissed into Jean's ear. "If Doctor Slesinger is heading for Sosnovka today, the Reich will crush him."

The sight of the plane touching the runway caused Izzy to relax. He had gone directly to the Moscow airport. The woman at the Aeroflot counter confirmed that a Doctor Oksana Zibrova was on the passenger's list of the incoming flight from New York's John F. Kennedy airport. Oksana was the first one off the plane. Having booked the flight at the last minute, she was forced to travel First Class. It turned out to be a blessing. The large, comfortably padded chairs were a welcome alternative to those found in the crowded coach section of the Aeroflot jet. Oksana had managed to even get some sleep on the flight that lasted a better part of the day. Therefore, when she stepped off the plane she looked human, as opposed to the disheveled creatures who had endured the flight in coach.

When she saw Izzy she sprinted to him, embracing him with a big hug.

"It is really you!"

Izzy pulled Oksana to him tightly. "I am so happy to see you. I've been living a nightmare."

When Izzy released Oksana from the hug she took a step back. Concern was etched on her face.

"Moscow is a long way from Buenos Aires."

"We need to talk," Izzy replied. "I think tonight we should stay near the airport. Tomorrow, there are things I need you to see."

A blood red Russian sun settled below the horizon as Izzy and Oksana checked into a hotel at the airport. They took several minutes to settle in their room and then headed for the hotel dining room. The temperature had fallen into the low thirties, typical for a late October Moscow night. Izzy had only packed a light sweater which offered little in the way of warmth. As a consequence he was quite chilled in the restaurant. Oksana noticed that he was shivering and suggested a first course.

"Order the *rassolnik*. It will take away the chill."

"*Rassolnik*? Never heard of it."

"Pickled vegetable soup. I'm sure you will love it."

Izzy made a face. "Let's skip the soup. What about *marozhnoye*?"

"Ice cream," Oksana laughed. "How about *pyelmeni*, in America I think you would call them meat dumplings."

"Sounds disgusting. I'm going to have the beef stroganoff"

Despite Oksana's word of caution, Izzy ordered the stroganoff. When the waiter placed the plate in front of Izzy, it took his appetite away. Chunks of beef swam among fried potatoes in a broth that was part brown and part white. Izzy looked questioningly at the waiter. "I. . . ordered. . . stroganoff." Izzy spoke the words slowly, the way Americans do when they travel abroad, somehow thinking that speed and understanding are linked.

The waiter looked puzzled. He spoke no English. Oksana explained to him that everything was fine and he disappeared. She then explained to Izzy that stroganoff is different in Russia.

The beef is boiled in sour cream and served atop fried potatoes. Just hearing the description made Izzy feel woozy. He looked at the plate in front of him and pushed it aside, all the while he was eyeing Oksana's chicken Kiev hungrily. She wound up splitting her plate in half and sharing it with him.

Immediately after dinner Izzy insisted on going someplace crowded and noisy. He had grown paranoid in the past several days and did not even want to risk a discussion in the safety of the hotel. He felt a crowded place among many people would be best for what he needed to tell Oksana. Outside the hotel, Oksana hailed a taxi cab. She gave the driver directions and he brought them to the famous Gorky Park. Oksana took Izzy by the hand as she headed towards the public beer drinking hall. Even though it was late autumn, the large concrete building was crowded, alive with a cacophony of voices. Izzy and Oksana found a small table and settled in for a long and private discussion.

Izzy held up his index finger and kept his voice just above a whisper. "One amino acid inside one particular protein alters the chromosome, which in turn alters the genetics of the cell. This altered cell, which is highly mutagenic, acts as the host for HIV. As the cell mutates, so does the virus."

"Host and target species combined?" Oksana pondered out loud. "Not possible!"

Izzy looked at Oksana with a steely gaze. He spoke with a quiet intensity. "Doctor Mengele did not live in our universe." Just Izzy's tone made Oksana shiver. "I want you to see something."

"Can't it wait until morning?" Oksana protested. "I am very tired. What is so important that I can not see it tomorrow?"

"We must move quickly," Izzy implored. "Or we will all find tomorrows in very short supply."

Chapter 14

It was a bit past one in the morning when Izzy and Oksana arrived at Doctor Chazov's clinic. Despite the late hour, Doctor Chazov was still hard at work. She was busy examining a four-year-old boy. His hands and feet were extremely swollen, almost grotesquely so. The boy's mother, who looked to be little more than a child herself, looked quite worried. She was a regular at the clinic. Having witnessed many other swollen children worsen and die, she could no longer hold back her tears.

Izzy immediately walked to the boy and examined his extremities. He didn't even bother introducing Oksana, who was silently reviewing any possible clinical diagnosis for the boy's swelling. She, like Izzy, concluded that it must be lymphadema. Izzy looked away from the boy and shook his head at Oksana. It was as if he were reading her mind. "At first I thought this was a lymphatic problem, like lymphadema. Skin is swollen, tender. . . But that's not it. This is an infection. The extremities are literally drowning in white blood cells." Izzy motioned for the boy's mother and she came close. Izzy turned his attention toward Lydia. "Can you ask her if he has had a fever?"

Before Lydia could ask anything, the boy's mother replied. *"Alexander nyevo' nyet temperatoo' ra"*

"No fever," Oksana translated.

"Damn strange," Izzy muttered under his breath. "Why isn't he burning up?" Izzy glanced towards Lydia. "I'd put him on a course of Augmentin, assuming that this is a type of infection."

"That will not help," Lydia advised. "Alexander needs PIRT-I9 to reduce the swelling. This is an effect of his HIV." Lydia escorted Izzy and Oksana to her office and at the same time had Alexander admitted to the clinic. She told her two guests that she would be back shortly and went back to seeing patients. Alexander's swelling was quite painful, and Lydia knew that it would take time for Heneke's medicine to take effect. Therefore, she personally prepared and administered a pain killer that allowed Alexander to get some sleep. His eyes were already closing as Lydia pulled the empty syringe out of the IV drip line and carefully discarded it in a medical waste container.

After finishing with Alexander, Lydia returned to her office. Izzy and Oksana were busy discussing the boy's condition. They paused as Lydia entered the office. "I did not think I would see you again so soon, Doctor Slesinger. Certainly not in the middle of the night."

"I'd like you to meet Doctor Oksana Zibrova," Izzy replied. "I needed her to see your clinic."

"You speak Russian," Lydia observed as she offered her hand to Oksana.

"I'm originally from Riga," Oksana replied. "Do you think it would be all right if I spoke with that boy's mother?"

Innessa Boku gazed blankly out the clinic's waiting room window. It had started snowing outside, blanketing the street with a cover of white. Innessa silently marveled at how a world that looked so peaceful, so beautiful, could actually be so cruel. But there was no escaping the fact that she was the one responsible for her son's illness. Now it was only a question of who would die first, mother or son? Unlike Doctor Chazov, Innessa held little faith in the discovery of a cure. She had seen too many others slip away in agony.

Innessa was so deep in her own thoughts that she didn't hear the door of the waiting room open. She jumped a little when Lydia tapped her on the shoulder. Innessa turned from the window and Lydia introduced Doctor Slesinger and Doctor Zibrova.

"Do. . . you. . . speak. . . English?" Izzy asked very slowly.

Innessa held up her hand and made a tiny space between her finger and thumb. "I speak a little."

"Good. We would like to get a bit of history if you don't mind."

Innessa consented and began to recount the details of her young life. At seventeen she was discovered by a modeling agency and signed to a contract. Deeply set brown eyes and perfect olive colored skin gave her an exotic look that was uncommon in Russia. Within half a year she had departed Moscow and was working the runways in Paris. Modeling brought with it a whole new life of easy money, sex and parties. With the parties came drugs, which Innessa initially was able to avoid. But the sex was unavoidable, available in any and every combination and perversity. It wasn't so much the sex that Innessa enjoyed, as much as the feeling of being desired. She had come from a very large family and had often felt ignored or invisible. Even though Innessa often woke up beside men she didn't know, they made her feel desired.

It was at a New Year's party that Innessa tried her first line of cocaine, just as an experiment. That experiment led to a three year addiction which drained her of every dollar she made. The drugs also burned her out. By the time she turned twenty-one, she looked thirty-five. Her modeling agent dropped her contract and Innessa fell into a deep depression. Her only outlet from the depression was harder drugs. A particularly bad trip on heroin landed her in the hospital where she discovered that she was about six weeks pregnant.

The pregnancy brought on an epiphany that saved Innessa's life. Even though the father could be any number of men, she decided to keep the baby. Not only would she keep this life inside her alive, she would start living her own life over again. With fierce determination, Innessa broke her drug dependency, gave up Paris, and moved back to Moscow.

Alexander was born a healthy eight pounds. However, he did not stay healthy for long. At twelve weeks he developed a fever and a jaundiced appearance. When he didn't respond to the typical antibiotic treatment, the family doctor ran a complete blood work, including a test for HIV. Innessa's world crashed into horror and agony when she learned the tests had come back positive. The doctor believed that Alexander's infant immune system was no match for the virus and tried to prepare Innessa for the worst.

Innessa wouldn't hear it. She sought out Doctor Chazov who admitted Alexander to the clinic. He was one of the first patients to receive Heneke's medicine, long before Heneke even knew if his hypothesis was sound. Alexander's body became a laboratory in the science of Mengele cells. Each time he became infected, the medicine forced the virus into retreat. However, each new flare up brought with it new viral antibodies. Heneke studied Alexander's blood and surmised that as the host cells mutated, so did the virus.

Alexander also offered proof that symptoms of illness could continue even if the virus was forced under control. Even though each new viral outbreak was rapidly contained by PIRT-I9, the periods of swelling and sickness were getting longer. Both Doctor Chazov and Heneke worried that a time would come when Alexander would not respond to treatment.

"How long has Alexander been swollen?" Izzy asked as Innessa finished telling about herself.

"Swollen, I do not understand."

"*O'pukhol*." Oksana translated swollen into Russian.

Innessa did her best to explain. "Alexander's hands and feet were better, but then they were not better."

A light bulb was beginning to switch on inside Izzy's brain. He had a feeling he knew what was causing the boys swelling. However, it hardly seemed possible in a Russian child. "Ask her how long ago?"

Oksana turned towards Innessa. *"Kak dol' go?"*

Innessa had to think for a moment. *"Pozavchera."*

"She says that it was the day before yesterday."

Izzy pulled his little notepad from his inside jacket pocket and wrote it all down. "Is there a good research library in Moscow?"

"A library?" Lydia asked. "Why do you need a library?"

"I believe I understand Alexander's problem, but I want to be sure before I say anything."

"The Lenin Library is the largest in the world. The medical section is particularly strong."

Izzy looked out the window. He could see the first rays of light touching the snow covered streets. It was almost morning, and neither he or Oksana had slept in over a day. However, Izzy was feeling revitalized. For the first time he felt as if this puzzle Heneke had dropped on him was beginning to make some kind of sense. "How do I get to the library?"

"The library does not open until 9 a.m." Lydia replied as she stared at the clock. It was just a bit before five in the morning. "Why don't you try and get some rest in here. Around the corner is a restaurant that will open soon for breakfast. We can get something to eat and I will call a car to take you to the library when it is open."

The dilapidating, rusty taxi pulled up in front of the library on Vozdvizhenka Street. Oksana paid the driver and followed Izzy out of the car. Izzy was amazed by the size of the library. It was at least three times the size of the New York Public library on 5th Avenue. Oksana saw the look on Izzy's face and spoke to it.

"There are over thirty million books inside. Every single book that is printed in Russian is cataloged. The research area maintains over 2000 journals from all over the world."

Much to Izzy's surprise, the library catalog system was as efficient as it was large. He quickly found his way to a copy of McGuire's Diagnostic Medicine and flipped to the section on blood disorders. Oksana stood in back of Izzy, reading over his shoulder.

"Sickle cell anemia?" Oksana questioned skeptically as she leaned over and whispered into Izzy's ear. "Sickle cell anemia does not affect Eastern Europeans."

"I know, but somehow Mengele cells and sickle cells are related. Alexander has the symptoms. His hands and feet are swollen. He looks anemic. And he has infections which resist antibiotic treatment."

A librarian approached and admonished Izzy, in Russian. He got the gist of what she was saying from her tone, and from the icy look she cast in his direction. He didn't need Oksana to tell him that the woman wanted him to keep his voice down. Izzy complied by lowering his voice and suggesting to Oksana that they leave the library. He had found what he was looking for.

As they walked down the steps of the library, Izzy began to explain what he was thinking.

"How could Mengele do something so advanced that we couldn't even attempt it? How do you devise a viable cell, genetically altered, yet still able to function and avoid bodily defenses? He needed some type of natural template. I'm betting that template was sickle cell anemia."

Oksana considered it skeptically. "In this model, would not Mengele need a large number of Negroes for experimentation? At least some would need to be afflicted with the disease."

Izzy paused, not wanting to mention Heneke, or what he had been told about Mengele's work. Therefore, he tried to frame it as best he could in his own hypothesis. "Suppose Mengele realized the genetic similarities between sickle-cell anemia and Tay-Sachs disease?"

Oksana's mouth dropped open. Tay-Sacks, the disease of eastern European Jews. Frighteningly, Izzy's theory could be grounded in the horrors of Auschwitz research.

"Consider," Izzy continued, "that sickle cell anemia is caused by a defect in the amino acid chain of hemoglobin. There are 600 amino acids in hemoglobin. Healthy cells have a glutamic acid in the chain.

Sickle cells contain a valine. Except for that one difference, they have 599 identical amino acids."

"You are guessing that Mengele used Tay-Sacks as a natural template?"

Izzy nodded. "I'm betting the house on it."

Oksana found herself shocked to be believing what Izzy was saying. "If you are right, what can we do?"

"Now we go and find Mengele's original notes."

Izzy and Oksana were on the first train for Cherkassy, which departed Moscow at nine in the morning. Izzy had decided not to tell Oksana about Jean Dulac, or his experiences at Brittany Pharmalogics. He also didn't mention he believed that the German Reich was looking for him. Oksana had been quite dismayed when he had rebuffed her suggestion to head to the airport and insisted on taking the train. Now that the train was safely out of the station, Izzy felt it was safe enough to discuss the woman they were looking for.

"I read Mengele's biography. It seems he entrusted his papers to a field nurse assigned to a medical unit in the Sudetenland. It appears that Mengele had some kind of relationship with this woman after he fled Auschwitz. From what's written, I'm guessing that she was maybe nineteen at the time. Mengele gave her instructions to get the notes back to Hitler in Berlin."

"Then should not we be headed for Berlin?" Oksana asked.

"She never made it back to Berlin. Russian authorities detained a young woman fitting her description in May of 1946. Records describe her as an unstable mute."

"It is very far from Sudetenland to Cherkassy. How do you know it was the same woman?"

"I don't," Izzy responded. "However, the Soviets kept very good records on people who they believed to be German sympathizers. This woman was carrying a leather satchel filled with papers written in German. When the authorities removed the satchel, the woman became hysterical. Therefore, they returned it to her. Before they did, the notes inside were studied. What the notes contained were unintelligible scientific writings."

"And what happened to the woman?"

Izzy shrugged his shoulders. "It's not in the records. There's a note that says the woman was taken to a little village called Sosnovka and left."

"Left? Left where?"

"No one knows. That's why were headed to Sosnovka."

It was a good thing that Izzy headed for Moscow to meet Oksana, instead of heading straight to Sosnovka. Ilya Babakov brought dozens of Reich operatives to search the little village. Ilya doubted that Izzy would be able to find a woman who hadn't been seen in over fifty years, but he was under orders to take no chances. After two days of extensive searching, Ilya gave the order to pack up and head back to Cherkassy. It was clear that Doctor Slesinger was not in Sosnovka.

A blood red Russian sun settled below the Cherkassy horizon as the train pulled into the station. This was now the third time Izzy had been there, and the place felt familiar. At the information desk, Oksana asked if there was any lodging nearby, other than the Hilton that was across the street. Izzy had mysteriously refused to go to the Hilton. The woman at the information desk gave her directions to an inn that was several blocks away. Oksana translated what the woman had told her and she and Izzy exited the station. They stood by the taxi depot, but after waiting for ten minutes and finding no cabs, they decided to walk to the inn.

They walked for several blocks, suddenly coming upon the 'Hill of Glory.' Izzy stopped to study the huge statue of the Motherland. Oksana pointed to the plaque and explained the statue was a memorial and common grave shared by Cherkassy's 14,000 war dead. Izzy stared at the statue for a very long time. When Oksana nudged him he responded with "in a minute." He touched his right hand to his head, then his heart, and reached out to touch the monument. Oksana watched and listened as Izzy began to repeat the words of the Kaddish, the Jewish memorial prayer.

"Yitgadal veyiskadash shemei raba. . . " What started out softly became silent. The only way Oksana knew that Izzy was praying was from the silent movement of his lips. When Izzy finished the prayer he turned from the monument, looking sadder than Oksana had ever seen anyone look. They continued onward toward the inn, both walking silently, lost in thought. Oksana thought about all of her fellow countrymen that the monument celebrated. Men and women who were opposed to the insanity of Hitler, and gave their lives fighting for mother Russia. And now here she was, still fighting against the same enemy.

The inn was only a block past the monument. As soon as they were checked in, Izzy and Oksana found their way to a restaurant that was nearby. They ate quickly, outlining their plans for the next day. When they got back to the inn they were both sound asleep in a matter of minutes. Unfortunately, morning comes early in Russia. With the first rays of sunlight Oksana awoke. Sleepily she got out of the bed and stared down at Izzy, who was still fast asleep. Oksana tried to rouse him, but he wouldn't budge. She pushed him, but all he did was roll over onto his stomach. In desperation she went to the bathroom and submerged her hand in cold water. Quickly, she returned to the side of the bed and placed her hand under the cover. Her fingers deftly lifted the waistband on Izzy's boxers and she rested her hand on a cheek of Izzy's ass.

Izzy almost broke his back as his eyes popped open and he launched himself towards the far side of the bed. He couldn't stop his momentum and fell to the floor with a thud. Oksana couldn't help but laugh. Izzy, however, did not find it funny. He stood up with as much grace as he could muster and snarled his way into the bathroom.

The village of Sosnovka sits 381 feet above sea level. A high pitched whine from the ancient taxi's engine made Izzy fidget nervously in his seat. The last thing he wanted was to get out and walk up a road that seemed to snake its way up Mount Everest. Since Izzy hadn't specified anyplace in particular in Sosnovka, the taxi driver stopped in the center of town. He let Izzy and Oksana off by a huge park. From the entrance, Izzy could see a concert stage. He shielded his eyes from the fierce Russian sun and caught a glimpse of a sandy beach in the distance. However, being the off-season, the park was completely deserted. Not a person in sight anywhere.

Oksana tapped Izzy on the shoulder. "Doesn't look like much of a place. Where do you suggest we look?"

Izzy looked up the road. Several hundred yards in the distance there were several large estates, but not much else. "Why don't we walk that way," Izzy said as he pointed towards the large mansions in the distance. Maybe we'll find someone in one of those that we could ask."

"Doubtful," Oksana replied. "Those are sanatoria. Many of Russia's ill come to Sosnovka for the peace and quiet."

"Let's still walk that way. Who knows what will turn up."

Oksana agreed and they set off. Izzy stared in wonderment at the estates they past. The homes were every bit as large as the mansions in Newport, Rhode Island. However, they were not nearly as ornate. Most were simple in their design, only set off by their sheer size. As they passed the third mansion on the left hand side of the road, an elderly man approached down the driveway. The man was dressed oddly. He wore a Russian army jacket over a hospital gown which just barely touched his knees. The man walked into the road and blocked Izzy and Oksana's path.

"Can I help you?" Izzy asked as graciously as possible. He suspected from the man's outfit that he was a patient in the sanatoria.

"*Vy zdyes parooski?*" The elderly man demanded.

Izzy knew from his book of Russian phrases that he was being asked if he spoke Russian. "*Nyet! Ya ne zdyes paroos'ki.*"

"American?" The man inquired.

Izzy nodded and the man spit on the ground. From behind a bush, a young woman in a doctor's coat appeared. She approached the elderly man and grasped him by the arm. She gave him a tug, which at first he resisted. She whispered something to him and he decided to head back up the driveway on his own.

"I must apologize for Mr. Spasov," the young doctor offered. "I hope he did not disturb you."

"Not at all," Izzy replied.

Oksana spoke to the doctor in Russian, asking if there were any restaurants in the immediate area. The woman pointed up the road. Oksana thanked the woman and she headed back towards the sanatoria she had come from. Oksana and Izzy continued up the road.

"You have been working on your Russian," Oksana commented.

"Not really. Just a couple of key phrases," Izzy replied as they crested a steep hill in the roadway. The road flattened out on the other side of the hill and the main district of Sosnovka came into view. It just kind of appeared on each side of the road. The first building, and largest, was an Eastern Orthodox church. The building was old, its white masonry exterior weathered and cracked. The small, golden dome had tarnished to murky brown, and the paint was peeling on the front doors.

Izzy stopped walking and studied the church for several moments. Something deep inside was pulling him closer to the building. Before he even realized, his hand was on the front door. He pushed down upon the brass handle with effort and moved the door open a crack. There was a tiny outer vestibule which opened into the sanctuary. Izzy stepped into the church and Oksana followed after him. The interior was very plain. There were ten rows of wooden benches, divided by a center isle. Each bench was covered with large cloth cushions which were quite worn. A large crucifix was mounted to the front wall of the church, and two small podiums stood at floor level in the front.

There was only one person in the church. She was an elderly, small, gray-haired woman, dressed plainly in a simple grey dress. She sat silently in the back, staring blankly at the crucifix. Izzy glanced in her direction but the woman paid him no attention. Izzy moved half way to the front and sat down on a bench to the left. It felt good to sit. A weariness had come upon him and it permeated right down to his soul. He put down his suitcase and placed his briefcase on top of it. With his right hand he patted a spot on a cushion. Oksana took a seat beside him. She had hesitatingly followed after Izzy, but with serious trepidations. As a child her parents had warned her to stay away from the churches in Riga. She was told that Jewish children were not welcome inside. Therefore, her heart rate quickened as she entered the building, yet she was curious as to why Izzy would enter a church. Now inside, her anxieties seemed to dissipate as she sat down.

For several moments they both sat in silence. The door creaked open and both Izzy and Oksana turned in their seats. It was the doctor they had seen in the driveway of the sanatoria. She stepped quietly into the church and walked to the old woman who paid her no mind. The doctor placed a hand on the woman's shoulder, yet the elderly eyes remained fixed on the crucifix. "Herta, *Tischzeit* ."

The elderly head nodded and the woman stood. She took a small step and almost stumbled but the doctor caught her. Together, they both departed the church, leaving Oksana and Izzy in solitude.

It was only one simple word but it caught in Izzy's head. Something about it wasn't right. *Tischzeit.* Izzy said it over and over again silently. At last, he said it out loud. *"Tischzeit?"*

"Excuse me?" Oksana replied, Izzy's voice snapping her out of her own silent thoughts.

"Tischzeit? What does it mean?"

Oksana shrugged her shoulders. "I do not know the word. I don't think it's Russian."

Izzy agreed. "Zeit means time in German, and Herta is definitely a German name."

"So?"

That old woman who was just here. That doctor spoke to her. "Herta, *tischzeit*, she said."

"So?" Oksana repeated.

"I don't know," Izzy replied. "It's a feeling, that's all. Seems strange to hear German in a Russian Orthodox church."

"I think you are imagining things."

"Probably," Izzy replied. "But we've got so little to work with. Maybe it will be a starting place and lead us in the right direction. The woman looked like she could have been the right age. Maybe she knew the woman we're looking for."

Herta Gerkhe was a day short of her twenty-sixth birthday when Doctor Joseph Mengele entered the small field hospital in Germany's north country. No one in the hospital recognized the bright young doctor who seemed to be a mysterious gift, and a skilled surgeon. The realities of Auschwitz were unknown on the Russian front, though rumors were widespread. Normally, a doctor returning from camps in Poland would have been thoroughly investigated. However, German casualties mounted by the hour and the field hospital needed Mengele's skilled hands.

Herte enlisted in the medical corps when she was twenty-four. After nearly two years of daily horrors—young men with missing limbs and worse—she was tired. Mengele was drawn to her immediately. The silky goldness of her hair, firm athletic figure, and deep blue eyes drew him in like a magnet. To him, she was the epitome of German perfection. Therefore, he kept his marital state a secret.

Herta didn't care much for Mengele. He seemed to be a human chameleon, taking on different personalities to suit the situation. It was as if there wasn't one Mengele, but many. However, Mengele was persistent. Whenever he wasn't operating, he was showering her with compliments and affection. More than anything, the war had made

Herta feel lonely. She had seen so many young men her own age die, she wondered if any would be left after the war. Mengele's persistence eventually wore her down, and soon she was spending nights with her limbs wrapped around Mengele in darkness.

Mengele said nothing of the camp that he had left behind. However, as the Russian troops gained more ground, he became increasingly nervous. A month after arriving at the camp, Mengele informed the hospital staff that he needed to leave. He seemed especially nervous as he pulled Herta aside and handed her a brown leather valise. He made her promise to get the valise to von Verscher in Berlin, and then he was gone.

Herta's curiosity got the better of her. That night she spent hours reading the notes inside Mengele's valise. Pages and pages of heinous atrocities. She read of dye injected into eyes, and of open vivisections performed on still beating hearts. People were placed alive on hooks and lowered into cauldrons of scalding water, their flesh boiled away to reach the skeletons below. It was more than Herta could bear. Many of the horrors were intentionally visited upon children with horrifying results. Herta's mind slammed shut, to the atrocities and everything else. She retracted into herself, becoming mute. She wanted to talk, but could find no words for the madness she had read about. With each passing day she became more remote, imprisoned in her own mind by a monster named Joseph Mengele. It was made it all the worse that she had been intimate with the fiendish ghoul.

Doctors at the field hospital labeled her condition as battle fatigue. She was evacuated to a civilian medical facility by ambulance. The doctors could not pry Mengele's valise from her fingers and gave up trying. En route to the hospital, the ambulance was hit by a mortar shell. The driver and his aide were killed, but Herta was unharmed. She crawled from the burning wreckage and started walking, her fingers still clutching tightly to the valise. A day later she was found by triumphant Russian forces.

Discovering that she was an affiliated Nazi, the Russians brutalized and raped her. The brigade commander ordered his men to take her prisoner and they forced her to march with them as they returned to mother Russia. On each and every stop, Herta was raped by her captors. Through it all she remained mute, only struggling when the valise was taken out of her sight. The Russians inspected the contents and deemed them of no importance. Therefore, they let her keep it. As the brigade reached Cherkassy, the commander ordered his men to abandon their prisoner. Herta was therefore cast adrift, a badly beaten stranger in a strange land.

She wandered aimlessly for several days. With each passing minute her reserves dwindled and she became weaker. Occasionally she would come across a discarded bit of food in the trash, but that was a rarity. During a particularly stormy night she found her way into a cow barn and collapsed. The farmer who found her the next day was appalled by her condition. He and his wife took her into their small home. They fed her, cleaned and bandaged her cuts and bruises, and gave her clean clothes. They sent for their doctor who came to the farm the next day. His diagnosis was that she was mentally infirmed and should be sent to a sanatoria. Herta remained mute, making no protest of his decision. On February 16, 1946, Herta Gerkhe, whose identity was unknown, became a ward of the Russian people. She was sent to a sanatoria in Sosnovka and settled into a kind of peaceful nonexistence.

For fifty-two years she lived a sheltered, quiet life. She had remained silent throughout the years. At the start she was given her own room, which remained exactly the same as the day when she arrived. The creaky wooden framed bed and mattress predated Herta's arrival by twenty years. In the corner of the room was an antique clothes chest. A red velvet chair which sat by the side of the bed could have easily been in a Norman Rockwell painting.

Herta looked as old as the room she occupied. Her once golden hair had turned snow white, and her smooth, clear face was wrinkled like a prune. Modern psychotherapy reached Russia in 1972. A team of hotshot doctors concluded that Herta was not retarded, and that her silence was a traumatically induced psychosis. While they did their best to bring her out of her subconscious prison, Herta was determined that she would never have to look at Mengele's horrors again. Therefore, she remained mute. The doctors went back to Leningrad, concluding that some people were so lost inside themselves that there was no way back out again.

The doctor at the sanatoria listened intently as Izzy described why they had come to visit. The doctor explained that the woman they had come to see never had any visitors. She had been at the sanatoria for over fifty years, her condition deemed hopeless. They had been able to determine that her first name was Herta, but nothing else. The court papers that had remanded her to the sanatoria listed her believed country of origin to be Germany. Therefore, what little was communicated by the staff was said in German. Sometimes she would respond and sometimes not. The doctor wasn't actually sure that Herta understood a word that she was saying.

"Can we see her?" Izzy asked.

The doctor agreed and led to Herta's room. They found her seated in the red velvet chair. A pleasant smile creased the old face. She was listening to a classical piece of music that came from the small speaker of a clock radio in a room across the hall. When Izzy and Oksana entered the room, Herta looked at each of them. Her eyes shifted back and forth, but remained distant and vacant. Izzy approached while reaching into his jacket pocket. He removed a white envelope and took from it a picture of Mengele that he had cut from a magazine article. He touched Herta's hand and held up the picture in front of her eyes.

The reaction was swift and immediate. Herta's entire body began to tremble as she grabbed the photograph from Izzy's hand. With jerky motions she ripped the picture into tiny pieces. Gingerly she stood from the chair, took one step, and collapsed.

Izzy tried to catch her but he was too late. Oksana knelt by Herta's side and placed her fingers on the old woman's neck. Her pulse was irregular and weak.

The doctor from the sanatoria ran from the room and headed for a telephone to call for an ambulance from the main hospital in Cherkassy. There was very little that anyone could do until the ambulance arrived. Izzy sat by Herta's side and held her hand. She opened her eyes and spoke for the first time in over five decades.

"Mengele," she said with quiet force. She then squeezed her eyes shut to try and force the memories away; memories that she hadn't confronted in a very long time. Izzy could feel her pulse getting weaker. He reached into his jacket pocket and pulled out the portable English-Russian dictionary. Izzy quickly looked up some words, which he directed towards the sanatoria doctor who had returned.

"*Kaan si rufen der Priester?*" The doctor looked confused and said nothing. In haste, Izzy had taken his German-English dictionary by mistake. He had told the doctor to call for a priest. However, she did not understand more than a few German words. But Herta understood very well. The thought of seeing a priest for last rights brought the faintest of smiles to her face. With all her effort she pointed a bony finger in Izzy's direction.

"*Sie Deutscher?*"

Izzy shook his head. "*Nein, American.*" He hesitated for a moment and then fumbled for the words to ask for the notes. "*Nur ich Mengele's papiere.*"

Before Herta could respond, two ambulance attendants entered the room. They lifted Herta onto a wheeled stretcher. As they fastened the retaining straps, Herta rolled her head in Izzy's direction. Her voice was little more than a whisper. "*Ich Haben die Augen niederslagen auf Heiland. Ich vergeben fur mein sundigen av stille.*"

Izzy flipped through the dictionary but there were too many words for him to remember. Oksana turned towards him and translated Herta's words. Izzy was unaware of the fact that she could speak German and it took him by surprise.

"She says, I have looked my eyes down on the savior. I am forgiven for my sins of silence."

Izzy looked at Herta, whose breathing had become very shallow. "Mengele's papiere?"

She nodded slightly and motioned for Izzy to move closer. He did, just as the ambulance attendants began to wheel Herta out of the room. Izzy ran next to her, moving his ear as close to her as he could.

"*Unter de bett*," were the last words that she said to him. Izzy watched as the attendants disappeared with the stretcher out the door. He returned to her room and knelt beside the old, wooden bed. A tattered leather case lay underneath, covered by dust. Izzy grabbed the valise and brought it out into the daylight. It was at that precise moment that Herta Gerkhe departed this world. However, she had insured that before she left, that the silence was shattered.

Chapter 15

Adolf Kaiser pushed open the laboratory door marked Trial Studies. The lab was restricted to authorized personnel, of which there were only five. Actually, it was only four since Doctor Heneke's unfortunate demise. At the center of the room was a padded leather chair, very much the type that was found in the office of most dentists. However, this chair was equipped with straps on the arm and foot rests. It had been installed at Adolf's request, as had been the soundproofing that was on the walls. The entire laboratory had been set up for human testing of PIRT-I9. Heneke refused to go near the place. He wanted no part in replicating the horrors he had witnessed Mengele carry out.

Adolf had no such reservations. As the president of *Verstaatlichung fur Duetscher*, the semi-political party that called for greater nationalistic pride from all true Germans, Adolf had watched his beloved Berlin become a true melting pot of peoples. It was a development that made him most unhappy and presented a situation he felt needed cleansing. Of all the peoples that Adolf hated, his greatest revulsion was saved for the homosexual population, followed closely by the Negroes and the Jews. It was by his hand that Mengele cells were introduced to the homosexual population, under the guise of free flu inoculations. He watched with glee during the late 1970s as infected men traveled the globe, infecting others as they went. The outbreak of disease and death in the United States made him downright giddy.

But that was just the beginning. Phase two was controlling the virus, that for some reason went hand in hand with the mutated cells. If the virus could be controlled, the disease would be forgotten, forgotten until it reached worldwide epidemic proportions. By then it would be too late. Only true Aryans, isolated genetically from other races would be spared.

The development of PIRT-I9 was slow and painstaking. At first, Heneke had believed the illness could be controlled by controlling the HIV virus. However, when he discovered that the virus was a consequence and not the real cause, he began to question whether the vaccine was really worth the effort. Adolf pressed him to move on with his research. Since Heneke would not use the clinical studies lab, Adolf assembled his own team. Volunteers were recruited by force from Berlin's homeless homosexual population. Adolf had lost count of the numbers that had been 'recruited' over the years. Even the ones who had survived the testing never made it back to the streets alive. In Adolf's mind he was simply relieving Berlin of some of its vermin.

On this particular day it was Jean Dulac who had been strapped into the chair. She sat limply, drugged unconscious, with her arms and legs tightly bound to the chair. Adolf's sister, Anna, was busy inspecting a drawer full of scalpels. She removed one from the drawer and held it up so that the light reflected off its surface. Adolf moved to the chair and peered down at Jean.

"Jean Dulac," Adolf said aloud as he began to pace little circles in front of the chair. "Claude Thomae's adopted little bitch. You have cost me many good men."

Anna came close and put the scalpel blade to Jean's throat. "I'm torn, Adolf," she said as she playfully touched Jean's flesh with the flat surface of the blade. "I know we should hold her hostage, but I'd rather slit open the jugular and watch a fountain of blood."

Adolf reached out and grabbed his sister's hand. "Patience, Anna, patience. We have had reports that Doctor Slesinger has eluded Ilya and his buffoons. Miss Dulac could be very important to us. Very important, indeed."

Anna reluctantly agreed and she put the scalpel back into its drawer. Unexpectedly, the door of the room pushed open and in walked Wolfgang Hauer holding a manila envelope. He had seen men strapped into the chair over the years, but never a woman. Therefore, the sight of Jean strapped down unnerved him.

"What is going on here?" he demanded to know.

"It is not your concern," Adolf sneered back. "Is that the report from America?"

"Not my concern? Everything that happens in this company is my concern. You promised me that this room would never be used again."

"Obviously you do not grasp the importance of this room. It is this room which has kept Mein Fuerher's dreams alive. This room that will restore an omnipotent Germany."

Wolfgang placed both hands on his temple and began to rub at the stress. "I have tolerated this *Schutzstafflen* madness of yours long enough. I am going to call a board meeting and have you replaced. You are a very sick man, Adolf. You need help."

While Wolfgang was speaking, Adolf silently motioned to his sister who deftly placed her hand back into the drawer and grabbed the scalpel.

"Of course I need help, Herr Hauer," Adolf cooed in a sugar coated tone. "I would hate for us to become enemies."

"Your family has always considered you *insen*, a lunatic. And your sister is little more than a common whore."

"A lunatic? You will pay dearly for those remarks!"

Wolfgang Hauer straightened his posture so that he towered over Adolf. He took a step in his direction. "Are you threatening me? Now that would be a switch. *Schutzstafflen* cowards usually terrorize little girls." Wolfgang paused and walked to the chair. He placed a hand on the strap that held Jean's right arm in place. As he unfastened it he continued to berate Adolf. "Or if not little girls, *Juden grobmutters.*"

The comment about Jewish grandmothers pushed Adolf past his breaking point. He nodded at Anna and she silently took two steps so that she was standing right in back of Wolfgang. He was busy releasing the straps that held Jean in place and had his back to Anna. She used her right hand to drive the scalpel into Wolfgang's back. Her expertise in anatomy allowed her to pick the most vulnerable spot and she pushed hard. The blade cut deep, ripping into the Wolfgang's heart. Anna rotated the scalpel blade in a sharp circle, ensuring that the blade ripped the heart into a useless pump. The tall, blond Aryan executive crumpled to the floor, his body already in death spasms.

Adolf knelt by the body and pulled the scalpel from the wound. He pushed the newly minted corpse over on his back and blood soaked the floor. Adolf held the blade in front of Wolfgang's now dull eyes and swiftly cut the letter S into his forehead, twice, side-by-side. Adolf dropped the knife and stood in disgust. He never dreamed that he would have to kill Wolfgang Hauer. It could create complications. Moving the body would be the easy part, and the SS would make it look like attack by neo-Nazi skinheads. The police would conclude that Wolfgang Hauer was in the wrong place at the wrong time. However, the death of the president of Kaiser pharmaceutics could slow the approval process for PIRT-I9 and that was something Adolf could not abide.

Adolf looked at his sister who was positively beaming with self-admiration as she fastened down Jean's arm again. This time she pulled the restraint even tighter.

"Anna, clean it up. Take the body to the spot. Make sure that they cannot trace it back."

Anna walked to her brother and gave him a hug. "I'm getting very good with a knife, aren't I?"

Adolf pulled back from his sister's embrace and frowned at her. "Just clean it up." Before leaving the room he picked up the manila envelope that Wolfgang Hauer had rested on a cabinet. He took one last look at the dead man and then left the room.

After leaving the facility, Adolf headed for the old city. He pushed his way through a crowd that was waiting for a table at very crowded pub called The Ale Haus. Ilya Babakov was already seated at a table. He spotted Adolf and waved him over. Even from a distance it was clear that Adolf was in an agitated state.

"Something is wrong?" Ilya questioned as Adolf sat across from him.

"Nothing I can't deal with. What about Slesinger?"

Ilya shook his head. "No sign of him in Sosnovka. He has disappeared."

Adolf reached across the table and slapped Ilya in the head. "*Dumkopf*, Slesinger went to Moscow to meet that woman doctor from New York. Our operatives followed him to the train station and watched him board for Cherkassy."

"I do not know what to say. Of course I will go back."

"Yes, you will," Adolf agreed. "And my sister is going with you."

"I do not like your sister," Ilya replied. "I will go alone."

"Don't argue with me. Anna is going with you."

"Nyet."

"Yes! She is going, period!"

Ilya decided to change the subject. "What have you done with Dulac?"

"Do I detect concern? That is hardly in your nature, comrade Babakov." Adolf's words were heavy with sarcasm. "Do not worry. She is our insurance policy in case you fail. One way or another I will get Slesinger."

"Or perhaps," Ilya countered. "He will get you. If he is capable of escaping Argentina. . . "

Adolf cut Ilya off. "Don't be an idiot. Brittany supported that operation with Dulac's help. Neither can bother us anymore."

"I hope you are right." Ilya finished his stein of ale, placed it back on the table, and departed.

Adolf watched him go, wondering for the first time who Izzy Slesinger really was.

While Adolf pondered Izzy, Izzy pondered Mengele's notes. He and Oksana spent hours pouring over the journals that were stored inside the valise. Grotesque and fiendish experimentation was explained in cold, detached, scientific language. Many times Oksana had to halt translating and steady herself. She did her best to keep from crying. The descriptions ripped at her heart, especially the ones that dealt with children:

"Patient is female, approximately eight years old. Used scalpel to expose and sever knee joint. Injected trial serum #682 into the marrow of tibia, fibula, and upper leg bones. . . " and then an entry from a several days later. "Girl's leg has become mysteriously gangrenous...considered amputation and rejected. Experiment incinerated in crematoria."

Izzy reacted with more anger than sadness. The journals were factual testament to the insanity and bestiality of the Holocaust. Izzy's father had bore his guilt of silence and inaction like an albatross. He was one of the few American Jews who realized that his lack of involvement, of not personally speaking out, cost European Jews their lives. He went to his grave with that bloodstain on his hands. It was a guilt that was always near the surface, in plain sight for Shana and little Izzy to see. Izzy's father did not take the entire bloodstain to his final resting spot. He left some of it behind, on his son.

After four hours, Izzy and Oksana could go no further. Izzy slammed one of Mengele's notebooks closed. He stood up, stretched his muscles, and walked to the window. "We have to go back to New York. I don't have the resources here to make sense of this. It's too complex a puzzle."

Oksana got up and joined Izzy by the window. "At least we now know why so many people want those journals. If they were destroyed. . . "

Izzy continued the sentence. "We would never be able to recreate them. Therefore, we need to make sure they get back safely."

"It's probably unsafe for us to go back to Moscow. We must get out of Russia by another way."

"I'm open to suggestions," Izzy responded as he turned from the window.

"Cherkassy has an airport with service to Leningrad. We will go there and then by boat to Helsinki, Finland. From Helsinki we will fly home to New York."

"Why don't we see all of Europe while were at it?" Izzy asked sarcastically.

"We have no idea how many people are looking for those documents. The KGB would be no more friendly than the German Reich. To die in a Moscow prison is still to die. We must serpentine our way if we are to be undetected."

By the time Ilya Babakov and Anna Kaiser arrived in Cherkassy, Izzy and Oksana were long gone. Izzy had used his Sheldon Kramer alias and credit cards to charge the airline tickets. Perhaps the cards should have made him suspicious. With Brittany's destruction documented in the media, surely credit card companies would have closed their accounts. However, Izzy thought nothing of it. He had still not told Oksana about actually meeting Heneke and his time at Brittany Pharmalogics. It was during the flight that he explained it all to her. She seemed especially troubled when Izzy told her about the blood on his pillow in the hotel, and the disappearance of Jean Dulac. Izzy defended himself by saying he had no idea what had happened to her, which was the truth. But deep inside he suspected what had happened, and he knew it wasn't good. He could also tell that Oksana understood the very same thing.

Cold, wind-swept rains pelted hard upon Leningrad's docks at the mouth of the Neva river. Fortunately, Oksana had made Izzy purchase a full-length, lined rain coat at a shop in the airport. She knew how brutal Leningrad weather was and impressed upon Izzy the need to stay warm and dry. He had resisted at first, seeing that the American made garment cost almost $600 when the rubles were converted to dollars. The same coat would have been $250 in America. At Izzy's favorite men's store, Moe Ginsky's on Manhattan's east side, it would have been even less. However, Oksana berated Izzy until he handed the coat and his credit card to the merchant. Standing in the rain, he was glad that she had been so insistent.

The rain coat protected his body, but his feet were less fortunate. A distinctive squishing sound emanated from his $150 Steinem leathers. He followed Oksana through the harbor area plagued by very cold, wet feet. And since his feet were cold, the rest of him was cold, and miserable. He carried his suitcase in one hand and his briefcase in the other. Mengele's notes had been taken from their old leather case and placed at the bottom of his suitcase for safe keeping.

Large cargo vessels, filled with Russian grain, clogged Leningrad's port on the Baltic ocean. Izzy watched as hundreds of cases of vodka were unloaded from a truck and stacked onto a pallet for transport onto a ship. Vodka and grain were two of the most important export products departing Leningrad. Ship traffic into the port had almost tripled since the demise of communism. But where the state once controlled the port, it was now run by the Russian mafia. The black market was a multi-billion dollar industry. One out of every six export dollars fell into the hands of organized crime.

Oksana had been a college student in Leningrad. She had put herself through graduate school doing questionable things for questionable people. Therefore, she knew the underbelly of the port city quite well. Izzy followed her to the shipping office of Andrei Khudyakov. Andrei was "the man" in Leningrad. All the old warehouses on the left bank of the Neva river belonged to him. Therefore, anyone who wanted anything came to him. Andrei's office was heavily guarded by half a dozen armed lieutenants. Oksana spoke briefly to his second-in-command, who slipped into Andrei's office. A moment later Andrei emerged from his office. He was a bear of a man, well over six feet and almost as large around. His face was covered with a thick brown beard which was even darker than the bushy mass on his head. He was dressed in a colorful woolen/silk sweater and gray Brooks Brothers gabardine pants.

"My tooris ti iz Ame'riki."

Andrei bellowed with laughter. "Speak English, Zibrova! An American tourist? You are as much a tourist in Leningrad as I am a czar in Moscow."

Oksana blushed red. "I did not think you would remember me. I was hardly more than a child."

"And now you are grown woman," Andrei said as he admired Oksana's dripping wet form. "What can Andrei do for you?"

Oksana glanced towards Izzy. "We need passage to Helsinki. Safe passage."

Andrei rubbed his beard. "Government?"

"Yes and worse."

Andrei walked to his office and held open the door. "Come inside to discuss this. I will order dry clothes for the both of you."

Izzy was about to state that he had a change of clothes in his suitcase for both of them. However, Oksana stopped him mid-sentence. Turning down Andrei's hospitality was a bad idea. Those who did rarely saw the sunlight of the next day.

Andrei walked to an antique Chinese cabinet and retrieved three crystal glasses and a crystal carafe filled with Armyanski

Cognac. Armyanski was consider the finest in the world. He placed the glasses on his desk and filled each with the dark, amber brandy. "Let us drink a toast. Then we will talk business."

Oksana and Izzy both lifted a glass.

"Nastrovia," Andrei offered and took a large gulp.

"Nastrovia," Oksana and Izzy replied. Izzy took a sip and the strong brandy immediately brought tears to his eyes. The smoothness of British Cognacs was nowhere to be found in this strong mash. Andrei laughed heartily and slapped Izzy on the back. This caused him to swallow the rest of his mouthful. His eyes opened wide in panic as he felt his throat melt away. It was several long moments before he could catch his breath normally.

Andrei laughed louder. "I like you, Doctor Slesinger."

Izzy looked at the big Russian in surprise. "How did you know my name?"

"Khudyakov knows everything. Before you stepped foot in Moscow, I knew you were coming. I know about the Reich, who would like to see you very dead. I know about the Brittany explosion in France. I know about the idiot, Ilya Babakov. I even know about your old friend, Ithamar Polansky."

Izzy nodded in amazement. "You're right. You do know everything."

"Cherkassy is filled with more Germans than Old Dusseldorf at Oktoberfest. You have found what they are after?"

Izzy nodded cautiously but said nothing.

"I will make you a deal. You give me the material and I will get you to Helsinki safely."

Oksana interjected herself into what had become a conversation between the two men. "Unacceptable. That material needs to get back to New York. With us."

Andrei walked to his door and opened it. "I believe I cannot help you. Our business is concluded."

Oksana walked to him and stared into his big, deeply set

eyes. "I had always heard Estonian's fought against the Nazis, not with them."

Andrei's entire demeanor changed and the anger showed on his face. His upper lip trembled and he had to fight to restrain himself. "You think because you are woman I will not kill you? I will kill you. My father was in a Red army brigade that was crushed by Rommel. But Estonians are strong. The Red army forced Germany from our land. And now you call Andrei traitor?"

Oksana knees were shaking but she did not give ground. "I say prove to me that you are not. The war is still going on, Andrei. Russian men, women and children are under attack. In Estonia, Bosnia, Siberia, Moscow. We are the only ones who can undo what has been done. The papers would be meaningless to you."

Andrei's face softened as he thought about Oksana's words. He had read the reports about the increase of AIDS in Russia and had witnessed victims of the disease first hand. When Oksana brought up the rising number of children in Kiev with cancer, Andrei relented. "I have a shipment of grain which is headed to Helsinki tomorrow aboard a cargo ship, the Ana Karina. I will speak to the captain and make sure that you are given safe passage."

Oksana leaned close and gave Andrei a Khudyakov style bear hug. She also kissed him on the cheek. Izzy walked to him and shook his hand.

"Thank you," Izzy offered.

Andrei squeezed Izzy's hand tightly. "You must save the Russian people."

Izzy squeezed back with as much force as he could muster. "We must save the entire world."

Izzy stood on the deck of the Ana Karina and watched her bow cut deeply into the dark, cold waters of the Gulf of Finland. Frigid arctic air turned his cheeks a deep shade of crimson. As the ship crested a wave, an even larger ship came into view. As the Ana Karina got closer, Izzy could see that it was a giant Russian superwhaler. To call the ship enormous was an understatement. Izzy had never seen anything that big. Back in Manhattan the military had mothballed an aircraft carrier named the Intrepid and turned it into a permanently harbored floating museum. The superwhaler was at least as long as the aircraft carrier, and twice as wide. It was hard to believe that anything that big could actually float. The whaler was more than a ship, a floating factory would have been a more accurate description, a floating factory of death.

It triggered a memory inside Izzy's head. He remembered a date he had gone on many years ago. A John Denver concert at Madison Square Garden. He had gone reluctantly. John Denver was not somebody he ordinarily listened to. There was one song which stuck in his head. Denver had introduced the song by telling everyone that it was written by some folksinger in Maine. At least that's what Izzy remembered. He walked to the bow of the Ana Karina with his eyes fixed on the giant factory ship and his mind searched for the lyrics to the song.

He couldn't find them. It was something about how it is the whales that die, but it is mankind that must measure the loss. It made him think of an article he had read about endangered species in National Geographic. The article's author, naturalist Douglas Chadwick, had written so eloquently about saving species, that his words were etched in Izzy's brain. "In the end, that's what motivates us. Not ideas like ecosystem management and biodiversity, however sound they may be, but the extraordinary human capacity for empathy, transfigured into compassion towards lives other than our own."

As the Ana Karina got closer to the whaler, Izzy could see whale blood pouring from the ship's discharge ports. He had seen documentaries on the slaughter of whales and could picture the men with long knives slicing into whale flesh not a hundred yards away from where he stood. In his mind he could hear the harrowing pitiful cry from the whales that were being stripped while they were still alive.

It gave Izzy reason for pause. "How much better the world would be without people?" He thought to himself quietly. He shuddered as the whalers brought him back full circle to Mengele. After all, that is what Mengele's work would eventually bring to a logical conclusion—no people. This was way beyond what could be imagined. Mengele had succeeding in genetically shifting the human system, a system that had evolved over tens of millions of years. Humans are very complex machines and even the slightest alteration can bring about devastating consequences.

Izzy thought of Lesch-Nyhan syndrome which was an extremely rare genetic childhood disorder. It affected only boys, and it was caused by a defect in the X chromosome. Lesch-Nyhan was characterized by bouts of self-mutilation, where the children would chew off their own lips or bite off fingers. The syndrome, which was caused by a missing enzyme, often resulted in death, if not from self injury then from kidney failure. The missing enzyme was responsible for the breakdown of metabolic wastes. Without that breakdown, the kidneys crashed.

Human genetic code is made up of approximately three billion DNA bases. One change in one base was responsible for Lesch-Nyhan. Izzy hypothesized that the same was probably true for Mengele cells. More than one change would have been well beyond anything that Mengele and Von Verscher could have pulled off. But they did pull it off. They had created a whole knew biological system for human beings, a system that eventually crashed. Worse still, this new system had the ability to mutate. It could go dormant, be passed between people by sexual contact, or be passed between mother and fetus. It had given rise to an entire new strain of virus which was now called HIV and contributed its own share of problems.

Izzy finally grasped the full significance of Ice-9. Freeze all the water on Earth and life vanishes. It might take decades, but eventually every human population would be touched by Mengele's altered genetics. With each passing generation there would be a huge population blowback. Izzy conjectured that parts of Africa were probably already six or seven generations removed from the original inoculations. In some countries the fatality rate was approaching forty percent. Another generation or two, at the same infective rate, and entire populations or countries would disappear.

Sexual abstinence was the only true prevention. Izzy contemplated it. Even if it was feasible, which it wasn't, it solved nothing. If people stopped having sex, mankind would become extinct. Sex had become a kind of damned-if-you-do, damned-if-you don't proposition. It was a catch-22 situation that only held one possible answer, human extinction. Of course, there was the possibility that a population could isolate itself from the infection and still reproduce. That had been Mengele's dream for the Aryan race. However, reality rejected that possibility on a planet that became more crowded and ever smaller each day. Sexual isolation in the twenty-first century was as unattainable as racial integration in the nineteenth century.

It was not lost on Izzy that Mengele cells presented another catch-22. The entire medical community was mobilized in a war against Human Immuno Virus, and the virus was the only marker for a compromised cell. There was no arguing that the virus could compromise a immune system, which in turn could lead to secondary infections. However, elimination of the virus would do nothing to prevent the human system from eventually failing. Until there was another way to detect a genetically altered cell from a normal, healthy cell, the HIV was needed. In fact, it would be of more help them harm. Izzy understood it to be a fact that the medical community would never accept.

The lights of Helsinki shimmered on the water as the Ana Karina approached the pier that was owned by Andrei. The sea had been turbulent for most of the day and the ship was way past schedule into the harbor. Oksana stayed below deck for most of the voyage. The interior of the ship made Izzy feel a bit claustrophobic. Therefore, he spent most of the voyage topside.

The Ana Karina churned through ten foot waves which caused her bow to rise and fall with each wave crest. At first Izzy had felt a little seasick, but it quickly passed, and seasickness was much preferred over feeling closed in.

Helsinki is a beautiful city. It combines old world European charm with the energy, technology and forward-thinking attitude of New York. While it was only the middle of October, the city was already deeply in the grip of winter. A fresh blanket of snow covered the sidewalks, but the streets were clean. Izzy nodded appreciatively as he stared out the window from the back seat of a taxi. In New York, it could take more than a week for roadways to be cleared of snow. And streets would be devoid of people.

The streets in Helsinki were abuzz with activity. Men and women in long woolen coats, ski parkas, and boots, freely traversed the downtown area. Pubs were alive with activity, as were a host of bookshops and coffee bars. Many people strolled down the streets with cellular telephones pressed to their ears. Izzy had heard that Finland was the cell phone capital of the world and it appeared that it was true. Even the concierge in the big, new Hilton hotel had a cell phone pressed to his ear when Izzy and Oksana checked in.

Immediately adjacent to the hotel was a public sauna. On their arrival, Izzy was too tired to consider anything but sleep. However, the next morning he inquired at the front desk and the sauna was highly recommended. Oksana cautioned him, explaining that Finnish sauna's are opened to the public. While sitting in the nude in a steamy room could be therapeutic, being naked among strangers often took some getting used to, especially for Americans.

"Are you saying I have a reason to be self-conscious," Izzy asked indignantly.

Oksana immediately shook her head. "Not at all. It is just that nudity makes most Americans a little bit crazy. Some feel self-conscious, others become aroused by the idea."

"Aroused? By sitting in a sauna?"

"Finland has a reputation. . . However, saunas do not mix men and women. They are separate."

Izzy pretended to wipe sweat from his brow. "What a relief. I'd hate to find myself naked next to some tall, blond Finnish goddess." Oksana had no reply for that comment and Izzy departed for the sauna next door.

The dressing room for men was very similar to those found in any health club in America.

Rows of gray metal lockers lined the walls, and there was a big, open shower room with many shower heads. The one peculiarity was the white, leather couches which sat by a long wall. Several naked men, of various ages, rested comfortably as they chatted in Finnish. One of the men stood, retrieved a pitcher of fruit juice and several glasses, and then returned to the group. Izzy hated to admit it, but he did feel a bit self-conscious. In America, men did not lounge around chatting in the nude. At least not straight, heterosexual men.

The man who had gotten the juice looked towards Izzy and noticed the half-bewildered look on his face. He stood from the couch and walked over.

"*Hyvaa humenta.*" The greeting was said warmly.

Izzy shrugged his shoulders. "Sorry, I don't speak the language."

"You are an American?" the man questioned in perfect English.

Izzy nodded. "From New York."

The man pointed towards a doorway that was covered by a heavy blue vinyl shower curtain.

"The washroom is through there, the sauna is on the other side."

Izzy thanked the man and headed into the washroom. His hands dropped instinctively as he found himself in the presence of a powerfully built, middle-aged woman. The woman chuckled as she watched Izzy try to shield his genitals. The last of his color drained away as she explained, in English, that she was there to bathe him.

"Bathe me? I don't think so. I can bathe myself perfectly well, thank you."

The woman took several steps closer and Izzy backed up a bit. "I have bathed many men. If I do not bathe you, you do not go into the sauna!"

"Why can't I bathe myself?" Izzy questioned in protest.

"You cannot reach all the spots I can," the woman replied. "After your sauna I will give you a massage."

For a moment Izzy thought about abandoning the sauna completely. However, his muscles ached for the relief that the steam would bring. He also knew that Oksana would question him on every detail. Having come this far he raised his arms high and let the woman bathe him. Izzy found that it wasn't all that bad. The woman rinsed him with a hand-held sprayer and then guided him to the sauna.

Long cedar benches were attached to each of the walls of the sauna. They formed a large box that could easily accommodate sixty people. Fortunately for Izzy, there was only one other man in the sauna when he entered. The steam enveloped Izzy's body and he breathed it in deeply. He found a spot on one of the benches, sat down, and immediately began to relax. He could feel the pores of his skin dilating and sweat broke out on his forehead. The aromatic scent of cedar that filled his nostrils made him think of the fireplace in his cabin in Vermont. In his mind he could see the snow covered hills of Mount Snow.

A deep, hacking cough snapped Izzy back to the sauna. He gazed across the sauna at its other occupant who was convulsed in a violent coughing attack. Without staring, Izzy clinically appraised his unknown companion. He guessed the man to be in his early thirties. The coughing had caused him to hunch over, with his face almost between his knees. Therefore, it was difficult for Izzy to tell what he looked like from that vantage point. However, the purple spots on his legs clearly indicated Kaposi's sarcoma. The coughing became more violent and Izzy decided to see if he could offer some assistance.

"Can I do something for you?"

Izzy's voice startled the man and he jumped a little. At the same time the coughing fit subsided and the man turned his face upward. It was a strong Nordic face, with bright blue eyes and a deep red beard. "Thank you, but I think I'll be fine now."

Izzy couldn't help but ask the question. "Kaposi's?"

The man nodded slowly. "How did you know?"

"I'm a doctor. I've seen it a lot in New York."

The man heard New York and immediately brightened. "New York? I read yesterday that your FDA is going to approve that new AIDS medicine, PIRT-I9. In Europe, it is only available in limited supplies in Germany."

Izzy nodded his head. "Would you mind if I asked you a few questions?"

The man patted the bench beside him and took a seat. He extended his hand and introduced himself. "Carl Vaalgren."

"Izzy Slesinger. How long have you had AIDS?"

"Not so long," Carl answered. "I was probably infected four years ago. Symptoms showed up at the beginning of the year, the Kaposi's showed itself a couple of months later."

"Do you know how you were infected?"

Carl paused before answering. "I enlisted in Special Services in the army at twenty-one. I was assigned to the Finnish peacekeeping force in Czechoslovakia. We had a lot of spare time on our hands." Carl paused again, seeming a bit embarrassed to continue.

"You were infected in Czechoslovakia?"

"At the Ruki and Kolena."

"Ruki and Kolena?"

Carl nodded. "It means, 'on hands and knees.' They were very secretive sex parties. Sometimes we'd have dozens of men and women. Things could get pretty wild."

"In Czechoslovakia?" Izzy asked with eyebrows raising. "If you had said Denmark or Holland. . . "

Carl shook his head. "Those places are tame by comparison. We had people from Egypt, Germany, France. One couple from Australia was incredible. The woman just couldn't get enough."

"How many parties did you go to?"

Carl tried to do the math in his head. "Don't know. Maybe a couple nights a week for six months."

"And how many partners per night?"

"It varied a lot. Some nights it would be two or three, some nights twenty."

"Twenty?" Izzy thought to himself. This one man could have had sex with hundreds of people, from a very diverse population set, and they could now all potentially be infected. It was a clear example of how easily Mengele cells could travel around the world.

"The biggest irony is that I've gone from orgiastic ecstasy to almost cloistered celibacy. My friends heard that I was HIV positive, and suddenly, I had no more friends. When I finally die, I will die alone."

Those words stayed with Izzy long after he had left the sauna. To die alone. But didn't everyone die alone? "Maybe some more than others," Izzy thought to himself. "The world isn't bringing us closer together, it's pushing us apart." Izzy pondered the double edge of technology.

The home computer had certainly made life easier, as had the internet. People could get anything their hearts' desired, without ever leaving their own homes. However, in this new wired society, society had very little value. It was every man and woman for oneself. The more Izzy thought about it, the more depressed he became.

The big FinAir 757 lifted off the runway in Helsinki and set a course for JFK airport in New York City. Izzy looked out the window and watched the plane spiral up into a sea of white puffy clouds. He turned in his seat and looked at Oksana who was busy rereading Mengele's papers.

"It is not a sin to die alone," Izzy mumbled softly. "The sin is to die lonely."

Oksana looked up from the papers. "Did you say something?"

Izzy shook his head. "Thinking out loud, that's all."

Izzy turned again and glanced back out the window. Just as the plane burst through the clouds and into bright sunlight he turned and tapped Oksana on the shoulder. She turned in her seat to face him.

"If I asked. . . would you?"

Oksana blinked. "Would I what?"

Izzy paused, realizing that this might not have been the ideal place to ask what had popped into his head, but there was no turning back now. "If I asked, would you marry me?"

Oksana's mouth dropped open in surprise. She couldn't decide if she should laugh or cry. "Marry you? You are asking if I would marry you?"

Izzy nodded. "What would you say?"

It was now Oksana who needed to pause. "If you ask me, I will say yes, or I will say no." It was a very coy response.

Izzy gathered all his nerve and forged onward. "Will you marry me?" He asked the question and his palms immediately began to sweat as he waited for a reply.

"Yes, Izzy Slesinger, I will marry you." Oksana said as she leaned close and kissed Izzy on the lips. "I will be very happy to become Mrs. Isaiah Slesinger."

Chapter 16

Anna Kaiser's mood became more foul with each passing minute. She and Ilya Babakov had spent two entire days searching Sosnovka. They had been able to trace Izzy's steps to the sanatoria, but the facility doctor could provide no information as to Izzy's current whereabouts.

However, the doctor did mention the episode with Herta and had explained that Izzy and Oksana departed with Herta's valise of papers.

"We have failed," Ilya said as he opened the driver's side door of the rental car.

Anna glared at him from the other side of the car. She yanked open the passenger door and angrily sat down. She slammed the door shut as Ilya started the ignition. "My brother will be furious. Sixty years of work in jeopardy." Anna made a fist with her right hand and slammed it into the passenger side door. "Mein Fuerher's dreams will be realized. We are going to go to America."

Ilya had started driving back towards Cherkassy. Anna's comment made him slam on the brakes. When the car was at a full stop, he turned to look at Anna in disbelief.

"America? Slesinger is probably half way there already."

"All the reason we must hurry," Anna hissed back. "We will fly into Dusseldorf and get Dulac for insurance. We will trade her for the papers if we have to."

"What if he won't trade?"

Anna laughed. "Won't trade? And let Dulac be killed? His naive love of humanity and misguided morality won't let that happen."

"What if he makes copies of the papers?"

The thought enraged Anna to the boiling point. "Then I will kill him with my bare hands." She lashed out with her fist again. This time she hit the glass of the side window and it exploded outward in a shower of sharp, flying shards.

The broken glass lay everywhere. It was on the ground, on the dashboard, and on the seats of Oksana's Saab. The glove compartment had been opened and papers were strewn around the floor of the car. All the road maps that Oksana kept in the seat pockets were missing. The fact that the stereo was intact proved that it wasn't the work of thieves out for a quick and easy buck.

Whoever broke the windows was looking for something specific. Oksana was too enraged by the violation of her property to consider the implications. Izzy, however, realized what the broken glass meant. It was clear that the Reich had connected him with Oksana. Therefore, her place was probably being watched as closely as his.

It took them quite a while to clean the broken glass out of the car. The attendant at the JFK airport lot didn't even blink when Oksana pulled up to the cashier's booth. Obviously, a car with broken windows wasn't all that rare in long term parking. Izzy's frazzled nerves were firing on all cylinders. Every moment or so he'd glance out the side window and turn back to make sure they weren't being followed. He would have preferred to glance in the side view mirror, but the Reich had ripped both side view mirrors from the car. It wasn't until the Van Wyck Expressway turned into the Grand Central Parkway that Izzy relaxed a bit, convinced that they weren't being followed.

Izzy had decided they needed to risk going to his apartment and Oksana had no objections. It wasn't until they were half way over Manhattan's Triboro Bridge that it dawned on her that Izzy's apartment might not be safe.

"What if they are waiting for you?" Oksana had also not yet realized that the Reich could be waiting for her.

"Gotta risk it. I need some files that I've got at home. I'll grab them and we can head straight to my office. Rich Levine increased security after Doctor Van Bassen shot himself in my office. Armed guards now check everyone at the door."

"How will I get in?" Oksana asked as she watched Izzy insert his key into the dead bolt.

"I'll get you cleared," Izzy replied as he touched a nervously sweating hand to the door knob on his apartment. He pushed the door open and jumped back, just in case an unknown assailant was waiting on the other side. With the door open, Izzy peered inside. He could see into the living room and part of the kitchen.

Everything looked in order and he tiptoed in. Oksana filed in after him. The first thing that Izzy noticed was his answering machine. The little light glowed a steady red, indicating that the machine was full and could hold no more messages. Izzy tapped the replay button and listened. The first message was from Shana. It was weeks old, from just after the state department had visited and explained that her baby brother was dead.

Izzy thought about calling her, but knew he couldn't. He was certain that the Reich would be watching her, or maybe he was being overly paranoid. Either way, he wasn't about to take a chance. Most of the other calls were from Rich Levine. However, the last call, which had come in several hours earlier that day, was from Doctor Polansky. The message froze Izzy by the machine.

"Isaiah, my friend. I know you have been in Europe hunting for

Mengele's notes. If you have found them we must get together. Your telephone is probably being monitored. Call my office from a secure spot and we will arrange to meet."

Izzy was dumbfounded. "How the hell does Ithamar Polansky know about this?"

"Who is that?" Oksana asked.

"My old molecular biochemistry professor at Yale. He was my mentor."

"When did you speak with him last?"

"I was in New Haven right after the Yontif. Yom Kippur was mid-September. Halloween's the end of the week. What's that? Six and a half, seven weeks."

"What did you say to him when you saw him?"

"Nothing," Izzy replied defensively. "I didn't know any of this six weeks ago." Izzy quickly gathered up files from his cabinets and bookcases. He grabbed a clean pair of pants from his closet in the bedroom and wrapped them around two clean shirts, three pairs of underwear, and some socks. He was moving very quickly, becoming more paranoid about being in the apartment by the second. Izzy emerged from the bedroom with a determined look on his face. "I'll meet with Polansky and then call Dave Dunlevy. He's got connections with the editors at *Nature*. I'll draft something for the December issue and have Dunlevy sign it."

Oksana liked what she heard. "I will help you trace back through the mutations and cellular shift. Doctor Chazov promised to send all her case histories to my office."

The meeting with Rich Levine lasted over an hour. Rich explained that he had been grilled by intelligence operatives from the CIA, CID, and the FBI. There had been an endless stream of questions, they all wanted to know what Izzy had been working on before his death in Argentina. Izzy filled Rich in as best he could, slowly explaining about the cell that Mengele had created, and how they were related to HIV and AIDS. The color drained out of Rich's face when he looked at the projected mortality numbers.

"These numbers can't be right."

Izzy nodded. "Brian Crighton ran those numbers."

"Crighton? The statistics guy? On the cover of Scientific America a couple of months ago?"

Izzy nodded again. "Bastards blew him up! They took out the entire Brittany Pharmalogics complex."

"Blew him up? What are you talking about?"

Izzy hesitated. "Better that you don't know."

Rich was incredulous. "Better that I don't know? An hour ago I thought you were dead. If you have forgotten, I run this place!"

Izzy tensed and looked Rich in the eye. "As far as you're concerned, I'm still dead. Killed in Argentina. You do not want these people thinking you know anything."

"What people?"

Izzy couldn't hold it back any longer. "Nazis."

Rich was stunned silent. He glanced at Oksana who simply nodded. "Nazis?"

"Yes," Izzy replied. "I can't stay here for very long."

"Where are you going?"

"I need to move quickly. And you don't need to know." Izzy stopped in his office, gathered more files and did a quick check of his computer. There was a single email recorded in his system. It had been sent several hours earlier on that day.

"You are in grave danger. Adolf knows that you are alive and he wants you dead. Trust no one. . . Heneke."

Shriveled brown leaves crackled under Izzy's feet as he walked from his car to the entrance of Temple B'nai Shalom in Woodbridge, Connecticut. Woodbridge, a small upper-class community was adjacent to New Haven. As soon as Izzy had crossed the town line the scenery instantly changed. Woodbridge was very rural, with only a handful of small businesses. The synagogue was among the largest buildings in town. As Izzy waited by the entrance he surveyed his surroundings. The only thing he could see in all directions were rapidly denuding trees.

He didn't have to wait long. A black Jeep Cherokee pulled into the synagogue driveway. It came to a stop in front of the building and Ithamar Polansky got out on the passenger's side. The driver also stepped down from the vehicle. He was a stranger to Izzy, a short man, maybe 5'8" at most. He had receding curly brown hair and the thickest neck that Izzy had ever seen. Doctor Polansky approached and immediately gave Izzy a bear hug.

"Isaiah, my friend. Thank the almighty that you are safe." The short man took a step closer and Doctor Polansky turned towards him. "Let me introduce Doron Katz. He is with the Mossad."

Izzy extended his hand and Doron clasped it in a vise-like grip. A little jolt of pain caused Izzy to wince a bit.

"*Shalom,*" Doron offered in a thick Israeli accent.

Ithamar approached the synagogue and slid the key into the lock. He pulled the door open and walked to the security panel and deactivated the alarm. "The rabbi of this congregation is a good friend. He is letting us use the sanctuary for our meeting." Ithamar led the way inside. Izzy admired the ornate stained glass windows while Ithamar searched for the lights. While Ithamar was searching in the back, Doron began speaking with Izzy.

"I must congratulate you. Mossad has been searching for Mengele's notes for thirty years. You accomplished in three weeks what we, the Germans, Russians, and Nazis have failed to do in over three decades. Tracking Herte Gerke to the sanatoria was a stroke of genius."

Izzy was amazed that Doron knew what he had done. "How do you know that?"

Ithamar finally found the switches. The lights flickered for a moment and then the entire sanctuary became bright. A moment later Ithamar was back. He returned just as Doron started to explain.

"It is complicated. We track the Reich's activities very closely. They were watching you, we were watching them."

"And now what can I do for you?" Izzy asked.

Doron pointed towards the front row of chairs. "Perhaps we should all take a seat."

Izzy shook his head. "I'd rather stand if you don't mind. I've been sitting a lot as of late."

"Fair enough," Doron agreed. "Mossad would like you to give us the papers. I will take them back to Tel Aviv as witness to the horrors of Auschwitz."

Izzy immediately rejected the request. "There is sensitive material in the journals. It must be carefully reviewed and dissected."

Doron was taken aback. He had assumed that Doctor Slesinger would automatically agree to his request. "I can assure you that Mossad will be very complete in our review."

"Complete?" Izzy asked sarcastically. "Israel is woefully ill-equipped to handle this inquiry."

Ithamar reached a hand out and pulled Izzy aside. He lowered his voice to a hushed whisper. "This is not a United Jewish Appeal pledge that you can push to the back of your desk for several months. You must give them those documents."

Izzy shook his head. "Can't do it. When we fully understand the notes we will be happy to share them with not only the Israelis, but with the world."

"So you will not cooperate?" Doron asked hotly. "This is what I should have expected from an assimilated American Jew. In Israel we understand the importance of *lador va dor*, from one generation to the next, we look after the ones who came before us. We do not abandon them."

Doron's words stung Izzy badly and he retaliated. "*Lador va dor?* Our difference is that you are trying to preserve the past and I am trying to insure the future. I won't deny the importance of your goals, but I'd gladly trade all the memories of the past in order to save lives in the present."

"What are you talking about?" Ithamar interjected. "What is in those papers?"

"Mengele somehow shifted cellular metabolism. He created a doomsday cell that is mutagenic and self-perpetuating. Those cells were injected into thousands of Africans, and God knows how many others."

Ithamar felt the sudden need to sit down. His fingers pushed down on a felt seat bottom and he collapsed into the chair. Izzy walked in front him and looked down into his old friend's face.

"Those cells are the host for HIV."

"You're certain?" Ithamar asked in a voice that was afraid of the response.

"Very certain," came Izzy's reply.

"I don't understand what you are saying?" Doron interrupted.

Izzy turned towards the Israeli operative. "I have a suggestion for you, Mr. Katz. Go back to Tel Aviv and contact Doctor Emanuel Meir at the university. I will transfer a copy of the documents to him, and him alone."

Ithamar looked at Katz and nodded. "Isaiah and I have much to discuss. You have things to do. I'm sure that Isaiah can drive me home when we're through."

Doron agreed and departed. When he was gone, Izzy filled Ithamar in on everything that he had discovered. It was a very long conversation. Despite his expertise in molecular biochemistry, or maybe in spite of it, Ithamar had a hard time accepting Izzy's hypothesis.

"So you believe that you can engineer a solution using gene therapy?"

"I doubt it," Izzy replied. "HIV is the most mutable virus we've ever seen. Why?"

"Because of changes in the mRNA. With each new split it changes at one site."

Izzy waved his hand through the air, dismissing Ithamar's comment. "Yes, but why? Some viruses mutate to become resistant to drugs, some mutate to jump species, but HIV is different...It mutates so rapidly in order to keep up with changes in its host."

"So, as the host changes, the virus changes." Ithamar paused to consider it. "I don't buy it."

"It's like dominoes. Mengele tipped over the first, and it started a chain reaction. If there was only one mutation, one protein change that differentiated from normal, healthy cells, then a gene therapy repair might. . . and I say might, be possible."

Ithamar walked onto the bimah in the synagogue. In the center of the elevated platform stood the arc that housed the Torahs. He squinted through the rolling metal doors of the arc and glimpsed the scrolls. Those scrolls represented almost 6000 years of Jewish history. If what Izzy said was even remotely correct, Jews had less time in front of them than in back. Not only Jews, everyone. Ithamar slowly turned from the arc and pointed his right index finger in Izzy's direction. "So we are doomed? That is what you believe?"

Izzy picked his words very carefully for his response. "I think some of us are doomed. But I also think that a resistance to the cellular mutation can be developed. Therefore, assuming either sperm or egg has that resistance, the resulting embryo should be free from mutation. However, should both parents be infected with Mengele cells, the child will also be infected."

"And all three will eventually die," Ithamar added with a very heavy heart.

Izzy nodded. "I don't see any other possibility."

Ithamar stepped down from the bimah and approached his old student and friend. "I am a very old man, Isaiah. I have witnessed atrocities which are beyond your imagination. The Shoah was beyond the comprehension of humanity, and yet it all happened.

You want me to believe this, and deep in my gut I think I do. But the world will not believe you."

Izzy nodded in agreement. "Then I will have to make them believe."

Ithamar grabbed hold of Izzy's arm. The elderly professor suddenly looked very fragile.

"Perhaps I should drive you home now?" Izzy suggested.

"I think that would be good. I'm sure Eda is worried and I suddenly feel tired. Very tired."

It was a short ride from the synagogue to Ithamar's home. During the ride, Ithamar closed his eyes and dropped his head onto the passenger side window. Izzy turned the radio on softly and tuned the dial to 99.1. The station, WPLR, was playing the Halloween song of the day. It was 'Bad Moon Rising' by Creedence Clearwater Revival. Izzy found himself singing along as the chorus rolled around. By the last line he was singing so loudly that he drowned out the voice of John Fogerty. Ithamar didn't even raise an eyelid through the entire song.

Izzy pulled his blue BMW up in front of the little house in Westville. The house that never seemed to change. The house that seemed a sanctuary from the kinder days of his youth. Placing a hand on Ithamar's shoulder, Izzy shook him. He did not move. Izzy shook him again and he knew. It was a bright moonlit night, two days before Halloween, and Izzy sat numbly behind the wheel. Then he began to cry.

Chapter 17

The ringing of the phone woke Adolf at three in the morning. He grabbed the cordless unit from its spot beside his bed and growled angrily into the mouthpiece. "Was?"

"Adolf, it's Anna. Babekov never arrived."

Adolf became wide awake. "What are you talking about?"

"Ilya is not here. I came in on Lufthansa last night. He was going to bring Dulac on the private jet."

"Why did you not go with him?"

"I wanted to get to New York as soon as possible and get back on Doctor Slesinger's trail. But now Ilya is over fourteen hours past due. I have already confirmed that our jet landed in New York on schedule."

Adolf began to pace the floor frantically while holding the phone away from himself. "Could Babekov have deceived me? Or defected? I should have known better than to trust a Russian." Adolf placed the phone back to his ear. "I am coming to New York. I will take the next available flight."

"What should I do until you get here?"

"Find Doctor Slesinger. And If Babekov or that girl turn up, kill them. Do you understand?"

"*Jawhol*. I understand."

Adolf clicked a button on the phone and the line cleared. He angrily grasped the plastic covered antennae and broke it. With all his might he threw the phone and its housing shattered against the wall. In a furry he retrieved his passport, two Glock automatic pistols, and quickly began to pack.

Anna glanced at the clock on the nightstand. It was a bit past eight in the evening and the long flight from Germany, combined with the anxiety of waiting for Ilya had put her on edge. She paced the floor of her room at the Waldorf like a lioness imprisoned for the first time. There was only one thing that would serve to release her and that would be a fresh kill. Anna stripped off her clothing and steamed herself in the hottest shower that she could bear. She dried quickly and picked an appropriate outfit for the hunt. The red satin underwire demi-bra was her favorite. It made her 38 C cup breasts sit up high and the underwire rubbed in just the right spot to keep her half-dollar sized nipples at attention. She took a moment to admire her neatly trimmed blond bush in the full length mirror and then donned matching red satin panties. A deep cut red blouse was tucked into a pair of skin tight black denim jeans. Anna finished by slipping her feet into a pair of blood red stilettos with three inch heals. The shoes pushed her to a height of almost 6'3".

Inside the bathroom was a small cosmetics case. Anna fished around until she felt the handle of what she was after. The knife was a switchblade. Anna released the mechanism and seven inches of razor sharp chromium steel sprang out. The tip was coated with dried blood, a memento from the last hunt. She touched the tip to her tongue. The salty taste enflamed her senses and increased her hunger. Hunger for fresh blood. This was the first time she had been in America and that added to the excitement. She had always wondered if American men would be as easy as those in Europe. Her brief discourse with Doctor Slesinger proved that at least some American men had the power to resist her charms. That thought only served to further arouse her. A kill without a satisfactory hunt was like intercourse without foreplay. It wouldn't be any fun if the hunted didn't at least struggle.

"*Yitgadal, yitkadash, shmei rabo. . .*" It was the second time that Izzy found himself saying the mourner's Kaddish in less than a week. The world was becoming more surreal and incomprehensible by the moment. "How could Ithamar Polansky be dead?" Izzy thought to himself as he watched the rabbi fill a shovel full of dirt and toss it into the grave. It wasn't a large funeral, maybe fifteen men and women from the Polansky's synagogue. They were all older, senior citizens who lived near the temple and Jewish graveyard. It was fortunate that Izzy was there. Without him they wouldn't have had enough to make up a minyan, the quorum of ten adult males needed to say the Kaddish. In Izzy's reform temple in New York they would have counted the women, but not here, not among the Orthodox.

Eda Polansky's eyes were red from the crying. She handed another woman her cane and reached for the shovel handle that the rabbi offered. She had to struggle to dig, but accepted no assistance. Izzy was the last in line. Ithamar had been like a second father. Izzy's lips began to tremble as he accepted the shovel. Guilt over the Holocaust had taken his real father, and now Mengele had reached up from the depths of Hell to claim Ithamar. At least that's the way Izzy saw it. He struggled to keep himself composed as he dropped dirt into the grave.

The rabbi gathered everyone around the grave and opened his prayer book:

At the rising of the sun and at its going down, We remember them.
When we are weary and in need of strength, We remember them.
When we are lost and sick at heart, We remember them.
When we have joy we crave to share, We remember them.
When we have decisions that are difficult to make, We remember them.
When we have achievements that are based on theirs, We remember them.

As long as we live, they too will live; for they are now a part of us, as we remember them.

It was with heavy heart that Izzy eased the BMW out of the cemetery lot. The drive back to New York passed in a blur. His mind was lost in days gone by. It had been Ithamar who had challenged him to push for excellence when he was at Yale. More importantly, Ithamar had been a good friend. He had accepted a brash, young New Yorker into his home, and into his heart. He saw potential in Izzy that Izzy didn't see in himself. It was in more than just academics. Ithamar preached a balanced life was best, with a time and place for everything that God had created.

Even though he knew his apartment might not be safe, he headed there all the same. Izzy was burnt out and tired of running. As soon as he stepped into the apartment, things went from bad to worse. There was an email response waiting for him from the editor of Molecular Bioproteins. Izzy had sent him a fifty-word abstract on the article he planned to write on Mengele cells, that's what Heneke had named them, Mengele cells. The journal was a small one, with a limited circulation. It would be a good launching pad for such a radical theory. The response that Izzy read silently was not pleasant.

From: Rkroop@mlbpt.com

To: Izzyman@nybell.net.

"Dear Doctor Slesinger,

Never in my 30 plus years have I read such an outlandish theory. Our journal has many African-American and German-American doctors on our subscription list. Your hypothesis would be offensive to both groups. We have no interest in pseudo-science, nor would we open ourselves to potential lawsuits from the pharmaceutical corporations you have libeled. It is my recommendation that you seek out professional help for dealing with your dementia.

With regrets,

Dr. R. Kroop, Senior Editor."

The response was pretty much what Izzy had expected. Even if it hadn't been, he was so numb from all that had happened, he simply didn't care. He fixed himself a sandwich and a cup of tea. He thought about calling Oksana and Rich Levine. He decided against it. Instead, he brushed his teeth, stripped off his clothes, and climbed into bed. Before turning out the lights he retrieved the copy of the Bible that he kept at the bottom of the nightstand beside his bed. He barely ever took it out. It had been a present from the Polanskys when he graduated from Yale, which now seemed a distant memory.

At that particular moment, Izzy felt a thousand years old. So old, that his youth seemed many lifetimes away. He lay awake in the darkness for a long time. He had a hard time shutting his mind off. However, the exhaustion finally got the better of him and he drifted off into a fitful sleep. He was out cold for exactly ten minutes when the ringing of the phone jarred him awake. He had trouble opening his eyes and groped for the phone in darkness.

"Izzy, it's Rich. Are you there?"

"Uh. . . huh."

"We've had two German experts working round the clock on the notes. I think I cried more today then I have in the past ten years. You can't imagine what they did. . . and to children."

Izzy did his best to will himself awake. "What about amino-acid chains?"

"Not yet. But we have found some things that might point in that direction."

"What type of things? Do you want me to come down?"

"No," Rich replied emphatically. "You sound dead. Get a good night's rest. We can go over this stuff tomorrow."

Izzy had half put down the phone when he heard Rich calling to him. He placed the phone back to his ear. "Did you say something else?"

"Yeah, one last thing. I want to remind you that tomorrow night is the fund raiser at the Waldorf."

"Can't I skip it this year?"

"It'll just be a couple of hours. Doris Rumplemeyer is coming especially to see you. Last year her foundation gave us almost $5 million."

"I hate this thing," Izzy moaned. "Where the hell am I going to find a costume at the last minute?"

"You won't have to stay long, I promise. As far as a costume, just throw something together."

Izzy's eyelids were getting heavier by the minute. "Okay. Is there anything else or can I hang up now?"

"Uh," Rich hesitated before replying. "It would be really good if you brought a date."

Izzy's mouth dropped open a bit and he shook his head a little from side to side. Before Rich could say another word, Izzy dropped the phone back into its cradle. A moment later he was sound asleep.

There was a real autumn crispness in the air as Izzy stepped out the front door of his building. A brilliant orange sun had just crept its way over the New York horizon and the rays glistened off frost that had formed overnight on car windows. Izzy took a deep breath and the cool air filled his lungs. It wasn't yet 6:30 and Manhattan was just coming alive for another work day. Izzy walked to Third Avenue, hailed a cab, and settled in the back seat. Five minutes later he was entering the elevator in Oksana's office building. He reached her door just as she walked in for the morning. She was surprised to see him, especially since he called from the car on his way back from New Haven and said that he was going to take a needed day of rest.

"Izzy, what are you doing here?" Oksana asked in alarm.

"So this is what it's like to be engaged." Izzy replied sarcastically. "It's everything I thought it would be."

Oksana pushed open her office door and Izzy followed her in. "Seriously, what are you doing here? You said you were taking a vacation day from the world."

"I've got a problem. I've got a fund raiser tonight which I can't get out of. They want me to bring someone."

"Tonight? I'm way back on appointments. I need to get caught up."

Izzy shrugged his shoulders. "Not a problem. I'll go stag. These things are always the same every year. Rich husbands get plastered by ten, and I wind up dancing with their wives."

A lot of men would have used such a comment to entice their girlfriends into coming along. However, for Izzy it was just a simple statement of fact. Each year he did go stag, and each year he did wind up dancing with rich, beautiful, married women. Women who made it quite clear that they were available for something a bit more intimate than dancing. Izzy imagined that was part of the motivation for Rich's asking him to bring a date. That way he would be able to avoid any embarrassing or confrontational situations.

Izzy's words were not lost on Oksana. She did not want her new fiance dancing with other women. In fact, a party inside Izzy's circle would be the perfect place to let the world know that Izzy was off-the-market. "What time is the party?"

Izzy had to stop and think. "I think cocktails start at seven, dinner's around nine, and then there's dancing."

Oksana nodded and at the same time checked her appointment schedule for the day. "Pick me up here at 6:45. I'll slip away to Saks at lunchtime and buy a dress and some shoes."

"It's a costume party," Izzy countered. "For Halloween."

"A costume party?"

Izzy nodded. "It's a fund raiser. Biggest one of the year."

"Okay, I'll think of something. But now you are going to have to leave. I need to get the office ready before my staff gets here."

"I owe you big time," Izzy offered as he leaned in and gave Oksana a kiss on the lips. "I'll wait out front at 6:45."

Oksana's very first patient was Virginia Mason, a middle-aged housewife from Queens who was being treated for AIDS-related sarcomas. Oksana reviewed Virginia's case history as she waited for the centrifuge to spin down a blood sample for testing. Virginia had contracted the original infection from her husband, who had gotten it from his secretary. The secretary had gotten it from her boyfriend, who had picked it from a prostitute.

Virginia's sarcomas had advanced very quickly, while her husband showed no signs of any AIDS-related diseases. It was difficult for Oksana to look Virginia in the eye, now knowing what she did about HIV. However, she tried to put on a brave front.

"We've run your blood and it's clean. The sarcomas appear to be receding."

"That's good?" Virginia questioned hopefully.

Oksana replied cautiously. "We will hope for the best. I want to increase your testing to once a week."

"I've read about a new medicine," Virginia commented as she began to put her clothes back on. "I think it's called PIRT-I9."

Oksana nodded. "It's experimental. We cannot yet use it in the United States."

"Are you sure? I thought I heard that the government was going to approve it."

"I will check on it." Oksana replied as she walked Virginia to the reception area. She left her there to make an appointment for the following week.

The morning passed in a blur of patients, and Oksana could not get Izzy's words out of her head. He had made it quite clear that Heneke's drug could make things a whole lot worse than they already were. Virginia Mason was a good example of how easily the infection could be passed, and how many lives it could touch. Oksana began writing an oncology paper in her head as she made her way down 3rd Avenue at lunchtime. At 31st Street she turned up towards 5th Avenue and came to a stop in front of Costume Mania.

Shopping for a Halloween costume in New York on Halloween is very much like deciding to go to Macy's Thanksgiving day parade, ten minutes before it starts. Costume Mania was packed with people of all different sizes, races, ages and sexes. Oksana walked through the front door and found people standing sixteen deep at the registers. A teenager with long, orange-dyed hair stumbled through the crowd. An axe was embedded in his head and blood gushed in spurts from the wound. People backed away, which was difficult to do in such a tight place. The young man stood up straight, pulled the axe from his head, and revealed the edges of a very realistic looking latex mask. The latex made a sucking sound as he pulled it off.

"Awesome," he stated as he took his place on the checkout line.

Oksana checked her watch and gave up. She headed back to the office and got there just before her assistant, Ellen Davies, took off for lunch.

"Can I ask you a favor?" Oksana asked.

"Anything," Ellen replied.

"Can I borrow one of your nurse dresses?"

"Sure. What do you need it for?"

"A costume party."

Ellen laughed. "It's about time you got out. I've got just the number. Baby blue, with a really high cut." Ellen held her hand at mid-thigh level. Ellen disappeared in the back and came back with the dress. She held it up for Oksana to look at.

"Looks kind of small," Oksana frowned. "Anything else?"

"It's supposed to be small," Ellen countered. "Makes men kinda big, if you know what I mean."

Oksana chuckled. "I don't know. . . "

"Live a little," Ellen countered. "It's not like you're married or anything. Give 'em a thrill."

At the Waldorf, Anna Kaiser was planning to give 'em much more than that. Adolf had arrived in New York and his sister told him of their good fortune, that Doctor Slesinger was going to come right to them.

"He is coming here? You're certain?" Adolf asked as he rummaged through his suitcase.

"Tonight. There is a fund raiser for his employer. The hotel manager was gracious enough to share the guest list with me." Anna threw her hair back and laughed wickedly. "Unfortunately, he won't be sharing anything in the future."

Adolf spun angrily towards his sister. "You can not simply kill every man you meet because it fits your fancy."

Anna got off the bed and strode over to her brother. Standing straight she towered over him.

"It wasn't simply to fit my fancy. He did not fulfill my sexual needs."

Adolf glared up at her. "The entire Munich soccer team wouldn't fulfill your needs!"

Anna became enraged at the comment. She balled up her fingers into a fist which she crashed into the side of her brother's head. The force of the blow actually lifted him off his feet and he crumpled instantly to the ground. He struggled onto to his hands and knees just as Anna placed a hard kick into his groin. Adolf immediately fell flat, his hands tucked underneath his body as the pain seared at his testicles. Anna turned toward her clothes dresser and retrieved her knife. She opened the blade and touched to the side of Adolf's neck.

"If you ever speak to me that way again, brother, it will fit my fancy to open your throat."

Now it was Adolf's turn for rage. He slipped his right hand into the waistband of his pants and pulled out a tiny, concealed handgun. He rolled away from Anna and pointed the barrel at his sister's forehead. "You are telling me what to do? You are telling me what to do?" Adolf forced himself to his feet as his sister backed away. "I would shoot you in the head, but what good would it do? You have no brains!"

Instead of retreating, Anna screamed back. "Go ahead, shoot me! See if you can get Slesinger by yourself."

Anna's words made Adolf pause. She was right. She would have a much better chance of capturing Doctor Slesinger than he would. "What have you planned?"

Anna folded up the knife and retrieved a long, brown wig from a drawer in the dresser. "It will be a costume party. I will go in costume. I will get Slesinger to leave the party with me."

Adolf liked what he heard. "I will wait out in the lobby. By the time anyone realizes that he is missing, it will be too late."

Izzy spent the entire day working on three dimensional computer models of protein chains. Most of Mengele's journals had been translated and it was clear that the focus on his work had been on finding an effectively lethal viral agent which could be used to decimate Africa. Shifting cellular proteins was not the focus. Mengele's new cell was an accidental creation. Therefore, tracing it backwards just became significantly harder. At least Mengele had documented which African viral cultures he was working with. There were hundreds of viruses which were tested. Viruses had been cultured from primates, rodents, amphibians, and insects. Healthy cells were exposed to individual viruses and to viral combinations. Unfortunately, there was no mention of which of the viruses had been successful.

"If it was caused by a mutant virus, we'll never find it," Izzy thought to himself as Rich Levine walked into the lab.

"Making progress?" Rich inquired.

Izzy spun his chair away from the computer monitor. He looked very weary. "This could take years, or decades. We may never find it."

"You'll find it," Rich said reassuringly. "It may take time, but you'll find it."

"What I need is to speak with Heneke. Why hasn't he contacted me again?"

"Are you certain the last message was from him? I've spoken to people in France. Brittany was completely obliterated in the blast. The authorities have given up on their hunt for bodies. That message might have been a trick."

Izzy thought about it. "Yeah, could be. But what would the Reich have to gain by making me believe Heneke is still alive?"

A cold shiver ran down Rich's spine. "Up until a couple of days ago I didn't even know there was a German Reich. This is all just so surreal."

Izzy nodded as he turned back towards the screen. He placed the mouse pointer on remodel and clicked. The computer screen turned blue and Izzy stood up and stretched. "The computer will remodel everything I've got so far. We'll see what we get in the morning."

Rich glanced up at the clock on the wall. It was 3:45 in the afternoon. "You're leaving before 6:00? This is a first."

"You're the one who said I needed to be at the fund raiser. I'm going home to shower and change."

Rich slapped himself in the head. "Shit! Forgot all about it. I'd better get it in gear if I'm going to get to the Waldorf by 5:30." Rich excused himself from the lab and Izzy gathered up his things and went home.

The costume ball was high on the 'A' list among New York's elite society. Tickets were $2500 per couple and the ball had been sold out since the end of the summer. The main ballroom at the Waldorf had space for 1200 guests. Ticket sales brought $110,000 into The Institute after expenses were paid. On more than one occasion there had been large endowment checks presented to Rich Levine from the wealthier of the guests.

Izzy dug through his closet and pulled out the makings of his costume. First he pulled out an old pair of tan cargo pants which had been in his closet for at least ten years. He slipped the pants on and found that they were actually a bit large in the waist. Fortunately, when he tucked his thick blue denim shirt into the waistband, the extra space disappeared nicely. Next was the tan leather aviator jacket that he had found in a consignment shop in Greenwich village for $25. Lastly, he reached up to the top shelf of the closet and retrieved his tan felt, fedora-style hat. He put the hat on and looked at his reflection in the mirror. Looking back at him was the spitting image of Indiana Jones.

It was the same costume that Izzy wore every year. Only this year his beard was gone, and his recent exploits in South America and Europe made him feel like he really was Indiana Jones. Before leaving the house he brushed his teeth. Nothing was worse than being at close quarters in conversation with someone who had bad breath. It had happened to Izzy at more than one ball and he promised himself he would never put anyone else in that situation.

Oksana was waiting in front of her office building when Izzy pulled up. She had a long red woolen coat over her outfit so Izzy had no idea how hot she looked in her skin tight nurse's outfit. Oksana settled herself in the front seat and appraised Izzy's costume. Even though she was from Russia, she immediately knew who he was supposed to be.

"Indiana Jones?"

Izzy nodded. "And you?"

"You will have to wait and see," Oksana replied with a twinkle in her eye.

The indoor parking garage at the Waldorf was filled with expensive machinery. Mercedes, Jaguars, BMWs and other exotics filled the spaces. Izzy squeezed his little beemer next to a bright red Ferrari. Izzy escorted Oksana into the hotel and they waited by the elevator. Waiting with them was another couple in costume. The man was middle-aged with a severely receding hairline and a bit of a paunch. He was dressed in business suit, with a cheap plastic mask covering his eyes. His companion was a young, busty blond.

She was dressed in skin tight black jeans, a skin tight red plaid shirt, and had a Stetson style leather cowboy hat on her head. She was also wearing high leather boots. Izzy glanced at her and smiled to himself. The investment bankers with their trophy wives or mistresses never ceased to amuse him.

Izzy eyes went wide when Oksana removed her coat and handed it to the coat check girl. The blue nurse's dress hugged her like a second skin. The hemline barely reached her thighs and the neckline plunged deeply to reveal more than a little cleavage. Oksana turned fully towards Izzy and appreciated the look on his face. She moved to his side and dropped her voice to a whisper.

"I was afraid that this might be too much."

Izzy chuckled and leaned in to give Oksana a quick kiss on the lips. "Too much? It's definitely not that!"

"You know what I mean! I do not want to embarrass you."

"Put it out of your mind," Izzy replied. "You could never embarrass me."

Izzy's comment put Oksana at ease and she relaxed. They were about to enter the grand ballroom when Izzy was stopped by Mrs. Helen Rumplemeyer, wife of billionaire financier, Roger Rumplemeyer. Mrs. Rumplemeyer, a petite woman in her early sixties, was dressed elegantly as Queen Victoria. The Rumplemeyer's had contributed large sums to The Institute over the years. Izzy knew both of them quite well. He also knew that Mrs. Rumplemeyer could be very confrontational.

"You there," she said as she pointed at Izzy, pretending not to know him. "You look exactly like Doctor Isaiah Slesinger. Except he has a beard, and always comes stag."

Izzy blushed a bit as he presented Oksana. "Mrs. Rumplemeyer, I'd like you to meet my fiancé, Doctor Oksana Zibrova."

"Fiancé?" Mrs. Rumplemeyer looked shocked as she turned towards Oksana. "However did you get him to propose?"

"It is quite a long story," Oksana replied.

Mrs. Rumplemeyer nodded and winked. "And I'll bet a good one. But I'd better be getting inside before my Roger sends out a search party." Mrs. Rumplemeyer motioned for Oksana to move closer. When she was close enough Mrs. Rumplemeyer whispered to her softly. "You're getting a good one, Doctor Zibrova. A bit wild around the edges perhaps, but a good one. Hold on to him. With both hands!"

Izzy and Oksana followed Mrs. Rumplemeyer into the ballroom. It was already very crowded, with a vast array of vampires, cowboys, harem girls, zombies, astronauts, and others.

The costume party made a perfect cover for Anna Kaiser. She improvised a costume from the clothing she brought with her. A short, tight black leather dress pushed her breasts upward and outward. Her legs were sheathed in black fishnet stockings with four inch stiletto pumps on her feet. The shoes were custom ordered, with the spiked heals reinforced with steel and metal points on the tips. To complete the outfit, Anna grasped a leather whip in her hand. She also wore the dark brown wig she had shown to Adolf, just in case Doctor Slesinger remembered her from the hotel restaurant.

Anna attracted a lot of stares, but her height and the whip made her seem more than a little intimidating. When she caught a glimpse of Izzy, she quickly made her way toward him. As she got closer she saw Oksana was latched onto Izzy's arm. That made her stop dead in her tracks.

Oksana's presence ruled out the possibility that she would be able to seduce Izzy away from the party. Therefore, she retreated to the lobby to find Adolf.

"I do not know what to do," Anna confided to her brother. Adolf was seated on a leather sofa in the lobby.

"You must create some type of a diversion," Adolf said at last. "I will sneak up on Slesinger and the woman."

Anna thought for a moment and a sly smile creased her face.

She whispered into Adolf's ear and he nodded in agreement. A moment later they were both standing in the grand ballroom.

Anna pointed to where Izzy and Oksana were standing. They were mingling with a group from The Institute which included Rich Levine, who was dressed as Batman. Anna slithered her way towards Izzy, as Adolf circled around from behind. Anna stopped twenty-five feet short of Izzy's group and promptly began to strip off her black leather dress. She let it drop and then removed her black underwire demi-bra which released her ample breasts. She was now only dressed in a black leather thong, the black fishnet stockings, and the four inch heels.

The crowd in the ballroom fell silent, and then loud chatter erupted. Men fumbled their way closer to Anna, her nakedness drawing them like a magnet. Rich Levine did not look happy. He could already see the headlines and photos in the morning edition of the New York Post. The ball was famous for its attractive, ambitious women who were out to snare a rich husband or sugar daddy. However, in all of Rich's years he had never encountered a woman so bold that she would strip off most of her clothes and make a public display.

"I'll take care of this," Rich said as he made his way in Anna's direction. Most of The Institute group followed after him, not wanting to miss how he was going to handle a tall, naked, bosomy brunette. Izzy did not follow with the group. He and Oksana stayed where they were, standing on the outskirts of the noise and chaos which grew louder by the second. It gave Adolf the opportunity to approach them unnoticed. When Adolf was directly in back of Oksana he reached into his jacket and pulled out a semi-automatic pistol. He placed the barrel at the back of her neck and leaned close to her ear.

"Make one noise and it will be your last," Adolf hissed.

Izzy sensed the danger and whirled around to see the gun pointed at the back of Oksana's head. He remained still, not knowing what to do. Adolf turned his head and looked into Izzy's eyes.

"You are both coming with me. We are all going to walk slowly out of the ballroom so as not to attract attention."

Izzy nodded. He and Oksana walked towards one of the exits with Adolf not a step behind. A moment later they were out on 5th Avenue. For a moment Adolf panicked, he had not planned this far ahead. The rental car was several blocks away in an underground lot. He decided that he had no choice but to make his two captives walk to the car. He hoped that Anna would realize where he had gone. If not, he was certain that she would find her way to the Gilly estate in Connecticut on her own.

"The notes won't help you," Izzy stated as Adolf started them down the street.

"And they won't help you," Adolf snarled back, "if I kill you here. No more talking!"

They had walked less than half a block when they passed an old, drunken man. The man was half curled in a ball, seemingly asleep or drunk. His clothes were tattered and the bill of a dirty Yankee's baseball cap was pulled low to cover part of his face. Oksana and Izzy stepped past him without incident. Adolf, however, couldn't resist spitting on him as he walked by. As Adolf sneered, the drunken man reached out and tripped him. As Adolf fell, the man stood up quickly. In his hand was his own pistol which he aimed carefully.

"Herr Kaiser, drop your weapon."

Adolf looked up and found himself face-to-face with Pieter Heneke. The blood drained from Adolf's face, certain that what he was seeing was a Halloween ghost.

"I said drop it," Heneke repeated. "I should have ended your madness years ago. I will shoot you."

Reluctantly, Adolf put down his gun. Izzy was as surprised to see Heneke as Adolf was. A silver Lincoln Town Car pulled up beside the street and the back door was pushed open from inside. Heneke stepped to Adolf's gun and kicked it into the street. He then nudged it into a grate covered storm sewer and listened for the splash. He walked back to the open door of the car and invited Izzy and Oksana to get inside.

"Doctor Slesinger, Doctor Zibrova. I think we should be leaving."

Without a word of objection, Izzy and Oksana got in the back seat of the car. Heneke followed them, keeping his gun pointed at Adolf as he closed the back door. The car zipped down 5th Avenue, leaving behind a furiously bewildered Adolf Kaiser. In the front seat of the car were Ilya Babekov and Jean Dulac. Jean smiled broadly at Izzy. The expression of disbelief on his face was priceless. Mouth half open, eyes searching for answers.

"This all must be a very great shock," Heneke began. "But not as much of a shock as it must have been to Adolf. He is not the only one who watches closely. We knew if we followed him, he would eventually lead us to you. "

Izzy continued to stare at Jean. "What happened? You just disappeared. Your pillow was soaked with blood."

"I was abducted by Ilya, who also set me free. It is all very complicated."

Back at the Waldorf things were returning to normal. Anna Kaiser put her clothing back on and was escorted by security to the hotel exit and told never to return. Out on the street she reunited with Adolf. He quickly told her what had happened and they both headed towards the car. For Anna it was especially difficult in the four inch heels. Inside the Waldorf, Rich Levine walked the entire ballroom a dozen times. He assumed that Izzy had decided to leave the party earlier than usual. Therefore, he rejoined the guests seated at his table and began eating, unaware that Izzy had been whisked away.

There was still heavy traffic on the lower level of the George Washington bridge and Ilya fought to get the big Lincoln into the lanes that led to the upper level. The cars on top of the bridge moved slowly, but at least they moved. Fortunately, as soon as the car was on I-95 in New Jersey, the traffic began to break up. Ilya took the second exit onto 9 West. A moment later he exited in Englewood Cliffs.

A heavy metal gate slid open and the Lincoln entered the property. The car severed a laser beam of light which automatically closed the gate. The driveway was long and steep. At the top was an enormous, Victorian style mansion which had been built on top of the cliffs that look over the Hudson River. Ilya stopped the car in front of the house. Half a dozen armed guards stood on the front porch. Each was armed with M-16 assault rifles and they all wore black cargo pants, black polo shirts, and black windbreaker-style jackets.

"We're here," Doctor Heneke said as he pushed open the back door and stepped out. Oksana and Izzy followed cautiously. Jean got out of the front seat and joined them. Izzy turned away from the house and looked out over the river. The night sky was bright, illuminated by the millions of lights burning in Manhattan. Izzy stared at the city for a long time, marveling at its beauty. It was the tall presence of Brian Crighton that snapped Izzy out of his trance.

"Beautiful, isn't it?"

Izzy turned and surprise returned to his face as he tilted his head skyward to look at the young mathematician. "How?"

"Long story," Brian sighed as he gazed towards the George Washington Bridge. "That's got to be the most frightening place on the planet right now."

Izzy looked towards the bridge. "You mean because of the traffic? It only seems that way to out-of-towners. Plenty of places worse than the GW."

"Not the bridge," Brian chuckled. "The city."

"The city?" Izzy repeated, waiting for more information.

Brian nodded. "Ground zero. The mother of all melting pots. From here, Mengele cells can touch every population on the planet."

Brian walked to the very edge of the cliff and pointed towards New York. "A young woman from Zaire has a brief fling with rock star from England after a concert at the Garden. The rock star has encounters with women in every American city he travels to, and then heads home and does it all over again in Britain."

Heneke called to Izzy and Brian from the front porch. Oksana, Jean, and Ilya had already gone inside, leaving Izzy to talk with Brian alone. "Gentlemen, we are about to get started."

The dining room inside the mansion was literally the largest that Izzy had ever seen. He guessed the big, round, white marble table could easily seat eighty people. At the present time there were only three; Anna Brovsky, Claude Thomae, and Rodney Bassett. Izzy ran to Claude and hugged him as tears welled in his eyes. Claude pulled him close and whispered in his ear.

"I am glad to see you too, mon ami."

Heneke came in from a side entrance with Oksana and Jean. "Let's all sit down," Heneke instructed. The entire group bunched tightly. Izzy sat in the middle chair, his eyes darting from scientist to scientist.

"Haven't seen ghosts before, av ya?" Rodney chuckled in his thick British accent.

Izzy's gaze fell on Claude. "CNN said you were dead. We saw the bodies, the destruction. Jean was hysterical."

"The whole thing was staged," Claude replied.

"Staged?"

"We knew that the Reich was planning an attack," Heneke explained. "But I also know Adolf Kaiser. We blew the place up and let him think that it was his people."

"I saw bodies." Izzy shot back. "And helicopters."

"Cadavers," Anna Brovsky interjected.

"The helicopters were ours," Claude added. "As were all the medical personnel. The media was kept at a distance. However, we did notify the French government about an hour before we detonated."

"The whole thing was a ruse?" Izzy couldn't believe what he was hearing.

"Better that they think all our work was destroyed."

Izzy rubbed both temples with the fingers of both hands. He could feel the early tremors of a massive migraine coming on. "But that facility cost you millions."

"Hundred of millions," Claude corrected. "But it couldn't be helped. We moved the computers, the lab gear, and the animals, everything that wasn't tied down. Still, it was a big loss."

"What now?" Izzy asked.

"That depends on what you have found. What was in those papers?"

Izzy spent the better part of two hours explaining what he had learned from Mengele's papers. He also stated that there was still some German left to be translated, but didn't think anything meaningful was going to be added. Each new fact sent Heneke deeper and deeper into depression. It was like he was reliving the whole experience of the experiments, of the horrors. Izzy also confirmed his deepest fear, that his theory was backwards. He spent half his life believing that Mengele shifted cellular biochemistry, creating a new type of cell. This new cell became the host to a new, never before encountered virus which was labeled HIV. However, now it seemed more plausible that Mengele had done something far simpler. It was entirely possible that Mengele created HIV by simply combining other viruses together. That would account for HIV's high mutagenicity. What he had labeled a Mengele cell was actually a healthy cell which had simply been corrupted into manufacturing more virus. It certainly was more in keeping with the accepted model of viral reproduction.

Izzy finally finished speaking. The group took several long moments to consider the new information. Heneke was the first to speak.

"So Mengele created HIV? That is what you think?"

Izzy shook his head. "No, I don't. Look at what happens when you attack HIV with protease drug cocktails like your PIRT-I9. The drugs somehow force the virus to break down to proteins which hide themselves throughout cells. Stop the treatment and the virus reassembles. Even if you don't stop the treatment the virus still reassembles, only it's a bit different than it was before."

"So what is it you believe?" Claude asked as he scribbled notes on a pad of yellow lined paper.

"I believe that Mengele's original viral soup added, subtracted, or substituted a protein in the cellular chain. This gave birth to a new kind of cell, and this cell became host to HIV."

"But where did the HIV originally come from?" Claude countered.

Izzy threw his hand up in the air. "Could have come from anywhere. Maybe it's naturally occurring inside our bodies and this new, Mengele cell simply switched it on."

Rodney Bassett got out of his chair and began to walk little circles. Claude knew the pacing indicated that Rodney was about to say something of importance. In fact, the entire group had come to learn that their British colleague could only elucidate his idea while moving. It was almost as if the analytical part of his brain switched off when he took a seat.

"So it's still the same problem we had before," Rodney stated as the circles became tighter and tighter. "We need to fix the cell in order to control the virus."

"No," Izzy replied. "It's much more complicated. Every time HIV replicates, the messenger ribonucleic acid changes a little. Every single time! Even if we can eliminate Mengele cells, the virus will adapt."

Heneke glanced towards Claude who nodded almost imperceptibly. Heneke then turned towards Brian Crighton. "We're going to need new probabilities, and a time-table."

"I'll do my best, but I'm guessing it could take years. And that's using the new data compression anagrams. Assuming that they even work."

Heneke did not like what he had just heard. But like it or not, it left him with only one option. "Then we will go underground and disappear. All of us. Until we have an answer we can present to the world."

"Excuse me?" Izzy questioned. "Disappear? I'm not disappearing anywhere. And the world needs to know about this now!"

Heneke stood from his chair and walked to the large bay window. He looked out towards the lights of New York City. "What will you tell them? That Mengele is responsible for HIV. You'll be labeled a madman."

Izzy got up and walked to where Heneke was standing. "I've been called worse. You can't honestly believe that your little group has the resources to do this alone."

Heneke turned towards Izzy. "We must do it! We must! And I want you with us!"

Izzy shook his head. "What happens when you're gone? How long until the Mengele cells shut you down?"

"Maybe tomorrow, maybe never. If you're saying you want to be project leader I will gladly have you. I'm certain the others feel the same."

Izzy glanced towards the table. Everyone except Oksana nodded, even Claude Thomae. "You're not hearing me. The world needs to know. The sooner the better."

Claude joined Izzy and Heneke at the window. "They will not believe you, or us, mon ami. Now is not the time."

Izzy turned to look at Brian, Anna, and Rodney. He screamed at them. "If not now? When?" The three of them remained silent and Izzy threw his hands in the air in disgust. "Do what you want. But I know what I have to do, with you or without you!"

Izzy stormed out of the room and Heneke shouted after him. "We will not support you. You will be on your own!"

Izzy was already a quarter mile down the road when Ilya

caught up to him in the car. In the back seat were Oksana and Jean, Brian Crighton was riding shotgun. It took a lot of convincing, but Izzy finally climbed in back and settled himself between the two women. However, he was so furious he didn't say anything. Brian swiveled around in his seat and looked at Izzy.

"We put it to a vote. Pieter, Claude, Anna and Rodney decided you're on your own."

"They did not let me vote," Oksana added, "But I would have told them that they are wrong."

"My father didn't like it, but I told him I supported you," Jean added from the other side.

Izzy rested his chin in his hand and shook his head. "What about you, Brian?"

"I'm a mathematician who deals in probability. There is no logic in waiting any longer. I will work with you to gather as much evidence as we can and we must present what we know. Waiting will only make it worse."

Izzy agreed. "But what if Heneke's right. It could get ugly for us."

Brian laughed. "Ugly? I'm the guy who passed up a $70 million dollar NBA contract. The world already thinks I'm nuts."

"And I am with you as well," Ilya added from the front seat. "In Russia, all we ever do is wait and things go from bad to worse."

Chapter 18

It was past midnight when Adolf and Anna reached the Buchanan compound in southeastern Connecticut. Gilly Buchanan, a transplanted Southerner, was a wealthy industrialist who had made a fortune supplying OEM parts to defense contractors. He also happened to be a white supremacist who had no love for Negroes. His seventy acre estate in the woods was a safe haven for skinheads, neo-Nazis, and an assortment of other hate groups. Southeastern Connecticut made for a great location. It was very rural, still almost wilderness, yet it was close to Norwich and New London.

The shipyard in New London used to be the largest employer. Thousands of white, blue-collar men had been thrown out of work, with little prospects in a white-collar, high-tech world. Resentment in the area ran high. Gilly funneled the resentment into hatred. He pointed to the nearby Indian tribes with billion dollar casinos as proof of how far the white race had fallen in America. He blamed loss of defense industry jobs on the Jews, who were secretly trying to weaken the moral fabric of America and dismantle its military capability. He blamed Blacks for sucking billions out of the economy in welfare payments that they didn't deserve. Therefore, when the neo-Nazi grapevine brought him news about Adolf Kaiser's plans, he offered his full assistance.

It was mostly young skinheads who stayed at the compound. For the most part they were in their late teens or early twenties. They spent most days drinking beer, having paint ball wars, or practicing with semi-automatic weapons deep in the woods. Gilly gave free room and board, paid for beer, ammunition, even gave them cash so they could go out whoring. He became like a father figure to an entire generation of displaced, angry, young white men. His reach extended far beyond Connecticut, with skinheads coming from all over the United States. On any given day there could be 700 or 800 people staying on the property. However, the inner circle of those who Gilly trusted was much smaller, probably less than a dozen.

Even though it was late when Adolf and Anna arrived, all the lights in the main house were still on. Gilly came out on the front porch, accompanied by five tough looking skinheads. The boys' hormones kicked in at the sight of Anna, still dressed in her black leather dress and pointed heels.

"Well, well, well, what do we have here?" The question came from a skinhead dressed in a black leather jacket. He was obviously Gilly's pointman. He was tall and muscular, with a couple days worth of beard on his face. He walked a tight circle around Adolf and Anna who remained calm and still. He stopped directly in front of Anna and smiled, showing off the yellowest teeth she had ever seen. "Never had me any German cunt before."

Without warning of any kind, Anna slammed her right knee into the young man's groin and he crumpled. She took a step to his side, lifted her foot, and drove the pointed steel tip of her heel into the side of his neck. She pulled her foot up and a fountain of blood sprayed from his mortally torn carotid artery.

"Shit!" one of the other skinheads cried as he ran to the side of his fallen friend. Half a minute later the blood spurts became a trickle and the young man lay dead. The other skinheads fell silent. Gilly took it all in, like a poker player studying a hand. Anna walked to him and stared into his eyes.

"Perhaps you would also like some German cunt?" she sneered with contempt, taking an instant dislike to Gilly Buchanan.

"My dear, I am a Southerner. In the South we know how to treat a lady. My apologies for that rude outburst. I assure you that it will not happen again." Gilly instructed the others to dispose of the dead man and then invited Anna and Adolf inside. Adolf had still not said a single word. Like Gilly, he remained silent to study and probe for weaknesses while Anna did the talking. Gilly led them into his private office and had them take a seat. Anna explained about their problem and Gilly offered men to help with Slesinger's abduction.

"Your brother doesn't say much. He a mute?"

Anna ignored the question. "We are going to need three of your best men, heavily armed."

Gilly continued to stare at Adolf. "A mute. I thought real Nazis didn't tolerate cripples."

Adolf simply blinked but said nothing. While Gilly concentrated on Anna, Adolf slipped his hand around the revolver that was harnessed to his waist. He lifted the gun, aimed at Gilly's forehead, and pulled the trigger. The bullet ripped into Gilly's skull and smashed out the back side. He was dead before his body even slumped over to the side and fell from the chair. Anna stared at her brother in amazement.

"What have you done?"

"He was an imbecile. The Reich does not need the assistance of American trash."

"Where will we get help?"

"We don't need help," Adolf replied. "I've had a chance to think it out. Heneke means nothing to us. He sought Slesinger out because the American is the only one who might be able to reverse Mengele's work. We eliminate Doctor Slesinger and Heneke has no hope."

"You think we can do it by ourselves?" There was more than a little skepticism in Anna's voice.

"I'll explain it on the ride back to New York."

Adolf and Anna left Gilly's office. They locked his door before they closed it. Most of the lights in the compound were now out. No one even noticed as they drove away in the darkness. It wasn't until morning that Gilly Buchanan's corpse was found.

A loud crashing sound woke Jean Dulac and she jumped up from Izzy's sofa on which she had been sleeping. She had taken the sofa, Izzy and Oksana had gone to the bedroom, Brian Crighton had stretched his frame out on the living room floor, and Ilya had taken the night watch. Jean and Ilya had agreed that one of the them would always remain armed and awake, just in case the Reich decided to make a move. The loud crash had been caused by Brian, who had removed the metal cover from Izzy's computer. When he pulled out the last screw, the cover slipped out of his hands and smashed to the floor.

"You are dismantling Izzy's computer?" Jean asked in hushed voice as to not awaken anyone else.

"Not dismantling, enabling," Brian replied as he slipped a tiny eyeglass screwdriver underneath the circuit board. "The chip guys build buses into their circuitry to keep the flow of data under control. But if I disable the buses we can get more clock speed."

Jean was lost. Computers were outside her element. "Do we need more clock speed?"

"We do if I'm going to run a new probability. Gotta ramp this baby up for more calculations per second."

Izzy stumbled out of his bedroom, dressed in a multi-colored terry cloth bathrobe. The sound of the shower in the bathroom had woken him. He lay awake for almost half an hour, wondering who could be taking such a long shower so early in the morning. The crash, and then the voices finally forced him to get out of bed. He was more than a bit disturbed to see that Brian had laid the guts of his computer open.

"That's a $3000 machine you're busy dissecting. God, Brian, I only bought the thing a couple months ago."

Brian looked up from his huddled posture over the circuit board. "Don't be getting yourself in a lather, Izzy. I'm fixing it."

"It wasn't broken!"

"Okay, I'm modifying. You should have gone with a Mac. Then I wouldn't need to be doing this."

Izzy was about to reply with a snide comment but the continuing sound of the shower had him distracted. "Who's taking a shower?"

Jean stared at Brian and then looked around the room. "Must be Ilya, he decided to take the first watch."

"Well, he's been in there forever," Izzy replied as he moved to the bathroom door. He knocked but there was no reply. He knocked again, only this time much louder. Still there was only the sound of running water.

Jean reached under the cushion of the sofa and retrieved her handgun. She motioned with her head for Izzy to move away from the door. Cautiously she moved over and placed a hand on the door knob. She twisted, finding the door unlocked. She pushed the door open and let out a loud gasp which brought Izzy closer. Ilya was face down in the tub. Only the hot water had been turned on and the bathroom resembled a sauna, with condensation dripping everywhere. Izzy moved past Jean and reached a hand inside the shower curtain and shut off the water. He was cautious, not touching the body, but inspecting with his eyes.

"I'm calling the police," he said after a protracted moment. "I don't want anyone touching anything."

It took a few minutes before Izzy was able to locate Detective Adam Rodman's card.

Twenty minutes later Rodman was in Izzy's apartment, accompanied by two uniformed officers and a forensics detective.

Rodman took pictures of everything in the bathroom. The bathroom window was open, but it was way too small for anyone to use for entry or exit. The forensics expert asked for Rodman's help, and together they lifted Ilya Babekov's body from the tub. The steaming hot water had kept his blood from coagulating and delayed the full effects of rigor mortis. Therefore, the body was still quite pliable. They laid Ilya's corpse down on the floor, on his back, and began an examination. There was no sign of struggle, no bullet or stab wounds, but the bruising around the shoulders gave the cause of death away. Ilya's neck was snapped.

While Rodman continued to gather evidence, Izzy huddled with Oksana, Brian, and Jean in the kitchen.

"How did they get in here without us hearing anything?"

"I don't know about anyone else, but I was beat," Brian replied.

"And we had the bedroom door closed," Oksana added.

"People break into my house, tiptoe through the living room, and viciously kill a 260 pound man who made a living as a soldier in the Russian secret forces. And none of us hears a thing?"

"It was my fault," Jean admitted out loud. "I should have stayed awake with Ilya. I know how dangerous these people are."

The phone rang which caused Izzy to jump. It was still before seven in the morning. No one would call at that hour. He picked up the receiver and pressed it to his ear. "Hello?"

"Doctor Slesinger, this is Adolf Kaiser. I'm assuming that you have found my gift?"

"You are very sick! "

"We could have killed all of you. That traitorous Russian scum was simply a warning. I would like to make you a proposition."

"I'm listening."

"I would like you to leave The Institute and come work for me."

"Drop dead," was Izzy's only reply before he slammed the receiver back into its cradle. Everyone in the kitchen was staring at him.

"Kaiser wants me to come work for him."

"You worry him," Jean stated. "With Heneke against him, he needs another scientist to continue perfecting AIDS vaccines."

Adam Rodman walked into the kitchen. He was in a pretty foul mood as he addressed Izzy. "Seven weeks ago a Dutch scientist puts a gun in his mouth and blows his brains out in your office. Now I have a dead Russian who slipped illegally into this country. You had better start talking, and I had better start liking your answers!"

The discussion lasted more than an hour, with Rodman filling his police notepad to overflowing. Izzy did his best to explain, with the others adding details that Izzy missed. They all did their best to keep the science simple so the detective would understand. Still, Rodman had a lot of problems with the story he was hearing and it had nothing to do with the science.

"Nazis? You want me to believe that Nazis are trying to kill off everyone but themselves."

"I know how it must sound, but it's true," Izzy stated seriously.

"And you say this Adolf Kaiser was responsible for the body in there?"

Izzy nodded. "That phone call a little while ago, that was him. He boasted about it!"

Rodman rocked back and forth from foot to foot. His gaze shifted from Izzy, to Jean, Oksana and Brian. He searched their faces for twitches, nervous ticks, anything that might suggest they were all lying, that they had conspired together to hide the real truth. He found nothing.

"What's it going to take to convince you?" Izzy asked.

"Some hard evidence would be a start. I'm finding it very hard to believe that two people could break in here and murder a man without any of you hearing a sound."

Jean replied to Rodman's comment. "Killing silently is easy, assuming that you know what you're doing. I can assure you that Adolf and his sister are very practiced."

"I'm calling an artist. I want descriptions on both of them. And I'm putting round-the-clock protection on you, Doctor Slesinger. You don't take a shit without me knowing about it!"

"We're all going to move into The Institute. We've got twenty-four hour security now, both in the lobby and patrolling the labs."

"Okay," Rodman agreed. "But I want to be kept in the loop. Anything happens, you page me!"

Izzy agreed and Rodman walked towards the door. He hesitated before leaving. "Forensics called the coroner. They'll come pick up the body. After they leave, the apartment will be sealed as a crime scene. You won't be able to get back in here for a couple of days."

It was a little after nine when Izzy and the others reached The Institute. Because of the stricter security measures, it took a long time to clear Oksana, Jean, and Brian inside. It became even more difficult to get them a full time security clearance and their own building passes. To complicate matters even further, security wanted no part of people requiring protection around-the-clock. The head of security explained there was no procedure for it. Scientists were not supposed to stay in the building past midnight, unless they had a critical deadline to meet. Security also explained that the staff was neither trained nor certified in personal protection. Such training was required by the union who wouldn't tolerate exposing untrained employees to additional hazards. After a great deal of argument from Rich Levine and Izzy, the head of security agreed to provide protection for one day. After that, Izzy and the others would need to find someplace else to stay.

Izzy spent the rest of the morning giving a tour of the facility to the others. Oksana found the liquid crystal holographic projector fascinating. It looked like a hollowed-out television, with liquid crystal projection screens covering all the interior surfaces. Izzy demonstrated its operation by projecting the double helix structure of human DNA. In the center of the box a three dimensional image of the DNA structure appeared. Its entire protein chain had been mapped out using different colors for each protein. By using a control joystick, Izzy had the ability to make the molecule rotate. He also had the ability to superimpose amino-acid chains on top of the protein chains. However, with the amino-acids there were big gaps which corresponded to information that was still unknown.

It was the Hygatchi super-computer that Brian fixated on. Hygatchi was the only bio-integrated computer in the world, using myelin in its data-transmitters. Myelin, the same substance in human nerve cells, could move lots of data quickly. A price tag of over $50 million made the computers extremely rare. The few that existed in America were owned by pharmaceutical companies. Therefore, mathematicians like Brian could only dream about running complex probabilities on a system that was capable of half a trillion calculations per second.

"You think they'll let me run a probability?"

Izzy nodded. "Right now we've got it working on transcription errors. After this trial is over I'll set you up with one of our programmers."

"That would be great," Brian beamed as he stared at the computer like it was a new found love.

Jean was the one who brought everyone back to the business at hand. "I'm thinking we need to find someplace safe to stay. Adolf and Anna won't wait long before making their next move."

They all sat in a circle, discussing and dismissing various places which could provide safe harbor. After ten minutes they had gone through all options and still couldn't think of an acceptable spot. Izzy wracked his brain and came up with an idea. He would call that Israeli agent he met in New Haven. The Israelis were experts in this sort of thing. Unfortunately, all Izzy could remember was the last name, Katz. He tried calling both the United Jewish Appeal and the Anti-Defamation League. Neither organization was able to offer any assistance. Out of desperation he called the office of the Israeli ambassador to the United Nations.

It was a very awkward phone call. Izzy did his best to explain without going into too many details. The ambassador's assistant, who sounded very young, spoke with deep Israeli accent. When Izzy mentioned that Katz was in the Mossad, the Israeli secret service, the line of the phone went dead. Izzy stared at it for a moment, puzzled over why they would have disconnected him. He put the phone back down and tried to think of other ways to reach Mr. Katz. It was less than half a minute when his phone began to ring. Instead of picking up the receiver, Izzy hit the speaker phone button.

"Hello?"

"Shalom. You wanted to speak with me?"

"Mr. Katz?"

"Yes. What can I do for you?"

Izzy explained about needing someplace safe to stay. Doron listened, hardly saying a word. When Izzy finished, Doron offered his help.

"We have a place. In Brooklyn. I will make the arrangements and I will call you back."

It was a small white house on a side street in Coney Island. From the front porch, Izzy could see the famous Coney Island boardwalk. He surveyed the neighborhood. There were only seven homes on the short block which terminated in a dead-end. Past the dead-end lay a vacant lot which was overgrown with weeds. In back of the house was a concrete playground. The playground, which had four basketball hoops and a wall for handball was surrounded by a fifteen foot metal fence. The entrance to the playground was on a different street at the opposite end of the fencing.

Doron Katz stood with Izzy on the front porch. He pointed his finger at the three houses across the street. "Relocated Russian Jews live in those homes." Doron turned to his right and pointed at the house next door. "That house belongs to us." He then turned to his left. "That house belongs to the New York Police department. They use it for undercover work. Right now it is empty."

Izzy looked up the street. "Seems like a good place. Not much traffic."

Doron nodded. "No traffic. None of the Russians owns a car. You see or hear one on this block, it could mean trouble."

"What about my car?"

Doron looked towards the curb in front of the house.

"On the street? No way. What if it gets stolen?"

"This is a quiet, Russian neighborhood. I do not think you have to worry. If you need to go shopping, always go in pairs. To get to Manhattan I would advise you to take the subway. We've seen quite a few people run off the roads in New York."

"Very reassuring," Izzy commented as he turned to enter the house. Doron walked towards the car he had used to transport Izzy and the others. He stopped before opening the driver's door and added a final comment. "I'm flying out to Tel Aviv this evening. I will be back in New York in three days."

Izzy nodded and entered the house. If it was small on the outside, tiny would describe the inside. The main living area was about 12 x 12. There was a harvest gold colored sofa up against the wall, obviously a survivor from an age long since past. A large poster of former Israeli prime minister Yitzak Rabin hung on the wall over the sofa. The only other thing in the living room was a twenty-one inch television, which was quite modern. There was an archway that opened into a small kitchen at the back of the house. Off to the left was a hallway with three doors. Two of the doors led into bedrooms, and the third was for the bathroom.

Oksana and Jean decided to share a bedroom, leaving Brian to bunk with Izzy. The two women thought it best that the men were together. If the Reich should somehow break in during the middle of the night, they would first and foremost be after Izzy. Even though Jean felt more than able to handle any kind of threat, Brian would present a more formidable appearance. An assailant would think twice before attacking someone who stood almost seven feet tall. Besides, Oksana was not terribly comfortable with the idea of another women in the same room with Izzy, every night, for what could be an extended period.

The first thing that Izzy noticed was the heavy iron gates that were over every window, excepting for the two front windows in the living room. The gates were the same type used in apartment buildings all over New York. They were supposed to prevent intruders from breaking in via a fire escape. However, these gates were much stronger and heavier. Worse, they were difficult to open.

Izzy walked into the bedroom and found Brian busy scribbling a new probability calculation on a pad of yellow lined paper. Izzy walked to the gate in the bedroom and used both hands to slide it open. It was difficult to move, and the latch took almost a minute to unlock.

"These gates might be good for keeping people out, but unfortunately, they are also very good at keeping us in."

Brian looked up from his yellow pad. "Huh?"

"Let's say someone breaks in. The back door in the kitchen is locked shut. That means the windows are the only route of escape. If we were in a hurry they'd be useless."

"Uh huh," Brian replied as he looked own at the paper again and continued on with his work. He was on the verge of establishing the parameters for his new AIDS probability and wasn't about to be distracted by thoughts of someone breaking in. He compartmentalized the images of Adolf and the Reich and tucked them away in a remote corner of his brain. It was as if they had been placed in a faraway state.

Tempers were beginning to boil over at the Buchanan compound in southeastern Connecticut. News of Gilly's murder spread quickly, transmitted by cellular telephone and CB radios. By midmorning there were almost 600 white supremacists gathered together in a large barn on Gilly's property. Gilly had converted the insides of the barn into a meeting hall. At the far end stood a podium, from which Gilly often extolled the virtues of white America to his followers. There was an abundance of both anger and fear, etched into the faces of many who had assembled. Mr. Buchanan, Gilly, had been their public benefactor, the sugar daddy of all sugar daddies. With him gone, what would become of them?

The crowd in the barn split into two halves as Terry and Leroy Hebb entered. The Hebb brothers were big, powerful men. Leroy stood 6'3" and weighed 260 pounds, and yet was called a runt by his older brother. Terry was almost 6'6" and close to 300 pounds. He was literally a giant of a man. He and his brother owned the largest independent waste disposal company in the southeast. Hebb Trash & Garbage owned the waste business in five southern states: Louisiana, Tennessee, Arkansas, Alabama, and South Carolina. It was probably the only waste company of its size that was free of mobster control or the unions. Terry made sure that it stayed that way by employing only good old white boys. At one time there had been talk of running Terry for an Imperial Wizard position within the Klu Klux Klan. He declined, primarily because he felt the Klan had become too gentle an organization, too accommodating.

The initial investment capital for the waste business came from Gilly Buchanan. Gilly became a second father to the two young men whose own father walked out when they were children. Most of the Hebb attitude came from Gilly, who encouraged Terry's strong arm tactics. Therefore, When Gilly's body was found, the first call went out to Terry. Ten minutes after the call, Terry and Leroy headed for their private chartered jet. It was a two hour flight from the little airfield in South Carolina to T.F. Green airport outside Providence, Rhode Island. Leroy rented a brand new Chevy pickup and let his brother get a little sleep on the ride to Connecticut. Unfortunately, the hour long nap only made Terry feel more tired and irritable.

The crowd hushed silent as Terry stood at the microphone. Terry's eyes shifted round the room, searching for the guilty party. "A great man has been taken from us. Taken! Where the hell is Bobby?"

Bobby Clampett, Gilly's head of security, sheepishly made his way towards the front. Bobby also hailed from South Carolina. He was an ex-combat marine sergeant who had been thrown out of the service for inciting his platoon to beat and humiliate a gay soldier. He was qualified on every type of hand weapon within the U.S. arsenal, and held little reluctance in using them. Even though he was a muscular 5'11", he looked tiny standing next to Terry. The fact that he cowered made him seem even smaller.

"And where the fuck were you when this happened?"

"The Last Tail," Bobby replied in a very soft voice.

Terry's anger exploded. "Out chasing pussy while some fucking kraut fucks Gilly?" Terry reached out with both his giant hands and placed one each side of Bobby's head. With all his might he began to squeeze his hands together like a vise. It wouldn't be the first time that he had crushed a man's skull with his bare hands. When he saw Bobby's eyes begin to bulge he stopped. He pulled his hands away and Bobby collapsed to the floor, gasping for air. "I'm giving you one hour to find the fucking kraut. One hour! Then you, me and Leroy are going to fuck him up!" Terry stormed off the podium with Leroy closely behind.

It didn't take long for Bobby to trace the license plate of Anna and Adolf's car to a rental company at J.F.K. airport in New York. He also got a list of skinhead and neo-Nazi organizations in the Big Apple. When the hour was up, he brought the information to Terry who studied it for a minute.

"Get some guns. A couple of automatic pistols, an AK-47, and bring a rocket launcher. Put 'em in the truck. Leroy and me will be ready in ten minutes."

While the Hebb's were speeding towards New York, Adolf and Anna Kaiser were headed for the Hamptons in Long Island. Adolf used his cell phone and called the estate of Franz Veldheim. Franz gladly agreed to assist Adolf in any way that he could. His friendship with Adolf went back many years. Franz came from a wealthy Austrian family, a family that heavily supported Hitler's doctrines of Aryan purity. During the 1960s, Austrians got caught up in the wave of social consciousness that was sweeping the rest of the world. All at once there were a million ideologies to choose from. Franz worked tirelessly to maintain the ideals of a pure Aryan race. His name was always in the press and by the end of the decade he had gravitated towards politics.

At about the same time, the Reich in Germany was crumbling. Anti-Semitism had fallen out of fashion with young Germans who were more in step with high-tech than Heil Hitler. Each passing day brought more immigrants and Germany was being transformed into a melting pot. Adolf had not yet become involved with the family business. He spent many years steeped in depression. He was arrested twice, both times for assaults on black men from France. He contemplated suicide on more than one occasion. His life changed when he read excerpts of a powerful, pro-Aryan speech delivered by a rising politician in Austria. The next day he was on a train towards Vienna.

Adolf spent the better part of five years working with Franz. When Franz was named Austrian ambassador to the United States, the two parted company. After five years, Adolf had tired of Austria. The family had offered him a position in the pharmaceutical business and Adolf was eager to return to Germany. He came back to a country that was seriously contemplating reunification between east and west. Adolf was opposed to reunification, realizing that it would weaken Aryan purity even further. He attended demonstrations and spoke out publicly. What he discovered was a large group of young men who had become disenfranchised with this new Germany. Almost single-handedly he organized them and the neo-Nazi skinhead movement was born.

Those were busy years, but Adolf remained in constant contact with Franz. On more than one occasion, Veldheim flew to Germany at Adolf's request. He delivered fiery, pro-Aryan speeches in order to keep the young skinheads' passion at a boil. One of those speeches was secretly taped by a reporter who had slipped into the meeting. The speech was printed in a Berlin newspaper, and then reprinted all over the world. It was quite an embarrassment to the Austrian government. It got worse when that reporter turned up dead, his young throat slashed from ear to ear, and a swastika cut into his forehead. While there was no direct link to Veldheim, the government was not willing to risk any more condemnation in the eyes of the world. Therefore, Veldheim was asked to resign.

The news shocked Adolf Kaiser. He was even more shocked when Franz told him that he had sold the family estate in Austria and was moving to America. When questioned, Franz explained that he wanted to be out from under the magnifying glass. While Adolf and Franz continued to correspond with each other, they hadn't actually seen each other in over ten years. Therefore, they were both a bit nervous about seeing each other again.

Neatly cropped rose bushes lined the quarter mile driveway that led to the stately, turn-of-the-century colonial. By Hampton standards, the 7000 square foot home was small. However, the grounds were immense. The entire fenced property measured just under six acres, with three being heavily grown woods. The manicured lawn covered a bit more than an acre and various gardens filled the rest of the space. A full Olympic sized swimming pool, with redwood deck, was in back of the house. To the right side was a helipad and helicopter.

Adolf shuffled his feet as he touched a finger to the doorbell. Before the door opened he glanced over his shoulder and stared icily at his sister. "On your best behavior!"

The door opened and a maid welcomed them into the house. The hallway opened into a grand dining room, replete with an antique rosewood table and eighteen matching chairs. There was also a matching wine rack that reached from floor to ceiling and housed many dusty bottles. Over the table hung a massive crystal chandelier. The maid had Adolf and Anna take seats at the table and promised that Mr. Veldheim would be with them shortly. Then she disappeared.

Franz Veldheim entered the room dressed in gray gabardine pants and a burgundy woolen Icelandic sweater. He had remained trim over the years and was taller than Adolf remembered.

The once brown hair had turned a solid gray, almost matching the color of the trousers. Adolf stood and extended his hand. Franz grasped it and squeezed hard in the familiar test of power.

Adolf winced which brought a smile to Franz's face. It also made Anna smile. She enjoyed seeing her brother in inferior positions and she took an instant liking to Franz Veldheim.

"So?" Veldheim said as he reached for a bottle of Riesling and pulled it from the wine rack.

He then stepped to Anna's side and nodded approvingly. "Could this be your little sister?"

Anna stood and found that she was actually looking up a bit. She extended her hand which Franz lifted gently and kissed. The gesture normally would have made her sick. Hand kisses were the cloying overtures of rehearsed seducers. Just the type Anna delighted in killing. But this was different, unrehearsed. This friend of her brother's was quite different, and exciting.

Franz handed Anna a glass of wine and then gave one to Adolf. He filled his own glass last.

"Have you found anything?" Adolf asked impatiently.

Franz took a sip of the wine. "This Riesling is from a small vintner near Cologne." He turned his gaze towards Anna. "Long legs, fine body. Delicious!"

For just a moment Anna felt herself blush. She also felt a tinge in her gut, and a bit of wetness between her legs.

"Have you found anything?" Adolf repeated.

Franz turned towards his old friend. "Relax, Adolf. You are tired. Drink some wine. Later we will have some schnitzel and talk about old times."

Adolf got to his feet and began to pace. "I have no time for your hospitality. I must find Slesinger."

Franz put down his glass and walked to Adolf's side. He placed a hand on his shoulder. "We will find him. I have already placed a call to my friends in the embassy. If he is being hidden in New York, we will find him."

It was almost midnight when Adolf and Franz finished getting caught up on twenty-five years. Franz showed Adolf to his guest room and then returned to the sitting parlor where Anna remained. An evening filled with good German wine had wetted her appetite for sex. She was seated in a white leather, swiveling recliner, silently sipping the last of the Riesling. The white leather of the recliner contrasted with the black leather garment she still wore. It was now a full two days since she had been able to change her clothes. The dress was the same one she wore to Gilly Buchanan's compound, and now she ached to strip the dress away.

Franz slipped back into the room silently, not sure if Anna was still awake. He stopped at the side of her chair, enchanted by the golden hair that fell half way down her back. "Anna, the maid has turned down your bed. You must be very tired."

Without saying anything, Anna rotated the chair so that she was now facing towards Franz. Deftly she moved her right hand to his gabardine encased crotch and her fingers slid open his zipper. A moment later she had claimed her prize which turgidly pulsed towards her face. She leaned forward and consumed it, running her tongue over and under the foreskin. Her lips and tongue pleasured Franz in a way he had forgotten was possible. As his climax approached, he tried to back away. Anna would not allow it. She clamped her lips tighter around his manhood, refusing to release him until she was rewarded with liquid protein.

The sound of shower water woke Anna from a deep sleep. When she opened her eyes she was a bit confused as to her location. Franz walked out of the bathroom dressed in a plush navy robe. A smile spread across Anna's face. While she remembered very little from the night before, it was obvious that she had been successful in seducing Franz. Or perhaps he had seduced her. He walked to the bed and kissed her lightly on the forehead. She returned the kiss by sliding her hand between the folds of his robe.

Franz chuckled and backed away. "Not this morning. I have arranged for a car to take you into Hampton Village after breakfast for some shopping. Both you and your brother need new clothes if you are going to go unnoticed."

After breakfast Franz gave Adolf and Anna a tour of the play-room in the basement. The room was actually a torture chamber, equipped with all sorts of restraining devices. Metal chains hung from concrete beams in the ceiling. Handcuffs had been welded to the metal chains. Anna inspected them closely and found little flecks of dried blood on the metal. She glanced at Franz who smiled in her direction. Could it be that he shared her passion for inflicting pain and suffering? That would be almost too good to be true.

Franz opened a door that led into a smaller room. He pointed towards the black metal machine built into the back wall. Anna and Adolf peered into the room. They glanced at each other, but neither knew what they were looking at.

"What is it?" Adolf asked.

"A medical waste incinerator," Franz replied. "This room is very effective in extricating answers, and even more effective in creating corpses. Corpses, I'm afraid, need to be disposed of discreetly."

Anna and Adolf were both very impressed. Franz glanced at his watch and then pushed his guests in the direction of the stairs. "I'm sure that the car is ready to take you into the village. I promise you will love it. It is an Aryan paradise."

Adolf looked at his friend skeptically as they all climbed the stairs. "An Aryan paradise? In America?"

Franz nodded. "Americans use economics to weed out the inferior. Here we have no Blacks, no Latinos, and the few token Jews are looked down upon. They are not allowed to join the best country clubs or marinas. Even if they have enough money, they don't stay in this community for long. They quickly learn that their kind is not welcome here."

"If only it were that simple everywhere," Adolf sighed.

"Enjoy the village, Adolf! You are among your own kind. When you get back I will have a surprise waiting for."

Going into Hampton Village was the first major mistake that Adolf and Anna made. Terry Hebb had called the bosses of every sanitation company with a contract in New York. He had given a very explicit description of both Adolf and Anna and had offered a finder's fee of $100,000 to any refuse worker who spotted them. Eastern Island Sanitation handled waste hauling for the businesses, restaurants, and private homes in the Hamptons. When their trucks rolled out at nine in the morning, each driver carried a description and photograph of both Adolf and Anna. The odds of them being in Long Island were slim, but no one was willing to pass up a chance at $100,000, tax free.

November was not a big month in The Hamptons. The tourists had long since left, and the seasonal homeowners had returned to their jobs and Central Park apartments in Manhattan. Therefore, Adolf and Anna shopped the boutiques almost by themselves. By eleven in the morning they had concluded shopping for clothes and were ready to return to Franz's house. However, the driver was not coming to pick them up until twelve. Anna stared out the window of the upscale furrier. Across the street was a coffee bar called Olde Bavaria. As she and Adolf left the furrier and waited at the crosswalk they were spotted by two garbage men who were emptying barrels into their truck. Both men raced to the cab of the truck and grabbed for their pictures and descriptions. When they both agreed it must be them, they called it in. Ten minutes later the dispatcher called back. He told the men to keep an eye on Adolf and Anna, to follow them in the truck if need be. But keep a safe distance.

Fortunately for the garbage men they did not have to follow in the truck for a long time.

Franz's home was only several miles outside the village. The men wrote down the address and departed. Both men smiled at each other knowingly. In their heads they were silently counting the money they were to receive.

The El-Al Boeing 747-300 touched down on the runway in London. The jet, which carried Doron Katz, was headed for Tel Aviv. London was a refueling stop where the plane would take on additional passengers. Passengers who had boarded in New York were allowed to get off the plane for what would be no more than an hour's wait. As soon as Doron was off the plane he was followed. He stopped to get a coffee and then entered a men's room. He put his coffee on a metal shelf above a sink and proceeded to the urinals on the opposite wall. He was busy relieving himself when a hand passed quickly over his coffee cup and dropped in a tiny white pill. The pill dissolved in the hot liquid without leaving a trace.

When Doron regained consciousness he found himself bound to an airplane seat. It took him a moment to clear his head. He was no longer on a commercial jet, but somehow had gotten on a private plane, a top-of-the line Learjet from the look of things. There were several young men with automatic weapons. Doron assessed the straps that had been used to bind him. They were sound. Therefore, he closed his eyes and pretended to still be drugged. His only chance for escape would depend on pouncing when the enemy least expected it. He had been with Mossad for almost four decades, and in that time had escaped from some pretty dicey situations. However, never had he encountered an enemy like Franz Veldheim.

Chapter 19

Izzy spent the entire day working on amino acid chains. His starting point was a comparison of sickle cell anemia and normal hemoglobin in a red blood cell:

Normal Hemoglobin
Valine-Histine-Leucine-Threonine-Proline-Glutamic Acid-Glutamic Acid-Lysine
Sickle Cell
Valine-Histine-Leucine-Threonine-Proline-Valine-Glutamic Acid-Lysine.

Izzy knew it was possible for Mengele to have discovered that a valine in place of a glutamic acid in the amino acid chain was responsible for sickle cell anemia. A similar replacement was responsible for Tay-Sacks disease, whose analysis was also within the capabilities of 1940s science. However, there was nothing in Mengele's journals that suggested he had accomplished replacement of an amino acid. Besides, The Institute had broken down the amino acid chains in the blood of hundreds of HIV positive patients and there were no anomalies. Izzy had traveled around the world, risked his life on numerous occasions, and the journals still didn't answer the mystery.

There was one peculiar entry in Mengele's journals that was repeated over and over again. Every couple of pages Mengele mentioned the "three little moons around the planet." No one at The Institute knew what to make of that. Rich Levine thought it must be a German code that Mengele used in case his journals fell into enemy hands. Izzy wasn't so sure it was code. It was repeated so often that it had to have significance. While he couldn't prove it, he was certain the answer was in that little phrase.

"You're not going to let this one go, are you?" Rich Levine questioned as he stared over Izzy's shoulder at the computer screen. "We're going to have to start calling you *spooky Mulder*." Rich's reference was to fictional FBI agent Fox Mulder from the paranormal television series 'The X-Files.' Like Izzy, agent Mulder was always chasing after hunches.

Izzy glanced back at Rich. "Then I'm supposing that would make you Dana Scully?"

Rich laughed. "The voice of scientific reason? I'll leave that role to your buddy, Dunlevy."

Izzy touched the computer screen. "Three little moons around the planet. It means something. I know it!"

"I'm telling you that it's German code. Maybe the CIA could break it, but we can't."

Izzy shook his head. If it's a code, why just this one repeated line? Everything else is straightforward. A lot of it is lousy science, but it's understandable."

Rich's pager beeped. "I don't know, Izzy. I don't know how you solve this one." Rich turned and walked back in the direction of his office.

Izzy, however, wouldn't let it go. He looked up at the clock which was rapidly approaching five in the afternoon. That meant in California it was a little before two. Izzy reached for his phone and dialed David Dunlevy's cellular number. Dunlevy picked it up the third ring.

"Dave, it's Izzy. I've got a problem."

"Can I call you back? I'm teaching my MB & B students right now."

"My brain won't work. Three small moons around a planet. What's it mean?"

Dunlevy repeated it. "Three small moons around a planet. I'll have to call you back."

Dave closed the cell phone, placed it back in his pocket, and turned around to face his students. All five were busy scribbling things in their notebooks. He watched curiously as his students exchanged glances and head shakes. These were his seniors in molecular biology and biophysics. They were the cream of the crop, the best young scientific minds that Dave had ever had. They were busy working out some type of problem, yet class had only started a minute before Izzy's call.

Vishnu Pajov's hand shot up in the air. Vishnu was the unofficial leader of the class. He was the best of the best. He was Pakistani and a scientific marvel. After graduation he was headed to Harvard for graduate work and a research fellowship. Many times Dave had mentioned Vishnu to Emily at home. He said his young student had a once-in-a-generation mind. The only one Dave could think of as a comparison was Izzy Slesinger. Vishnu was that good. Emily often shuddered at the thought of another Izzy Slesinger in the world.

"Yes Vishnu?"

"We've got the answer," Vishnu replied. "At least we think we do. Your question was a bit vague."

"My question? I didn't ask a question."

"Three moons around a planet," Vishnu shot back. The others in class nodded in agreement.

"Really," Dave replied with bemusement written on his face. "Enlighten me."

"Nucleotides. The triplet rule demands there be three nucleotides for each amino acid in a hemoglobin protein."

Dave's mouth dropped open. It was so obvious. That's probably why Izzy couldn't see it. Dave excused himself from the class and walked out into the hall. He flipped open the cell phone and touched *69. The phone automatically redialed Izzy.

"Izzy, I know what it means."

Izzy sat straight up in his chair and a chill ran down his spine as he listened. "What?"

"Nucleotides. Apply the triplet rule."

"You're a fucking genius," were Izzy's only words. He dropped his phone and whirled towards his computer. His fingers danced on the keyboard.

Valine coding: Guinine-Uricil-Guanine

Glutamic Acid Coding: Guanine-Adenine-Guanine.

Izzy grabbed the phone but Dave was no longer on the line. Having no one to speak to he shouted the news at the top of his lungs. "I've got it, you bastard! Now I know what you did."

When Izzy screamed, security came running. Rich Levine was right behind them.

"What? What?" Rich asked.

"I know what Mengele did," Izzy replied in a more normal tone of voice.

Rich shook his head and the security guards left Izzy's office.

"You going to keep me in suspense?"

"An amino acid is huge. I kept asking myself how Mengele could have possibly pulled off a substitution in a chain and still have a viable cell. The answer is he didn't. He went a lot smaller and targeted a nucleotide."

"And that's good news?" Rich asked with more than a touch of dread in his voice.

"Of course it's good news!" Izzy shouted back. "What's wrong with you?"

Rich Levine held up his index finger. "Had Mengele succeeded in changing just one amino acid, just one mind you, the search for it could have taken years. But if it's really down to a nucleotide, you might never find it. The permutations are limitless. Did he change one, two, or three of them." Rich paused to think for a second. "Maybe they're not changed at all, but simply reordered. How do you find something like that?"

"I don't know. But the first step is to see if I can produce a viable, reproducible cell." Izzy sat back down at the computer and accessed the work he had already completed. "Take a look at what happened when I modeled cellular division using a single replacement of an amino acid in blood hemoglobin."

Rich Levine stared at the screen as data began to appear.

Transcription error 101, Transcription error 209

Transcription error 5, Transcription error 31,

Transcription error 12.

"See what I'm talking about?" Izzy questioned. Let's assume Mengele was able to alter an amino acid in a cell. The new cell might be able to carry on functions like respiration, but it can't divide itself. It's not viable."

"Which of the amino acids did you try replacing?"

Izzy pulled out his list. "We've worked through the first 16. None of the offspring are viable."

It took Izzy about an hour to work through the sub-menus in the program. The system had been designed to model amino acid chains and wasn't well suited for nucleotide adaption. Brian Crighton knocked on Izzy's door at a little before six p.m. He had been given access to the computers and had lost himself in chaos theory calculations. Izzy motioned for Brian to come into his office.

"By the look on your face I'm guessing that you've figured out the probability of the Knicks winning a championship and it's not good."

"Not exactly. I've just extrapolated a time-line for the continued effectiveness of Heneke's protease inhibitor."

Izzy was almost afraid to ask. "Do I want to know this?"

"Probably not. 36 months, maybe 48. And then all hell is going to break lose."

"Meaning?"

"The virus will be completely therapy resistant."

Izzy looked stunned. It was the worst possible news. Even if he could somehow reverse the damage inside the cell, the virus itself was marching towards invincibility. Eliminating a cellular host might do nothing to prevent disease. In fact, it could very well make things worse.

Brian touched his finger to the window. "It's dark outside. You know what Katz told us about traveling at night. Could be vampires out there."

Izzy walked to the window. Brian was right, it was very dark. "Shit! I feel like a prisoner."

Brian nodded. "But better a live prisoner than a dead victim."

Izzy picked up the phone. "I know a police detective. I'll call and see if he can give us a lift back to Brooklyn."

Detective Rodman was only too happy to be of assistance. He called Izzy's office from The Institute's security desk at a little past 7 p.m. Izzy shut off his lights and walked out with Brian at his side. Izzy's computer program was still running. Forty minutes after Izzy left, a message appeared on the screen:

No Transcription errors.

Chapter 20

The front gate on Franz Veldheim's property slid shut and the big black Mercedes with tinted windows continued up the driveway. The car passed by the front of the house and continued to follow the road to the back of the house. It was a crisp, cold, moonless autumn night. The silence of night was shattered by the sound of a car door slamming, and a voice screaming *"Schnell! Schnell!"* Then there was only silence.

Inside the estate, Anna and Franz were finishing a late dinner. Adolf had excused himself to get in some night time firing practice on Franz's outdoor target range.

"You promised a surprise," Anna cooed seductively.

The phone that sat atop the credenza rang three times and was silent. It was a secret code, alerting Franz that people were in the playroom. A fiendish smile spread across his face. "Come Anna, let me introduce you to your surprise. We will get Adolf later."

Two muscular, dark-bearded Arabs kept a careful eye on Doron Katz. The men had shackled Doron's hands behind him with handcuffs and sat him in a big wooden chair, with big wooden arms. It was the only seat inside Franz's torture chamber. The Arabs both brandished automatic weapons. The only words either had spoken was the order of '*Schnell*.' They had been waiting with the Mercedes when the private jet touched down at the Hampton's airport. Doron was blindfolded and then hurried off the plane and into the car. Until he saw Veldheim walk into the room, he had no idea who had abducted him or why.

Franz tried to walk towards Doron but the Arabs blocked his path.

"One million Deutschmark," the bigger of the two demanded.

"*Morgan fruh.*" Franz told them that they would be paid tomorrow morning.

The Arab leveled his gun at Franz. "*Nein. Jetzt oder nie!*"

"Now or never? I do believe I'm being threatened."

"Believe it," the shorter Arab responded in clear British English. "We want our money."

Franz nodded. "Very well. Wait by your car. I will bring you what you have earned."

The two Arabs discussed it among themselves and agreed. A moment later they disappeared out the door. For the moment Franz ignored Doron and pulled Anna by the hand. He stopped when they were in front of a closed circuit television screen. Franz touched a button under the screen and it illuminated with the image of the two Arabs standing by their car.

"Arab mercenaries. Highly trained at these kind of abductions. They're not cheap, but there is no way to trace their activities. The best part of this is they are expendable."

The taller of the two Arabs paced nervously by the car. The shorter struck a match and lit a cigarette as he leaned against the front bumper of the Mercedes. On the other side of Franz's property, a three foot, steel kennel door was lifted automatically. Five Austrian Kuvatz made their way in a pack towards the main house. The agile, Saint Bernard-sized hunters had been trained from birth as human killing machines. Every shred of their normally docile behavior had long been beaten out.

The attack was swift, grisly, and efficient. The two largest dogs went for the taller Arab, and the three others went for his companion. The attack came with so much surprise that neither of the men could so much as scream. Within seconds, both had been knocked to the ground. Five sets of powerful canine teeth tore at flesh and zeroed in on two exposed necks. Spurting blood sent the dogs into a frenzy of biting and tearing. It was so vicious that Anna had to turn away from the monitor. Despite her love of mutilating victims, it was even more than she could bear.

As soon as it was over, the dogs fell silent. One by one they gave each body a final sniff. Satisfied that both prey were dead, the dogs headed towards the kennel, knowing that they would each be praised and rewarded.

Franz left the monitor and finally turned his attention to Doron. He motioned for Anna to join him. "Do you know who we have here, my dear?"

Anna studied Doron's face. His features were also Semitic, but she had never seen him before. "Another Arab?" she guessed.

Franz laughed. "She thinks you are an Arab, Doron. I do not believe Mr. Arafat would be so confused."

Doron said nothing as he silently eyed Veldheim, looking for weaknesses.

"No, no, Anna! Who we have here is Mr. Doron Katz of Israel's Mossad. Mr. Katz was the one responsible for planning the capture of Eichmann." Franz took several steps so that he was directly in front of the chair. He looked down at Doron who refused to meet his stare. "But we have no hard feelings. That was ancient history."

Finally Doron spoke. "Why am I here, Veldheim?"

Veldheim's right hand opened and he enclosed it around Doron's throat, pushing him farther back into the chair. "I want Doctor Slesinger, and I want him now. Do not try to lie that you don't know what I'm talking about. The Reich follows your every move."

Doron considered his options and decided to lead with his

head. He thrust himself outward and upward. It was a quick movement that broke Franz's grip on his neck. Once standing, Doron sent a powerful head butt directly into Franz's nose. The tall Austrian staggered backward, blood pouring from his now crushed nostrils. Doron would have followed up the attack if it weren't for Anna. She ran to Franz as she pulled a small pistol from the leg holster underneath her skirt. She aimed the gun at Doron's forehead and started to pull the trigger. Franz knocked her arm upward just as the gun discharged. At the same moment, half a dozen of Franz's security men burst in and subdued Doron Katz.

Doron Katz's last hour was not a pleasant one. Adolf had returned from the firing range and personally supervised the interrogation and torture. All the Mossad training in resistance and pain management that Doron had received over the years was no match for Adolf's heinous nature. Doron was subjected to unspeakable atrocities and still remained mute. However, when electric probes were inserted into his chest he became very vocal, swearing obscenities in German. Every fifteen seconds Adolf increased the voltage, which caused Doron's musculature to spasm in contractions. Adolf pushed the regulator past the quarter position and Doron's entire body began to jerk. Another click and Doron howled. His jaws clenched together, almost severing his own tongue in the process. The blood flowed freely down his throat and he gagged. He would have choked to death if Adolf hadn't of shut off the current.

"Are you ready to tell me what I want to know?"

Doron nodded feebly. "Brooklyn, by the boardwalk." Tears streamed down Doron's face.

"Now that wasn't so hard, Mr. Katz." Adolf's voice was syrupy sweet. "You would like me to send you home?"

The gash in Doron's tongue, along with his previous beating made it hard for him to speak. "To Yisrael?"

Adolf shook his head as he placed his hand back on the electrical current regulator. "To your God," he replied as he moved the device to its highest setting. Doron's heart was immediately shocked into an arrhythmia which was followed closely by a massive myocardial infarction. In the next tick of a second he was gone. He died with his eyes wide open, but they emptied immediately upon death. It was proof that the eyes really are the gateway to the soul. All that was left of Doron Katz was a shell. Adolf bent over the restraining table and looked into the lifeless eyes. "Your death was easy. Doctor Slesinger's will be hard!"

Detective Adam Rodman listened intently as Izzy recounted the events that he had neglected to share when Ilya Babakov was killed. It was hard to believe that he could have done it all in less than eight weeks. He had been to Argentina, France, and Russia, along with a trip to California and several to Connecticut. It was the science that Rodman had the most trouble with, so Izzy explained that slowly. Oksana and Brian listened, chiming in when they thought Izzy had gotten too technical.

"This all started with Doctor Heneke's message about Ice-9, written inside the cover of Vonnegut's paperback."

"I remember that," Rodman nodded. "You didn't understand the Ice-9 reference."

"I do now. A nucleotide is made up of three things; a phosphate, a nitrogen base, and a sugar. I believe that Mengele used a virus to cannibalize the sugar."

"And what does that mean?"

"It means that there is now a fundamental difference in the human nucleic acid of these altered cells. It's nucleic acid that carries our genetic information."

Brian could see that Rodman was lost. "It's like trying to tell the difference between Sprite and Seven-up. Almost the same, but not quite the same."

Izzy nodded his head. "That's right. Except there's a problem with the cell that's almost the same. First, it somehow acts as a host for HIV. Second, after hundreds, or thousands, or billions of multiplications it becomes unviable and you get cancers." Izzy stopped in order to frame the words for his most important point. "Let's not forget Ice-9. For some reason, all human cells prefer the cannibalized sugar."

Izzy's pronouncement took Oksana and Brian off-guard.

"When did you come up with that?" Oksana questioned.

"I worked it out last night. I'm going to call Dunlevy and see what he thinks." A tiny tear welled in the corner of Izzy's right eye. He used his hand to brush it away. "I wish Ithamar were here. He's probably the only one in the world who could see this thing straight."

"What I want to know is can you fix it?" Rodman asked.

For some reason the question struck Izzy as funny and he began to laugh. The laughter grew louder and it caused Izzy's whole body to shake.

"I said something funny?"

Izzy tried to control himself as he looked into the eyes of the black detective. "Fix it? First I'd like to know what 'it' is. It's impossible to come up with an answer if you don't first understand the question."

Rodman nodded. "So what do you do next?"

"Next, I take it to the world."

The front door burst open in a shower of splinters and four of Veldheim's heavily armed men charged into the house. They were dressed in camouflage fatigues, stolen from the Austrian army. Each man brandished a military style automatic weapon. Detective Rodman thought about reaching for his shoulder holstered revolver, but realized it would have been both foolish and foolhardy. Therefore, he tried to remain calm.

"You are all coming with us," one of the men screamed as he aimed his weapon directly at Oksana.

Rodman nodded and they all started towards the front door. Izzy was the last one out, with Veldheim's point man directly in back of him. Two gun shots rang out from behind. Jean Dulac had sprung from the kitchen with her pistol, taking down two abductors. As one of the men fell, he trained his weapon on Jean and pulled the trigger with his last heartbeat. A single bullet slammed into her shoulder and she dropped her weapon. The firing stopped. The fallen man in the doorway was dead.

The lead terrorist, whose gun was aimed at Izzy, didn't even look back. He just kept pushing until Brian and Adam Rodman were in one car, and Izzy and Oksana in another. He and his remaining accomplice split up and jumped into the front passenger seat of each vehicle. Both cars used in the assault had separate drivers ready at the wheel. As soon as the doors were shut, the cars were gone.

Bobby Clampett's inspection and surveillance of Veldheim's estate took a little more than an hour. Terry and Leroy Hebb waited in the truck while Bobby serpentined his way around the perimeter. He had a pair of high powered, night-vision binoculars and used them to identify and mentally chart all buildings, structures, and people. By the time he returned to the truck, Leroy was on edge. He had smoked an entire pack of cigarettes since they had parked the truck at a gas station that was about half a mile from Veldheim's. Leroy was certain that he could have finished the job in half the time it took Bobby. Therefore, he was more than a little bit agitated when Bobby finally reappeared.

"What the fuck? You shoulda been back twenty minutes ago," Leroy wailed as Bobby jumped into the truck's bed.

Terry slid the back window of the cab open and turned so he was looking at Bobby. "You gonna tell us what you found?"

Bobby was busy transferring mental notes to his clipboard. "Can't do it."

The veins in Terry's neck began to bulge. "Hell you say. Why y'all not?"

"The place is crawling with paramilitary Nazis. They got dogs, guns, and a copter that has gun mounts. You want to take that place, we're gonna need more guys. A lot more guys."

Terry brought his hand smashing down on the front dashboard. He hit it so hard that the vinyl split, and the blow triggered the passenger side air bag. The explosive charge went off and the bag shot out, smashing Leroy back into the back of his seat. He screamed as he tried to fight his way forward. While the bag deflated rapidly, it wasn't fast enough for Terry who was now livid with rage.

"No, no, no,' he screamed as he plunged his nine inch hunting knife into the air bag. The bag made a hissing sound as the air rushed out of the slash mark. Leroy pushed his door open and jumped out of the truck. Terry got out on the other side, slamming his door closed. He paced back and forth, kicking his foot into the ground every few seconds. He stopped right in front of Bobby Clampett. "Not gonna wash, Bobby. Not gonna wash at all. We're gonna spike the road and wait. Anyone tries to get in or out, we've got them. We'll use them as bargain chips with this guy Veldheim. He gives us those two fucking krauts, and we give him whoever we grab."

Bobby averted his eyes from Terry's stare and looked down at the ground. "What if no one tries to go in or out?"

Terry stretched out a big hand and pushed Bobby backwards. "You better fucking hope that doesn't happen. Now get in the truck."

Five minutes later, Leroy was spreading spikes across the private roadway that lead up to the gate to Veldheim's estate. Terry parked the truck on the side of the road and instructed Bobby to set up the legs for one of the AK-47s. Bobby did what he was told, setting the tripod in the back of the truck. He mounted one of the guns and inserted a round of ammunition. Bobby pivoted first left, and then right. He set a night scope on top of the gun's barrel and targeted Veldheim's front door. He guessed the distance to be over half a mile, and the house was elevated on a hill. It was beyond the accurate firing range for this type of weapon. Bobby looked away from the sight and set his gaze on the bazooka and the box of mortar shells that lay on the floor of the truck. A smile spread across his face. "When the going gets tough," he thought to himself, "Bring in a bazooka."

The two gray Lincoln Town Cars exited the Southern State Parkway at exit 65. It had been a straight run from Brooklyn to Long Island, with hardly any traffic. Still, Izzy had been staring at the muzzle of a high-powered automatic weapon for over two hours. Oksana sat by his side. Every time Izzy tried to turn and look at her, the gunman ordered him to "face forward, no talking!" He only hoped that she was holding up as well as he was. He thought about Jean Dulac. Her sharp shooting had eliminated one of their abductors. He thought he heard her scream out when they were being pushed out the door, but he couldn't be sure.

The first of the cars turned up Veldheim's private driveway, and then the second followed. There were several pops from the first car and then a loud hissing. Three of the tires were punctured by spikes. The driver of the car in the rear, Izzy's car, immediately threw the transmission in reverse. He touched his foot to the accelerator. Before the car actually moved backwards, it was struck by a round of bullets. The radiator was sliced into metallic Swiss cheese and antifreeze poured out onto the ground. The driver would have kept going if the engine didn't immediately overheat and stall.

The driver who had been guarding Adam Rodman and Brian Crighton jumped out of the first car. He trained his pistol towards the massive hulk of Terry Hebb. Before he could even flinch, Bobby Clampett sent two bullets deep into his brain. As he fell, Leroy rushed to the car in the rear. He pointed the other AK-47 at the driver. Terry Hebb stared menacingly in the direction of both cars.

"Y'all get your asses out here now!" Terry shouted.

Both cars emptied quickly. Terry had everyone stand with their backs to him, legs spread, hands up against the cars. Bobby stayed with the gun on the truck, and Leroy frisked everyone while his older brother watched. Leroy was especially thorough in patting down Oksana. He let his hands play on her frame until his brother pulled him away. Leroy disarmed the two remaining neo-Nazis. However, when he tried to pat Rodman down, Rodman kneed him in the groin. Leroy collapsed, writhing in pain. Terry had to step over his brother to get to Rodman. The older Hebb towered over the detective.

"Well, well. We got us an aggressive little nigger." Terry made a fist and punched Rodman in the stomach. Even though Rodman's physique was like steel, he grunted from the force of the blow. However, he stayed up. It was the second blow that did the damage. Terry's second fist landed just below Rodman's throat. It fractured one of the neck bones and immediately started an internal hemorrhage. Rodman dropped to his knees, gasping for air. He bent his head forward and began throwing up blood. Terry Hebb turned towards Izzy and Brian.

"Y'all understand I got no problems killing the lot of ya'. Now who are ya' and what the fuck are you doing here?"

"Scientists," was the only word that Izzy got to say. Their presence on the private roadway had not gone unnoticed. Alarms went off all over Veldheim's property. Veldheim had busied himself dressing in proper Austrian attire for Doctor Slesinger's arrival. When the alarms sounded he ran to the security control room, only one leg dressed in Lederhosen. It was difficult to make out anything but shadows in the darkness, and Veldheim released a patrol. Three heavily armed Nazis, dressed in paramilitary outfits made their way to the front gate in a golf cart. They were fifty yards from the gate when they started firing their weapons.

Izzy instinctively crouched while reaching out and pulled Oksana down with him. Brian dropped flat and Terry Hebb ran into the space between the two cars. The two Nazi hijackers reached for their pistol holsters. Bobby swivelled his AK-47 on its tripod and began firing. The two men were sliced to pieces. Bobby then expertly sighted all three men in the golf cart on the road beyond the fence. Three shots was all it took to silence their fire.

Leroy had jumped into the back seat of the first car when the shooting started. Bullets shattered all the windows and a torrent of glass had rained down upon him. When he got out of the car he was shaken, but otherwise intact.

It took several moments for Terry to gather his wits. He walked to his brother, picking up the AK-47 that Leroy had dropped when he jumped into the car. He handed the gun back to his brother and pointed at Izzy and Brian and Oksana. "Watch 'em. They move and you do 'em!"

Terry walked to the truck. He looked at Bobby and pointed towards the house. Bobby nodded and knelt to lift the bazooka. Terry put himself behind the wheel and started the engine. He dropped the clutch and the wheels spun and squealed. The truck rocketed forward and crashed through Veldheim's front gate. He ran directly over two of the men who had fallen from the golf cart, which had crashed into a tree. Terry slammed on the brakes and the truck screeched to a halt. Terry looked back through the cab windows.

"Fuck 'em, Bobby! Fuck 'em good!"

A mortar shell burst from the bazooka and obliterated the front frame of the house. When the smoke cleared it was easy to see directly into the dining room, which was burning. Terry Hebb lifted a fist and laughed. He put the truck back in gear and headed back down the driveway.

Inside, it was chaos. Franz surveyed the destruction with Anna and Adolf. His front hallway had been turned to rubble. The heavy, antique wooden door was now a pile of splinters and toothpicks. The explosion from the mortar shell started a fire in the dining room. Franz used a handheld fire extinguisher to put out the flames. He was too late to save six of the antique chairs that went with the dining table, and the table itself was singed from the heat. Franz tried to get his eight other security officers to follow the truck down the driveway. All of the men refused, claiming that it was suicide.

Franz returned to Adolf and growled at him. "Who did this?"

Adolf looked at Anna. "Could this be the work of Heneke?"

Anna shook her head. "I do not believe so. Even if Brittany had been a ruse, they would not be this bold."

"Then who?"

Anna had no answer. Therefore, Franz decided to get an answer on his own. He went to his security office and turned on the speaker that was in a tree, by what was left of the front gate.

"This is Franz Veldheim. What do you want?"

Terry had just stopped the truck and returned to Leroy's side. Bobby pointed from the back of the truck towards an intercom which was mounted on the now half-mangled fence post. Terry walked to it and pressed a fat finger on the talk button.

"I want the kraut and his sister."

There was silence for a moment. Franz then replied. "Who are you?"

"None of your fucking business," Terry growled.

"They are guests of mine. What business do you have with them?" Anna and Adolf walked into the security room just in time to hear the response.

"I've got a little present for them from Gilly Buchanan."

Anna immediately turned and slapped her brother in the head. "What have you done?"

Adolf paced around the little room while Franz waited for an explanation. Adolf filled him in quickly, explaining that the people outside were very likely white supremacists. From the sound of the voice, Adolf concluded they were probably Southern Klansmen.

"And what am I to do?" Franz asked.

Adolf was very cool with his response. "Why, you turn us over to them. Doctor Slesinger is at the bottom of that hill. Anna and I are expendable. Doctor Slesinger must not be allowed to escape. He must be silenced!"

Anna returned to her room and slipped out of the flowing black dress she had purchased in the little Hampton's boutique. Her leather bodysuit was more revealing and a much larger distraction. They were going to need every advantage if they were to come out of this alive. She pulled on her knee high black boots, the ones that had been custom ordered with steel toes built in. Before leaving the room she grabbed hold of a thin metal cylinder that looked like breath freshener. She pushed the cylinder into her cleavage so it would not show. When she returned to what was left of the front door, Adolf was waiting.

Adolf had also changed his clothes. He was now dressed in the uniform of an S.S. officer, replete with Nazi arm band and aviator's cap. In his hand was a Glock semi-automatic pistol.

Before slipping a ten-bullet magazine into the pistol, he checked to make sure that he had loaded it with armor-piercing bullets. Franz gave both Adolf and Anna hugs. He watched as they both walked onto the driveway and headed down the hill.

Terry Hebb appraised Anna and Adolf carefully as they approached. Bobby Clampett kept the truck mounted AK-47 focused on them. Leroy, however, was less cautious. He took one look at Anna and his mouth began to water. He stepped forward and blocked Anna and Adolf from advancing. Terry walked to his brother's side. He pointed the rifle at Adolf and made him drop his gun. Leroy walked over and frisked them. He spent more than a moment running his hands over Anna's legs and ass.

"This is all very simple," Terry stated. "You killed Gilly and now you have to die."

Leroy walked back and whispered something into his brother's ear. Terry glanced at him and shrugged his shoulders. "Okay, take her off into the woods. You can do her there."

Leroy grabbed Anna's arm and began to tug. She offered very little resistance, figuring that she and Adolf would be much more successful if they were able to split the men up. They hadn't moved ten feet when Bobby Clampett jumped down from the truck to protest.

"How come he gets to get his dickie wet and I don't?" he wailed.

Terry looked disgusted. "You want a piece, too? Fine, go with them. But I'm giving you both just fifteen minutes to finish this. Make it quick."

A smile spread across Anna's face. This was working out better than she could have hoped. Fifteen minutes? She was sure her two doltish 'would be' rapists would be dead within ten. They walked about two hundred yards into the woods. Anna walked between the two men, both hands busily rubbing at their crotches. They reached a tiny clearing and Leroy made Anna stop. She immediately loosened the top of her bodysuit and slid it down to her waist, exposing her breasts for both men to see. The thought of a double-kill had her very excited and her nipples were taut and erect.

Leroy let out a low moan as he slapped Bobby on the back. "The bitch wants it more than we do."

Anna just smiled. She turned towards both men and shook her breasts from side to side. The movement caused the metal cylinder to fall from her cleavage. Anna made an obvious move to try and hide it with her foot. Leroy saw it and knelt to pick it up. He held it up in front of her face.

"What's this?"

"It is not for you."

Leroy lashed out and slapped Anna hard across the face. "Let's try that again. What's this?"

Anna pretended to hesitate. "It is German."

Leroy raised his hand again. "What's it do?"

"It enhances sexual pleasure."

Leroy looked at the cylinder closely. He popped off the top and noticed that it came equipped with a spray nozzle. "How's it work?"

"It's absorbed through the tongue. It goes right to the nerve endings in the penis, making them more sensitive."

"I gotta try it," Leroy laughed.

"Me too," added Bobby.

Anna stopped them. "The effects are limited. You should not use it until you are ready for penetration."

Leroy and Bobby couldn't strip their clothes off fast enough. Anna removed her dress all the way. She had Bobby lie on the ground and she straddled him so that his mouth was buried in her crotch hair. Then she instructed Leroy to move closer. When his engorged penis was near her mouth, she opened and sucked him in. Leroy's right hand was still tightly clenched to the cylinder. Anna tightened her thighs and shifted forward. Her dripping pussy was over Bobby Clampett's nose and her anus was flush up against his mouth. As she bore down, she cut off his air supply and he began to struggle.

Leroy was oblivious. He could feel the tension of a powerful orgasm building in his loins. Anna could sense it as well. She released her mouth suction for a moment and pulled off of Leroy's pulsing prick.

"Spray it now," she screamed, and then sucked his cock deeply again. She fastened her lips tight, even used her teeth a bit to make sure he wouldn't move. Leroy opened his mouth and lifted the cylinder. He held it close as Anna had instructed and aimed for the back of his throat. A spray of liquid fire squirted from the dispenser as the inside of Leroy's mouth burst into flames. He screamed, which triggered the swallowing mechanism. Fiery liquid poured down towards his stomach. Leroy tried to move back, but Anna had him secured by his penis. She held him for about five seconds and then open her lips. Leroy had made just the one scream. He immediately collapsed, his body already entering into violent death spasms. The flames were actually shooting out of his mouth, accompanied by the black acrid smoke of burning flesh.

Anna was so excited by it that she could hardly control herself. She jumped up and watched Leroy Hebb burn up from the inside. Then she turned towards Bobby Clampett, who was lying unconscious from a lack of oxygen. Anna stood there naked, excepting for her high black boots.

In her mind she pretended to be a German soccer star and planted her steel toe right boot into the side of Bobby Clampett's head. That first blow shattered his skull and drove bone fragments into his brain, killing him instantly. However, Anna did not relent until she split his head open and could see the contours of his brain.

Terry had dismissed thoughts of his brother, Anna and Bobby. He was trying to get Adolf to plead for his life, but Adolf wouldn't do it. Terry held the AK-47 against Adolf's temple, but Adolf didn't even flinch.

Adolf looked up into the eyes of the big Southerner. "A man would have killed me by now!"

Terry backed off several feet, keeping his gun trained on Adolf. "What's your hurry? I want to enjoy your death." Terry looked in the direction of the two cars that had been disabled. He had put Izzy, Oksana, Brian and Adam Rodman into the first car. He wanted to make sure that he had an audience for Adolf's execution. Even in the darkness he could see the look of disgust on Oksana's face. Izzy was seated behind the wheel and it wasn't possible to see any expressions. He had allowed the tall guy to get into the back seat and attend to the nigger, whose condition was deteriorating. All and all, Terry Hebb felt quite good about himself.

Anna waited in the woods for an opportunity. It came as police sirens wailed in the distance.

The gunshots and explosion had prompted Franz's usually reticent neighbors to call the police. They were now on the way towards the Veldheim estate. The sirens distracted Terry for a moment and Anna charged from the rear. She hurled herself against the giant man with all her force. It took Terry by surprise and he stumbled forward. Anna attacked again and jumped onto his back, wrapping her right forearm around his neck. Terry swirled to dislodged her and Adolf's bullets tore into his chest.

They continued through him, exited, and tore into Anna. As Terry fell to his knees he returned fire.

Only one bullet found its target. The shell hit Adolf in the throat, just below the Adam's Apple. It had a downward trajectory and shattered his spine before it exited between his shoulders blades. Miraculously, the bullet missed his spinal cord. However, the bone fragments tore it badly. Adolf toppled over and lay motionless. His body wanted to convulse in death spasms, but the nerves that transmitted those signals were torn and useless. He had entered the space between life and death. His last pitiful thought focused on how his entire life's work had been ruined.

Back in the house, Franz was nearly apoplectic. He had watched Terry Hebb's gunfire illuminate his security monitor and saw Adolf fall. His security staff had abandoned him, taking the helicopter. He could hear the police sirens getting closer. The only entrance and exit for the property was through the front gate. He grabbed a gun and headed down the front driveway. His plan was to run past the carnage at the front gate quickly, then disappear into the woods. Anyone who tried to stop him would get shot.

Franz stopped twenty yards short of the mangled front gate. From where he stood he could see the bodies of Adolf, Anna and Terry Hebb plainly. His anxiety skyrocketed, but there was no other way. He picked a line to the right of the bodies, almost on the very edge of the private roadway and started running.

Oksana and Izzy had turned their attention to Adam Rodman after the shooting. Rodman's vital signs had become erratic and he desperately needed to get to a hospital. It was Brian Crighton who pointed out the figure running toward them. Izzy and Oksana turned in their seats and Oksana let out a gasp.

"Franz Veldheim?"

"Who?" Izzy asked.

"He used to be a politician in Austria. Russian Jews considered him to be very dangerous. He's an apologist for Nazi war crimes."

Franz was now less than a half dozen yards from the car. Izzy did the only thing he could think of. He opened his car door just before Franz got to it. The Austrian slammed into the door at full speed. The door bounced him backwards, more dazed then hurt. He dropped his pistol by the open car door. Izzy saw it and jumped on it before Franz could react. Izzy picked up the gun and pointed it towards the former Austrian politician.

"Put your hands up and don't move," Izzy shouted.

Franz did exactly as he was told, which took Izzy a bit by surprise. He was worried that he would actually have to fire the gun and at least wound Franz Veldheim to stop him. Three police cruisers roared onto the private roadway and came to a stop behind the two disabled cars. Six uniformed officers from the South Hampton police force jumped out of their vehicles with weapons drawn. All six officers took positions that surrounded Izzy.

"Drop your weapon," one of the officers shouted.

Izzy did exactly as he was told. Oksana and Brian climbed out of the car and approached the officer who was in charge. Oksana informed the officer of Adam Rodman's condition. The officer immediately called for an ambulance, as others checked the dead bodies. Franz Veldheim tried to talk his way out the situation. However, Izzy, Oksana, and Brian all spoke against him. In the end, the officers concluded that everyone was going to have to come with them to the police station.

The ambulance arrived and two paramedics transferred Adam Rodman from the back of the car to a wheeled gurney. They started an IV and rushed him to the ambulance. The police draped sheets over the bodies and called for the coroner. One team of officers stayed with the bodies, the others escorted Izzy, Oksana, Brian, and Franz Velheim to the back seat of their cruisers. It wouldn't be until daylight that they would find the bodies of Leroy Hebb and Bobby Clampett.

The interrogations lasted for several hours. By the time they were over, Franz Veldheim had been charged with many counts of murder and conspiracy to commit murder. It was almost daylight when a police lieutenant informed Izzy that they were free to go. However, he also advised that they were going to need to make themselves available for further questioning and depositions.

The police let Izzy use the phone and he tried calling Rich Levine at The Institute, but the line was busy. It was odd to get a busy signal from the switchboard, but Izzy didn't even think about it. His mind was reliving the events of the past evening. He had seen people get shot on television, and the movies. However, he had never seen it happen in front of him, and at close range. He had also never seen anyone target a house with a bazooka. For everything he had been through in last two months, this had been the worst. He hoped this was the end of it. He was tired of playing Indiana Jones and just wanted to be a scientist. If he were to solve the puzzle of Mengele's legacy, it would require a full time effort.

The phone at The Institute stayed busy. Oksana suggested they take a taxi cab back to the city. It was just the start of morning rush hour and traffic was worse than usual. On the ride home, they had a long discussion on what the next step in the AIDS battle should be. The cab driver picked up on the conversation. He was a black man from Antigua. He glanced back towards Oksana and asked her what she thought of the story in the New York Times. Oksana had no idea what he was talking about.

"I be speakin about AIDS. Paper says the Germans invented it as a weapon. I'm not believin' it." The cab driver reached across the front seat and grabbed hold of the morning paper. He handed it through the sliding window that separated the front and back seat of the cab. Izzy grabbed hold the paper and the headline drained the blood from his face. There it was in black and white: "AIDS targeted at Africans by Nazi doctor." The reporter's byline stated that the article had been reprinted from the *L.A. Times*.

Izzy had no one to blame but himself. When Doron Katz had

moved everyone to the safe house, Izzy had sent a copy of all his findings to Dave Dunlevy. Obviously Dave found Izzy hypothesis credible and wasted no time in calling the media. Izzy scanned the entire two page article in under ten minutes. The blame for AIDS was laid in front of Germany's front door, and there was no absence of malice. The article made it clear that the intent of Mengele's work was to wipe physically superior Africans off the planet.

Izzy couldn't believe his eyes. This wasn't an article about science, or the need for a new research direction. It was a historical diatribe aimed at placing blame and stirring up controversy. In other words it was typical 'Dunlevy.' However, even Dave couldn't have guessed at the firestorm of trouble that he released.

The first thing Izzy did as soon as he got home was try The Institute again. The phone line was still busy. Izzy was at a complete loss and neither Oksana nor Brian had any suggestions. They were ill equipped to be at the center of what was now an international incident. It was still early enough in the morning for the tail end of the news. Izzy flipped on the television and went immediately to CNN. The first thing he learned was that sixteen African nations had severed diplomatic ties with Germany. The German government was caught completely off guard. Germany's prime minister called the accusation insanity. He promised that Germany would hold Dave Dunlevy and his associates responsible for defaming the German people.

CNN switched its coverage to Moscow where Russia's president was about to address the politburo. The President stood at the podium and the room fell silent. His statement was short and a CNN reporter translated into English. "The Russian scientific community doubts the veracity of the American claim that HIV is hosted inside human cells. However, should we find this to be true, Russia reserves the right to take any and all punitive actions against those responsible for our suffering." The President left the podium and the scene shifted to a reporter who was standing outside the

Kremlin. The reporter's face looked weary and haggard.

"We have just learned that Russian troops are beginning to mass on the eastern border."

Izzy stared at the screen in disbelief. "Don't they realize you can't hold modern day Germany accountable for this?"

Brian stepped to Izzy's side. "Maybe not. But suppose it was your ancestors who were injected. You'd be plenty pissed."

Izzy spun angrily towards Brian. "And how does blowing Germany off the map fix anything?"

Brian shrugged his shoulders. "Didn't say it would."

The television screen changed again. This time CNN was in New York, where early morning fires destroyed several BMW dealerships. Izzy picked up the remote control and turned the set off in disgust. He searched around the apartment for the security alarm for his BMW, and his keys. Then he remembered that the car was still parked on the street in Brooklyn, by the safe house. "This is way beyond blame and geopolitical borders. We all better get down to The Institute before David makes this worse than it already is."

When they arrived at The Institute, things had already gone from bad to worse. Izzy and the others had to fight their way through a sea of reporters. Rich Levine stood near the security desk, answering questions as best he could. Unfortunately, there was very little that he understood and The Institute's investigations into Mengele's notes were still inconclusive. Rich practically jumped for joy as he saw Izzy coming toward him. Rich ran to him and hugged him tight, leaving the reporters to themselves.

"David called me. I told him I hadn't heard from you and then this started yesterday. When the police found the body of that Israeli agent, I feared the worst."

Once inside his own office, Izzy tried to make a list of things that he needed to do. Oksana watched him scurry about like a mouse caught in a maze. Brian immediately went back to the computers and began working on probabilities. The press was going to want to see a projection of just how far reaching Mengele cells were at the present time, and how much further they would spread. Izzy decided to open his email first, hoping that maybe Heneke had changed his mind and was willing to speak out. What Izzy found was a box full of hate mail. The letter from Avery Wells, a research scientist at the Scientific Institute for Technology in Newton, Massachusetts was typical:

"Doctor Slesinger,

My colleagues and I are were shocked by your hypothesis that was presented by pseudo-scientist David Dunlevy. As a doctor of virology, with a specialty in retroviruses, I find your claims both illogical and irresponsible. In the real scientific community we do not present our findings in the national media. We write well-documented research studies and submit them for peer review. Your bombastic tabloid technique has done irreparable harm to the well established and accepted HIV/AIDS hypothesis. You have put many lives at risk, not to mention billions of pharmaceutical research dollars. In short, we find you and your associate in California to be an embarrassment to the entire American scientific community."

With Disdain

Avery M. Wells, Ph.D., E.E.D

Izzy let Oksana read the letter and then he went in search of Rich Levine. He found him in his office, jumping between a half-dozen phone calls and conversations. Izzy walked to Rich, pulled the phone out of his hand, and replaced it in its cradle.

"How do they know I'm involved? There was nothing in *The Times* article."

"Dunlevy," Rich replied. "He was on *Good Morning, America*. He gave you credit for the Mengele cell hypothesis, right in front of the whole world."

Izzy threw his hands in the air and couldn't help but laugh. "Great. Can it get any better?"

"Lots," Rich replied while trying to hide a smile. "Dunlevy looked directly at the camera while pointing a finger. I'm going to quote him directly because it was so unforgettable." Rich pointed his finger at Izzy and tried to look stoic. "Ladies and gentlemen. I must tell you that Nazi geneticist, Doctor Joseph Mengele, did not live in our universe. Be afraid. Be very afraid!"

Izzy placed both hands over his face while shaking his head. "He didn't?"

Rich nodded. "He did. I thought Stone Phillips was going to shit right on camera."

"I swear, I'm going to California and I'm going to ring his neck."

"No need to do that. He's coming here."

"Here?"

"Well, not exactly here. To New York. The NIH has called an emergency meeting to diffuse the situation."

"When?"

"Don't know," Rich replied. "It's been less than twenty-four hours since The *L.A. Times* broke the story. I'd definitely say that it will be this week. No one wants this hanging over Thanksgiving."

Izzy nodded and turned to leave the office. He stopped and turned back towards Rich. "That thing Dunlevy said, he got it from me. And I got it from Pieter Heneke."

"What's that?"

"The thing about the universe. Except he did live in our universe. He left us a legacy. . . Mengele's legacy. And if we're not all very bright, and very clever, it will outlive mankind."

Chapter 21

It was snowing hard as the presidential limousine pulled up in front of the Bundesrat council chambers in Bonn, West Germany. German President Helmut Sleiden had called an emergency meeting of the federal council's upper chamber. He had also instructed the chancellor to call an emergency meeting of the lower house, the Bundestag, in Berlin. At nine o'clock in the morning, seventy-eight of the seventy-nine council representatives were assembled. For six decades Germany had tried to escape its Holocaust bloodstain. The farther they got away, the more there was something to pull them back. If it wasn't insurance settlements, it was slave labor reparations. No one was more tired of it than President Sleiden. He worked diligently to annul the bloodstain, trying to leave it in a Germany of the past, a Germany he and many others would have liked to forget.

Dave Dunlevy's article brought it all back, and then some. The German media pounced on the article in the *L.A. Times* and ran with it. Within one day, Germany was in a state of chaos, the likes it hadn't seen in fifty years. With Russian troops massing to the east, and African nations demanding answers and accountability, President Sleiden was stretched very thin. The scrutiny was not just external, but also came from within. Calls came from every state's representative, demanding a full investigation. The last thing Germany needed were newly discovered Holocaust atrocities to put it back under the world's magnifying glass.

The council's majority leader called the roles. Only the representative from the city of Kempten was absent. The majority leader paused and called the name of the Kempten representative again:

"Kaiser, Adolf."

There was silence. Many other representatives took it as a bad sign. Adolf was one of the few who never missed a meeting. He was one of only four members from the Social Nationalistic party, and was a well known neo-Nazi supporter. He had launched many a filibuster on the lack of German pride in the council. While his family business was small, it was a leader in its segment of the pharmaceutical industry. Therefore, his absence during this crisis was most suspicious.

The majority leader called for an opening statement. Protocol was forgotten as seventy-eight men and women stood behind their seats. President Sleiden made a further breach of protocol as he took charge of the meeting, "I would like to hear from Bernhardt Weser of Dusseldorf."

Everyone except Mr. Weser took their seat. Mr. Weser was a middle-aged, conservative industrialist. His views were often those shared by many. "I spoke with Karl Kaiser, CFO of Kaiser pharmaceutics. He verifies that Doctor Heneke created PIRT-I9, but has no knowledge of these supposed aberrant cells. I was hoping Herr Kaiser of Kempten could confirm this, but I see he is absent from this meeting. However, I have been informed that a massive shipment of Kaiser's drug was shipped to Africa just last week, and it was shipped for free. Surely that proves Kaiser's intent to help eradicate this horrible disease."

Joseph Bremer, a young outspoken lawyer from Hamburg jumped to his feet. He cast an angry glare towards Weser. "And if a war on the virus makes the disease worse in the long run, is this really an act of charity?" Bemer paused to give his next words added effect. "Or a continuation of genocide?"

Chaos broke out in the chamber as all seventy-eight members began screaming to be heard at the same time. It took five minutes of heavy gavel banging from President Sleiden to regain control of the meeting.

"Meine Herren, gentlemen. We must maintain a sense of decorum. If we of the Bundesrat cannot weather this crisis, how will Germany?" The question restored order, at least momentarily. "The Council recognizes Doctor Ingrid Morgan of Nurnberg."

Doctor Morgan, a forty-eight year-old former gynecologist cautiously rose to her feet. She was the only physician in the Bundesrat, in a sea of lawyers and professional politicians. Unlike many in Germany who had already written off the American hypothesis as anti-German lunacy, Doctor Morgan was willing to subject the existence of Mengele cells to scientific scrutiny. "There can be no argument that Human Immuno Virus, HIV, destroys a human being's immune system. Is it possible that the virus is connected to an even larger cellular anomaly? While it is highly unlikely, the possibility does exist."

Mr. Weser, the industrialist, jumped angrily to his feet. "Do you realize what you are saying? We've spent billions on reparations. If we let the world lay the blame at our feet, there will be nothing left of Germany for ourselves."

Doctor Morgan replied icily. "In Nurnberg our children study the trials, our atrocities. While I doubt that Mengele could muster the science to target Negroes, I do not doubt for one moment his intent."

The chamber exploded in cacophony of shouts. It took President Sleiden's threat of contempt to quiet the room. He then let Doctor Morgan finish.

"You speak of reparations. If the Americans are right, the world is paying reparations to Germany, in human lives." Doctor Morgan paused to regain her composure and control the emotions in her voice. "Nurnberg is very close to the Czech border. We've seen a marked increase in their cancer rate. The etiology is very similar to that described by the Americans. We've always attributed the increases to environmental factors, air pollution, contaminated water, tainted food. Unfortunately, we've seen the same kind of increases in Germany."

The silence that followed Doctor Morgan's comments was chilling. If the American's were right, Africa was a harbinger of a world yet to come. A world with no people.

Hans Shumann, the representative from Berlin, and a member of the military cabinet, jarred the assembly with his analysis of the present situation. "Meine Herren! As we meet, the Russian are assembling troops. If we do not prepare for an attack, our deaths will come much sooner than from this disease."

Joe Breman answered Shumann's remark. "The Russians simply want accountability. If rattling a saber in our direction calms them, let them rattle away. However, we must work quickly to determine the veracity of the American claims."

President Sleiden agreed with Herr Breman's assessment. "We will send our finest scientific minds to the meeting in New York. Calls will be made this morning, and those chosen must be ready to leave this evening. At the same time I suggest you all return home to your towns and cities for the duration of this crisis. Go home and calm the fears of your neighbors. Assure them that this republic is not Weimar, and that we will weather this as a united people. If there is some sort of unseen emergency, we will contact you at home."

The President stood aside and the majority leader put it to a hand vote. Unanimously, the Bundestag voted to end the emergency session and go home.

Unfortunately, the streets of Germany were anything but peaceful. After the initial shock wore off, the finger pointing began.

Berlin had become Germany's equivalent of New York. It was a melting pot for a cornucopia of immigrants and races, and it was also a powder-keg waiting to explode. Homosexuals, Blacks and liberals called for complete German accountability. Conservatives openly mocked the Mengele cell theory as an idiotic impossibility. The nationalist saw it as a plot hatched by the American pharmaceutical industry, who was obviously jealous of Heneke's new drug. The neo-Nazi's saw it as threat to bring down Germany.

Mengele cells were on every German's lips as snow began to pile up on the campus of Berlin University. *The mensa*, or cafeteria served as both a commissary and a meeting area for the students. Shortly before lunch, skinheads from 'students for nationalism' found themselves in direct confrontation with several other groups. What started off as finger pointing deteriorated in pushing, and then things turned ugly. By the time the police and news crews arrived, sixteen young men and women were injured, and one Black student lay dead, the victim of a skinhead's bullet.

Scene after scene of violence played out on a special afternoon news broadcast. One man, in Dusseldorf, could not bear to watch Germany implicated in another horror. He doused himself with gasoline and lit himself afire in the old town. Horrified townspeople and tourists watched him burn to death. As evening approached, the government feared violence and looting after sunset. Therefore, Germany's first postwar curfew was imposed nationwide. As darkness fell, and the streets emptied, a feeling of dread pervaded from Hamburg in the north, to Munich in the south.

Chapter 22

It was a little before three in the afternoon when Dave Dunlevy stepped out of cab and walked into the circus of reporters that swarmed The Institute. Things had calmed a bit from the morning, mostly because the established medical community had labeled the Mengele cell hypothesis pure nonsense. The *New York Times* featured an analysis from researchers at Sloan-Kettering, NYU, and the Columbia School of Medicine. There wasn't a single scientist who had a kind thing to say, or found anything even remotely plausible in Izzy's supposed discovery.

Rich Levine had to sign David in and ushered him past security. Izzy and Oksana had gone to Coney Island Hospital to visit Jean Dulac. Fortunately, she had been able to call the police after being struck by the bullet from the Nazi's assault rifle. It had ripped through her right shoulder, just missing a major blood vessel. The police found her barely conscious when they arrived.

"Nice little crowd you got here," Dave joked. "Very low key."

"Be afraid. Be very afraid."

Dave looked questioningly at Rich. "Too much?"

Rich nodded. "Way over the top. Unless mass hysteria was what you were trying for."

Dave became a bit defensive. "I got the world's attention, didn't I? That's what Izzy said he wanted, the entire world's attention."

"Well you got it, Davey! You spelled it all out for them. Couldn't have made it any plainer if you had actual pictures of Mengele injecting blood serum into Africans or South Americans."

Dave threw both hands in the air. "Say what you want. But I'll bet Izzy agrees with what I did."

Rich shook his head as they stopped at Izzy's office. "Don't be too sure about that."

Dave stuck his head cautiously around the corner of Izzy's door. "Where is he?"

"He's out."

"I can see that. I didn't travel 3000 miles to find him out."

"He told me to tell you that he will be back soon. Take a seat, or if you want I'll take you up to the cafeteria."

"Not hungry," Dave replied. "I'll wait for superbrain Slesinger right here."

At the hospital, Jean was overjoyed to see Izzy and Oksana. She tried to sit up in bed. Oksana made her remain flat. Jean's upper right arm and shoulder had been casted. Izzy almost started crying when he saw her.

"I should have done something," Izzy remarked as he leaned over the side of the bed and gave Jean a kiss on the forehead.

"You did exactly what you were supposed to," Jean replied.

"How do you figure that?"

"You're alive, aren't you. My father and Pieter Heneke chose you from thousands."

Izzy seemed to brighten a bit. Oksana shook her head.

"You'll listen to her when she tells you that, but you won't listen to me."

Izzy nodded. "You're both right."

Jean reached out with her left hand and grabbed a hold of Izzy's wrist. She moaned as she pulled him closer. She wasn't satisfied until his face was over hers and he was looking down into her eyes. "Izzy, you are that 'once-in-a-millennium' mind. If you wind up getting yourself killed, none of us may have any hope left."

"Adolf Kaiser and his sister are dead. Franz Veldheim is in custody. I don't think I have to be worried about being killed anymore."

Jean disagreed. "You have merely cut off the snake's head. It will grow another. Do not let your guard down."

Oksana drew close and smiled. "I will look after him, at least until after the wedding."

Jean's eyelids were becoming heavy. She smiled in response and nodded. A moment later she was asleep. Izzy turned and kissed Oksana deeply. Five minutes later they were both seated in his convertible and headed back towards Manhattan.

Izzy found Dave Dunlevy deep in concentration when he returned. Dave had accessed Izzy's files on Mengele cells and was trying to come up with a reasonable number of variables that they would need to attack. Izzy walked into his office with Oksana at his side. Dave ignored him and moved right to her.

"The future Mrs. Slesinger, I presume?"

Oksana did not find Dave's wit amusing. "Do you know how many burned out German car dealerships we passed?"

Dave looked perplexed. "Should I?"

"I would think you would feel a bit responsible, and embarrassed."

Dave glared at her. "As I've already explained to Doctor Levine, your fiancé wanted this on the world stage."

Izzy had to laugh. "On the world stage, yes. An international incident, no."

"Better that, than no reaction at all. This way they can't sweep it under a rug or ignore you. Now that we've exchanged our usual pleasantries, can we get back to work?"

Oksana excused herself, having had all of Dave Dunlevy that she could stomach on a first meeting. He was even more arrogant than Izzy said he was. Izzy walked over to the computer screen to see what Dave had added. Dave joined him and pointed to the nucleotides that he had mapped out.

"For every nucleotide it's one of two sugars, either D-ribose or 2-deoxy-D-ribose. We've got a fifty percent chance of guessing right for each protein."

"No," Izzy countered. "The sugar is only part of the molecule. We also have to consider that there are five bases, cytosine, uricil, thymine, adenine, and guanine." He counted them off on his fingers to make sure that he hadn't forgotten any.

"But your hypothesis says the original virus attacked the sugar."

Izzy stared at Dave like he was from some other world. "My hypothesis? That and a buck doesn't even buy you a cup of coffee in this town. I'm guessing it's a sugar. It could also be a base, and it could be the phosphorus in every nucleotide molecule. The only thing I know for certain is alterations in the nucleotides don't necessarily result in transcription errors in replicated cells. At least that's what our cellular model is telling me."

"How comfortable are you with the model."

Izzy shrugged his shoulders. "It's a model. We both know modeling can only take you so far."

"It worked pretty well for the genome guys. They've mapped out DNA completely, all 1.3 billion sequences."

Izzy did not look impressed. "Not going to be much help to us. And they only had four bases to sequence, and most were repeats."

"I'm assuming you've got a next step figured out?"

"All I know is that we have to start where Mengele started, with a healthy cell. There is no way to back trace this thing. I couldn't even guess how many subtle mutations have taken place over the years. Maybe trillions."

"You think we can model our way to the end?"

Izzy reached out and slapped Dave on the back. "Gonna have to, Davey. Gonna have to. I just wish to God I had Heneke around to back me up, and Claude. With all three of us, they'd have to listen."

The NIH finally set a date for the symposium. It was to be held on the Sunday before Thanksgiving at the main diplomatic hall within the United Nations in New York. Invitations were mailed to 500 top scientists, 200 diplomats, and 180 translators. Despite protests from journalists, the meeting would be closed to the media. No government was willing to risk presented information starting a worldwide panic. Germany was especially insistent on requiring an intergovernment panel for review and dissemination of provable data.

It left Izzy very little time to get a presentation ready. He and Dave Dunlevy worked almost around the clock. Oksana had spent all the time she could afford away from her hospital duties, and therefore, had little time to offer. Brian Crighton was busy with his own problems. He was trying to come up with a working model for a worldwide infection rate, but the sexual practices of each culture presented too many variables. Therefore, he had to prepare multiple probabilities.

"Doctor Chazov's clinical data from Russia, you want that on transparencies or slides?" Dave was digging through the mountain of data that Izzy had brought back from Europe. There seemed no way to organize it all into one coherent presentation.

Izzy looked up from his computer screen to look at the pile of paper that Dave was holding. "We're going to need to condense it."

"I've got files on over 5000 case histories. And it's taking forever for the computer to translate the Russian."

Izzy thought for a moment before responding. "Maybe if we collate by type of cancer, gender, and age."

Dave nodded. "That'll work. I should be able to crunch that in an hour or two."

"Good. There's a really good slide house on 14th Street. We can drop the stuff off after we leave tonight and pick it up in the morning."

Detective Adam Rodman had spent three days convalescing in

South Hampton hospital in New York. The beating he had taken at the hands of Terry Hebb had fractured his breastbone and ripped open a blood vessel. Fortunately, the surgery was minor and his powers of recuperation were strong. He was discharged on the third day, to the care of fellow officers from the NYPD. The police commissioner had personally sent the escorts who brought Rodman home. Authorities in New York were very anxious to get Rodman fully debriefed. They were more than a little bit nervous about the upcoming medical symposia at the U.N. The last thing anyone wanted was an act of terrorism to deal with.

The meeting was small, just the Police Commissioner and Adam Rodman's captain, Mark Ovitz. Adam's doctor had confined him to bed for ten days. Therefore, the meeting was held in his apartment in the Bronx. Adam was pretty zonked out on pain medication, but he did his best to stay propped up in bed and concentrate. His girlfriend, Cassandra Winfrey, wished the two men would leave so that Adam could get some rest. However, she held her tongue and stayed out of the way.

"So we've got a list of sixty-eight hate groups connected with neo-Nazis or white supremacists operating in New York City. Do you know which of these groups was responsible?" Mark Ovitz had a pad out to write down names.

"Not from New York," Adam answered in a whisper. His injury made speaking difficult.

"Well, that settles it," the commissioner interjected. "This is not a local matter. I'm calling the Feds. Let them handle this. We'll take a secondary support position."

"Okay, Adam," Captain Ovitz said as Rodman's eyes started to close. "That's all we need. Get some rest and I'll check on you in a couple of days."

Adam fought through the haze in his head and made a small motion with his right hand to draw his captain closer. Captain Ovitz moved beside his bed.

"Something else?"

"Protect Slesinger."

Captain Ovitz placed a hand on Adam's bed. "We've got it covered," he assured.

Sunday, November 20 was a day the world would not soon forget. By 6 a.m., Izzy was in his office, dashing around like a crazed rat on LSD. The symposia was two and half hours away and he was certain he had forgotten a million details. Oksana and Dave arrived a little bit past seven. Brian Crighton walked in the door just behind them. They found Izzy sitting in his office, mumbling to himself while he stared absently into space. Oksana stepped into the office and placed her hands on his shoulders.

"Izzy, are you all right?"

Izzy turned his head to look at her. "Last night was Saturday."

"Yes, it was," Oksana replied. She answered as if Izzy had asked a question. Perhaps all the stress had made Izzy forget what day it was.

"I guess that a couple of thousand people had sex last night, with people they didn't even know Saturday afternoon. Add in the hookers and it could be tens of thousands, and that's just in New York. This is ludicrous. We can't stop this."

Oksana didn't know how to respond. Dave walked in and saw the empty, vacant look in Izzy's eyes. It was the same kind of look that he had just before the organic chemistry final at Yale. A forlorn Slesinger stare that spoke of impending doom.

At a little bit past eight, a heavily armed entourage of police officers and vehicles gathered in front of The Institute. Being a Sunday, the streets of the lower East side were practically deserted. It was a short ride from The Institute to the United Nations. The FBI had cordoned off several surrounding blocks and only allowed in authorized personnel. A procession of limousines formed a line that stretched almost three city blocks. The Feds proceeded cautiously and double or tripled checked invitations and ID's. Washington had made it very clear that this was a powderkeg situation which could easily escalate into global military action.

Even as the scientists arrived at the U.N., Russia was building her forces on the eastern border. If Mengele's notes implicated the Nazis of inoculating Russian prisoners of war, or worse, civilians, things could get ugly. The President ordered the U.S. Military to raise troop readiness to Defcon 3. While the Pentagon doubted that Russia would do anything harsh, there was no room for error, or to be caught off guard. The sooner this situation was diffused, the better off the entire world would be.

Doctor Joseph Granger was the chairman of the National Institute of Health. His staff had hand picked six experts from around the world to question Doctors Slesinger and Dunlevy after their presentation. Unlike typical peer review meetings, there would be no questions from the floor. Doctor Granger had to be truthful to himself—this was so unlike a typical meeting that it almost fell into the *twilight zone*. It was almost more than he could handle, despite thirty years in public service. As moderator, it would be his job to make sure that the meeting didn't get out of control.

Doctor Granger adjusted his microphone on the podium as scientists began to file into the room. Armed security stood at the perimeter, heavily armed with automatic weapons. Deb Petersen, Joe's executive assistant, approached him with a clipboard in hand. Doctor Granger took it from her and studied the names on the list.

Doctor Drexel Grey from the North Star foundation in Baltimore, Maryland. North Star was a think tank, pure research. Drexel was a virologist who had pioneered the use of monoclonal antibodies in the treatment of cancer. Twice nominated for a Nobel prize, it was difficult to argue that there was a better American inquisitor.

France's PhillipYves-Piccard was the other virologist on the panel. Doctor Piccard was more of a clinician, having used gene therapy to treat more cancer patients in his clinic in Paris than had been treated in the entire rest of the world, combined. His cure rates were better than sixty percent, and he was revered throughout Europe. He had also been one of Claude Thomae's closest friends. Therefore, he wanted to learn the truth about the accident at Brittany that had claimed Claude's life. More than eight weeks had passed since the explosion and still there was no body, and no accountability.

Johannesburg's Doctor Lisette Antoine was the only public servant on the panel, representing South Africa's Ministry of Health. As the youngest member of the panel at thirty-six, she had seen more real world deaths, in a country that had experienced more than its share of AIDS. Thanks to her educational programs, South Africa had an infective rate that was a fifth of other African countries. Still, with millions already dead, and tens of millions at risk, any new findings needed to be considered.

Germany was represented by the husband and wife team of Ingrid and Wecker Kohler. Both geneticists, they were considered in Germany to be the modern equivalent of von Verscher. They were both cool, detached research scientists, who had spent their lifetimes studying genotypical differences in the races. It was a controversial choice, especially considering that several of their published papers hinted at a genotypic superiority in people of Aryan background. However, they were also both brilliant, and Doctor Granger was in no position to challenge their selection.

Doctor Granger touched his finger to the last name on the list. "Lidia Chazov? Who is she?"

"A Russian medical Doctor," Deb replied. "Very well respected in Soviet circles. Doctor Slesinger insisted that we include her on the panel."

Doctor Granger handed the clipboard back. "I can remember the names."

By 9:30, the entire room was filled with invited scientists, politicians, analysts, security and translators. Even though the NIH had gone out of its way to invite researchers who were fluent in English, more than 100 interpreters were still needed for the symposia. The panel of experts took their places behind the table that had been set up for them. Right from the outset it was clear that this was no ordinary meeting. There was very little chatter as the assembly took its seats, and there was no exchange of pleasantries between scientists on the panel. Deb Petersen had placed Phillip Piccard next to Ingrid and Wecker Kohler. The Frenchman would not stand for being seated next to the Germans and demanded his spot be changed. Fortunately, Drexel Grey offered to change seats and the first incident of the day was avoided.

Doctor Granger could feel his stomach tying in knots. He wished the meeting was already over. Izzy felt the same way. He massaged both temples, hoping to keep any migraines at bay. He and Dave had been sequestered in a meeting room and they were busy explaining their materials to the audio-visual staff. Dave handed over the slides and transparencies and they were whisked up to the projection booth. The U.N. staff had installed a special high definition projection screen at the front of the auditorium, just in case any diagrams of cellular structure were to be projected.

At exactly 9:58, a platoon of secret service agents entered with the Vice-President of the United States. The former senator from the South was no stranger to the NIH. He was the President's point man on cancer, and an expert on its environmental causative factors. As soon as he was settled, Doctor Granger sent a messenger to get Doctors Slesinger and Dunlevy. A moment later they both walked onto the floor, accompanied by Brian Crighton. The three of them took seats at a small half-circular table that had been placed to the right of the podium. The table had been oriented away from the audience and towards the panel of experts.

Doctor Granger took a big gulp of water and tried to calm himself as he flipped the switch on his microphone. "Ladies and Gentlemen, distinguished colleagues, I would like to thank you for attending this special symposia on HIV. Our format for this meeting is a bit different. We have established an expert panel who will direct questions to our presenters, Doctor Isaiah Slesinger of New York's Viral Research Institute, Doctor David Dunlevy of the California Technical Institute, and noted mathematician, Brian Crighton. Because of this format, we will not be taking any questions from the floor."

Loud grumbles emanated from many of the seated guests. Doctor Granger let it pass and then started things by calling Izzy to the podium. Nervously, Izzy stood. For a moment he was frozen in place. Dave gave him a nudge and Izzy moved to the lectern. Izzy had rehearsed his beginning a thousand times, and still he had to grope for the words.

"Let me begin by saying that nothing we present today is in conflict with accepted HIV/AIDS assumptions. We do not deny that the virus will cause impairment of human immune systems. Nor do we deny that these impairments allow for secondary infection and death. However, we will present irrefutable data on the existence of a symbiotic relationship between the virus and a genetically altered cellular host." Izzy paused and looked towards the projection room. "Can I have the first slide, please."

The lights went down and a slide flashed up on the screen.

Population 2003	**Genotypic Positive 2040**	**Genotypic Positives**
North America	8%	89%
South America	11%	91%
Africa	43%	100%
Asia	14%	89%
Europe	10%	91%

Izzy let the numbers sink in before he began to elaborate. "My colleague, Brian Crighton, has taken into account both variability of sexual habits, and natural immunities. You can all see that the entire human race becomes unviable within four decades."

The auditorium exploded. Half the scientists jumped to their feet and started shouting things towards Izzy. The calmer half remained seated, but they shouted as well. Fifty armed police officers moved towards the floor of the U.N. Doctor Granger pounded a gavel on his gavel pad, but it was meaningless. The crowd was out of control and about to get violent. Izzy could see scientists in the audience pointing fingers at each other. It was Dave Dunlevy who restored order to the hall. He walked to Izzy's side and put his hand under the podium. He found the switch that controlled volume for the public address system and rolled the knob towards its highest setting. Immediately, the feedback began and a loud, mechanical shrieking filled the hall. Dave continued to roll the volume up. He stopped when the pain in his own ears forced him to cover them with his hands. The loud, high frequency sound painfully distracted the entire audience. They were all looking toward Dave, pleading with their eyes for him to make it stop. Mercifully, he pushed the knob back to its original setting and there was a loud sigh of relief. Secret service agents started heading in his direction.

"This is the way it is," Dave began. "Yesterday, we were all different. Chinese, American, Russian, South African, Jew, Gentile, White, Black. Today, there are only two types of people. Those with normal cellular function, and those with abnormal cellular function. In a short while, none of us will have any cellular function, if we do not find an adequate solution."

The audience was so stunned by the straight forwardness of his statement, they remained silent for the rest of the presentation. Izzy's portion, which dealt strictly with science, lasted approximately fifteen minutes. He realized that the audience would only be able to contain itself for a brief period, considering the nature of the material. Brian Crighton followed Izzy with an even briefer presentation of mathematical probabilities, most of which went over the audiences head. When Brian finished, Doctor Granger opened the symposia to his expert panel.

Drexel Grey leaned close to his microphone. "Gentlemen, I am certain that I am not alone in my skepticism. Explain to me how you are linking your Mengele cell to cancer?"

"It's quite simple," Izzy replied. "Somatic mutation, by definition, requires the alteration of a cell's genetic makeup. That is exactly what we have here. However, when we say cancer, we do not necessarily mean tumors. We are talking about cells, that over time, lose the ability to carry on basic cellular function.

Doctor Antoinne asked the next question. "In your article in *The Times*, you claim that people started dying from this decades ago."

"That's correct," Dave responded. "We believe there is a correlation between infection, and disease spikes in various populations. These go back decades, and they're not all cancerous conditions.

"Can you give us examples?"

Dave nodded as he glanced through his notes. "Addison's disease, glomerulonephritis, pernicious anemia, and there are many others we believe will be linked to this cellular anomaly."

Wecker Kohler had heard more than he could stand. "In America, I believe the proper term for your data is bullshit." His comment brought on chuckles, and a smattering of applause. "It seems very convenient that you have chosen to pair conditions with long gestation periods and your supposed discovery. A discovery I might add that is undetectable by any known science."

"Systemic lupus erythematosus," Dave shot back. "predominantly seen in the last decade in young women. The disease has an etiology characterized by cellular infiltration, fibrinoid necrosis, and there is evidence that nuclear material is altered." Dave put special emphasis on the word altered.

Izzy completed the explanation. "Death from S.L.E. is rapid, sometimes within weeks."

Ingrid Wecker took over for her husband. "You have said nothing about the mechanism of how these conditions happen." Ingrid paused and glanced at her husband. He nodded for her to continue. "Could it be that it is fairies from the Black Forest?"

The entire room filled with laughter. Dave, however, couldn't see the humor. "If memory serves, those fairies were rounded up and disposed of at Auschwitz."

A hush instantly fell over the entire room. Even though Dave had promised to keep the discussion focused on science, he had clearly slipped over the line. So much so that Wecker and Ingrid Kohler dismissed themselves from the podium and left in a huff. Doctor Granger was now down to four experts, and an audience that was growing more hostile by the minute. A secret service agent sitting next to the Vice-President likened the proceedings to the animated claymation television show, 'Celebrity Death Match.'

Doctor Lidia Chazov did her best to help Izzy by distracting the audience's attention away from Dave's last comment. "I would like to ask a question of Mr. Crighton."

Brian leaned towards his microphone. "I'm ready."

"One of your probabilities projected a timeline on Doctor Heneke's protease inhibitor, PIRT-19, can you explain that?"

"It's a game of cat and mouse. Heneke's drug works in two ways. First, it blocks receptor sites in blood cells from being attacked, and it also fractures the virus into individual proteins. These proteins hide themselves in the cells, and somehow, have the ability to realign in a different matrix. I believe that Heneke's drug will be effective in any infected patient for a period of four years. After that time, the drug will no longer be able to shatter the virus. It is also possible that the timeline will be shorter for African populations. They do not possess the HIV resistant gene in their mRNA, to the same extent as other populations."

Lidia Chazov asked a follow-up question, which she directed towards Izzy. "Doctor Slesinger, do you believe that it is possible to cure a patient?"

Izzy paused, not knowing if he should reply truthfully. After several long moments, he decided to answer candidly. "I believe that science has the ability to halt a further infection, if we can understand the first cellular shift."

"You did not answer my question."

"No," Izzy stated. "I do not think we have the ability to cure a patient, of either the virus, or its underlying host. Maintenance is the best we can offer, and eventually, that will not be enough."

Now it was Phillip-Yves Piccard's turn to lose his patience with Izzy. "Gentlemen, if my good friend, Claude Thomae, were here, he would explain to you all the problems with your fictional Mengele cell. Since he is not here, I must speak on his behalf. It is my professional opinion that your Mengele cell quackery eclipses even cold fusion as the biggest hoax perpetrated on the world."

Two-thirds of the audience stood and applauded Piccard's remarks. Doctor Granger was thinking that it was time to end the symposia, before things turned really ugly. While the audience stood and applauded, a door at the back of the auditorium was pushed open and a three men walked inside. They weren't noticed until they reached the security line at the front of the hall. Everyone in the first few rows recognized Claude Thomae. His presence shocked them silent. After several terse moments, security allowed them to approach Doctor Granger. At Thomae's side were Rodney Bassett and Pieter Heneke.

The three men had a brief conversation with Doctor Granger, who had stepped away from the podium. The applause from the audience had been replaced with chatter and confusion. Finally, Claude broke away from the others and walked to the lectern.

"Most of you know me," he began. Claude lifted his hand and angrily pointed toward Phillip Piccard. "How dare you presume to speak for me? This is so beyond your intellectual grasp, it is simply ludicrous that you were placed on this panel, Phillip. Now be a good boy and shut up!"

Piccard was so embarrassed that he had no other option. Claude stepped away from the lectern and Pieter Heneke took his place. Pieter held up his right hand and extended the index finger. "One man! I could have picked anyone. I could have picked any of you. I picked Isaiah Slesinger. I am an old man. I was there with Mengele. I saw the genesis. I needed the best amino-acid scientist in the world. Claude and I have gotten far more than we could have hoped for."

Izzy had to purse his lips together to keep his emotions intact. He had prayed for Heneke to stand up with him. To add his voice so the world would believe. So the world would understand and fight back against Mengele's madness.

Pieter raised his other arm and opened both hands, showing the palms to the audience. "My hands are empty. You have been given all that we know. A few will believe, most won't. Those who do believe, must act. Humanity is in your hands." Heneke paused and glanced at his watch.

"As I said, I am an old man and it is past my lunch hour. Therefore, I suggest we conclude this here. I am certain that Doctor Slesinger will make himself available in the coming days and weeks to continue this discussion."

Heneke stood back from the podium and walked to Izzy. He embraced him in a bear hug and then led him from the auditorium. Claude and Rodney followed him, as eventually did Dave Dunlevy and Brian Crighton. Whether Doctor Granger liked it or not, the symposia had come to an end.

Chapter 23

They all gathered together in the visitor's solarium, adjacent to the intensive care unit at New York University hospital. Rodney Bassett, Brian Crighton, Claude Thomae, Dave Dunlevy, Lidia Chazov, Pieter Heneke and Izzy waited like nervous hens for Oksana to sign the discharge papers for Jean Dulac. Oksana had cleared it first with Jean's surgeon, who recommended quiet bed rest for at least two or three days. The automatic metal doors swung open, and Jean walked out with Oksana by her side. Jean's arm was in a sling, but that didn't stop her from giving everyone a hug. She saved the biggest hug for Izzy.

"So you told the entire world?"

Izzy nodded. "Now we have to wait and see. Even with your father, and Pieter, I'm skeptical."

Claude walked to his daughter's side. A big smile was written on his face. "Doctor Dunlevy has told me that he has a student named Vishnu, he claims he is a second Izzy Slesinger."

Jean frowned at her father. "I hope that's not aimed at me."

Claude frowned. "And why not? It is my right to see you married. I'm not getting any younger."

Jean ignored the comment as she turned to look at Oksana, who was busy staring out the window at the East River. "Speaking of marriage, I believe we have an engaged couple in our midst."

Izzy immediately began to blush as Oksana turned from the window and walked to his side. She whispered into his ear and he nodded his head in agreement.

Izzy gathered everyone around him and he made the big announcement. "We are going to get married the weekend before Yom Ha'Shoah. We want our anniversary to be a constant reminder to us of the six million who will never be forgotten."

It had all come full circle. The little boy from Brooklyn, whose own legacy had been an albatross of guilt, was finally free. He had stood up straight and looked directly into the eyes of a heinous madman, and hadn't blinked. The remaining question was if it had done any good? Perhaps they were all too late already and just didn't know it yet.

It was Dave Dunlevy who broke the atmosphere of seriousness that Izzy's comment brought to the group. He slapped his old college roommate on the back, and then hugged Oksana, which she accepted graciously. She had started to warm to Dave. He was sort of like a warped, vinyl record album; outdated, relatively unplayable, but of great sentimental value.

"Dizzy Izzy Slesinger getting married? If that doesn't prove miracles can still happen, I don't know what does!"

Everyone laughed, including Oksana and Izzy himself.

Epilogue

The National Institute of Health deliberated for two days, and then rejected the presented hypothesis on the cellular anomaly labeled 'Mengele Cells.' Doctor Granger wrote the article himself, which was published in *The New York Times*, and reprinted around the world. Within one day of its release, Russia called back its troops on the Eastern front. The United States lowered its defense readiness to Defcon 4, and the world settled back to its everyday troubles. A massive earthquake in the Ukraine distracted the world's attention, as did a historic 'land for peace' deal in the middle east.

It was easy to forget about HIV/AIDS. People were far more interested in their own lives, than in wondering if or when Africa was going to cease to exist. Americans couldn't grasp the interconnectedness of the planet. To the rest of the world, the brotherhood of humanity had been disproved in a never ending series of conflicts, wars, ethnic cleansing, and barbarisms. If Africans were going to become extinct, it was Africa's problem.

Over the next sixty days, many of the front-line medical journals published articles debunking the possibility of a human host cell. Pons and Fleishmann at least had a modicum of support for cold fusion, Izzy and Dave had no one outside their own little group.

Heneke begged Izzy to leave The Institute and come work at Brittany's new complex in New Jersey. Izzy refused, explaining that his own resources in Manhattan were more easily customized for a nucleotide or nucleoside search. Even if the world would not believe, Izzy was determined to find an answer.

It was on the Tuesday before the Superbowl that Dave Dunlevy called from California. Dave was ecstatic. The NIH had mysteriously agreed to fund Cal Tech's research on "the viral hosting abilities of human cells." Perhaps their warning had gotten through after all.

"That's great," Izzy agreed. "And I've heard inklings from Lydia Chazov that the Russians are about to start a huge research project of their own. We're going to beat this bastard, Davey. Mark my words, we're going to beat him!"

"I read his biography you gave me," Dave replied. "You know they never found his body."

Izzy immediately knew who Dave was talking about and disagreed. "You're wrong. They exhumed the body of Helmut Gregor and identified him from dental records." Helmut Gregor was Mengele's assumed name in South America.

"No. The coroner concluded that it could be his teeth."

"And what exactly does that have to do with the cost of tea in China?"

"Nothing," Dave replied. "You told me to read it and I did. End of story."

It was a harbinger of things to come. At the end of the week, Izzy came home to find a small, yellow manila envelope slid under his door. It had no name, no return address, and no post mark. Izzy picked it up and smiled, assuming that it must be another one of Heneke's little messages. "More Ice-9?" He thought to himself as he slipped a finger under the flap and broke the seal.

"Herr Doctor Slesinger,

How better to be remembered than by having a cell named for

me. As I lie here, awaiting my death, I must tell you that everything you know about my work is wrong.

Ihre ergebene

Doctor Joseph Mengele"